2.

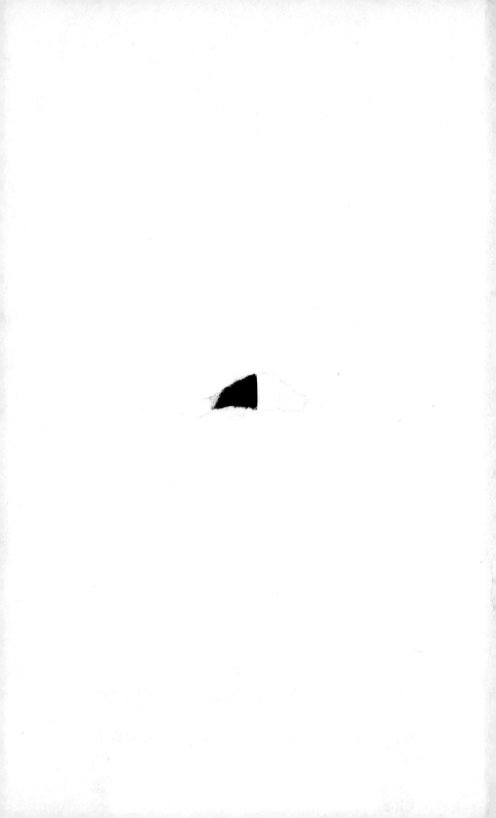

*Down an English Lane*

*Down an English Lane*

MARGARET THORNTON

First published in Great Britain in 2006 by
Allison & Busby Limited
13 Charlotte Mews
London W1T 4EJ
*www.allisonandbusby.com*

Copyright © 2006 by MARGARET THORNTON

The moral right of the author has been asserted.

A catalogue record for this book is available from
the British Library.

10 9 8 7 6 5 4 3 2 1

ISBN 0 7490 8156 2
978-0-7490-8156-0

Printed and bound in Wales by
Creative Print and Design, Ebbw Vale

MARGARET THORNTON was born in Blackpool and has lived there all her life. She is a qualified teacher but has retired in order to concentrate on her writing. She began by writing articles and short stories for magazines and has since gone on to have fifteen novels published, most of which are set in Blackpool. Her family sagas range from the late Victorian period, through to the Twenties, the Second World War, and the Fifties and Sixties. She has two children and five grand-children.

**Also available from Allison & Busby:**
*Above the Bright Blue Sky*

**Previously by Margaret Thornton:**
*It's a Lovely Day Tomorrow*
*A Pair of Sparkling Eyes*
*How Happy We Shall Be*
*There's a Silver Lining*
*Forgive Our Foolish Ways*
*A Stick of Blackpool Rock*
*Wish Upon a Star*
*The Sound of Her Laughter*
*Looking at the Moon*
*Beyond the Sunset*
*All You Need Is Love*
*Sunset View*
*Don't Sit Under the Apple Tree*
*Wednesday's Child*

*Dedication*
For my friends and fellow members
of the Romantic Novelists Association (RNA).
I am thankful for their friendship and
advice over the years

PART ONE

# Chapter One

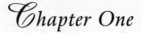

'Maisie... Hey, Maisie Jackson, stop daydreaming and come and give us a hand with these sandwiches...'

Maisie glanced across the church hall towards her friend, Audrey Fairchild, who was calling to her through the kitchen serving hatch. She laughed. 'OK; sorry, Audrey. I was miles away just then. Thinking about the concert tonight and hoping it'll all go off all right. Especially my solo...'

'Oh give over! You've sung on your own dozens of times. You'll be fine, you know you will... Are you sure that's all you were daydreaming about?' Audrey's blue eyes twinkled mischievously as she smiled – a very knowing smile – at her best friend.

'Of course! And what else would I be thinking about?' retorted Maisie. A secretive, little half smile played around her lips, but she was determined not to give anything away. After all, she was only fifteen years old – she kept trying to remind herself of this – and it was far too young to be imagining herself in love. At least, that was what everyone would say if they knew. But Maisie had felt this way about Bruce Tremaine for ages now, even before he had joined the RAF more than two years ago. And, as the old saying went, absence had made the heart grow fonder; Maisie's heart at any rate. She did not know how Bruce felt about her, but he had written to her regularly all the while he had been away and she had written back. Friendly chatty letters had passed between the two of them, fortnightly at least, and that surely must mean that he did think something about her. But perhaps only as a friend...said the more commonsensical voice in her mind; a voice she immediately tried to quash.

Now, at the end of August, 1945, Bruce was coming

home, just in time for the Victory concert which was to be held in St Bartholomew's church hall that evening. Before that, in the afternoon, there was to be a tea-time party for all the children in the little market town of Middlebeck. Maisie and Audrey, with their friend, Doris, from the farm, were now preparing for this event, assisting the ladies from the church congregation and the local Women's Institute.

Maisie straightened the red checked cloth she had put over one of the tables and went into the kitchen at the rear of the hall to assist with the sandwich making. Audrey and Doris were working hard, Audrey buttering the bread – or, to be more correct, spreading the bread with margarine – which Doris then spread with salmon paste before cutting the slices into four triangular pieces. Ada Nixon, Doris's mother, had expertly cut all the loaves into thin slices, none of the girls, as yet, being expert enough to be in charge of a bread knife.

'We don't want doorsteps,' Ada had declared, 'especially not on a special occasion like today. And sandwiches look much better – much more party like – when they're cut in triangles.'

'What can I do?' asked Maisie. 'I've put all the cloths on the tables, like your mum told me to do, Audrey. Corner-wise; they look classier like that, don't you think, than putting them on straight?'

'It's only kids that'll be eating off 'em,' laughed Doris, 'and they're not going to bother what the cloths look like, or the sandwiches neither. Here, Maisie; you can take over from me for a while. We've nearly come to the end o' t' salmon paste. I'll go and ask me mam if she wants us to start on t' boiled ham.'

'Very well then...' Maisie took over with the salmon paste, made from tins of pink salmon – the red variety was too precious to use on sandwiches – mashed together with a knob of salad cream and soft breadcrumbs to make it go further.

Audrey cast a sideways glance at her friend. 'I was only teasing, y' know.' She lowered her voice. 'But you are looking forward to seeing Bruce again, aren't you?'

Maisie nodded silently. 'Mmm... Don't say anything to anybody, will you, Audrey?' she said in a low voice. 'People would think I was silly, I know they would. They'd tell me I'm just a schoolgirl and that I'm not old enough to know what it's all about. Being in love, I mean... Because I do love him, Audrey. I think I've loved him for ages.'

'I shan't tell anybody, don't worry,' said Audrey. 'I can keep a secret.'

'And it's got to be a secret until I know how he feels... Oh, Audrey! I've got butterflies in my tummy already, thinking about tonight.'

'Well, you would have anyway, with the concert,' replied Audrey. 'So have I! I know I'm not actually taking part on the stage, but I'm anxious that the kiddies should do their best and not get stage fright.'

'I don't think little 'uns do get stage fright,' said Maisie. 'They just like dressing up and showing off a bit. I know our Joanie's really looking forward to it.'

'Oh, Joanie's a natural,' said Audrey. 'She learned her part straight away, ages before any of the others, and she's really got herself into the part of Alice.'

The Sunday School children of St Bartholomew's, including Joanie, Maisie's nine-year-old sister, were to act scenes from *Alice in Wonderland*, which Patience Fairchild, the rector's wife, had adapted from the book with the help of her daughter, Audrey; and it was Audrey who had been largely responsible for the production of the playlet. She was now a Sunday School teacher, and the enthusiasm she had brought to this task made it clear that the career she had planned for herself, that of an Infant teacher, would be an ideal choice. That was in the future, though, several years hence. Audrey still had her School Certificate year to do, then two years in the Sixth Form before she could apply for Training College. So had Maisie, although she had no desire to become a teacher...

'I'm glad our Joanie's enjoying herself,' Maisie said now.

'I'm looking forward to seeing her performing on the stage. What about Jimmy? He's not got a speaking part, has he?'

'Oh no; he's happy enough to be one of the playing cards, with the rest of the lads,' replied Audrey. 'He's quite a comic though, your Jimmy; he has the others in fits of laughter.'

'Yes, I'm sure he does,' said Maisie dryly. 'He acts the fool in school as well, from what Anne Mellodey tells me.' Anne Mellodey had been Maisie and Audrey's favourite teacher at the village school across the green, and now she had Jimmy Jackson in her class. 'Never mind, he'll maybe settle down eventually. I know he's only mischievous, not real naughty, like he used to be when he was a little 'un.'

As far as settling into the school was concerned, however, and into their new life in the town of Middlebeck, Joanie and Jimmy had shown no difficulties at all. Their former life in Armley, in the city of Leeds, was now well and truly a thing of the past.

Maisie had been the first of the family to come and live in the town, high up in the northern Yorkshire Dales, as an evacuee at the start of the war. Her mother, Lily, and the two younger children, escaping from a brutal husband and a disastrous marriage, had followed a couple of years later. Now Lily ran a successful little draper's shop on the High Street and her three children lived with her; Maisie, aged fifteen, and Joanie and Jimmy, who were nine and eight years old. The family were now known as Jackson, Lily having managed to get a divorce from her former husband, Sidney Bragg, on the grounds of cruelty. Jackson was the name of Maisie's beloved father, Davey, who had died, to Lily's great sorrow, when the little girl was four years old.

Maisie had been forced to grow up very quickly, first of all in Armley, trying to protect herself and her mother from the sadistic behaviour of Sidney Bragg and his son, Percy; and later, in Middlebeck, where she had stayed for a considerable time with the rector, the Reverend Luke Fairchild and his wife, Patience. She felt, sometimes, quite mature for her fifteen years, and she knew that people seeing her for the first time might think she was several years older than that.

Her thoughts were wandering again now to the coming evening, when she would put on her new dress to sing in the concert. She would feel very grown-up then, and she knew, too, that the colour and the style really suited her.

'You look beautiful, our Maisie,' her mother had said in a hushed voice, when she had tried on the finished dress. Tears had appeared momentarily in Lily's eyes. 'Your dad would've been real proud of you, love,' she whispered.

It was not often that Maisie's father was mentioned now, but she knew that her parents had been blissfully happy during the few years they had spent together until Davey Jackson's untimely death. Lily's subsequent marriage to Sidney Bragg had been a disastrous mistake, but not entirely unproductive, because out of it had come the 'little 'uns', Joanie and Jimmy, who were now developing into much more lovable children, belying the bad behaviour of their earlier years.

And now Lily had a man friend again; a much more suitable one this time, in Maisie's eyes. Arthur Rawcliffe was due back in Middlebeck this weekend following his demob from the Army Catering Corps.

'You're miles away again, Maisie...' teased Audrey. 'But I'm not going to ask you what you're thinking about this time.'

Maisie realised she had been staring into space, her knife poised over the now empty dish of salmon paste. 'I wasn't, actually,' she replied. 'I wasn't thinking about...that.' She would have said 'him', but Doris had just come back with a plateful of ham; and Doris, although she was a good friend, could not see into Maisie's mind – nor did Maisie want her to – in the way that Audrey was able to do. 'As a matter of fact, I was thinking about my new dress that I'm going to wear tonight.'

'Hang on a minute,' said Doris, 'then you can tell us both about it... See here; this boiled ham, it's special, like. It's home-cured, from one of our own pigs, and me mam says it's to be used sparingly. She's cut it into dead thin slices, and she says we've to spread a bit of this pickle stuff on it to make it go further.' She placed a jar of bright yellow, homemade piccalilli on the table.

Audrey pulled a face. 'I don't think the kiddies will be all that keen on the taste of pickles.'

'No...well, maybe that's the idea,' laughed Doris. 'The sandwiches that are left will be for the helpers' tea afterwards. I know me mam's rather partial to boiled ham and pickles.' The boiled ham, indeed, looked and smelled very tempting; pink fragrant slices, moist and with not a trace of fat, were piled on the willow pattern plate.

'Come on, girls; let's get moving,' said Doris. 'You carry on buttering, Audrey; I'll see to the ham, an' you can spread a bit of this yellow stuff on it, Maisie... Now, tell us all about this dress of yours? What colour is it?'

'It's pink,' said Maisie, 'but not a pale pink; it's a sort of deep coral colour.'

'It'll look lovely with your dark hair and brown eyes,' commented Audrey.

'An' it's a long dress, right down to my ankles. I've never had a long dress before,' nor had any of them, 'but Mum says we can always shorten it later, so I can get more wear out of it. She's made it herself from a paper pattern. Mum's got real good at this make-do-and-mend stuff lately; but this is proper new material, a sort of silky cotton. We've got it in blue and green an' all in the shop, but the pink was my favourite. Anyway...it's got wide shoulder straps and a squarish neckline, quite low...' She demonstrated, placing her hands tentatively on the gentle swell of her breasts. 'And a nipped-in waist and a full skirt.'

'You mean...you'll have bare shoulders?' asked Audrey.

'Yeah...sort of. Well, yes, I will. But there's nothing wrong with that, Audrey; it's for this special concert, isn't it? And I'll be able to wear it as a sun-dress later. I can always put a cardigan over it,' she added. Audrey was looking a mite disapproving.

'It sounds lovely,' said Doris, looking a tiny bit envious, but not unduly so. She was a good-natured girl, quite contented with her life and work on the farm, and it was very rarely that one saw her disgruntled or unhappy. Maisie knew, though, that Doris and her mother were very seldom able to afford new clothes. They did not need them on the farm, and it was not often that they left its environs. But money, or the lack of it, was quite a problem, as Ada Nixon was a widow with her two sons and daughter all living at home. Pulling their weight, of course, on the family farm, but by no means well off.

Maisie felt a shade guilty; and conscious that she could be giving the impression that she was showing off, she decided to change the subject. 'Yeah...it's OK,' she said nonchalantly, 'but I'll be glad when my solo's over and done with, I can tell you. Are your brothers coming tonight, Doris?'

'They both say they're coming,' replied Doris, 'but I think our Ted's only coming so as he can have a laugh at me doing my recitation, the rotten so-and-so!'

'He won't laugh,' said Maisie indignantly. 'Why should he? I bet he'll be dead proud of you. What are you reciting?'

'Ah, it's a secret,' said Doris. 'You'll have to wait and see. Actually...folks are supposed to laugh, 'cause it's a funny poem, y' see – a humorous one, I mean. But our Ted would kill himself laughing anyway, seeing me up on t' stage.'

'So there's only me that won't be on the stage tonight,' said Audrey, sounding a little regretful. 'Even our Tim's going to do a piano solo. Mum's managed to persuade him. She really wanted both of us, him and me, to do a duet, but I didn't want to. I get real scared in front of an audience; anyway, I haven't had much time to practise, with producing the play for the children and everything.'

'We'll have you up on the stage to take a bow, Audrey Fairchild,' laughed Doris, 'whether you're scared or not. You've worked harder than any of us for this 'ere concert, training them kids. Gosh! I don't know how you handle 'em. My Sunday School class are little divils! Oops...!' She put a hand to her mouth. 'I mustn't let yer mam hear me say that, Audrey.'

'She's too busy,' laughed Audrey, glancing across the kitchen to where Patience Fairchild, the rector's wife and Audrey's mother through adoption, was occupied in adding the finishing touches to the large bowls of trifle; sprinkling the mock cream that covered them with tiny multi-coloured hundreds and thousands. 'Mum's not all stiff and starchy, though, even though she's married to the rector. Neither is Dad for that matter. Of course you know that, don't you, Doris? Actually, you've known them a lot longer than I have...'

Maisie noticed that her friend, Audrey, was looking a little pensive; not unhappy, but just thoughtful. A day such as this, of course, celebrating the end of the war in Japan as well as in Europe, must remind her forcibly of the losses she had suffered during the course of the war. The deaths of both her parents, her mother's through illness, but her father's as a result of the blackout in Leeds. But how heartening it was to hear Audrey referring to the rector and his wife, her adoptive parents, as Mum and Dad. It had been very hard for her at first, and for Timothy, their second adopted child, to get used to the names; but the arrival of baby John Septimus in the September of 1941 had made all the difference.

He was the natural child of Patience and Luke, the one they had never expected to have, coming as a great blessing after twelve years of marriage. As John grew from a baby to a toddler, and now to a sturdy little boy of almost four, learning as he developed to say 'Mama' and 'Dada', and then 'Mummy' and 'Daddy', it had come naturally to Audrey and Tim, also, to start saying Mum and Dad.

Maisie looked across at Patience Fairchild, the woman who had taken her into her home and made her so very welcome in the September of 1939. Maisie had loved her very much; and she still did. Patience had been a substitute mother to her until the time that her own mother, Lily, had come to live in Middlebeck, and the two of them, Maisie and Patience, had become very close. She was still Aunty Patience to Maisie; she knew that that was how she would always think of her, although she called the rector Luke, as did most of the folk in the parish who knew him well.

In Maisie's eyes Patience looked just the same, not a day older than she had six years ago, although she was now in her mid-forties. Her hair was a deep and glossy auburn, with just a few silvery wisps showing at the temples, and the bright blue of her eyes was the exact colour of the dress she was wearing; a blue background with white polka dots and finished off with a red belt. Patriotic colours, such as most of the women, both old and young, were sporting today.

Patience became aware of Maisie's glance and she looked up, smiling at her enquiringly. 'Yes, Maisie, love? Are you ready for another job to do?'

'Yes, I think so, Aunty Patience. We've just about finished all the sandwiches. D' you want some help with these trifles?'

'No, thank you, dear. They're just about ready, and we're not going to dish them out until the children have finished their sandwiches and cakes. Some of them might prefer to have just the red jelly... Is there something the matter, Maisie?' Patience was looking at her concernedly. 'You seem rather preoccupied.'

'No...not really,' replied Maisie. 'There's nothing the matter. I was just thinking that today, well, it's a sad day, sort of, for some people, isn't it, as well as us celebrating the end of the war. Audrey and Tim; it's them I was thinking of, really. It's sure to remind them of their parents... Of course I know that you and Luke are their mum and dad now, and that they're very happy...'

'I know exactly what you mean, my dear.' Patience put an arm around her and gave her a quick hug. 'You're always a great girl for thinking things through, and, do you know, you and I always seem to think alike.'

'Great minds, eh, Aunty Patience?' smiled Maisie.

'Of course! Yes, as you say, Audrey and Tim are sure to have memories today, but let's hope that the pleasant ones outweigh the not so pleasant. Although none of us must ever forget... It's a day of mixed feelings for a lot of folk; for your friend, Doris, as well. She's always bright and cheerful, bless her, but there must be times when she thinks about her father... That tragedy all came about as a result of the war.'

Maisie nodded, remembering how Doris's father, Walter Nixon, had been killed, not by enemy fire, but on a training exercise in his army camp in the south of England, by a stray bullet. He had not even needed to have joined up at all as he was over forty years of age and, moreover, he was a farmer in a reserved occupation.

'Yes... Doris as well, of course,' said Maisie thoughtfully.

'But let's not be down-hearted,' whispered Patience in her ear. 'Come along; let's make sure that we've got everything ready. It won't be long before the hordes descend on us.'

'Audrey...' she called to her daughter, 'and you as well, Doris. I think the next job is to put a selection of sandwiches on big plates to put in the middle of the tables. Allow three sandwiches each...'

'Supposing some take more than three?' said Maisie. 'I'm thinking about our Jimmy actually. He can be a greedy little pig when he gets going, and I can just see some poor little kid only getting one.'

'Mmm...good point,' agreed Patience. 'But we'll be circulating, won't we, to make sure there's fair play? And I suggest we don't put the cakes out until the sandwiches have gone.' She laughed. 'That's what my mother used to say when I was a little girl. "Bread and butter first, Patience, and then you can have your cake." And I've never forgotten it.'

'And you've never let us forget it either, Tim and me and little Johnny,' said Audrey, with a sly grin at her.

'No; children don't change much over the years,' said Patience, smiling, 'nor do mothers' words of wisdom... Now, girls, I'll leave you to get on with that little job, and I'll go and help Mrs Hollins and Mrs Spooner with the big jugs of orange squash. And there are some little sausage rolls that Mrs Campion has made. I think it would be a good idea to hand those round, then we can make sure

that nobody takes more than one... Oh help! They're
beginning to arrive already, and we did say not till half
past three...'

——

It was early for a tea-party – too soon after dinner, some had
said – but it was necessary because the hall would need to be
cleared afterwards and the chairs re-arranged ready for the
evening concert. And whether the children had eaten a midday dinner or not, they all tucked in with gusto to the
delectable treats on offer. The sandwiches and tiny sausage
rolls, each one no more than a good mouthful, were soon
demolished, and then it was time for the cakes to be handed
round. Mouth-watering offerings, home-baked by the
members of the Women's Institute and the women of the St
Bartholomew's congregation; jam tarts; fairy cakes; iced
buns decorated in white and blue, with a red cherry in the
middle; chocolate clusters; and almond tarts and moist
gingerbread for the children with a more sophisticated taste.
    Maisie, going round from table to table, handing out cakes
– 'Just one each at first' – was viewing the scene with great
interest. The grown-up helpers were pretty much the same,
plus one or two new ones, as she remembered from her early
days in Middlebeck. Mrs Muriel Hollins, with her co-
workers – her minions, as they were often referred to – Mrs
Jessie Campion and Mrs Ivy Spooner were very much in
evidence. At the start of the war they had been stalwart
members of the WVS, as well as the WI, whose job it had
been to organise the evacuation scheme in their town. They
appeared very little different now, some six years later. Mrs
Hollins was just a shade plumper, maybe, and certainly a
shade bossier; although she was jovial today, rather than her
usual bossy self, determined that the children should have a
whale of a time.
    'Now then, tuck in and enjoy yourselves, boys and girls,'
she boomed at them. 'Isn't this fun! And how smart you all
look today. I can see a lot of mothers have been busy on their

sewing machines.' Suddenly, she burst into song, to the amusement of many of the children who started to giggle behind their hands.

*'Red, white and blue; what does it mean to you?*
*Surely you're proud; shout it aloud, Britons awake...'*

But her rich contralto voice was really quite a joy to listen to. Maisie knew that Muriel Hollins, also, would be singing a solo at the concert that evening.

There was, indeed, an abundance of red, white and blue in the church hall, not only in the Union Jacks and the bunting and streamers strung across the room, but in the clothes of all the children and a goodly number of the adults. Maisie knew that her mother's draper's shop had run out of the special red, white and blue ribbon which they had ordered for the occasion. It now adorned the heads of the girls, both the big and the little ones, setting off all kinds of hairstyles; plaits and pony tails, bobbing ringlets and straight short hair finished off with a fringe.

There had been a run, as well, on the red-and-white, and blue-and-white gingham that Lily had in stock. The majority of the smaller girls wore gingham dresses, and there were several boys, too, wearing shirts of the same material. Others wore white shirts, many with red or blue bowties.

The grown-ups, also, had risen to the occasion. The WVS ladies were not dressed in their usual green today, which they had proudly worn when occupied on their wartime duties. It would have been too hot for such clothing; besides, the war was over and it was time now for a bit of frivolity. Mrs Hollins wore red, not really a good choice for such a florid-faced lady, although it could be said that her dress matched her complexion. Maisie had never seen her so excited. Mrs Spooner wore a mid-blue dress with a white lace collar and a pretty white lace-edged apron; sensible attire for a sensible lady; and Mrs Campion looked like a stick of rock in vertical red, white and blue stripes.

Miss Amelia Thomson, the spinster lady who lived in the house across the green, opposite to the Rectory, was more soberly clad, as one might have expected. Her ankle-length dress was of navy-blue crêpe de Chine with tiny white spots, but she had actually trimmed it with an artificial red rose pinned discreetly to one side. The woman had mellowed considerably over the long years of the war, Maisie thought to herself, remembering the forbidding person whom she and Audrey had met on their first day in Middlebeck.

'Maisie, Maisie...' shouted a little piping voice, near to her elbow. 'Cake for me...please,' he added, as he knew he should. It was Johnny Fairchild, bouncing up and down with excitement, but being kept in check, more or less, by his adoptive brother, Timothy, who was sitting next to him. A couple of Tim's friends seemed to be finding the child highly amusing; and Johnny, knowing he had a captive audience, was acting up for all he was worth. He was normally a very well-behaved little boy. It didn't help, though, that Maisie's mischievous brother, Jimmy, was also at the same table.

'Yes, Johnny; which cake would you like?' asked Maisie.

'That 'un,' said Johnny, laughing and pointing to an iced bun with a cherry on the top.

'You mean, that one...please,' said Maisie, frowning a little at him. 'Say it properly, Johnny.'

'Please can I have that cake, Maisie?' he asked, more quietly, with a twinkle in his blue eyes, the legacy of both his mother and his father. Her heart leapt with a surge of affection for him. How like his mother he was with his shock of auburn curls and his winning smile; but you could see Luke there, too, in his finely drawn features. He would be a handsome lad when he grew up.

The rector was still a handsome man. Maisie could see him now, out of the corner of her eye, standing at the side of the room and smiling indulgently at his son, but not wanting to interfere. He would know it was unlikely that Johnny would get too much out of control. She gave him a quick meaningful grin and turned back to his son.

'That's better, Johnny. Take the paper case off the bun...
That's right. And you, Jimmy...' She frowned at her brother.
'Don't encourage him to be silly. Now, think on! Be a good
boy.'

'What, me? I'm always good!' replied Jimmy, to guffaws
of laughter from the rest of the table.

'Shh...' she admonished them. 'Mrs Hollins and Mrs
Campion are coming round to see who wants some jelly and
trifle. They won't give it to silly boys and girls.'

Sure enough, the two women, Muriel Hollins in the lead
bearing the trifle dish, and her second-in-command, Jessie
Campion, following behind with the dish of jelly, were
already doing the rounds. The lads fell quiet. Some of them
had been in Mrs Hollins's Sunday School class and knew her
as something of a dragon.

Audrey appeared at Maisie's side with a large jug. 'Now,
boys; who's ready for some more orange squash?' she asked.

'Me, me, me!' shouted Johnny, bouncing three times on his
chair. Audrey scowled at him in a pseudo-stern manner, and he
added, angelically, 'I mean...can I have some, please, Audrey?'

She ruffled his ginger curls fondly before half filling his
cup. 'Good boy, Johnny. Just try and calm down, eh? If you
get too excited Mummy might not let you stay up for the
concert tonight.' Johnny would be there, though, as she well
knew, as there would be nobody left in the Rectory to look
after him.

She poured the squash into the other cups that the boys
were holding out, then put the jug down. 'Do you know
what this reminds me of?' she said to Maisie. 'All the kiddies
sitting round the tables...'

Maisie nodded. 'I can guess what you're thinking about.
The day we arrived in Middlebeck, eh? When we were poor
homeless little evacuees...' She gave a mock sniff of despair.
'Oh dear, oh dear... But it all turned out OK, didn't it?'

'I know it's not just the same, not really,' Audrey went on.
'We sat at long trestle tables, if I remember rightly...'

'And we weren't even here, were we?' said Maisie. 'We

were in the Village Institute, not the church hall.'

'Goodness, so we were. I'd forgotten that...'

'And it was a sad time, wasn't it, all of us feeling lost and bewildered, and wondering where we'd end up? And today's a happy occasion.'

'Yes...' Audrey nodded thoughtfully. 'It brings back memories, though, seeing the same people that were there then; Mrs Hollins and Mrs Campion...and Miss Thomson.' She smiled reminiscently, shaking her head. 'I was frightened to death of her at first, but really she was just a prim and proper old lady who wasn't used to children. She's quite nice to us all now, isn't she?'

Maisie nodded, recalling that Audrey had spent a not very happy couple of months staying at Miss Thomson's house across the green, until circumstances had changed and she had been moved to the Rectory to be with Maisie.

'And I'll never forget how you took care of me that first day, Maisie,' Audrey continued. 'I was a real misery, wasn't I, weeping and wailing and making a fuss?'

'You were homesick,' said Maisie, 'that's all. None of us had ever been away from home before, without our parents. But as for me...well, it was more of an adventure, really.' And a happy release, she recalled, from Sidney Bragg, her stepfather, and his loutish son, Percy.

'Then we met Doris,' said Audrey. 'She was kind to us, wasn't she?'

'That was the next day at Sunday School,' said Maisie, 'when we were all put into Mrs Spooner's class... And there were four of us at first,' she added in a low voice, glancing towards Timothy.

'I know; I hadn't forgotten,' said Audrey. 'That's why today is a little bit sad, as well as happy.'

Both girls were remembering Ivy Clegg, Tim's sister; the two Clegg children had been amongst several evacuees from Hull. The four girls – Maisie, Audrey and Ivy, the evacuees, and Doris had formed a close foursome. Then, that first Christmas of the war, Ivy and Tim's mother had taken her children back to Hull. It had been the time of the 'phoney war', but all too soon the bombing raids had started on the major cities. Ivy had been killed, along with her mother and father, and Timothy, injured, but the only one of the family to escape death, had been brought back to Middlebeck, where he had been fostered and then adopted by the rector and his wife.

Maisie smiled consolingly at her friend. 'Cheer up, eh? Tim's happy enough now, isn't he?'

'Yes, and so am I,' replied Audrey. 'You know I am. But memories are precious, too, aren't they, Maisie? We can never forget...'

Audrey moved away to the next table with her jug of orange squash, and Mrs Hollins and her partner arrived to dish out the trifle.

'Just jelly for Johnny, and for you, too, Jimmy,' said Maisie in a motherly way. Lily, busy working in the shop, was not there to see to Jimmy. 'We don't want you being sick and missing the concert.' The same applied, of course, to the rest of the children, but they were not her immediate concern. To her surprise both boys nodded in agreement.

'I'm so full I could burst,' said Jimmy.

'Me too!' piped Johnny. 'I could burst, I could burst...'

'Well, we mustn't have that,' said Mrs Hollins, laughing. 'What a mess it would make...'

The dishes were soon scraped clean, and whilst the tables were being cleared and an army of ladies prepared themselves for the mammoth task of washing up, Mrs Hollins, a veritable Jack of all trades, seated herself at the piano.

'Come along, boys and girls,' she shouted. 'Pull up your chairs and we'll have a sing-song...'

And soon the roof of St Bartholomew's church hall was almost raised from its rafters by the strains of, *'Run rabbit, run rabbit, run, run, run...'*

# Chapter Two

The stage in St Bartholomew's church hall was used only rarely for concerts. If there were meetings of some importance then the rector and his spokesmen from the church council might sit up there, the better to command the attention of the audience. And during the recent elections the Parliamentary candidates from all three of the main parties – Conservative, Labour and Liberal – had used the stage as a rostrum. They had found themselves, however, addressing gatherings which could be described as 'only fair to middling'. It had been regarded as a foregone conclusion that the Conservative candidate, a businessman from Leeds who had held the seat for years, would be returned once again. And so he was, but with a vastly reduced majority. And countless other seats, in all parts of the country, had been lost to the victorious Labour party.

'Poor old Winston!' was the cry on the lips of many people. 'And after all he's done for our country. What a shame...' But politics were not openly discussed. What went on between the voter and the ballot box was strictly confidential. There would have been many more surprises if the folk of Middlebeck could have seen the crosses on the voting papers. As well as the 'Poor old Winnie' brigade, there were countless others who were thinking, if not saying outright, 'It's time for a change...well, maybe next time.'

But on this day politics was forgotten as the stage was being prepared for its proper purpose, that of putting on an entertainment. The red velvet curtains were somewhat faded and not used to a great deal of opening and closing – they must have been there since the first war, many folk remarked – but after a slight adjustment to the pulleys and runners they were soon in working order again. There were even a couple of spotlights which were rigged up for the infrequent concerts by able men from the church congregation.

There were two small cloakrooms to the right and left of the stage which served adequately as dressing rooms, one for the men and boys and the other for the women and girls. It was a tight squeeze in the women's room, but everyone was in good humour and the feeling of excitement and anticipation was palpable.

'You look lovely, Maisie,' said Audrey, with not a trace of envy. 'It's a real glamorous dress, just like a film star's.'

'Thank you,' replied Maisie. 'You don't think it's too... well, daring, like? A bit too low at the front?'

'No, of course it isn't. I thought it might be when you described it, but it's just right. It's a gorgeous colour, and that coral lipstick you're wearing matches it exactly.'

Maisie rubbed her lips together a little self consciously. 'You don't think it's too bright? It was Mum's idea, actually. She never really liked me wearing it before, but she said with me being on the stage it would give me a bit more colour.' She did not need any artificial colour on her cheeks, however, as the excitement, tinged with nervousness, that she was feeling had heightened them to a rosy glow.

'I'm dead nervous,' she said, clutching at her stomach. 'Talk about butterflies; it feels more like baby elephants doing a dance in my tummy! But at least I'm getting my solo over with quite early in the programme. I wouldn't have wanted to wait till the second half.'

'Good luck, anyway,' said Audrey. 'Oh no; you're not supposed to say that, are you, when you're going on the stage? You're supposed to say "Break a leg", aren't you? But I think that sounds silly. Anyway, I know you'll be just great.'

Patience popped her head round the door at that moment. 'Choir members, would you make your way up to the stage, please? The concert is just about to start, after Luke has welcomed everybody.'

The men and women of St Bartholomew's church choir,

including Maisie and a few other girls of a similar age, assembled themselves in their correct order – sopranos, altos, tenors and two bass singers – behind the curtain, as the Reverend Luke Fairchild welcomed everyone to the Victory concert.

'...and what a lot we have to celebrate and be thankful for this evening. So, on with the show, starting off with our own church choir.'

Applause broke out as soon as the curtains, somewhat hesitantly and jerkily, were drawn back to reveal the choir members, the men resplendent in dark suits with red bow ties, and the women in long dresses of varying styles. Rarely were they seen in such magnificence. Mr King, the elderly choir master and organist, but just as competent on the upright piano as the church organ, announced that the opening item would consist of songs by the well-loved Ivor Novello.

There were audible sighs of, 'Aah, lovely...' from some members of the audience, then the choir started to sing, 'Keep the Home Fires Burning'. After the opening chorus, one of the bass singers sang the verses and the audience joined in heartily with the choruses.

*'There's a silver lining, through the dark cloud shining,*
*Turn the dark cloud inside out, till the boys come home.'*

The sentiment of the song brought tears to a few eyes plus cheers and frenzied clapping, and this was only the start of the evening.

'And that song, of course,' said Mr King, when the applause had died down, 'was written by Mr Novello in 1914, at the start of the last war. And it is just as applicable today. How happy we are that our boys have come home and that some of them are here tonight.' He had to wait for another burst of clapping before his next announcement. 'And now for some gentler numbers from the same great composer. Here is our very own Maisie Jackson to sing for you that lovely song from *Perchance to Dream*; 'We'll gather lilacs...'

Maisie stepped forward into the spotlight, and as she did so she felt the fluttering sensation inside her ease a little. Because there, in the second row, smiling encouragingly at her, was her mother, with her old friend Mrs Jenner, who owned the draper's shop, sitting next to her. And Audrey and Doris were there in the wings, and the thought of them rooting for her gave her confidence. She started to sing, trying to remember all she had been taught about the correct way to breathe: deeply and from the diaphragm so that she did not lose control.

> '*Although you're far away, and life is sad and grey,*
> *I have a scheme, a dream to try...*'

It was becoming a little easier as she went on. She was aware that her first few bars might have been a trifle wavery, but she started to gain in confidence as she heard her voice reaching the top notes quite easily without straining, soaring out into the hall over the heads of the audience. She was afraid to stare around too much at the rows of people in front of her in case she forgot her words – that would be dreadful, especially as she knew the song backwards and inside out with constant practising – but she could not resist taking a fleeting glance.

Bruce's parents, Archie and Rebecca Tremaine, were plainly visible in the middle of the front row, just in front of her mother, as befitted their importance as the local squire and his wife. The title was largely a courtesy title afforded to Archie as the biggest landowner in the area. The Tremaines lived in the aptly named Tremaine House, and the land surrounding it included the Nixon's farm where Doris lived with her mother and brothers. Archie and Rebecca were smiling at Maisie, but she knew it would be considered unprofessional to smile back. And so, after her eyes had lighted on them briefly she looked away again.

She could see that Bruce was not with them. She felt a tiny pang of disappointment, but then it would not be his style, she told herself, to take an important seat with his parents. He would be more likely to sit further back, perhaps with others of his own generation. That was if he knew anyone well enough. Bruce had been educated at a public school in North Yorkshire, and not at the local grammar or secondary school like most of his contemporaries in the town; and so had never had a chance to make close friends in his own neighbourhood; and for the last two years, of course, he had been away serving in the RAF.

> *'We'll gather lilacs in the spring again,*
> *And walk together down an English lane...'*

The chorus was familiar now to many people, after being sung and played on the wireless countless times, following the production of the play in London's West End earlier that year. And as she sang the familiar words Maisie caught her first glimpse of him.

He was sitting about halfway back on an end seat near to the aisle, leaning forward as though he wanted to get a better look at her. And even at that distance and in the dim light she could tell that he was smiling. His dark eyes were glowing with pleasure and delight...at being home again, no doubt, she told herself. She must not read too much into his smile, but it was so good to see it again. After letting her glance linger on him for only a few seconds she looked away again; she fixed her eyes on a point near the back of the room to enable her to focus her attention on her song.

But her thoughts still kept wandering back to Bruce. 'And walk together down an English lane...' The words assumed a greater significance as she recalled the first time she had met Bruce Tremaine...

She was an evacuee. It was only her second – no, her third – day in Middlebeck if she remembered rightly, and she had been exploring the countryside behind the church with

Audrey. Then Doris, their new friend from the farm, had joined them, anxious to teach these city kids some of the lore of the country. And then Bruce had suddenly appeared on the scene, chasing after Prince, his boisterous collie dog, who had frightened Audrey, causing her to fall down and spill her blackberries...

Maisie realised now that she had started to fall in love with him, just a little bit, on that very first day, even though she was angry with him – or, rather, with his dog – for frightening her friend, and though she was only nine years old. He had seemed posh to Maisie, especially the way he talked. She had never met anyone like him, especially not a boy. She had not been keen on boys at all at that time, comparing every one that she met with her loathsome stepbrother, Percy. But she had soon realised that Bruce was different; he was kind and considerate and ever such good fun, and not the slightest bit snooty towards her and her friends, in spite of being a few years older and, moreover, the son of the squire.

Her song came to an end to ecstatic applause from the audience and shouts of 'Well done, Maisie love...' She was well known now in the little town of Middlebeck and popular with her own peer group. Feeling thankful that it was over, she gave a slight bow to acknowledge their ovation, then took her place amongst the other sopranos.

The choir then sang 'Waltz of my Heart' and 'I can give you the Starlight' from the musical *The Dancing Years*, with the audience, though unbidden, joining in with the more familiar words. The last song, 'Rose of England', was another one very appropriate to the occasion.

Muriel Hollins was the soloist this time, a majestic figure in midnight blue satin, with a white rose anchored to a spot just above her magnificent bosom, which rose and fell visibly with every breath she took. She had a rich and melodious contralto voice, which had been known to cause amusement amongst the choir boys at practices, when she insisted on demonstrating how a certain phrase should be sung. But the young boy choristers were not included in that night's performance – Ivor Novello was not considered to be their forte – so there was no giggling. And certainly none from the members of the audience who, once again, were moved by the patriotic sentiments.

> *'Rose of England breathing England's air,*
> *Flower of Liberty, beyond compare;*
> *While hand and heart endure to cherish thy prime,*
> *Thou shalt blossom to the end of time.'*

When they had taken a bow – well, two and three bows to be accurate – the ladies of the choir retreated to their dressing room to refresh themselves with drinks of orange squash. There were seats reserved for them in the hall so that they could watch the rest of the concert if they so wished; but Maisie chose to stay with Audrey to help her to get the children ready for their *Alice in Wonderland* scenes. The girls, that was, because the boys who were taking part were in the other dressing room, the male one, in the charge of a lad called Brian. He was Audrey's co-producer, a sixth-former at the grammar school in Lowerbeck, which complemented the school which Maisie and Audrey attended. Maisie believed that Brian Milner rather fancied her friend, but Audrey chose not to give too much away when it came to affairs of the heart, and she did not take kindly to teasing.

'You were brilliant, honest you were,' Audrey told her 'We felt real proud of you, didn't we, Doris? Oh...where's she gone?' She turned round looking for their other friend. 'Oh, there she is at the other mirror, doing her hair ready for her poem. She's on soon.'

Maisie glanced across at Doris. She was not within hearing distance – there was quite a racket going on anyway – so she leaned towards Audrey. 'He's here!' she whispered in her ear. 'I've seen him; about halfway back, at the end of the row.'

'Oh...! No wonder there's such a gleam in your eye,'

replied Audrey. 'Shall you go and say hello to him at the interval?'

'I think I'll wait till the end,' said Maisie. 'We're only having a ten minute break, aren't we, just to stretch our legs and so on? And I don't want to appear too eager, you know; as though I can't wait to see him.'

'Which would be quite true...' Audrey grinned slyly.

Maisie shrugged, aware that she was letting her feelings show too much, something she had been determined not to do. 'Well...yes; it's good to see him again,' she said, with an air of nonchalance. Her cheeks felt hot and Audrey was looking at her knowingly.

'Joanie...come over here, love,' Maisie called to her sister, 'and I'll help you to fix your hair ribbons.'

'Doesn't she look just perfect in that dress?' said Audrey, taking the hint from Maisie and changing the subject. 'Just like the pictures of Alice in the books. Your mum's been busy, hasn't she, Joanie?'

Joanie nodded. 'She's done nothing but sew just lately, hasn't she, Maisie? My dress, and Maisie's an' all.'

Joanie, as Alice in Wonderland, was wearing a mid-calf length dress of pale blue cotton, with puffed sleeves, a white collar and trimmings and a white apron tied around her waist. She had been growing her hair especially for the performance, and Maisie brushed it for her now. It was a pale golden colour, straight and shining, and fell to just below her shoulders. Her sister fastened it back with kirby grips, then secured the blue ribbon bows, one at each side of her forehead.

'There now,' she said, kissing her lightly on the cheek. 'You'll do. In fact, you look lovely.' They were not, as a family, much given to a lot of hugging and kissing. But Maisie, over the years, had been amazed at the transformation of her once naughty, grubby, and not very likeable little sister, into this pretty, polite, and friendly nine-year-old girl. And Jimmy was shaping up quite nicely too.

'Aw, give over, Maisie! Don't be soppy,' said Joanie; but

she could not disguise her pleased smile. 'Are we on soon, Audrey?' she asked. 'Have I time to go to the lav?'

Audrey laughed. 'Yes; you'd better go. We're on after Doris's poem, and she's next. You four girls who are being the playing cards, you've all been to the toilet, have you? Because you won't be able to sit down when you've got these costumes on.'

The four girls nodded in unison, then Audrey and Maisie placed the large cards – the three and four of hearts, and the three and four of spades – over their heads. The numbers of the playing cards were painted on both the front and the back, and the cards were secured at the shoulders and sides with tapes. Audrey and her friend, Brian, with Maisie sometimes assisting them, had spent many evenings at the Rectory designing them.

Maisie shrieked with laughter when Doris turned round from the mirror. 'Goodness, Doris, what a scream you look! You'll bring the house down before you even start to speak.'

Doris's flaxen hair was done up in two plaits which, somehow, she had made to stick out at an angle on either side of her head. Each plait was finished off with a bright pink bow, with a third bow on top of her head. Her cheeks were normally rosy, but she had heightened their colour with dabs of rouge like a Dutch doll. Her dress was of pink and white gingham, one that she had used to wear a couple of summers ago, but she – or her mother – had altered the bodice to fit her increasing bustline, and the shortness of the skirt did not matter. Layers of stiffened petticoats underneath made it stand out, revealing her shapely, rather plumpish, legs and her feet in white ankle socks.

'I told you they were supposed to laugh,' said Doris. 'Oh heck! D'you think I've overdone it? I feel sick. Oh... Oh dear! I can't go on...'

But Maisie and Audrey knew that it was mostly just banter. Doris would be fine once she got on to the stage.

''Course you can, don't be daft,' said Maisie, giving her a push. 'Luke's announcing you now. Go on; get a move on.'

Doris grimaced as she went through the door. 'I still don't know what she's going to recite,' said Maisie. 'Come on, Audrey; let's go to the front and listen, shall we?'

'No; I'd better stay here and keep an eye on the children,' said Audrey. 'I can hear well enough from the side of the stage. You go...'

Maisie tiptoed out and stood by the side wall, not allowing her eyes to stray further back down the hall, but fixing them on the stage. The laughter and applause greeting Doris's appearance was beginning to die down, and she grinned at them, all trace of nervousness, if there had ever been any, completely gone.

'Matilda,' she announced in a confident voice, 'by Hilaire Belloc.' And then, ghoulishly and leaning confidingly towards her audience, 'Matilda, who told lies and was burned to death!' She paused for effect, and some members of the audience responded with a reciprocal, 'Aahh...', knowing, from the girl's appearance that this would be a poem to evoke laughter and not a feeling of horror.

> 'Matilda told such Dreadful Lies,
> It made one Gasp and Stretch one's Eyes...'

Doris was a born actress, thought Maisie, as she watched her friend's expressive face and meaningful gestures, but no one seemed to have realised it before. There had not been much opportunity for concerts and play-acting during the war years, such performances as there were having been held during daylight hours because of the blackout regulations.

> '... And therefore when her Aunt returned,
> Matilda, and the House, were Burned.'

Maisie clapped till her hands were stinging and she gave a cheer, along with several others, as her friend bowed and grinned then left the stage.

It was time then for the last act before the interval, the

scenes from *Alice in Wonderland*. Maisie stayed where she was. Joanie would not want her fussing over her again. She was still forcing her eyes to look straight in front and not allowing herself to turn round, but once the Mad Hatter's tea party commenced she was thoroughly engrossed. Joanie was an enchanting Alice and word perfect too, and the boys who played the Mad Hatter, the March Hare and the Dormouse made the audience laugh, though not always in the right places. The Hatter's top hat was a shade too large and kept falling over his eyes, and the Dormouse, a tiny little lad, kept waving to his mother in the third row.

In the next scene Maisie was relieved to see that Jimmy behaved himself very well. He was one of the playing-card gardeners, the two of spades, engaged in the task of painting the white roses red. Fortunately, he was concentrating on doing just that and not splashing the paint all over himself and his mates which, at one time, would have been a pleasant diversion for him. The card worn by the Queen of Hearts – a twelve-year-old girl who shouted, 'Off with their heads!' in a very imperious voice – had been drawn and painted expertly by Audrey. The whole performance, indeed, was a great credit to her and Brian and there were cries at the end for the producers to come onto the stage and take a bow.

Brian emerged from one dressing room and Audrey, rather more unwillingly, from the other. As they stood in the centre of the stage, smiling and bowing a little to acknowledge the applause, Brian took hold of her hand. Maisie saw the blush which crept over her friend's cheeks, but she also noticed that her blue eyes were extra bright and sparkly as she turned to smile shyly at Brian and then at her mother and father, both standing proudly at the side of the piano.

'Well done, everyone,' said Luke. 'Very well done indeed. And now we will have just a short ten-minute interval before we start the second half of our programme.'

When Audrey came down from the stage she was surrounded by folk who wanted to congratulate her on the children's performances. Maisie could see that her friend was quite pink-cheeked with pleasure. This was her moment of glory and well deserved, too. Maisie added her own praise as well.

'That was great, Audrey. I'm really proud of you. I'm amazed at the way you've got our Joanie to do her part; she was terrific.'

'Yes, she was,' agreed Audrey. 'But I told you, she's a natural. It had very little to do with me; she just seemed to know what to do.'

'And all the others played their parts so well; it was obvious they were enjoying it.'

'Well, that's the most important thing at their age, isn't it?' Audrey laughed. 'As for me, I shall enjoy the rest of the concert much more now that that's over. Anyway, I'd better go and help the girls to get out of their costumes.'

'No... I'll do that,' said Maisie quickly. 'You stay and talk to these ladies.' A few of Luke's more elderly parishioners were smiling fondly at Audrey. She was very popular with them and had a pleasant manner which enabled her to associate with both the young and the old in her father's congregation. Already she was becoming quite an asset to him.

'Are you sure?' said Audrey. It was clear that she was enjoying her triumph, in her own quiet way.

'Of course I am,' said Maisie. She grinned. 'Off you go and chat to the old ladies,' she added in a lower voice. 'They'll love it.'

Maisie was feeling, suddenly, rather nervous and shy at the thought of encountering Bruce again. Besides, she was all dolled up in her finery ready for the next appearance of the choir near the end of the programme. It would be better to wait until the end. Without a backward glance she went back into the dressing room to help the playing card girls with their costumes, and the Queen of Hearts, too, with her more elaborate regalia and cardboard crown. Joanie, though, wanted to stay in her *Alice* dress, minus the apron, and there was no reason why she should not do so. The children all hurried out to the seats reserved for them to watch the rest

of the concert, and Maisie busied herself tidying up the
costumes and props that had been used for the *Alice* scenes.

Audrey popped her head round the door. 'Come on,
Maisie. There are three seats at the end of a row near the
front, so you and me and Doris can sit together.'

'All right then,' said Maisie, joining her friends just as the
lights in the hall were dimmed. 'I'll have to leave you,
though, before the choir goes on again.'

'Our Timothy'll be playing soon,' whispered Audrey. 'I
knew you'd want to listen to him.'

'Yes, of course I do,' Maisie whispered back, as Luke
stepped forward to announce the start of the second half.

The next act was a conjuror; quite a competent one. He
was a middle-aged man who was also in the choir, and he
had the audience suitably impressed with his yards and yards
of silken handkerchiefs, his card tricks and the climax at the
end, a rabbit in a top hat.

Maisie leaned close to her friend and whispered in her ear,
under cover of the applause, 'Did you...er, did you see Bruce
in the interval?'

'Er, yes... I did, actually...' Audrey replied.

'Did you speak to him?'

'Only to say hello, that's all.' Audrey sounded quite off-
hand, almost impatient, in fact.

'Who is he sitting with? 'Cause he's not with his mother
and father...'

'No, I know he's not...'

'Who is he with then?'

But Audrey did not answer. She was looking ahead, her
eyes fixed on the stage instead of turning to look at her
friend. Then, 'Hush, Maisie,' she said. 'I'll tell you later.
We'll have to shut up now while Mr Carey does his poem.'

The audience had heard Albert Carey's monologue, 'The
Green Eye of the Yellow God' before, on more than one
occasion; but as a highly regarded church warden of many
years standing they gave him the attention and respect due to
him.

'There's a one-eyed yellow idol to the north of
   Kathmandu,
There's a little marble cross below the town;
There's a broken-hearted woman tends the grave of
   Mad Carew,
And the Yellow God forever gazes down.'

Loud, if not rapturous applause followed the last verse as
Albert Carey bowed and left the stage.

Maisie was beginning to sense some sort of a mystery.
'You said you'd tell me who Bruce is sitting with,' she
persisted.

Audrey was silent for a moment, then she said, 'He's with
a friend...from the RAF. He's wearing his uniform...and so
is his friend.'

'Oh, I see... And did he introduce you to the other young
man?'

Audrey looked at her oddly, then, 'No, why should he?'
she said. 'I told you, we only said hello.'

'I just thought he might've done, that's all...'

'Well, he didn't,' Audrey snapped, but immediately she
regretted it and turned and smiled at Maisie. 'I'm sorry... I'm
feeling a bit on edge. It's our Tim next and I suppose I'm
feeling nervous in sympathy with him. I hope he'll be OK. He
played his pieces beautifully before we came out.'

'I'm sure he will.' Maisie squeezed her friend's arm, her
perplexity about Bruce being put aside for the moment.

Then Luke announced, 'And now here is Timothy
Fairchild to play for us,' and Timothy took his seat at the
piano.

'Aw, bless him!' said Maisie, smiling fondly. 'Doesn't he
look grown-up?' Timothy was now eleven years old, due to
start at the grammar school in Lowerbeck at the beginning
of the September term. He was, in point of fact, only four
years younger than Maisie, Audrey and Doris; his sister, Ivy,
having been a friend and class-mate of theirs. But the older
girls had always made a fuss of him.

'My first piece is "Sonata in C" by Mozart,' he announced, quite confidently, in a voice that was still quite shrill and piping. He had recently joined the ranks of the boy choristers at St Bartholomew's and had been found to have a pleasing voice.

The first movement of the sonata was a popular one with budding pianists and familiar to the audience, many of whom had played it in their youth. Or attempted to play it, because it was not as simple as it at first appeared. The runs and cadences were quite tricky, but Timothy managed them all with scarcely a slip or wrong note.

Maisie found herself remembering the skinny knock-kneed little boy with the wire-framed glasses who had clung so desperately to his big sister when they were first evacuated to Middlebeck. She and her friends had tried to comfort and protect him then; and now he was Audrey's adopted brother. He had matured considerably since those early days and was no longer so nervous or self-effacing. His sandy hair still stuck up like porcupine quills, being unmanageable if it was allowed to grow longer; but his glasses, which he still needed for his short-sighted pale blue eyes, were more adult ones with a tortoiseshell frame. And that evening he was wearing his first pair of long trousers, grey flannels, with a crisp white shirt and red bow tie.

'And now I would like to play, "Butterflies in the Rain"', he said, smiling, as the applause for his first piece died down.

That, too, needed a good deal of dexterity and neat fingering, and he played it with even greater confidence. As he passed the three girls, on his way to join his parents, he grinned and uttered a very relieved, 'Whew! I'm glad that's over!'

'You were terrific!' said Audrey, sticking her thumb up in the air. 'Wasn't he, girls?'

'I'll say,' echoed Maisie and Doris.

'I'd better go now,' said Maisie, 'and tidy my hair and re-do my make-up. The choir's on again soon.'

'OK, see you later,' said Audrey. She gave her a

sympathetic sort of smile, and Maisie wondered why.

For the last item of the evening the choir had put together a medley of patriotic songs and ones that had been very popular in recent years. What other way could there be of concluding a concert to celebrate the end of the six long years of war?

'Wish me luck as you wave me goodbye'; 'I'll be seeing you'; 'The White Cliffs of Dover'. How familiar these songs were, having been heard time and again on the wireless and in dance halls all over the country, and sung by the Forces' own favourite, Vera Lynn. It was impossible to stop the audience from singing along, although they did not know the words to all the verses.

'A Nightingale sang in Berkeley Square'; 'Deep in the heart of Texas' (one introduced by the American GIs); and, inevitably, 'There'll Always be an England'.

> *'There'll always be an England,*
> *And England shall be free*
> *If England means as much to you*
> *As England means to me.'*

As everyone joined with great enthusiasm in the final verse, the lights in the hall went on again. There was frenzied clapping and cheering until Luke raised his hand as a signal for them to be quiet, if that were possible.

And Maisie, unable to contain herself any longer, looked to the centre of the hall. She could see Bruce at the end of the row, where she had picked him out dimly before; but now that the lights had gone on she could see he was wearing his blue airforce uniform. And sitting next to him, also dressed in airforce blue there was...a girl! A young woman, to be more correct, several years older than Maisie. A blonde-haired young woman, and as Maisie watched she turned and smiled at Bruce. And Bruce smiled back at her.

Maisie felt sick with the shock and had to restrain herself from gasping and crying out, 'Oh no...!' But she knew she must smile, like everyone else was doing, and they still had one more song to sing.

'Ladies and gentlemen,' said Luke. 'We would like you all to join with the choir to sing, "Land of Hope and Glory". You will find the words on the back of your programmes.'

It was a thrilling finale, jubilant and joyous, with several folk in the audience waving Union Jacks high in the air, but it was an emotional moment as well. There was scarcely a dry eye in the audience or choir as they sang the final words.

*'Wider still and wider shall thy bounds be set,*
*God who made thee mighty, make thee mightier yet.'*

Maisie's eyes were moist too, but not solely with the patriotic fervour that was gripping everyone. Why had she not realised? Of course; that was why Audrey had been behaving so oddly. And she, Maisie, ought to have known. What a complete and utter fool she was...

# Chapter Three

Maisie grabbed hold of her friend's arm. 'Why didn't you tell me? I've just seen him…with that girl. And I feel such a fool!'

Audrey's blue eyes were filled with concern. 'I'm sorry, Maisie; honest I am, but I didn't know what to do. I didn't want you to get all upset, because you had to sing again with the choir. Anyway…we're jumping to conclusions, aren't we? We don't know that this girl is anyone special.'

'I saw them look at one another,' said Maisie, 'all moony and soppy. Oh, Audrey, I'm such a stupid idiot! I don't even want to go and speak to him now, but I suppose I'll have to…won't I?'

Audrey nodded. 'I think so, or else it'll look funny, won't it? Listen…let's go and get our cups of tea, and then we can go and say hello to him, sort of casual like. I'll come with you. Just act normal, like you used to when we all went around together.'

There was a smaller hall leading off the main one where the Infant Sunday school and informal meetings were held. It was there that refreshments were being served, cups of tea and, as it was a special occasion, homemade shortbread biscuits rather than the usual Nice or digestives. Maisie and Audrey – Doris had gone to find her mother and brothers – collected their tea and biscuits from the table where Mrs Spooner and Mrs Campion were busy pouring out and went to mingle with the crowds of people. Some were standing and some were sitting in little groups, with everyone trying to balance a cup and saucer and a large biscuit without spilling the tea.

They caught sight of Bruce and his friend standing on their

own at the side of the room. It was Audrey who led the way to them.

'Hello again, Bruce,' she said. 'Did you enjoy the concert?'

'Indeed we did,' replied Bruce. 'What a talented lot you are... Hello there, Maisie. I saw you up on the stage, of course, but...it's lovely to see you again.' He smiled at her, just at her, it seemed, and his brown eyes were so warm and friendly. But she knew that that was all it was; he was pleased to see her again, because she was a friend. Immediately he turned to the young woman at his side who was looking quizzically at Maisie.

'Let me introduce you to my friend, Christine; Christine Myerscough. We met at the camp, didn't we, darling? And we are...well, we are very good friends. Christine...this is Maisie and this is Audrey.'

'How do you do?' The young woman shook hands with each of them. 'Pleased to meet you,' she said. Maisie had the feeling that that was not considered to be correct in posh circles, although a lot of people said it. Christine smiled at them, but it was a cool smile and did not reach her silver-grey eyes...which really were rather lovely, Maisie had to admit to herself.

'How do you do?' said Maisie, flatly, but trying to smile. She did not say, 'Pleased to meet you,' because she wasn't, but she felt that something more was required.

'Have you...have you known Bruce for a long time?' she asked. (Because he had been writing to her, Maisie, and his letters had not tailed off...not until very recently, she recalled.)

'Oh, for about six months,' said Christine. She smiled up at him. She was a small person, only five feet or so in height, much shorter than Bruce. 'But it seems like much longer, doesn't it, darling?' Maisie noted the 'darlings' uttered by both of them, and she felt a stab of anguish, and of anger, too.

'Yes...' said Bruce briefly, and then he went on, 'These two young ladies have been friends of mine for a long time, haven't you, girls? Ever since they came to live here at the start of the war.'

'Oh... I see.' Christine looked curiously at the pair of them, her delicately pencilled eyebrows shooting up into her forehead. 'You were evacuees then, were you?'

'Yes, we were, actually,' said Maisie, unable to prevent a shade of belligerence creeping into her tone. 'But we both live here now, in Middlebeck, don't we, Audrey? Audrey lives at the Rectory.' She gave a satisfied nod. 'The Reverend and Mrs Fairchild are her mum and dad.'

'Adopted ones,' explained Audrey.

'Oh, I see...' said Christine again. 'That's very interesting.'

'And Maisie's mother, and her little brother and sister, lived with my parents for quite a while at Tremaine House,' said Bruce. 'Mrs Jackson was in charge of the land girls, but she has a draper's shop now, on the High Street.'

'Oh, that's all very...interesting,' Christine repeated. 'It's so nice to meet your old friends, Bruce. And you are the girl who sang at the beginning of the show, aren't you?' She turned to Maisie, smiling indulgently and arching her perfect eyebrows. Maisie nodded.

'What a sweet voice you have, my dear. I do wish I could sing... And you're the girl who produced the play, aren't you?' she went on, looking now at Audrey. 'How very clever of you. I used to love *Alice in Wonderland* when I was a little girl. What very talented little friends you've got, Bruce.'

'Come on, Audrey,' said Maisie suddenly. She could feel herself boiling up inside and her fists clenching into balls. 'I must go and find my mum and our Joanie and Jimmy. 'Bye, Bruce... Bye...er, Christine.'

'Cheerio then,' said Bruce. 'Great to see you both again. See you soon, I expect.'

'Are you home for good now?' asked Audrey.

'No...but I'll be at home for a little while. I'll be seeing you...'

Audrey hurried to catch up with her friend who was already halfway across the room. 'Ohhh...' sighed Maisie, when Audrey stopped her in mid-flight. 'What d'you think about that then? How dare she...patronise us like that, as though we're a couple of silly kids?'

Audrey smiled. 'Well, I suppose she did, a bit. But perhaps she was just trying to be nice. I take it you're...not very impressed with her?'

'You're dead right I'm not! I can't stand her; I hate her!' Maisie stormed, but she had the sense to lower her voice.

'Aw, come on, love,' said Audrey anxiously. 'I know you're upset, you're sure to be, but you'll have to try and come to terms with it. She's probably all right really. She must be feeling awkward, being here for the first time and not knowing anyone.'

'She didn't seem like that to me,' muttered Maisie, 'and I'll tell you something; I don't think she's right for Bruce.'

'Well...you're sure to think that, aren't you? You'd think that about anybody that Bruce had met.' Audrey cast a worried glance all around, but nobody seemed to be watching or listening to the two friends. 'Er...shall we go and find your mum and the kids? I want to tell Joanie how pleased I was with her, and Jimmy, of course; I mustn't forget him, he behaved so well.'

'Hang on a minute, Audrey,' said Maisie. 'I know you think I'm being biased because I'm jealous about...Christine, and perhaps I am. But I really think she's not right for Bruce, or his family. I mean...she talks quite ordinary, and she's got a Yorkshire accent. I think she was trying to hide it, but she has!'

Audrey laughed. 'So have we. You're sure to have if you've always lived in Yorkshire, and probably she has, just as we have. Bruce didn't say where she was from, did he? I know he talks nicely, but that's because he's been to boarding school. But his parents don't talk as posh as he does, certainly not his father.'

'No, it's not just that,' said Maisie, shaking her head a trifle impatiently. 'I felt she was trying to act a bit refined, sort of, but that underneath she's really quite...ordinary. She wants him, Audrey; I know she does, and she's determined to get him. She knows he's the squire's son and...well, that's what I think.' Her voice tailed away, sounding very dispirited and disillusioned.

'So there you are! I've been looking all over for you...' Brian had appeared at their side, smiling delightedly when he saw Audrey. 'My mum and dad want to say hello to you, Audrey... Hi there, Maisie. I enjoyed your song.'

'Thanks, Brian,' she replied. She turned quickly towards Audrey. 'I'm going to find my mum now, and our Joanie and Jimmy. Actually... I'm ready to go home now. I feel...' she shrugged wearily, 'just dead tired.'

'I know; it's been a hectic day,' said Audrey, smiling understandingly at her friend, but unable to keep the elation out of her voice at the appearance of Brian. 'See you tomorrow...' The next day was Sunday; they were sure to see one another at church. 'Have a good sleep...and you'll feel better in the morning.' Audrey reached out and squeezed Maisie's hand as she hurried away.

'Mum...' She caught up with Lily and the children in the main hall, where they were talking to Luke and Patience, who was holding a very tired little Johnny by the hand, and young Timothy. 'Are you ready to go now? I mean – you know – when you've finished talking?'

The adults looked at her in some surprise, her mother with a little frown of annoyance. 'In a moment, dear,' said Lily. 'There's no hurry, is there? I was just congratulating Tim on his piano solo. Didn't he play well? Not that I'm an expert on piano music, or any sort of music, come to that. But it was a real treat, and he says it's the first time he's played in front of an audience.'

'Yes, he played brilliantly,' said Maisie, aware that her opening words might have been rather abrupt. 'Well done, Timothy... Sorry if I butted in...' She looked apologetically at her mother and at Patience and Luke. 'It's been a long day and I suddenly felt very tired.'

Lily still looked a trifle annoyed, but the rector and his wife nodded as though they understood. 'I'm sure you must be exhausted,' said Patience, 'after all the excitement of the day; the tea party and then the concert, and I know you were anxious about your solo. But it was very good, and we were all very proud of you, weren't we, Luke?'

'Indeed, we're proud of them all tonight,' replied Luke. His kindly glance took in Joanie and Jimmy as well as Maisie, and his sons, Timothy and little John. His hand rested briefly on Tim's sandy hair, then he stooped down and ruffled John's auburn curls. From the colouring of the two boys one might believe them to be natural brothers. 'And you are not the only one who is tired, Maisie. It's certainly long past this young man's bedtime, isn't it, Johnnie?' Johnnie nodded, then gave a wide yawn; and Joanie and Jimmy, also, were fidgeting.

'Yes, I reckon it's home-time,' said Lily. 'Have you got all your belongings, Maisie?'

'I'll just get my coat from the cloakroom on the way out,' replied Maisie. 'Goodnight, Aunty Patience, goodnight Luke, Timothy…'

'Good night, God bless…' said Luke and Patience simultaneously.

—

'That was not very polite, Maisie,' said Lily, as they left the church hall. 'You could see I was talking to Luke and Patience.

'Sorry, Mum,' mumbled Maisie. 'But I've already said sorry, haven't I? You don't need to keep on about it. Anyway, Joanie and Jimmy were ready to go. I could tell they were.'

'That's beside the point. Anyway, we'll say no more about it. I can see that you're tired, love… There's nothing else the matter, is there? I thought you might have wanted to stay a bit longer to talk to Audrey and Doris.'

'Why should I? Audrey was with her boyfriend anyway,' Maisie answered abruptly.

'Oh… I didn't know she had one,' said Lily. 'D'you mean that nice-looking boy who was standing on the stage with her? Well, fancy that!'

'He's quite nice looking, I suppose,' said Maisie with a shrug. 'He's called Brian Milner.'

'Mmm... Audrey's very young to have a boyfriend,' said Lily. 'And so are you, Maisie.'

'But I haven't got one, have I?'

'No...but it's too soon to be thinking about boys while you're still at school. There'll be plenty of time for that later.'

'I don't suppose you thought that when you were going out with me dad, did you?' retorted Maisie. She surprised herself with her outburst. It was very rarely that they mentioned Maisie's father, but Maisie knew her mother had been only sixteen or so when she had first met him.

'It was different then,' said Lily. 'I left school when I was thirteen, you know, to go and work at the mill; that's where I met your dad... Anyway, never mind all that now. I can see you're upset about something.' She looked at her daughter concernedly. 'You mustn't be jealous, love, because Audrey's got friendly with a lad before you. It'll probably come to nothing. The rector and Mrs Fairchild won't want her distracted from her school work. Like I said, there's plenty of time.'

'I'm not bothered about that,' said Maisie crossly. 'Why should I care about Audrey and Brian Milner?'

'All right, all right, love. I just wondered, that's all,' replied Lily. 'I see Bruce Tremaine had a young lady with him an' all tonight. Of course, he's several years older than you girls, isn't he? I always thought when he was knocking around with the three of you, before he joined the RAF, that he should find a girl of his own age. I know he only thought of you as children though...' Maisie was not answering and Lily looked more closely at her. She was staring fixedly ahead as they walked down the High Street, her lips pressed closely together.

'Oh... Maisie,' said Lily, suddenly realising what might be the problem. 'You're not upset about...? It isn't Bruce, is it?' The fact that her daughter didn't answer made Lily realise that that was, indeed, the case. 'Oh, lovey... I never realised you felt like that. But...he's years older than you.' She took hold of her daughter's arm. 'He's too old for you, darling. Besides...'

Maisie snatched her arm away. 'Leave me alone,' she cried. 'You don't understand; nobody does...'

She set off running down the street, her long pink dress billowing around her legs, not stopping until she reached the draper's shop. She let herself in with her own key and fled upstairs to her attic bedroom. When Lily arrived home she was lying on her bed, sobbing as though her heart would break.

—

'Oh dear, that poor girl; poor Maisie,' said Patience, shaking her head. 'I guessed what was the matter with her. I don't think she was tired... Well, she might have been, I suppose, but that wasn't all it was.'

She and Luke were enjoying a late-night cup of tea before retiring. The boys had gone to bed as soon as they came home, and Audrey had arrived back soon afterwards looking happy and starry-eyed. She, too, had gone straight to bed and, tactfully, her parents had not asked her any questions.

Luke regarded his wife quizzically. 'What do you mean, dear? I noticed that Audrey and Brian Milner appeared to be getting rather friendly tonight, and I expect he's brought her home, judging by her pink cheeks. You don't mean... Maisie isn't feeling jealous, is she? Did she "fancy" Brian, as they put it?'

Patience laughed. 'No, no...not Brian. You've got the wrong end of the stick, Luke. I'm surprised; you're normally such a perceptive soul. No... I've known for ages that Maisie has had what you might call a "thing" about Bruce Tremaine.'

'Oh dear! Are you sure?'

'Pretty sure. I know they wrote to one another whilst he was away; and I've noticed that certain look in her eyes whenever she mentions him. And she does seem to mention him rather a lot.'

'She's only young though,' said Luke. 'And so is Audrey, of course. They're only fifteen. And Bruce must be – what? – almost twenty-one now, isn't he?'

'Yes; he'll be twenty-one in November. Rebecca was telling me that they were planning to have a party for him. But she didn't mention anything about him having a lady friend when I spoke to her a couple of weeks ago. Perhaps the young woman was as much of a surprise to Archie and Rebecca as she is to the rest of us.'

'Maybe she is.' Luke nodded. 'I spoke to them briefly at the interval, Bruce and Christine, I mean, and I thought she seemed a nice sort of girl. She's very pretty, and he's obviously very taken with her.'

'Well, she would be on her best behaviour, talking to the rector, wouldn't she?' smiled Patience. 'I've only had a brief word with them both myself... but I sensed a sort of calculating gleam in that young woman's eyes. She wants him, Luke, I could see that, and she'll be determined to hang on to him.'

Luke chuckled. 'I know you are intuitive, my dear, but don't you think you're being a tiny bit imaginative? And jumping the gun as well. It might just be a casual friendship.'

'I don't think so; not as far as she is concerned at any rate. I've always thought that Bruce is a very innocent sort of lad. He had a sheltered boyhood, stuck away in that boarding school. I don't suppose he's ever had a girlfriend before.'

'You don't know that. He's been in the RAF for a couple of years now, so he's sure to have had a few corners rubbed off him. Don't worry about him. He's a sensible lad, and I'm sure he can take care of himself. And I know you're concerned about Maisie, but she'll have her heart broken many more times before she's through. She's only fifteen; she'll get over it.'

'I hope so,' replied Patience, deciding it would be best to say no more to her husband at the moment. It was true that Maisie was young in years, but circumstances had forced her to grow up quickly and she often showed the maturity of a much older person. Patience had seen the pain tonight in the girl's eyes and she knew that she was hurting very badly.

—

'That's girl's in love with you,' said Christine, when Bruce's parents, somewhat reluctantly, had gone to bed, leaving them alone in the sitting room.

'Which girl?' asked Bruce, with an air of innocence that was not assumed. 'I don't know who you mean, darling.'

'Oh, come off it, Bruce, of course you do!' Christine sounded impatient and she pulled away from his encircling arm. 'That girl who sang the song; the one with the soulful brown eyes. She's crazy about you; I can tell that she is.'

'What? Maisie Jackson...'

'Yes, Maisie; that's the one. I remember that was what you called her.'

'Don't be silly, darling; of course she's not,' laughed Bruce. 'Maisie? She's only a kid; she's only fifteen. Honestly, Christine, how could you possibly think...?'

'Because it's true. I'm a woman, aren't I, and I know. Feminine intuition, my darling. Don't tell me you haven't noticed the way she looks at you?'

'No, I can't say that I have,' replied Bruce thoughtfully. 'We've been friends for a long time; I told you so...' He chuckled. 'Actually, I don't think she liked me very much at first. She was very wary of me; she was of all boys. Apparently she'd had a bad experience with an awful stepbrother – I don't know all the details because it was never really talked about – and I know her mother was married to a brute of a man when she first came to live up here. Maisie had had a rough time...'

'She seems to have recovered well enough now,' remarked Christine. 'What happened to her brute of a stepfather? I take it he's not still around?'

'He was in prison the last I heard. He was doing a stretch for burglary and for beating up his wife. He came up here and had a go at Lily when she was living here, in Tremaine House. As far as I know he's still in gaol; it's the best place for him.'

'Oh, I see...' Christine suddenly went very quiet. 'Poor Maisie...' she muttered, but Bruce was not altogether sure that her utterance was sincere. 'So you befriended her, did you, the little evacuee girl...and her pal? Audrey, isn't it, the girl from the Rectory?'

'Yes... Maisie and Audrey.' Bruce smiled reminiscently. 'But a lot of water has flowed under the bridge, as they say, since those days.'

'And you're interested in rather older girls now, aren't you, darling?' Christine looked up at him teasingly in the enticing way she had, her lovely silver-grey eyes alight with amusement and desire. And, as always, he was powerless to resist. He bent to kiss her lips and she reached for him hungrily, her mouth opening beneath his, her hands cradling his head to draw him closer to her.

He drew away from her after a few moments. 'Steady on, darling. I don't think we should; not here, with my parents upstairs.'

'Where then, Bruce?' Christine demanded. 'Your mother has seen to it that we have separate rooms.'

'Well, of course she has! What else did you expect? You surely didn't imagine that she would...?'

'No, no, I suppose not.' She shook her head irritably. 'No, of course I didn't. It would be highly improper, wouldn't it? No, I guessed when you invited me to come and meet your parents that we would have to behave impeccably.' She shrugged away from him then, reaching for her shoulder bag and taking out a slim red packet of Du Maurier cigarettes. She lit one with her silver lighter and handed the packet to Bruce.

'Thanks, I will. You've got me into all sorts of bad habits,' he remarked, leaning towards her while she touched the flame to his cigarette.

'You are ridiculous, darling,' she chided. 'I can't believe you didn't smoke until you joined the RAF. What about that public school of yours? Don't tell me you didn't have a crafty drag or two in the dorm? I've heard all sorts of tales about what those public school toffs get up to.'

'Wildly exaggerated, I'm sure.' Bruce drew deeply and blew out an expert smoke ring. 'See how good I'm becoming... No, there was very little extreme behaviour at my school, believe it or not. And we were kept well away from any girls.'

'It wasn't just girls that I was thinking of,' said Christine slyly. 'I was thinking more of the boys...'

'Then you're barking up the wrong tree,' said Bruce vehemently. 'There was nothing of that kind, I can assure you.'

'I'm glad to hear it,' she said.

She smiled contentedly as she puffed away on her cigarette, looking around the Tremaine's elegant sitting room. 'I must say it's a lovely place your parents have here, Bruce. I'm very impressed...'

Her eyes took in the deep pile floral carpet, the floor length green velvet curtains which matched exactly the green background colour of the carpet, and the large three-piece suite; two enormous armchairs and the huge sofa on which they were sitting, dark green with chair back covers of cream linen edged with crochet work. A Dresden shepherd and shepherdess stood at either end of the mahogany mantelpiece, with a golden clock under a glass dome in the centre. There was no fire in the hearth as it was summertime, and the grate held a tasteful arrangement of leaves and fir cones. The house was gently heated throughout, when required, by a central heating boiler which Archie Tremaine had had installed just before the start of the war; one of the few houses in the area that could boast of such a commodity.

'Your father owns a lot of the land around here as well, does he?' Christine went on. 'The outlying farms, they belong to him, do they?'

'Only the Nixons' farm now,' replied Bruce. 'There were a couple of others, but my father sold them to the tenants. Walter Nixon might well have bought his farm as well, but he was killed during the war. It's still run as a family concern though. Ada, Walter's widow, is very competent, and she has her son, Ted, to help her as well as young Doris. That's the girl who was in the concert – she's a friend of Maisie and Audrey – the one who did the poem about Matilda. She's quite a scream, is Doris.'

'Yes, I'm sure she is,' said Christine, with an eloquent lift of her eyebrows. 'How many more little girlfriends are you going to trot out of the woodwork, darling?'

'That's the last one, I promise,' laughed Bruce easily. 'But to get back to the Nixons that I was telling you about...' As if I am really the slightest bit interested, thought Christine, trying not to look too bored.

'The eldest son, Joe, has just been demobbed – I caught a glimpse of him there tonight – so no doubt he will go back to working on the farm. They've had a land girl helping out, but the girls will all be going back home before long, I dare say, as the male farmhands return. They've done a marvellous job, though.'

'I'm sure...' replied Christine, on an exhalation of cigarette smoke. There were three land girls still billetted at Tremaine House, and she had been surprised to see how Bruce's mother treated them, almost as though they were members of the family.

'My father would like to sell the Nixons' farm as well, to the family of course. They've been invaluable tenants, and I know he'll be willing to help Ada financially if she would like to own it.'

'But there is still a good bit of land apart from that, isn't there?' asked Christine, in a casual tone, not wanting to appear too inquisitive.

'Yes, quite a fair acreage...'

'How does it work, Bruce? I know you have two older sisters...' Both were married and living a good distance from north Yorkshire, he had told her. 'But as the only son of the squire, it would all come to you, wouldn't it?'

Bruce burst out laughing. 'Good gracious, darling! We don't belong to the nobility.'

'But your father is the squire…'

'It's only a sort of courtesy title, really. It doesn't mean very much. He just happened to be the largest landowner in the district at one time, as were his father and his grandfather, although the estate was much larger in those days. There was a good deal of touching their forelocks and bowing and scraping went on then, I dare say, but times have changed now, thank goodness. Dad doesn't care for any of that nonsense – he's very liberal-minded – but he goes along with it when they refer to him as the squire.'

'Oh…I see,' said Christine.

'Anyway, what does it matter to us? My father isn't going to "pop his clogs" as they say round here, for many a long day, or so I hope, nor my mother.' He stubbed out his cigarette in the cut glass ashtray on the occasional table at his side, and put his arm around her again.

'What shall we do tomorrow, darling?' He did not give her time to answer. 'Church in the morning is obligatory, of course.'

'Is it really?'

'Oh yes… And then it will be the usual Sunday roast and all the trimmings that my mother insists on. And after that… how about a walk up to Middleburgh Castle; that's the ruin you can see up on the hill? Do you fancy that?'

'Yes, why not?' she shrugged. So much for asking her what she wanted to do tomorrow… 'It's all the same to me… How far is it?'

'Oh, just a couple of miles…and two miles back again, of course.'

'Is that all?' She gave a sardonic little laugh. She was not a great walker, or had not been until she joined the WAAF, since when the drilling and marching and square bashing had played havoc at first with her legs and feet. Back home in her native Bradford all the walking she had done had been around the shopping streets.

'You'll manage it easily, darling, and I shall be there to help you along. So long as you have some comfortable shoes to wear.'

'Of course I have; my WAAF regulation ones. They're well broken in by now.'

'So they are... I'm sorry about asking you to wear your uniform tonight, Chrissie, but I thought it would look better if we "flew the flag" together, so to speak.' She had been relieved to shed the serviceable black shoes, though, when they returned home, and to replace them with her frivolous red velvet slippers; they had been purchased long ago at Brown Muff's store in Bradford when such fripperies were still obtainable. And to take off her heavy blue jacket, too. It was a vastly inferior one to the uniform which Bruce wore as a Flying Officer.

'You will be able to dress up in your "civvies" tomorrow when we go to church,' Bruce continued. 'I shall feel so proud of you, darling. I'm longing to show you off to everyone.'

She smiled at him. 'And I'm proud of you too, Brucie. I'm only sorry that I have no family to show you off to.' She had told him, soon after they had met, how her parents had been killed in a car crash when she was a small girl, and that she had been brought up by her maternal grandmother. When her grandmother died, a couple of years ago, she had been left more or less alone in the world, apart from a few friends, and it was then that she had joined the WAAF.

Meeting Bruce six months ago had provided the fillip to her life for which she had been waiting. She was looking forward confidently to the future, but she knew that she must play her cards right.

———

Rebecca Tremaine knew she would not sleep until Bruce and his young lady had come upstairs. She knew it was foolish of her to fuss over him. He had been away from home for many years, apart from the long holidays, ever since he went away to boarding school at the age of thirteen. Surely, by now, she should have ceased to worry about him, especially now that the wretched war was over.

She had not been overly concerned about him whilst he was at school, knowing that he was in safe hands in the place that had been vetted by herself and Archie. Since he had joined the RAF, however – something he had been determined to do as soon as he was eighteen – she had had little peace of mind. She had been proud of him when he had been awarded his wings, but her pride had been overshadowed by her anxiety for his safety. She was relieved that she did not know when the bombing raids over Germany had been taking place; and Bruce had phoned home frequently – he had always been such a considerate and dutiful son – to let his parents know that he was safe and well. One blessing was that he had not been old enough to join the RAF at the time of the Battle of Britain. By the time he had enlisted, and had been accepted for officer training, there had been early signs that the war might be in its latter stages, and that Britain – please God – might be the victor.

Rebecca strained her ears as she heard footsteps on the stairs, then the sound of voices saying goodnight and doors closing. Archie, who she had believed to be asleep, was stirring at the side of her and when he turned over she could see that he, too, was awake.

'They've just come to bed, Archie,' she whispered, 'our Bruce and Christine.'

'Give over worrying about him, Becky,' grunted Archie, his voice muffled by the covers. 'He's old enough to look after himself. And she seems a nice sort of lass.'

'Do you think so?'

'Of course I do... Don't you?'

'Well...yes, I like her well enough, I suppose. But it was such a surprise – a shock, really – when Bruce wrote and asked if he could bring her home with him. We didn't even know he had a girlfriend, did we?'

'I shouldn't fret about it if I were you,' said Archie. 'He had to start sometime. And I dare say this girl will be the first of many. Now...shut up and go to sleep.' He leaned across to kiss her cheek, then humped the bed covers over himself as he turned round again. 'Goodnight, love. Have a good night's rest.'

'Goodnight, Archie...' she replied. The first of many? she thought. Perhaps her husband was right. He usually was, about so many things. But this time Rebecca did not think so. She guessed that Christine Myerscough might well be around for quite some time, maybe for ever...

# Chapter Four

The Reverend Luke Fairchild always tried to have some time alone in his vestry before the start of a service; to collect his thoughts and run his eye over his sermon for a final time, and to have a few moments in silent prayer. This morning, more than usually, he felt that he needed the solitude, and so he had left the Rectory a few minutes earlier than he normally did. His church wardens, Thomas Allbright and Albert Carey, who had served him and the congregation faithfully for many years, would join him about ten minutes before the service began, but for the moment he was on his own.

There was little quietude to be found in the Rectory nowadays. Even when he closed his study door, insisting that he did not want to be disturbed, the needs of his family had to come first, whenever there was a problem or a dilemma. That was how it should be when he was at home. He was the head now – he and Patience together, of course, because he regarded her in all family matters as equal with him – of what was quite a large family. And for that he had never ceased to give thanks to God for finally answering his and Patience's prayers.

For many years following his appointment to the living of St Bartholomew's church in Middlebeck, he and Patience had rattled around in the large Rectory like two peas in a jar. It had been designed, in Victorian times, for a large family such as was common in those days, not least amongst the clergy. But although he and Patience had prayed and longed for a child – and played their part enthusiastically, too, in what they hoped would lead to a conception – none had arrived. When the war started in 1939, they had both been more or less resigned to their childless state.

And then young Maisie Jackson had come to live with them. She had brought such happiness to them with her liveliness and warmth of personality, and also by her need to be loved and protected. Then, only a couple of months later, Audrey Dennison had come to live with them as well. She was a very different sort of child from Maisie in many ways; in her home background – a happy one, whereas Maisie's had been quite appalling – and in her more retiring and nervous disposition. But she, too, had needed love and care in those early days of the war. When her parents, separately, but both in tragic circumstances, had died, Luke and Patience had known that they must adopt her. Now Audrey was their dearly loved daughter and a great blessing to them, as was Timothy, who they had taken to their hearts and into their lives some time later.

And then, in a miracle too great at first to be believed, there had arrived their very own son, John Septimus, born when Patience was forty years of age and Luke just a couple of years away from fifty. Luke knew that he had, indeed, been blessed beyond measure in his home, his lovely wife and his happy family life.

But this morning, on this last Sunday in August, as he contemplated the service he was about to conduct, to give thanks for the final victory of the war, Victory over Japan, Luke's heart was heavy and his mind burdened with conflicting thoughts. Yes, he rejoiced in the victory and in the cessation of bloodshed and strife; but at what a dreadful cost had this victory been won.

Luke was by no means a pacifist. If he had been then he would not have served in the First World War, as he had done, as a second lieutenant in the Shropshire Light Infantry. And at the start of this recent war he had had thoughts at first of re-enlisting; he had been only in his early forties. But his bishop – and his wife, too – had told him, in no uncertain terms, that his place was here in his parish. And so he had remained, to be a leader to his flock, and to offer comfort and advice to the many members of the congregation who suffered tragedy and bereavement, or just weariness and depression during the long years of the war. There had been problems a-plenty in the little town of Middlebeck and Luke had known he was in the right place.

But he was a peace-loving man and he abhorred war and all that it entailed. What was war, when all was said and done, but a demonstration of man's greed and the desire to possess what he believed was rightfully his, and to subdue others to his own way of thinking? His wife had often said that if women were left to sort out the affairs of state then there would be no conflict between nations. It could all be resolved over a cup of tea. A very simplistic view, but maybe there was something in what she said.

Did the end justify the means? This was what he often asked himself. Archie Tremaine had been of the same opinion, he recalled. His son, Bruce, had become a pilot late on in the war. How they had hoped and prayed, Becky and himself, Archie had told him, that the war would be over before he was old enough to enlist. Alas, that was not to be; and Archie's concern, once the young man had started flying – apart from his constant anxiety for his son's safety, of course – was that he could have been involved in the devastating attacks against the city of Dresden. Bruce had never actually told them so, but Archie had wondered and had asked himself whether such an onslaught, killing thousands of innocent people, could ever be justified. Luke had empathised, knowing how he would have felt if a son of his had been involved.

And now Luke was asking himself the same question over the recent catastrophic assault on Japan. He had followed with mounting dread the news of the 'Forgotten Army', the British troops still fighting in the Far East. There had been furious resistance by the Japanese against any attempt to land in their country. The Allied leaders knew that over a million British and American prisoners of war would be massacred if Japan was to be stormed in November, as had been planned.

And then, on the sixth of August, the war in the Far East had been brought to its conclusion when a US Army Air Corps bomber had dropped the first atomic bomb on the city of Hiroshima. This had caused eighty thousand deaths. And the second bomb dropped on Nagasaki on the ninth of August had resulted in forty thousand more. On the fourteenth of August the Japanese had accepted the demands of the Allies; and in Britain, on the fifteenth of August the day had been celebrated as Victory over Japan day.

And their own Victory tea party and concert for the folk of Middlebeck had taken place yesterday. How trivial it all seemed, Luke mused, when one considered the global situation. The Second World War – and after the first it had been believed that there would never be another one – had resulted in over forty million deaths throughout the world.

But men and women must be given a chance to celebrate. They needed to give thanks and to look forward with renewed hope to what the future might bring; but never must anyone forget at what a tremendous cost this victory had been won.

Luke bowed his head in prayer... Lord, help me to think aright, and to set aside my depressing and gloomy thoughts. Help me, please, Lord, with the words I say, that I may, through You, offer comfort and hope for the future...

———

Later, as he looked around his congregation from his place in the pulpit – six feet above contradiction as his wife often joked – he found that his melancholia had lifted. The opening hymn, 'For all the saints who from their labours rest', had been sung heartily by the choir and congregation, and he could almost feel the raising of everyone's spirits.

For Luke there was always a sense of pride and quiet joy when he glanced down at his beloved wife sitting in her accustomed place in a pew near the front. That had been her place ever since he had been rector of the parish. And now an added joy was that she was accompanied by Audrey and little Johnnie, who was sitting between them. The little boy would go out during the sermon as it was asking too much of a small child to be still and quiet for the whole of the morning worship. A few of the teenage girls, including Audrey, had a rota and they took it in turns, Sunday by Sunday, to look after the young children who had come to church with their parents. Patience and Luke had agreed that John should get used to the idea of church attendance at an early age; and in September, when he was four years old, he would start at the afternoon Sunday school.

Patience looked very attractive, and elegant, too, in her leaf-green costume with the white collar, and a white straw hat trimmed with a green ribbon on her short auburn curls. Audrey, keeping a watchful eye on Johnny as he made a tower of the hymn books, was wearing the same sky blue dress as she had worn the previous night at the concert, and how well it complemented the colour of her eyes. She gave a knowing little smile at Luke as she met his glance, as if to say, Don't worry; I'm keeping an eagle eye on him...

Timothy was not with them as he was in the front row of the choir stalls, looking angelic, as all the choir boys did, with their white surplices and ruffles around their necks. He was taking his duties as a chorister very seriously, his eyes seldom straying from the music in front of him and his mouth opening wide, like a hungry little bird, to enunciate the words clearly, as Mr King, the choirmaster, had taught them to do.

Luke smiled to himself. Timothy, once so timid and unsure of himself, had come on by leaps and bounds during the last year. Luke glanced covertly at the row behind him where Maisie was sitting. What his wife had told him last night about the girl's fondness for Bruce Tremaine had surprised him. He still tended to remember Maisie as the odd and shabby, but delightful, little girl who had come to share their home six years ago. It was incredible to think that she might be old enough to consider herself in love... But then, so might Audrey; they were much the same age. He remembered, however – although it was many many moons ago – the pangs of young love and how they could hurt.

Maisie looked very much in control of herself this morning, he thought. She was singing away cheerfully, in her usual confident manner, and not letting her eyes wander into the congregation, as he was sure she must be wanting to do, for a glimpse of the young man that she...what? Luke asked himself. That she loved...or was it just a schoolgirl crush?

Bruce was there, sure enough, dressed in his uniform as he had been the night before, sitting quite near to the front with his parents and his lady friend, Christine. She was not in uniform this morning, but dressed in a pink and white candy-striped cotton frock and a white straw hat with a large brim. She looked very stylish, but very demure, too, with her eyes downcast at the hymn book in her white-gloved hands.

The hymn before the sermon, 'Lord of our Life and God of our Salvation' was one of Luke's favourites.

*'Lord, Thou canst help when earthly armour faileth,*
*Lord, Thou canst save when deadly sin assaileth,*
*Lord, o'er Thy church, nor death nor hell prevaileth;*
*Grant us Thy peace, Lord...'*

He knelt down in the pulpit for a few quiet words of prayer whilst the choir and congregation sang the final verse...

*'Grant peace on earth, and after we have striven,*
*Peace in Thy heaven.'*

The words were singularly appropriate for the occasion, he thought, as he stood to deliver his sermon. 'Now, Lord, may the words of my lips and the meditations of all our hearts be always acceptable in Thy sight...' he prayed aloud as the members of the congregation bowed their heads.

He glanced around at them, these folk who looked to him for spiritual guidance, and often for guidance in more worldly matters as well. He sometimes felt inadequate and unworthy of such a responsibility, and yet, somehow, he always managed to find the appropriate words of advice or comfort. The appointment of a rector, or of any minister of God, was for the 'cure of souls'. That was the ancient wordage and the one that was still used in the Church of England.

'My text this morning,' he began, 'is not taken from the Bible as is usual. Instead I would like to remind you of the words that our King, George the Sixth, spoke to us in his first Christmas broadcast of the war, when spirits were low and we were full of anxiety for the future...

'I said to the man who stood at the gate of the year, "Give me a light that I may tread safely into the unknown". And he replied, "Go out into the darkness and put your hand into the hand of God. That shall be to you better than light and safer than a known way."

'Those words still apply now when we stand on the threshold not of war but of peace...'

By the time Maisie left the church building, after chatting for a few minutes in the vestry with some of the other choir members, most of the congregation had dispersed. Luke was still at the door bidding farewell to his flock; it was his custom to stay until the last one had departed. She shook his hand and heard his sincere, 'God bless you, Maisie, my dear.' Then, as she turned away she caught a glimpse of Bruce with his parents and Christine, standing near the gate talking to Miss Thomson.

She slowed her steps. She had been hoping not exactly to avoid him, but she did not want to come face to face with him. She had willed herself not to look at him there in the congregation, although she had noticed him when the choir had processed past the end of his row during the first hymn. To her relief, at that moment she also noticed Miss Foster, the headmistress of the school, and Anne Mellodey chatting to two other ladies. Anne lifted her hand in greeting as the two women said their goodbyes and moved away.

'Hello there, Maisie. I've been looking forward to seeing you; you had disappeared last night when I was looking for you. I wanted to tell you how very much we enjoyed your song; well, we enjoyed all the concert, of course, didn't we, Charity?'

'Indeed we did.' The headmistress nodded. 'Your solo was delightful, my dear; and as for your Joanie, I felt so proud of her, and Jimmy too. It is so nice to watch a concert that one hasn't produced oneself, isn't it, Anne?'

'So it is,' replied Anne Mellodey. 'Yes, we were very glad to be members of the audience last night and not to be taking part in any way... How are you, Maisie? I haven't seen you for quite a while, not to talk to at any rate. You are looking well, and I can see you have been enjoying the sunshine.'

'Yes, I'm...very well, thanks.' Maisie was relieved that the tears she had shed the previous night had not done too much damage to her face. She had bathed her red eyes in cold water and had been determined to smile and put on a happy face. It seemed as though her efforts had been successful. 'And I've been enjoying this lovely weather, as you say.' Her face and arms and her bare legs had turned a pleasing shade of brown. 'So have all of us. I managed to persuade Mum that she needed a holiday, and she actually agreed to leave the shop – Mrs Jenner looked after it for a few days – while we went off to Scarborough, me and Mum and the kids.'

'Very nice too.' Anne smiled. 'Miss Foster and I spent a few days in the Lake District, didn't we, Charity? It was lovely and peaceful in Grasmere... Your mother is keeping well, is she, Maisie? I haven't seen her just lately.'

'Yes, very well indeed...' Maisie stopped short, deciding not to say that her mother's friend, Arthur Rawcliffe, was due home very soon. Anne's fiancé had been killed in the second year of the war, during the Battle of Britain, and since then she had spent most of her time, both in school and out of it, in the company of her friend and colleague, Miss Charity Foster. Not a very exciting sort of life, Maisie often thought, for such an attractive and personable young woman. Anne, she guessed, was still only in her late twenties.

'Maisie, come and have tea with us this afternoon,' said Miss Foster suddenly. 'Then we can all have a good chat together. That's a good idea, isn't it, Anne?' Her friend eagerly nodded her agreement.

'Unless...unless you are seeing some of your other young friends, of course? Audrey or Doris or...anyone else?'

'No...no, I'm not.' Maisie shook her head decidedly. 'Thank you very much; I would love to come for tea. What time shall I come?'

'Oh, mid-afternoon, about three o'clock, shall we say? We will look forward to seeing you. Now, Anne and I had better hurry back or else our shoulder of lamb will be burned to a cinder.'

'And I'd better go and give my mum a hand with the vegetables,' said Maisie. Sunday dinner was a ritual in most Yorkshire homes.

She walked with them to the church gate, and then the two teachers crossed the green to the schoolhouse on the other side, whilst Maisie made her way to the draper's shop halfway down the High Street.

—

'Miss Foster and Anne have invited me to tea this afternoon,' she told her mother as they ate their Yorkshire pudding, served in the customary Yorkshire way as a separate course before the main meal, with lashings of gravy. 'That's OK with you, is it, Mum?'

'Of course it is,' replied Lily. 'It'll be a change for you. You've always had a soft spot for Anne Mellodey, haven't you, love? Such a nice young woman... I hope she's not going to be left on the shelf and turn into an old spinster like Miss Foster. Such a pity her fiancé being killed, and she's never met anyone else, has she?'

'There's not been much chance of that, has there, Mum, with all the men away at the war?'

'No, I suppose not...'

'And, do you know, I never really think of Miss Foster as an old spinster – not like Miss Thomson is, I mean. She's always seemed so lively, especially for a headmistress, and not a bit old-fashioned and stuffy.'

'Too old to be a bosom pal of Anne Mellodey though. That young woman wants to get herself out of a rut before it's too late... Anyroad, I suppose it's none of our business, is it?' Lily smiled at her daughter. 'I'm glad to see you're looking more cheerful today. Got over it, have you?' She did not wait, however, for Maisie to answer. 'I thought you would. There's plenty more fish in the sea, remember that, love, when the time comes... Mind you, you've got to be careful where you cast your net. You don't want to make a silly mistake like I did, but I reckon you've got too much common sense for that... By the way, I'm expecting Arthur to call this afternoon. He should be back in Middlebeck by now, all being well.'

Maisie knew that the imminent return of Arthur Rawcliffe, due to be demobbed from his three years in the Army Catering Corps, was the reason for her mother's cheerfulness and her bright eyes and pink cheeks. Nor did she begrudge her mother this happiness. Arthur was a decent fellow, and she knew that Lily would never again make such a disastrous mistake as she had done when she married Sidney Bragg.

'Very nice, Mum,' she replied. 'Now I know why there's such a gleam in your eye.'

'Oh, give over! Don't be silly,' scoffed Lily.

'Will he be staying here?' Maisie asked innocently, although she knew what the answer would be.

'Of course not! Whatever are you thinking of, Maisie?'

'He could have my room, and I could sleep on the settee. I don't mind, honestly.'

'No, it's quite out of the question. He'll be staying with his sister at the other end of town until... Well, we'll have to see how things work out, won't we?' Lily stood up, looking red-cheeked and flustered. 'Now, let's get these dishes cleared away, Maisie. You've finished your puddings, have you, Joanie and Jimmy?' A needless question, as it looked as though the children's plates had been licked clean. 'Right then; we'll go and see to the roast beef...'

Anne Mellodey had been living at the schoolhouse with Charity Foster for six years. She had joined the staff at Middlebeck school as one of the two teachers who had been sent – or, rather, had volunteered – to take charge of the evacuees from Armley. Her colleague, Dorothy Cousins, had returned home to Leeds after the first Christmas of the war, because the majority of the children had gone back. The anticipated air raids had not taken place, parents were missing their children, and vice versa. It was in 1940 that the air raids had started with a vengeance, and many parents had had cause to regret their decision.

But Anne had stayed, and now, after living in the little town of Middlebeck for so long, she had no desire to live or to teach elsewhere. She doubted, though, at times, the wisdom of remaining at the schoolhouse. Miss Foster had offered her a home in the first place, anxious to play her part in the evacuation scheme, and it had seemed more appropriate to have a fellow teacher staying with her rather than one of the pupils. The two of them had soon become firm friends as well as colleagues, in spite of the age difference. Anne had known, deep down, that she really should think about finding somewhere else to live. After all, Miss Foster would not go on teaching for ever; she had been almost sixty years of age when the war had started. But the older woman had seemed glad of her company, Anne was contented, and so the years had drifted by...

And then Charity had dropped the bombshell which, in her heart of hearts, Anne had been long expecting. They had settled down at the fireside after returning from the Victory concert in the church hall, with their drink of cocoa, which had become something of a late-night ritual. They had talked about how much they had enjoyed their evening out; how rewarding it was to see some of their old pupils, and present ones as well, singing and dancing and acting on the stage, knowing that they, as teachers, had been partially responsible for nurturing the talents that the children displayed. And then Charity had told her...

'Anne...' she said. 'I have some news for you, my dear. I hope it won't come as too much of a shock, but...' Charity's brown eyes, so warm and yet so shrewd, looked earnestly into her own; and Anne knew at once what the news must be.

'You have decided to retire,' said Anne. 'Is that it?' She smiled questioningly at her friend.

'Yes, that's it,' said Charity. 'I really feel that the time has come. I'm sixty-six years old now, and I think it's time to call it a day.' She gave a little laugh. 'I'm like an old war horse, aren't I? And that was the reason I've kept on, of course. I wanted to stay till the war ended. And now...well, it's time to let go and make room for someone younger, someone with new ideas...'

Anne could not think of her as an old war horse. She had the stamina and the strength and vigour, but Charity did not seem old. She looked very little different from the time Anne had first met her six years ago; a small woman, only five foot or so in height, with her mass of silver-grey hair drawn into a bun at the nape of her neck. She was slightly plumper now, maybe, and a few lines had appeared at the corners of her mouth and eyes, but she was still full of fun and vitality.

'Yes... I see,' said Anne. 'I can't honestly say that I'm surprised. I knew, at the back of my mind, that this would happen. But it's still a shock; the thought of you not being there at the helm. Nor here, living in this house... The house goes with the job, doesn't it? I mean...'

'Yes, and that is why I am telling you, my dear, because this will affect you as well. I admit I've been rather selfish. I should have encouraged you to look for a place of your own;

I knew I couldn't stay here for ever. But I enjoyed your company so much, and we get on so well together.'

'And I wouldn't have wanted to go anyway,' Anne told her. 'I've been very happy here. And after...after Bill was killed I was so glad of your friendship and comfort. This was like a safe haven to me; that's the reason I've never looked anywhere else. But what about you, Charity? Have you thought about where you will live?'

'I have given it some thought, yes... I want to stay in Middlebeck of course. All my friends are here. I've lived here for twenty-six years, incredible though it seems, and I certainly wouldn't want to return to Sheffield. But it would not be fair to the school – to the children and teachers and to whoever takes over my job – to live too near... There are some little bungalows between here and Lowerbeck; a newish estate, built just before the war started. Do you know where I mean?'

Anne nodded. 'Yes, there's a duck pond there, and a nice little park.'

'Yes, that's right; it looks an ideal spot to retire to. And there are one or two of them for sale at the moment.'

'It's a couple of miles or more, though, from Middlebeck,' said Anne. 'And there are no shops near, are there? And the bus probably only runs once a day... Sorry, Charity. That's dreadful of me, being so negative, but I was just thinking that it might be rather lonely for you, moving away from your friends.'

'Ah, well now... I have another idea, you see. What I intend to do is to buy a little motor car; one of those nice little Austins, maybe. I'm hoping the petrol regulations will be relaxed soon, and, to be honest, it's something I've always wanted to do.'

'But you can't drive, can you?'

'I can soon learn!' Charity sounded brimful of confidence. 'But finding somewhere to live, of course, is the most important thing. As a matter of fact, I've put in an offer with the estate agent, Leadbetter's on the High Street, for one of the bungalows. So...as soon as we go back to school next week I shall send in my notice to the Education Office and... Bob's your uncle, as they say!'

Anne stared at her in some amazement. She was certainly not letting the grass grow beneath her feet. New house, new car, plans for a new life; and she, Anne, had known nothing about it.

'I'm sorry,' said Charity. 'I realise it has been something of a bolt from the blue. And here I am going on about my plans, and I know you must be thinking, What about me? But I haven't forgotten about you, Anne, please don't think that. There is something else I want to say...' She paused and leaned forward in her chair, looking intently at Anne and half smiling. 'How would you feel about applying for my post, for the headship of Middlebeck school?'

Anne gave a gasp of astonishment. 'What, me? Oh no... I couldn't possibly. For one thing, I'm far too young to be considered, surely. And...well, I'm a newcomer, aren't I?'

'After six years I don't think you could be considered a newcomer, my dear. And as for being too young, it isn't always age and experience that interviewing panels go for. They sometimes want someone with a fresh outlook and new ideas. Anyway, you've had ten years' teaching experience, haven't you? You are by no means wet behind the ears.'

'But...what about Shirley.' She was the third member of the teaching staff. 'Shouldn't she be considered? She has been here longer than I have.'

'No...' Miss Foster shook her head. 'I am quite certain that Shirley would not want any more responsibility. She is a married woman, and now that Alan has been demobbed I should imagine they will be wanting to start a family; that is what she has hinted to me.'

Anne felt a pang of not exactly jealousy or bitterness but more a quiet sorrow. It was more than five years since Bill, her fiancé, a young pilot who had only a few months previously been awarded his wings, had been shot down and killed. The anguish she had felt for a long time afterwards had subsided to a dull ache, but she knew she would never forget him. She realised, however, that she would not be unwilling to enjoy male companionship again, even something deeper, maybe; but she had not actively sought it, nor had any come her way over the past years. How did Charity Foster regard her, Anne wondered? Did she think of her as a war 'widow' as Charity herself had been? The headmistress had told her, soon after they had met, how her own fiancé, Jack, had been killed in the First World War. Charity had been older than Anne was, in her late thirties, and she and Jack had waited several years to be married, as couples did in those days. But it was not to be; and Charity, resigned to her spinsterhood, had accepted the position of headmistress at Middlebeck school. She had remained at her post for twenty-six years. Anne gave an inward shudder. She was not sure that that was what she wanted for herself.

'You have gone very quiet,' said Charity. 'I've shocked you into silence, have I?'

Anne smiled. 'Yes, I suppose you have. I will have to give it some thought... When would you be leaving?'

'At Christmas; that is giving them a full term's notice. The post will be advertised – nationally, I dare say – within the next couple of weeks.'

'And there are sure to be lots of applicants?'

'I should imagine so, although one can never tell. Not everyone wants to bury themselves in a little backwater in the Yorkshire Dales. I know we don't see it like that. It is home to us, but I know that is how a lot of folk regard it, especially those from the big towns and cities. A shortlist will be drawn up, and then...well, it will be up to the interviewing body to choose the best applicant; or the one they consider to be the best applicant.'

'And...who would be on the panel?' asked Anne.

'Well, the rector, of course. The school was once in the control of the church, you know. It is aided now by the Education Authority, but the rector still has quite a lot of say. And I think they would invite me along as a matter of courtesy. The others, I should imagine, will be members of the North Riding Education Committee.'

'I wouldn't stand a chance,' said Anne.

'Now, now – that's defeatist talk,' retorted Charity, 'and you know what Queen Victoria said about that, don't you?' The words of the old queen, to her generals at the time of the Boer War, had been widely quoted during the early days of the recent conflict, when it had seemed, for a time, that Britain might be facing invasion and defeat.

'Yes, I know what she said,' smiled Anne. '"We are not interested in the possibility of defeat; it does not exist." It was over a rather more grave issue though, wasn't it... At the moment I am not at all sure about whether I want to apply. It would be a big decision. I need time to think about it.'

'Of course you do. I have rather sprung it upon you, haven't I? But having made my own decision and set the wheels in motion, I thought it was only fair that you should know.'

'And...is it to be kept a secret, about your retirement?'

'No; I don't see any need for that.' Charity laughed. 'You know what the bush telegraph is like here, and once the natives get wind of it, it will spread like wildfire.'

'I will give it serious thought,' said Anne. 'But in the meantime I will need to be looking around for somewhere else to live. I can't count my chickens, can I? That is, if I do decide to give it a go...'

The best plan, she thought, would be to find somewhere to rent. Like Charity, she had been careful with her money and had saved quite a tidy sum; enough, maybe, to at least put a deposit on a small property. But it would be best not to burn her bridges, she decided, just in case she was granted the tenancy of the schoolhouse. She had already decided, albeit unconsciously, that she would apply for the post.

—

Anne had had a fondness for Maisie Jackson ever since the day she had first met her on the train bound for Middlebeck; and she knew that the feeling was mutual. She had noticed her at the school in Armley, of course, in the playground or corridors, but as she had not been in Anne's class they had not become acquainted.

What Anne had been most impressed by on the day of the evacuation had been the little girl's bravery and determination to be cheerful. She must have been feeling confused and apprehensive, as all the children were – and the grown-ups, too – at leaving behind their homes and families. Although Anne had discovered, later, that for Maisie it had been more of a fortunate escape from her dreadful home circumstances. But the child had hidden her own feelings and had taken it upon herself to look after Audrey Dennison – now Audrey Fairchild – who had been most unhappy at leaving her home and loved ones behind. Chalk and cheese they had been, those two little girls; Maisie shabbily dressed in her too-short gabardine raincoat, pixie hood and scuffed shoes, and Audrey, looking as though she was going to a party, in her best coat and patent leather ankle-straps, rather than on an evacuation train to goodness knows where. Because the children, at least, had not known where they were bound until the teachers had told them, when they were nearing their destination. For security reasons, it was said; there had been so much red tape in those early days of the war.

Anne had been pleased when Maisie and Audrey had been placed in her class of nine to ten-year-olds at Middlebeck school, along with Doris Nixon, the girl from the farm, and Timothy's sister, the girl who, so tragically, had returned to Hull and had then been killed in a bombing raid. A close little foursome they had been, she recalled. She had been fond of all four of them, but her affection for Maisie had been foremost, although she had tried, as an impartial teacher, not to let it show.

She was glad that Maisie and Audrey had remained firm friends over the years, and Doris too, although the girl from the farm had drifted away slightly from the other two. After the scholarship examination Doris had gone to the local senior school, now called the Secondary Modern, whilst her two friends had been awarded places at the Girls' High School. Consequently, Doris had left school at fourteen to work on the family farm, whereas the other two still had years of study ahead of them.

Maisie had always seemed the most mature of the girls, and this was still the case. She and Anne had progressed beyond the stage of pupil and teacher and were now good friends. Anne had watched her progress with interest and affection. She could tell when she was happy and she was aware, too, when something was troubling her young friend.

And something was at the moment, she was sure of that. Moreover, she had a good idea as to what it might be. She had been pleased when Miss Foster had invited the girl for tea. It was good at times to unburden oneself to someone outside one's own family. And if Maisie wanted to do that, then she, Anne, would be ready to listen.

Maisie knocked at the door of the schoolhouse at precisely three o'clock. The house did not adjoin the school, but was at the other end of the playground; a greystone building dating from over a hundred years ago, the time when the school was opened, when Middlebeck was still a village.

Anne opened the door quickly, looking bright and summery in a floral patterned cotton skirt and a white blouse, with Clark's openwork sandals revealing her toes. Her bare legs and arms were brown and her dark hair shone as though it had been newly washed. Her blue eyes smiled welcomingly at her visitor; she did not look a day older than she had when Maisie had been in her class.

'My goodness, you're prompt,' she exclaimed. 'Right on the dot.'

'Old habits die hard,' said Maisie. 'Aunty Patience used to make sure that Audrey and I were never late for school. We had no excuse, though, had we, living just across the green.' She followed Anne into the living room which opened off the tiny hallway.

'Sit down and make yourself at home,' said Anne. 'You have no coat or cardigan, have you? It's such a lovely day again. We've lit a fire though, because we need it to heat the water, but we don't need to sit too close to it, and I've opened the window.'

A vase full of roses and sweet peas, from the small garden patch at the rear of the house, stood on the window sill, delicately perfuming the air, and the rose-patterned curtains lifted gently in the breeze. Maisie sat down in the chintz-covered armchair nearest to the mullioned window. The little room did tend to get rather warm at times, but it was a cosy and homely place with its oak-beamed ceiling and delft rack, along which was ranged a selection of blue and white plates. The wooden shelves on either side of the stone fireplace were filled with books belonging to Miss Foster and Anne, along with photographs, ornaments and holiday souvenirs. Maisie noticed an exotic creamy-pink shell, from Scarborough or Whitby, maybe; not found on the beaches there, but for sale in several of the gift shops; and a china model of a country cottage; Wordsworth's 'Dove Cottage', she guessed; Anne had mentioned that they had visited Grasmere recently.

'Where is Miss Foster?' asked Maisie. Although she now called Anne by her Christian name she would not have dreamed of calling her former headmistress Charity, nor had she been invited to do so!

'She has gone to have a rest,' replied Anne. 'At least that is what she said, but I think she is giving us a chance to have a little chat together, just the two of us. She will be reading I expect, certainly not sleeping. She is still as lively as ever. She will join us later when we have our tea. Now, Maisie, what's new?'

'Nothing much…' She gave a slight shrug. 'I told you we've been on holiday, and now…well, I suppose I'm looking forward in a way to going back to school. I know a lot of girls don't say that, but…'

'But you have never minded school, have you? That's the right attitude to have, or else school can become such a drag.'

'I've been helping my mum in the shop and trying to amuse our Joanie and Jimmy some of the time. But now, I must admit I won't be sorry to see this holiday come to an end.'

'It's an important year for you and Audrey,' said Anne. 'School Certificate next June. I don't need to tell you to work hard, because I know you will; you always do. You don't find it hard to study, though, do you, like some girls do?'

'No, I suppose not... I've managed exams and all that without having to do too much swotting. I like school well enough, but not enough to think of being a teacher, Anne, if you don't mind me saying so. I don't think I could ever do that.'

Anne laughed. 'Why should you? We are all different, Maisie, and we all have to make our own choices. Is Audrey still sure she wants to be a teacher?'

'Yes, she seems to be...'

'And what about you? Have you any ideas about a career? You could go a long way with a good brain like yours.'

'No, I've no idea at all.' Maisie shook her head. 'I feel sort of...lost and bewildered at the moment. I don't know what I'm doing or even what I'm thinking.' She suddenly knew that she had to confide in Anne. 'That's why I want to get back to school, to help to focus my mind.' She looked across at her friend. 'D'you mind if I tell you something, Anne? It's sort of...personal, although some people do know about it – my mum and Audrey – but they think I'm being silly, I know they do. And I suppose I am, really... You see, I thought I was in love with somebody; I know I was. Well, I still am, but now I know that I've been a complete idiot.'

Anne nodded gravely, and Maisie could see the concern in her eyes. 'Yes, by all means tell me about it; I'm glad that you want to. But I think I can guess... It's Bruce, isn't it?'

'Yes...' breathed Maisie. 'Oh dear, is it so obvious? D'you think everybody knows? D'you think they'll all be laughing at me? Or feeling sorry for me and saying, "Poor Maisie"?'

'No, I don't think so at all,' replied Anne. 'I guessed

because I know you very well. I know you and Bruce have been friendly over the years, and you told me once that you were writing to him. But you haven't had a great deal to do with boys, have you, Maisie? Bruce came along when you were feeling vulnerable and in need of friends, and he was kind to you, wasn't he?'

Maisie nodded. 'I know I'm only fifteen. That's what my mum says, and I know it's what everybody would say, that I can't know what it's like to be in love at my age. But I do, I really do…and I know, now, that he only thought of me as a friend; as a kid, I suppose. And it hurts, Anne; it hurts so much.'

'I'm sure it does…' Anne smiled sadly. 'I know what it feels like to lose someone, too.'

Maisie looked at her in horror. 'Oh, Anne! How dreadful of me! I'm so sorry; I was forgetting about you and Bill. Well, no, that's not true; I hadn't forgotten about it, how could I forget? But I've been so wrapped up in my own concerns that… I'm really sorry. I know this doesn't compare at all with what happened to you.'

'It's all right, dear,' said Anne. 'Losing Bill was terrible and I thought I would never get over it. But the pain subsides to a certain extent. And although it's an awful cliché, life has to go on. You'll get over this. I know it's painful… I saw Bruce last night with a young lady, and I guessed that you might be upset. But there will be somebody else for you. Maybe quite a few somebodys before you meet the right one.'

'D'you think so?'

'Of course I do. Bill wasn't my one and only boyfriend. When I was in the sixth form I was madly in love – or imagined I was – with a lad I met at a dance hall. My parents didn't like him, and they tried so hard to convince me that he was not a suitable friend for me to have. He was an apprentice plumber. Not that that was what mattered to them; my parents were not snobs, although they did hope for someone – what shall I say? – rather higher up the career ladder. But they were right, not because of the job he did, but because they knew he was so wrong for me. I wouldn't listen, though...'

'And...what happened?'

'He chucked me, to put it bluntly. He was two-timing me and I found out and that was that. I thought my heart would break, but I was going to college soon afterwards so I had other things to think about. I went out on a few dates after that – my friends' brothers and that sort of thing – but I didn't think seriously about young men again until I met Bill. Then we both knew that that was it.'

Maisie began to feel quite ashamed of her reaction to what she had regarded as Bruce's infidelity, although it was really nothing of the sort. She knew that now. It was her first experience of heartbreak over a member of the opposite sex, and it hurt like mad. But Anne's loss of her fiancé had been a tragedy, not to be compared with her own disappointment which, seen in that context, seemed quite trivial.

'I'm sorry...' she said again. 'I shouldn't have gone on like that. But I couldn't tell Mum all about it...'

'No, I realise that.' Anne smiled. 'And I'm very honoured that you wanted to share your problem with me. Now... I have something to tell you as well.' She decided it would be good to get Maisie thinking about something else other than her own heartache. 'Not the same sort of thing, but there are going to be a few changes of one sort and another round here, Maisie.'

'Oh...you've not decided to go back to Leeds, have you, Anne?' Maisie looked a little crestfallen, and it was gratifying to Anne to see the girl's reaction.

'No, not at all. I go back from time to time to see my parents, and I always will, but my home is here now, Maisie, as yours is. And I guess it always will be. No; the big change is that Miss Foster has decided to retire at Christmas.'

'Oh goodness! That is a surprise,' said Maisie. Then, thinking about it more rationally, she said. 'Although I suppose she must be...quite old by now.'

'Yes...well, elderly at least,' replied Anne, laughing, 'but I don't think she would like to be told that. Anyway, she's decided to go...and the other news is – guess what? – that she would like me to apply for the post.'

'Of headmistress?'

'Yes, that's right.'

'Gosh!' said Maisie. 'And...are you going to?'

'I think so,' said Anne, smiling in a confident way. 'Yes, I'll have a try, but if it doesn't work out, then I will realise it was not to be. There may be a lot of applicants.'

'But you will be as good as any of them,' replied Maisie staunchly.

'Thank you for the vote of confidence,' laughed Anne, 'but I expect it will be a tough contest... It's not a secret, by the way, about Miss Foster's retirement, but she might want to tell you the news herself. If she does then...well, you can't pretend that you didn't know, but we can say that I just mentioned it casually.'

'OK,' grinned Maisie. 'I've got it... Now, can I help you with the tea, Anne? Setting the table or anything?'

'Yes, thank you. You can put the cloth on and the cups and saucers and cutlery. Charity and I prepared the food earlier...'

Miss Foster joined them for the meal of afternoon tea; thinly cut boiled ham with salad and triangles of bread and butter, followed by tinned peaches and evaporated milk, and finished off with homemade fruitcake and gingerbread. The cloth was Miss Foster's best lace-edged one, with napkins to match, and they ate and drank from delicate china patterned with wild flowers, using silver cutlery that gleamed with recent polishing. It was all what Maisie termed very posh. She felt almost like a Junior schoolgirl again, aware that she must be on her very best behaviour. But the two adults did not treat her as a child and the conversation flowed quite naturally. And as Miss Foster seemed to realise that Maisie would already know about her retirement, that little hurdle was surmounted.

Anne thought, as the girl said goodbye at five-thirty –
evening service started at six-thirty and she had to get ready
to sing in the choir – that she seemed to be in a more positive
and cheerful frame of mind than she had on her arrival.
Young love could be devastating in its effect, she pondered,
but Maisie was a sensible girl and she would learn to put it
behind her.

And Maisie's thoughts, surprisingly, were no longer solely
of herself, but of Anne as well. Her friend and Miss Foster
were too much in one another's pockets, she mused. Like a
couple of old spinsters, except that Anne Mellodey was not
old, and neither did she look or act as though she was. So it
was perhaps as well that the two of them would be parting
company. But Maisie had reservations, too, about her friend
applying for the headship, although she would not have
dreamed of saying so. What Maisie hoped was that Anne
would meet someone who might help to take her thoughts
away from Bill. She did not want to see her mouldering away
in the schoolhouse for years and years.

# Chapter Six

'Jenner and Jackson' read the sign in gilded letters over the door of the draper's shop in the High Street. Lily had been the manageress there for four years, following the couple of years she had spent working at Tremaine House, helping Rebecca Tremaine with the land girls. Formerly, the rather faded sign had read 'Jenner's High Class Draper's', harking back to a time, twenty or more years before, when many shopkeepers had described their businesses in such terms. In truth, the little shop and living premises above still belonged to Eliza Jenner, an elderly lady in her mid-seventies, but not, in appearance, looking much more than sixty.

It was in 1941 that Lily, anxious to find a home where she could have all three of her children with her, had first become acquainted with Mrs Jenner. They had got on well together from the start, and Eliza had been only too happy to have the little family living above, with Lily taking charge of the shop. They lived there rent free and Lily was paid a weekly wage for her services, but the property and its proceeds belonged to the Jenners, Eliza and her husband, Cyril.

The elderly couple had gone to live in a small house near the railway station where Cyril could tend a small patch of garden to the rear; this had been his chief occupation since his Home Guard duties had come to an end. Eliza, until very recently, had gone into the shop two or three mornings a week, anxious not to let go of the reins entirely. And it had been at her insistence, last year, that the sign above the door should be changed. Lily Jackson's name should be included, she maintained, as the woman had proved to be worth her weight in gold.

Lily had been happy there right from the start, but more

so, on a personal level, since she had become friendly with Arthur Rawcliffe, the man who owned the bakery next door to the draper's shop. She had first met him when she had gone in to buy her bread and cakes; they had chatted about the restrictions and how they were affecting both their businesses. Bread had never been rationed throughout the war, but the only loaf available was what was called a National wheatmeal loaf, made from unrefined flour; somewhat unpalatable to those used to pure white crusty loaves and cobs. Arthur had told her how he was having to make do with dried egg in his cakes, when he could not get what had become known as the shelled variety. Dried fruit, too, had been in short supply, and so cakes – wedding cakes in particular – were darkened by gravy browning, made moist with grated carrot, and flavoured with rum essence.

Arthur had had his hands full running the shop and caring for his wife who was ill with tuberculosis and never left the room upstairs. He had been helped, however, by his elder sister who served in the shop and his brother-in-law who worked in the bakehouse.

Mrs Rawcliffe had died early in 1942, and it was then that Arthur had decided to join up. He was just over the compulsory call-up age of forty; nevertheless he had felt that he wanted to do his bit. There had been nothing to keep him at home after the death of his wife – they had had no children – and Flo and Harry, his sister and brother-in-law, had offered to take over the running of the shop in his absence. The upstairs flat had been rented to a young woman with two children who had come to the country town to escape the bombing in Hull; and when Arthur came home on leave he stayed with Flo and Harry.

It was during one of his early leaves that Arthur had decided to further his tentative friendship with Lily, the attractive young woman who ran the draper's shop next door. Bertha had been dead for more than six months and he could not go on mourning her for ever, especially as he was still in his early forties.

Their relationship had developed slowly at first. Arthur had come to learn something of Lily's disastrous marriage and had realised he must proceed with caution. Lily, moreover, was a very moral sort of person, and until her divorce from Sidney Bragg had been made absolute, she had not permitted anything other than a chaste kiss or two. Nor would she admit, until she was a free woman again, that she was fond of Arthur – extremely fond – as he was of her.

And now at the end of August, 1945, Arthur was coming back home for good. His wartime service had not taken him very far; no further, in fact, than to Catterick Camp near Richmond, less than twenty miles away. He had enlisted in the Army Catering Corps and his talents had been put to good use in the Officers' Mess.

Lily looked at herself in the mirror over the mantelpiece with a critical eye, patting her short dark curls into place, and fingering the stray silver hairs by her temples. There was nothing she could do to disguise them nor did she want to. She applied a touch of pink lipstick, the only make-up she needed to wear. Her skin had taken on a natural healthy glow since she had been living away from the grimy city, and her brown eyes had begun to shine again as they had done in her youth. She was not dissatisfied with her appearance, especially when she recalled the way she had looked at the start of the war when she had been married to Sid: dull of complexion, with greasy lack-lustre hair and dark-rimmed eyes that had lost their sparkle. But those days were long gone, and now, at last, the future was full of promise.

She sat on the settee, idly turning the pages of a magazine, awaiting Arthur's arrival. It was fortuitous that Maisie was out, having tea with the ladies at the schoolhouse, and Joanie and Jimmy were at a birthday party. They were going home after Sunday school finished with one of Jimmy's pals and would not be back until after six o'clock. Joanie had been invited as well because she and the boy's sister were in the same class at school. Lily had not planned it that way; it had just so happened that she was on her own. Arthur seemed kindly disposed towards the children and she had never tried to hustle them out of the way when he was there. If he wished to continue their friendship and if it should lead to a more permanent relationship, then he must know that her children could not be ignored.

A knock at the back door, the entrance used when one was not entering through the shop, told her that he was here. With a final pat at her hair and a straightening of the seams on her new nylon stockings, she hurried down the stairs. Arthur stood on the threshold with a bunch of red roses in his hand.

'Hello, love,' he said, kissing her on the cheek. 'I've brought you a few flowers, see. Best get 'em in water, quick; I want 'em to last.'

'Oh, Arthur, they're lovely,' she exclaimed, kissing his cheek in return. It was the first time he had brought her flowers and she was very touched. He was not one for sentimental gestures or for throwing his money about. She read into his words that he had spent good 'brass' on those roses and, like a true Yorkshireman, he wanted value for his money. 'And how nice it is to see you again. Come on in...'

'Grand to see you too, love.' He wiped his feet cursorily on the doormat and followed her through the stock room and up the stairs. 'You're looking real bonny today; a sight for sore eyes. Where are the children?' he asked as they entered the living room.

'Er...they're at a party, and Maisie has gone out to tea.'

'All the better! Come here then...' He put his arms round her and kissed her more thoroughly on the lips. 'I've missed you, Lily. Aye love; it's grand to be home for good.'

'It's only three weeks since you last saw me,' she said, smiling. 'But I agree. It's good that you're back to stay.'

They stood, fondly appraising one another. 'You look... different, Arthur,' she said. 'It's odd to see you in civvies.'

'You'll soon get used to it,' he chuckled. 'I couldn't wait to get rid of that there battle-dress. Talk about itchy!' He was dressed in grey flannel trousers and a checked sports jacket, with a cream shirt and striped tie. He looked smart and, somehow, younger. 'This lot feels a bit strange, I must admit, after wearing uniform for so long. But wait till you see my demob suit!'

'I've already seen a few of them around,' said Lily. 'Is it a grey one with white stripes?'

'No; I could've had one like that, but they make you look like a ruddy spiv! No, it's brown... I thought it'd match my eyes.' He grinned at her. 'An' it's sort of checked. Not exactly Savile Row, but at least it's free. I mustn't grumble, I suppose. I can't wait, though, till this lot grows again.' He ran his hands through his regulation army haircut. 'I feel like a bloomin' convict.' Lily realised that it was just a figure of speech, but she could not help her thoughts flitting to her ex-husband, not long out of gaol.

'Don't they all,' she smiled. 'Never mind, Arthur. It'll soon grow.' Before he joined the army he had sported a fine head of light brown wavy hair which he had worn rather longer than was usual. His crowning glory, she supposed, and maybe he had been deservedly proud of it because it was his only outstanding feature. Arthur was short in stature, no taller than Lily herself at five foot five or so, and inclined to be corpulent. His stomach, protruding slightly over the waistband of his trousers, his toffee-brown eyes and the kindly expression on his unremarkable face put her in mind of the teddy bear that Maisie had once owned.

'Come and sit down, Arthur,' she said, taking hold of his hand and leading him to an armchair, 'and I'll go and make us a cup of tea.'

'Ne'er mind the tea,' he said. 'I reckon I'll be staying to a proper tea, like, won't I? Boiled ham and best cups and saucers an' all that? It's what I've been looking forward to.'

'Of course,' she laughed. 'Just you and me, as the children are all out. We'll have it in a while. Well, if I can't make you a cup of tea I'd best go and get these flowers in water.' She buried her face in the deep red petals, breathing in the sweet fragrance. 'They're beautiful, Arthur. Thank you so much.'

'Well, special occasion, isn't it.' He laughed. 'Don't expect 'em every time, mind.'

Feeling very light-hearted she went into the kitchen and reached for a glass vase from the top shelf of the cupboard. Not real cut glass; she had never been able to afford that. But this one was not too bad as a substitute – Woolie's best – and the long-stemmed roses looked just right in it. She placed it in the centre of the sideboard and sat down in the chair opposite to Arthur.

'So...what's the news?' she asked. 'You're staying with Flo and Harry, are you, for the moment? And what about the bakery? You'll be taking up your former position there, will you?'

'Hey, steady on; one question at a time.' Arthur held up his hand. 'Aye, I can't wait to get back to the bakery. I suppose you mean will I be in charge again, don't you? It was always my business as you know – well, mine and Bertha's – and Harry worked for me for a wage; so did Flo. But he's been such a godsend while I've been away, and Flo too, of course...so what I've done is this. I've asked 'em if they'll go into partnership with me, equal shares in the bakery and the shop.'

'And...they've agreed?'

'Yes, they have. They were surprised, like, but they didn't need much persuading.'

'It's very generous of you, Arthur,' said Lily, 'but it's no more than they deserve. They've worked their socks off while you've been away. And it can't have been easy for Harry, leaving home at five o'clock in the morning to get the ovens going. It isn't as if they're living on the premises, like you were. I suppose it'll be just as difficult for you, though, won't it, whilst you're staying with them?'

'Ah well, I've got news on that front an' all,' said Arthur. 'Pamela's given me notice; she's leaving next week.' Pamela was the young married woman with two children who had been renting the upstairs premises ever since Arthur joined the army. 'I'd never have asked her to go, you know, and she's not been under any pressure. I know she liked it here and there was some talk of them staying here permanently; well, in Middlebeck at least. But her husband's being demobbed quite soon, she hopes – he's been in the Far East, poor devil – and her mother's not been too well, so they've decided to move back to Hull. She's going next week, so everything's hunky-dory, as you might say.'

'So it is,' agreed Lily. 'It's worked out just right for you. So...you'll be moving back next door, of course?'

'Yes...for the moment. There's nothing definite, not just yet.' He was looking at her intently. Then he moved across the room and perched on the arm of her chair. 'Lily, I'm not much good at this sort of thing. I'm just an ordinary chap... you know that, don't you? But you and me, we get on well together, don't we? And I want us to have a future together. But I sometimes wonder how you really feel about me. Y'see, I know how I feel about you...'

She turned and looked at him, into his warm brown eyes, alight with affection, but holding a question, too. 'I'm very fond of you, Arthur,' she said. 'And – yes – we do get on very well.' She had an idea what he was going to say and was trying to make it a little easier for him. She knew it was often hard for him to show his true feelings, except in a jokey kind of way.

'Lily...' Suddenly he moved from the chair arm and knelt on the carpet in front of her. He took hold of her hand. 'Lily... I think I love you... Well, no, that's not right, is it? That's not want I meant to say. I know I love you and... and I want you to marry me.' He looked at her almost pleadingly. 'Will you...will you marry me, Lily?'

She was taken aback for a moment, although she had realised what he was leading up to, and she had known, too what her answer would be. When she saw the look in his eyes changing to one of puzzlement and uncertainty she answered at once. 'Yes, Arthur,' she replied simply. 'I will marry you.'

He did not kiss her at once, as she might have expected. Instead he breathed a small sigh of relief. 'Whew! I thought for a moment that you were going to say no. It would've served me right, I dare say, for taking it for granted. Not that I shall ever take you for granted, Lily love. That's not what I meant... Oh heck! I'm getting meself all tongue-twisted now.' He reached into his jacket pocket and drew out a small black box. 'Here you are,' he said. 'I've got you this. I hope it's the right size and that you'll like it. Happen I should've waited and let you choose your own, like, but I wanted so much for you to say yes that I just couldn't wait.'

'Oh, Arthur...' She leaned forward and kissed him on the lips. 'You are such a kind, lovely man...' She opened the box to reveal the ring, his choice of ring, nestling on its cushion of white satin. It was small, but exquisite; a diamond encircled by tiny sapphires, like the petals of a flower. 'It's beautiful...' she gasped, not having to feign her delight at all. It was just what she might have chosen for herself. She held out her left hand. 'Put it on for me, please, Arthur.'

He fitted the ring onto her third finger, which had been ringless since she had discarded Sidney's worthless band of gold. It fitted perfectly and Arthur sighed again. 'Well, that's a relief, I must say, although they did say at the shop as I could have it altered... Eeh, Lily love; you don't know how happy you've made me.' He did kiss her then, long and hard, and she found herself responding to him more fervently than she had done before.

It had been difficult for her at first, when their friendship had developed to the holding hands and then to the kissing stage. Memories of Sidney – dreadful memories – would loom into her mind unbidden. She had been almost afraid to return Arthur's affection. She had believed there would never be anyone else for her; her experiences with Sidney Bragg had put her off men for ever, or so she had thought. Then, too, there had been the sweet and loving memories of Davey Jackson, Maisie's father; her childhood sweetheart and young husband. Nobody could ever replace Davey in her

heart and mind. She was not sure, even now she had agreed
to marry him, that she loved Arthur. But she felt she had
done the right thing in accepting him. Her fondness for him
would grow. He was a good man and worthy of her care and
affection. The two of them had to look to the future now and
leave the past with its memories, both the happy and the sad
and torturous ones, behind them.

She had not told him she loved him, though, and he had
not asked her. He had not said the words, 'Do you love me,
Lily?' She guessed he had the wisdom not to push her too far
at the moment; perhaps it was sufficient for him to know
that she cared enough to want to marry him. She had every
confidence that it would be a successful marriage. She
surmised, too, that he would not want to wait too long
before they tied the knot.

'Let's go and sit on the settee, shall we?' he said, getting up
and pulling Lily to her feet. 'I reckon I've been on me knees
long enough. We'll make ourselves comfy, eh?' They sat
down and he put his arm around her. 'About me moving in
next door,' he said. 'Yes, I shall be doing that before long.
But it'll seem odd, won't it, you here and me there, with only
a wall between us, and us planning to get wed?'

'What d'you mean, Arthur?' Lily asked with a puzzled
frown. 'We can't very well... I mean, we can't knock the wall
down.'

'Oh, I'm not suggesting anything improper, love. But I
don't want us to wait too long, if you see what I mean.
There's no point, is there? It's a bit of a problem, though.
Er...shall I come and live here? After we're wed, I mean?'

She smiled. 'That would be the usual thing to do, surely.
You don't want to go on living next door on your own, do
you?'

'No, of course not. But this is your home, see, and I
wouldn't want to presume. What I mean is this...it's up to
me to provide a home for my wife, isn't it?'

She patted his hand. 'I know full well what you're getting
at, Arthur. But this is my children's home as well as mine,

you know. And we haven't mentioned them yet. How do you feel about Joanie and Jimmy? They can be a couple of scallywags, you know. Maisie's never been much trouble. Actually, she was asking about you earlier today.'

'Aye, your Maisie's a grand lass. And I don't forsee any problems with the other two. They never seem to mind me being around, do they? Bertha and I wanted kids, you know, but it wasn't to be...'

'The little 'uns have got their attic bedroom,' said Lily, 'and so has Maisie. And...my bedroom is quite big enough for two,' she added, feeling just a little embarrassed. 'And the living room and kitchen are adequate. Your place is pretty much the same as mine, isn't it? There wouldn't be any more room than there is here.'

'It's a pity we can't combine the upstairs accommodation,' said Arthur thoughtfully. 'You know, make it all one. Like I said, there's only a wall between us. But I know this property belongs to the Jenners, doesn't it?'

'Yes, it does,' agreed Lily. 'I'm just the tenant, really... But I've had some other good news this week, Arthur. It's been an amazing week, one way and another. I was going to tell you... And then, well, you took the wind out of my sails good and proper, didn't you?'

'I certainly did,' said Arthur, kissing her cheek. 'Go on, tell me then. What's your good news?'

Lily took a deep breath. 'I can hardly believe it really,' she said. 'It's so amazing...Mr and Mrs Jenner are going to leave this property to me – the shop and the living accommodation – after they have...gone, of course. I know that might be a long time ahead, and it's something I don't really want to think about. I've become very fond of Eliza, and both she and Cyril, they've been so good to me.'

'That's great news,' said Arthur. 'And it's no more than you deserve, like you said about Flo and Harry and the bakery. The Jenners couldn't have kept the draper's shop going without you. I take it they've no family then, no close relatives to inherit their worldly goods?'

'No...they have no children. Cyril had a sister and Eliza had a brother, apparently, but they're both dead now, and from what I gather the nephews and nieces don't bother to keep in touch.'

'Hmm...' Arthur nodded thoughtfully. 'They've made a will, have they, stating what they want to do?'

'Yes, so Eliza has told me. I argued with her, of course. I said I certainly hadn't expected anything of the sort; that I'm not a relation and they must think carefully about it. But she assured me that they had done so and that it was what they both wanted. And that I was to regard this as my permanent home.'

'You know what they say though, love, about a will. Where there's a will there's relations. Those nephews and nieces may very well come crawling out of the woodwork if there's any sign of money or property, especially if it's not going their way.'

'Don't be such a Job's comforter, Arthur,' laughed Lily. Like many Yorkshiremen she knew he had a sceptical streak, unwilling to take everything at face value. 'There was no mention of money, just this property. And they have their little house that they live in as well. I've no idea what they intend to do with that; so maybe the relations are included, who knows? Anyway, as I've said, it could be years and years before I inherit.' She laughed out loud. 'Goodness, that's an amazing word. I never expected to inherit so much as a brass farthing, not from anybody.'

'Well, it just shows that you never know what's round the next corner. How old are Mr and Mrs Jenner? Seventy-odd, I suppose?'

'Yes; they're both seventy-five or thereabouts, but very hale and hearty. They could well live till they're ninety; I hope they do. At least I know that my future's secure, mine and the children's. Even more so, of course, now.' She stopped suddenly; she must not give Arthur the impression that she was marrying him just for the security he could give her. She stretched out her hand, admiring the floweret of tiny gemstones twinkling on her finger. 'It's lovely, Arthur, really lovely...and I'm so very happy.'

It would be her third marriage, she was thinking, with a feeling of incredulity, but the first time she had had a real engagement ring. Davey had given her a token ring of semi-precious stones, all that he could afford, but she had cherished it as if it were worth a thousand pounds. It was too small now, but she sometimes wore it, when she was feeling sentimental, on her smallest finger. Sidney Bragg had not bothered with an engagement ring at all, and the wedding ring, she had guessed, had been the cheapest he could buy. Always supposing it had been bought at all...although she didn't think he had been into thieving at that stage. That had come later.

'Are you going to tell your three our good news when they come in?' asked Arthur. 'We're not going to keep it a secret, are we?'

'Of course we're not...going to keep it a secret, I mean. I shall wear this with pride.' She waggled her fingers, seeing the light catch the stones. 'But let me choose my own time to tell the children, Arthur, if you don't mind. It won't make any difference to Joanie and Jimmy. I doubt if they know what an engagement is, but I shall tell them that we're going to get married quite soon and that you will be coming to live here. As for Maisie...well, she's going through something of a crisis at the moment, at least it seems like it to her.'

'Oh, what's up with Maisie then?'

'Calf love, I reckon, although she thinks it's more than that. She'll get over it, no doubt, but she thought she was in love...with Bruce Tremaine; you know, the squire's son?'

'Oh aye? Well, there's nothing like aiming high, I suppose.'

'She's been friendly with Bruce ever since she was a little girl,' replied Lily, a shade indignantly, 'and there's nothing snobbish about the lad, nothing at all. Bruce Tremaine is a grand young man. But she's just a kid really, Arthur; she's only fifteen and he's nearly twenty-one. Anyway...he brought his lady friend to the concert last night. And from all appearances it looks as though the two of them are quite serious about one another. And Maisie...well, she was upset to say the least. So I don't want to make matters worse by flaunting my happiness in her face.'

'Oh dear, poor Maisie! Yes, I see what you mean. She's quite grown-up for her age, isn't she? I can imagine how it hurts. Poor kid; I'll try to be extra nice to her.'

'Don't say anything about it, though, will you? About Bruce? I think she's realising that she's made rather a fool of herself.'

'Don't worry; my lips are sealed. Now, let's start thinking about you and me, shall we? We've got a wedding to plan.'

---

Maisie dashed in soon after five-thirty, seemingly in a much more cheerful frame of mind.

'Good to see you again, Arthur,' she said. He had told her when they first met to call him by his first name, although her younger sister and brother referred to him as Uncle Arthur. 'You've finished with the army then now? Back to Civvy Street, eh?'

'Aye, that's right,' he said, smiling at her and shaking her hand. He did not attempt to hug or kiss her; Lily had told him a little of her experiences with her stepfather and his son and he knew he must tread carefully. 'Back to the old routine. I'll be starting at the bakery again tomorrow.'

'My goodness! No rest for the wicked, eh? So... I suppose we will be seeing quite a lot of you, will we?' Maisie raised her eyebrows, smiling impishly at him.

'You can be sure of that, Maisie,' he chuckled, casting a glance at Lily by his side. 'That's right, isn't it, Lily love?' She just nodded serenely.

'That's good then,' said Maisie, grinning at them. 'Now, if you'll excuse me, I must go and get ready for church.'

She was on her way again within half an hour, like a gust of fresh air breezing in and out. 'Bye, Mum, bye Arthur... See you soon I expect...'

Arthur laughed. 'I thought you said she was upset,' he remarked as the sound of her footsteps on the stairs died away. 'She seems OK to me.'

'Putting on a brave face maybe,' said Lily. 'Anyway, time will tell...'

# Chapter Seven

B ruce Tremaine was concerned about Maisie. They had
been good friends for several years, ever since she had
first come to Middlebeck as a nine-year-old girl. She had
been wary of him at first, he recalled, but he had known
from the start that she was a tough little kid who had already
received more than her fair share of hard knocks. She had
become fond of his dog, Prince, and the animal had often
accompanied them on walks through the country lanes
around Tremaine House and the Nixons' farm; Maisie,
Audrey and himself, and sometimes Doris as well.

He had seen them only irregularly as he had been away at
boarding school, and each time he came home the three girls
had grown a little in stature and in maturity as well. But he
had thought of them as little girls, sort of kid sisters, and it
had come as something of a shock to him, returning home on
this present leave, to see how grown-up they had suddenly all
become. They were very attractive young ladies, all three of
them. There was Doris with her slightly buxom fresh-
complexioned, 'milkmaid' kind of beauty; Audrey, blonde
and blue-eyed with a Dresden china sort of prettiness; and
Maisie, a contrast to the other two with her deep brown eyes
and dark hair and winning smile; an arresting loveliness
which forced you to take notice of her. He had to admit that
Maisie had always been his favourite of the three friends, the
one who had seemed to be more on his wavelength. He had
corresponded with her ever since he had joined the RAF, but
not with the other two girls. She had shown an interest in his
progress on the training course and had sent congratulations
from all three of them when he had been awarded his wings.
She had kept him in touch, too, with anecdotes and news

from home and he had come to look forward to her letters more and more. He could not have explained, even to himself, why he had not told her in his letters about his developing friendship with Christine.

It had come as a great shock to him after the concert when Christine had told him that she believed that Maisie was in love with him. He had poured scorn on the idea, choosing to believe that Christine herself might be the tiniest bit jealous. It was a trait he had noticed in her once or twice before, although he had never given her cause to be jealous. It was true, though, that Maisie did seem to be avoiding him; or it might just have been that there had been no opportunity for them to get together and have a chat about old times. Chrissie would not have liked that, and whilst she had been staying at Tremaine House, Bruce had thought it only right that he should spend all his time with her. Now she had returned to the camp in advance of him. Her demob was imminent and she wanted to say goodbye to the friends she had made. Bruce was staying for a few more days in Middlebeck before returning to the camp in Lincolnshire. He intended to stay on and make his career in the RAF. As for Chrissie, she would be returning to Bradford, her home town, and her office job at the woollen mill. But he hoped that, before long, he and she would be together for good. Christine Myerscough, he had decided, was the girl with whom he wanted to spend the rest of his life.

But the fact remained that he was anxious about Maisie and he decided, the very day that Christine had departed on the morning train back to Lincoln, that he must go and see her. The secondary schools were not due to start until the following week, so he guessed that she might be helping out at her mother's shop on the High Street.

'Jenner and Jackson' read the sign over the door. Bruce was pleased that Lily Jackson was now being given credit for the hard work she had put into the shop. Goods were still in short supply, but there was an attractive display in the window. Red, white and blue was the theme, in accordance with the recent VE and VJ celebrations. There were hanks of knitting wool and swathes of ribbons and dress materials in those colours, interspersed with baby clothes in white and pale blue, floral aprons and men's working shirts, all toning in with the same patriotic colours. A pair of gaily striped blue and white gents' pyjamas hung at the back and below it, more modestly displayed in a corner, a pair of ladies' knickers – the old-fashioned 'directoire' type with elastic at the waist and knees – in bright scarlet. A large union Jack formed the backdrop, with portraits of King George the Sixth and Queen Elizabeth at either side.

Bruce had noticed on his way down the street that some windows still sported pictures of Winston Churchill, with slogans such as 'This was our Finest Hour', but the elderly statesman was now being forced to take a back seat. As he would not be twenty-one until November, Bruce had not been able to vote in the recent election. He was not at all sure, either, as to which way he would have voted. Nobody was supposed to know how others cast their votes. His parents' generation were still secretive about it, but Bruce had a sneaking feeling that his father, if not his mother, might not have voted for the 'grand old man'. There was something of the radical now about Archie Tremaine. There had been open and sometimes heated discussions in the Officers' Mess; it had been no secret that many of the young men, with similar backgrounds to his own, were ready for a change of direction.

He peered through the glass of the shop door and saw that Maisie was alone in the shop, occupied in tidying a shelf behind the counter. He pressed the latch and opened the door and the bell sounded with a welcoming ping. Maisie looked round and he saw the look of open-mouthed surprise on her face for just a moment, before she smiled.

'Bruce... How lovely to see you...' She looked inquiringly behind him and out of the door. 'Are you...er...are you on your own?'

'Yes, there's just me,' he replied. 'You meant am I with

Christine, I suppose?' He noticed that she gave a curt nod. 'Chrissie's gone back to camp. She's being demobbed soon, you see, but I have a few more days leave. So I decided I must catch up with my...old friends, and spend some time with my parents, of course.'

'Yes...of course,' replied Maisie. It seemed for a moment as though there was going to be an awkward silence between them, but then she started to chat in her usual carefree and friendly way. 'What about you, Bruce? Are you staying in the RAF, or are you getting demobbed as well?'

'Oh, I'm staying on,' he replied, 'I have always wanted to fly, ever since I was at school.'

'Yes, I remember. You used to talk about it,' said Maisie. 'But now that the war's ended there won't be any need, will there, for fighter planes?'

'Not as such, no. But we have to retain our fighting forces – the army and the navy as well as the RAF – even though there is no war at the moment. One never knows where or when skirmishes might break out, and there are bases in Germany now, of course, with peace-keeping forces.'

'But you are staying in Lincolnshire, are you?'

'For the moment, yes. There are plans for me to be an instructor now, training new pilots, and I'll be doing test flights. Yes, they'll still need the RAF, Maisie... Anyway, that's enough about me. It really is great to see you again. I'm sorry if you thought I was neglecting you...and Audrey, but Chrissie has only just gone back this morning, and I had to spend my time with her, seeing that I had invited her to Middlebeck...to meet my parents.'

'I quite understand,' Maisie said, politely. She did not ask any questions about Christine, and Bruce decided it would be best not to mention her again.

'So...what about you, Maisie? Back to school soon, I suppose? I notice the Juniors and Infants have already started.'

'Yes, my brother and sister went back earlier this week. We start on Monday, Audrey and I. Don't remind me that it's an important year, Bruce, because I know that.'

'I wouldn't dream of doing so,' he laughed. He had noticed a slight grimace of annoyance at his mention of the word school. Perhaps this new, grown-up Maisie did not like to be reminded that she was still, in actual fact, a schoolgirl. And likely to be so for two or three more years, he guessed. It would not be surprising, he pondered, if she were to kick out against the restraints, later, if not sooner. 'I used to hate it when people asked me, "When are you going back?", and now I'm guilty of doing the same. I am truly sorry, deeply sorry...' He grinned at her.

'It's OK; you're forgiven,' she replied easily.

'So...how about us going on one of those rambles we used to enjoy?' he continued. 'You and Audrey, and Doris, too, if she can be spared from the farm.' He thought it would be best to make it clear from the start that he did not mean himself and Maisie alone, just in case she had any strange ideas of the kind that Christine had suggested. 'And Prince; that goes without saying. The old boy's still as sprightly as ever, I'm glad to say.'

'Yes, I see him out with your father sometimes,' said Maisie, 'and he barks and wags his tail when he sees me. Yes... I'd enjoy that and so would Audrey. And we'll ask Doris; her mother might be able to spare her for an hour or two. We could take a picnic, couldn't we? Like we did once before, d'you remember...oh, years ago, and we went up to the castle on the hill.' She looked positively elated at the memory and any previous sign of awkwardness seemed to have vanished.

'Yes, that's right,' said Bruce. 'We had young Timothy with us as well. He was limping rather, because it was not all that long after his...accident, but he was really game, insisting he could keep up with us all.' It was the bombing of the poor little lad's home in Hull that he was recalling. 'Perhaps Tim would like to come as well. Or does he not go around with you and Audrey any more?'

'Not as much,' said Maisie. 'He's got his own friends now,

but I'm sure he'd like to spend some time with you, Bruce. We'll ask him. So…what day would you suggest?'

'No time like the present,' he replied. 'How about tomorrow, early afternoon?'

'Great,' said Maisie. 'I'll summon the troops then. And I'll raid my mother's cake tin and take something to drink as well.'

'How is Lily?' asked Bruce. 'Is she around? I see you are in charge this morning.'

'She's fine. On top of the world, actually,' said Maisie. 'She and Arthur have just got engaged, and there might even be news of a wedding soon. She's gone to have a look round the market; she should be back soon.'

'That's good news,' said Bruce. 'About her marrying Arthur, I mean… And you are pleased about it?'

'Of course,' said Maisie, smiling brightly. 'Why shouldn't I be?'

They looked at one another for a brief moment and Bruce could see a touch of defiance in her eyes. He remembered that it would be the girl's second stepfather, and maybe her mother's engagement was evoking memories of the first disastrous situation that Lily had got them into, with her hasty re-marriage. But Arthur Rawcliffe, from what Bruce knew of him, was a very different sort of person; strong-minded and reliable and a good businessman, too. He reflected again, though, on how Maisie had matured of late. There must be times, surely, when she wanted to rebel and make her own decisions, instead of succumbing to the pressures and ideas instilled in her by the adults around her.

'No reason at all,' replied Bruce now. 'Arthur's a good sort, and I wish your mother all the best… By the way, Maisie, I must thank you for the letters you've kept on sending me. Letters mean so much to servicemen when we're away from home. And yours are so bright and full of fun; they were a real tonic.'

She gave a slight shrug of embarrassment. 'It's all right. I quite like writing letters. Thank you for yours as well… But

I won't... I mean, now that the war's over an' all that, perhaps I won't write any more? It might be best, don't you think?'

'Yes, I think so, Maisie,' he agreed. He guessed that her reasons for not wanting to write any more had little to do with the end of the war. Besides, Christine might well be annoyed, and rightly so, he supposed, if he was corresponding with another young woman. 'Anyway, you will have quite enough to do with your schoolwork... Sorry, sorry.' He lifted his hand in a gesture of apology. 'I'm not supposed to mention that, am I?'

She laughed. 'It's OK. I will be busy with choir practices and homework and everything. And we're going to do a pantomime at church – next January, probably – now that there's no blackout restrictions. Audrey did really well with the children in *Alice in Wonderland*, but I'm trying to persuade her to be in it this time, instead of helping to produce.'

'Yes, she did do well,' agreed Bruce. 'And I shall look forward to the pantomime. I must try and get home to see it. What's it going to be?'

Maisie tapped her nose. 'It's a secret yet,' she smiled, 'until it's been cast.'

'Oh, I see. Very hush-hush, is it? Well, I expect you will have a leading role...I don't think I told you how much I enjoyed your solo the other night. It was very remiss of me; I meant to tell you at the time. It was first-rate, Maisie. Jolly good show, as some of my RAF mates might say.'

'Thank you...' she murmured.

'Such an evocative song,' he went on. 'Well, all Ivor Novello's songs are nostalgic, aren't they? And that line about walking down an English lane... It reminded me so much of the countryside round here.'

'Me too...' said Maisie quietly.

Their eyes met and held for a few seconds. 'Maisie...' said Bruce. He was not sure what he was about to say to her, the moment was so full of poignancy; but it was interrupted by the ping of the shop doorbell and the entrance of Lily.

'Hello there, Bruce,' she called brightly. 'Nice to see you.' He turned to greet her, and the moment of magic was broken.

'Hello, Lily,' he said. 'I'm catching up with old friends, as you see. And I've been hearing about your exciting news. Congratulations on your engagement! I'm sure you and Arthur will be very happy.'

'Thank you, Bruce,' she replied. 'That's very kind of you. I'm sure we will too...'

'I've tidied the boxes of ribbons, Mum,' Maisie broke in, 'and dusted the shelves, like you said. I'll go upstairs now that you're back, if you don't mind. I've a few things to sort out...for next week.' She moved out from behind the counter towards the door that led to the upstairs rooms.

'OK, love,' said Lily. 'You've been a good help.'

'Cheerio then, Bruce. Good to see you.' Maisie turned to take her leave of him. 'See you tomorrow then. What time did we say?'

'We didn't,' he replied. 'Two o'clock suit you? At the village green?'

'Fine, I'll tell the others. See you then...'

———

Maisie averted her face as she left the shop and hurried up the stairs. To her shame and annoyance, she could feel tears pricking at the back of her eyes. 'You silly, stupid idiot!' she castigated herself. She had been getting over it very nicely, or so she had thought. For all she had known, Bruce had already returned to his camp; and then to come face to face with him like that, it had been too much.

She had conducted herself very well, though, she thought. She had been determined that nothing in her demeanour – either the tone of her voice or the look in her eyes – would give him a hint of how she felt about him. Because one glance at him had told her that she still cared very deeply.

Everything had been going on all right, then he had looked

at her and said her name...and that had been her undoing. If her mother had not come in at that moment she felt that she might well have blurted it all out, about how much she thought about him and how upset she had been on seeing him with Christine. It was just as well that they had been interrupted; saved by the bell, you might say. She felt her cheeks start to flush now when she considered what a fool she might have made of herself.

And yet there had been that look that had passed between them. What had it meant? She doubted that she would ever know. She flung herself down in an armchair, biting her lips and blinking hard. No, no, no! She was not going to give way to tears again. Her mother might well come upstairs at any moment, and she must find her acting perfectly normally. As she had said, there were things she had to sort out for next week for the return to school; books, pens and pencils and so on, and her school uniform. There was no use in sitting here moping, or dreaming of what might have been... She sighed deeply, then stood up with an air of resolution and climbed the second flight of stairs which led to the attic.

Her room was at the back – the one she had chosen when they had first moved in – and from the high vantage point she could see over the rooftops of the houses which lay at the back of the High Street, and over to the distant hills. Not too far distant, though. The ruins of Middleburgh Castle were only a couple of miles away, on top of one of the nearer hills. Down below she could see the silver stream rippling through the meadows, a tributary of the river which ran through the dale. And just visible above a clump of trees, the tall chimney stacks of Tremaine House where the squire and his family had always lived...and where Bruce lived at the moment.

Had it been foolish of her, she wondered, to agree so readily to go on a ramble with him? But it might have seemed churlish to refuse, to say that she was too busy, especially as the invitation had been given to her friends as well. She was determined, however, that she would keep her distance from Bruce. She would walk with Audrey, and Doris, if she was able to go with them, and allow Bruce and Timothy to have some time together. Tim, she knew, hero-worshipped the young pilot who had served in the latter years of the war and had – thank God – come back safe and sound. If Bruce wanted to speak to her personally, then he would have to make the opportunity to do so. And if he didn't...then she would know that the look that had passed between them had meant very little to him. Bruce was just a good friend, and that was how she would make herself think of him.

The day started well with everyone in high spirits. They met outside the Rectory gate; Maisie, Audrey and Timothy, and Bruce and his collie dog, Prince. They were to meet Doris, who fortunately could be spared for a few hours, at her farm gate, just up the lane behind the church.

They took the short cut through the churchyard to the small gate at the back. The warm summer weather was still continuing, but now, with the start of September, the sun was lower in the sky, shining more directly into their eyes and seeming more powerful than it had at the height of summer, although the long shadows cast by the gravestones across the grass and the path told that autumn was not far away.

In the lane which led to the Nixons' farm the blackberries hung in the bramble hedges, purple-ripe and glistening; deep red hawthorn berries too, and large juicy rose-hips, loved by the birds. 'But dangerous for us to eat,' Maisie remembered that Doris had warned them, the 'townies' from Leeds, when they had first arrived. She had been their tutor in many aspects of country lore. So unschooled had they been, she and Audrey, that they had scarcely been able to tell an oak tree from an ash; or differentiate between cows and bulls, she recalled, much to Doris's amusement.

It had been during the same week of the year as it was now that they had taken their first walk along this very lane. Now, as then, the outer leaves on the trees were yellowing, the start of the time of year known in the country as 'back-end'. 'It's feeling a bit back-endish...' was a phrase often heard on the lips of country folk. It was the time of year when the farmers had to be prepared for anything. The mellow sunny days might last a while and give an Indian summer, or the autumn rain might start and continue in a deluge, filling the rivers and streams and even overflowing to flood the fields.

As they climbed the first stile, Prince bounding over ahead of them all, they could see Doris waving to them from the farm gate.

'Glad you could make it,' said Bruce, when they drew near to her, 'although it's quite a busy time on the farm now, isn't it?'

'All seasons are busy, one way or another,' replied Doris. She was already an experienced farmhand, just as willing and able as her brother, Ted – so Ada, her mother, had admitted to Maisie – and Joe, who had recently left the RAF to resume his work on the farm again. 'Ted and Joe are getting the last of the hay into t' barn.' In the nearest fields they could see the tripods holding the pyramids of pale yellow hay, and at the back a barn door stood open revealing the hay stacked high inside.

'Our Ted and Joe did a fair bit of grumbling, mind,' said Doris, "cause me mam was letting me go, but she said it could count as me half-day; I usually have it on Saturday, y'see. But I dare say she'll let me have Saturday off an' all. I've been helping her with the cheese-making this morning, and that's summat that our Ted and Joe are no good at. Aye, it's a busy time sure enough. There's potatoes and root crops to be gathered, and the last of the apples and pears. I'll have to get stuck in again tomorrer, but it's nice to have a bit of freedom... Where are we going then?'

'Oh, up to the castle, I think, if everybody agrees,' said Bruce. 'I intended going up there with Christine on Sunday, but we didn't get any further than the waterfall. It was such a nice day, so we just sat and took our ease.'

It was the first time he had mentioned Christine, and no

one made any comment, except to agree that they would climb up to the castle ruins. I bet she didn't want to walk so far, that Christine, Maisie thought to herself. She didn't look as though she was well suited to a country life.

Their path took them through a little wood, no more than a copse, where oak and sycamore trees grew closely together. On the fringes grew the mountain ash, making a vivid splash of colour with their bright red berries and feathery pale green leaves against the dark shadows in the middle of the coppice.

Then they were at the waterfall, not a huge cascading torrent but a much more gentle splashing and tumbling of foaming water over peat brown rocks and boulders. As they had done many times before, they crossed the river by the stepping stones, knowing just which ones to choose to avoid getting their feet wet. Prince did not care about wet feet. He bounded ahead and arrived on the opposite bank before any of them, shaking himself and wagging his tail and panting; laughing at them it seemed as he watched them tread much more carefully than he had done across the glistening stones.

The moorland ahead of them was brown with bracken and the heather which had almost finished its flowering. Here and there, though, there was still a patch of purple, sheltered by an outcrop of rock, and the golden gorse bushes added a touch of brightness to the dark-hued landscape. Dull and sombre it might appear in the dark shades of early autumn, but Maisie had learned to love the moorland in each and every season of the year.

Now, walking on her own for a while as they took the path across the moor, she found pleasure, as always, in the scene around her; the criss-cross pattern of drystone walls separating the further fields and the lazy, seemingly motionless, sheep grazing on the distant hills. She could hear the rippling sound of the waterfall and the river they had crossed, the far distant hoot of a train, although from here no railway line was visible, and the lone cry of a moorland bird – Bruce had once told her it was a curlew – wheeling high above.

She felt the wind more keenly on her face as they climbed higher although the sun was still shining. But the clouds were no longer still as they had been an hour or so ago; they were racing across the sky and the approaching ones were edged with grey.

'D'you think it's going to rain,' said Audrey, hurrying to catch up with her.

'I don't know; I hope not,' replied Maisie. 'I'm not really prepared for it, are you? I've got a headscarf and my cardigan, but not a proper coat. It didn't look as though we would need one.'

'No, nor have I,' said Audrey. 'Aren't we silly? You'd think with living in the country for so long that we would remember how quickly the weather can change. But it was such a lovely day earlier on. I bet Doris has come well prepared though.'

'What's that?' said Doris. She had been walking behind with Bruce and Timothy, and now they all stood together in a little group. 'Come prepared for the rain? Is that what you mean? You bet I have. I've got me waterproof jacket in here.' She patted the haversack on her back. 'Be prepared, that's my motto, like the Boy Scouts.' She laughed. 'Haven't you got any raincoats?' They shook their heads. 'Oh dear; you're still a couple of town mice, aren't you?'

''Fraid so,' said Maisie, with a shrug. 'What about you boys? But I don't suppose a drop of rain will worry you, will it?'

'My jacket's waterproof,' said Timothy precisely.

'And so is mine,' said Bruce. 'But let's look on the bright side, eh? The clouds are still quite high in the sky. Come on, best foot forward everyone; we'll soon be at the top...'

The view, when they reached the ruins of Middleburgh Castle was well worth the climb. There was Middlebeck, nestling in the valley and the silver ribbon of the river. They could make out the tower of the church, the roof and tall chimneys of Bruce's home and Doris's squat grey farmhouse.

'Shall we eat our picnic?' said Doris, who was always hungry. 'Come on, before it rains,' she giggled.

'Don't keep saying that!' said Audrey, glancing anxiously at the sky. 'You'll make it rain… Actually, I think the sky's clearing a bit…'

'Wishful thinking,' said Doris, through a mouthful of bread. She was already seated on a rock with her coat as a cushion, tucking into a ham sandwich and taking a gulp from a bottle of Tizer. The rest of them made themselves comfortable and took out the provisions they had brought.

'Tim and I haven't got very much,' said Audrey. 'Only a packet of crisps each and an apple. Mum's expecting us back before tea.'

'Nor have I,' said Maisie. 'Only some of me mum's gingerbread and a bottle of lemonade; Mum made that as well.' She lifted the bottle to her lips and took a drink. 'Mmm…that's good. Here, would you like some?' She wiped the mouth of the bottle and handed it to Audrey. 'Have a swig, you and Tim. It'll be all right; I haven't got a deadly disease.'

Audrey looked doubtful, but she took the bottle, wiping it again with a clean handkerchief before she took a gulp. 'Mmm…it's delicious,' she agreed. 'You have some, Tim. Wipe the top first…' They drank with such relish that Maisie feared there might be none left for her, but it was a large bottle.

'What about you, Bruce?' she asked, rather shyly, when she had had another drink. 'Would you like some? And… haven't you brought anything to eat?' He was sitting staring out at the distant landscape.

He shook his head. 'No; I've had quite a decent lunch, and Mother will be cooking a meal this evening.' He patted his stomach and grinned. 'I have to keep fit, you know. Can't afford to put on any extra weight in my job. But I'll have a taste of your lemonade, please, if you don't mind, Maisie.'

'Have what's left,' she told him. She tried not to watch him too obviously as he tilted the bottle. He was wearing an open-necked shirt and his Adam's apple moved visibly in his brown throat as he gulped at the remaining liquid.

'Nectar for the gods,' he said, smiling at her as he handed back the empty bottle. 'Oh no...' He glanced heavenwards and held out his arm. I do believe... Yes, it's raining.'

'Well what did you expect?' retorted Doris. 'I told you so.'

'Perhaps it will only be a shower,' said Audrey hopefully.

Bruce grimaced. 'I'm afraid we're in for a real downpour.' He stood looking thoughtfully up at the sky. '"Why did you promise such a lovely day..."' he murmured.

'"And bade me venture forth without my coat,"' added Maisie quietly, finishing the quotation that she knew. He looked at her and smiled, and once again the glance that they exchanged was full of meaning, or so it seemed to Maisie.

'What the heck are you on about?' asked Doris.

'It's a poem...' said Maisie. 'I remember hearing it at school.'

'For heaven's sake!' said Doris. 'We're going to be caught in a flippin' rainstorm, and you two stand around babbling poetry! Come on, let's get going before we all get soaked.'

Quickly they gathered up their belongings, clothed themselves as adequately as they were able and set off on the trek back to civilisation. The journey down took far less time than the upward one as they hurried and stumbled along the moorland path, over the bridge – instead of the treacherous stepping stones – alongside the river and through the wood, back to the lane near Nixons' farm. By this time the five of them, and Prince, too, were drenched; but as they stood at the farm gate they laughed, able to see the funny side of it.

'Ta-ra,' called Doris, dashing in through the gate. 'See you sometime, folks. Thanks for inviting me...' She ran off with a cheery wave.

'You'd better come home with me,' said Bruce to the other three, 'then you can have a rub down and my mother will make you a warm drink. We don't want anyone catching a chill.'

'We'll be OK,' said Audrey. 'Actually, Mum might be rather worried about us.'

'Then phone her from our house,' said Bruce, 'and you

too, Maisie, and let them know you're back safe and sound.'
Audrey and Maisie looked at one another and nodded. They
didn't need much persuading.

Maisie laughed. 'We look like a couple of drowned rats,'
she said. The rain was still pelting down. It had got worse as
they had made their descent and now it was a deluge.

'Come on then; let's run for it,' said Bruce. The four of
them and the dog raced up the lane to Tremaine House.

Mrs Tremaine, neat and tidy as always in her pleated skirt
and pale blue twin-set, was full of concern. The girls went to
the bathroom and dried themselves with her big fluffy
towels, then she lent them each a cardigan to replace their
sodden ones. Then they sat by the Aga stove in the kitchen,
with Bruce and Tim, feeling the comforting warmth and
enjoying a cup of milky cocoa.

'I've rung your mothers, all of you,' said Rebecca
Tremaine, coming to join them, 'and I'll ask Archie to run
you home in a little while.'

'Thank you very much, Mrs Tremaine,' said Maisie, and
the other two nodded their thanks, but nobody seemed to
want to talk very much.

Maisie was wanting to ask Bruce when he would be
returning to his camp, but she felt too shy to do so in front
of everyone. It was Rebecca who told them he would be
returning in three days' time. 'And we hope you will all be
able to come to Bruce's twenty-first celebration,' she told
them. 'His father and I are planning to have a party for all
the family and friends. It will be sometime near the end of
November, we're not quite sure when, but you will all be
receiving invitations.'

'It will depend on when – and if – I can get leave, Mother,'
said Bruce. He did not sound all that excited about it,
thought Maisie. In fact it seemed as though he did not like
the idea at all.

'Oh, surely, for your twenty-first, dear...' said Rebecca.
'An important event like that. They're sure to let you have
leave.'

'There's nothing sure at all in the RAF,' said Bruce. But that was the end of the discussion because Archie Tremaine came in at that moment from the fields, clad in his gumboots and oilskin coat. He agreed readily to take the three of them back home.

———

There had been no chance for her to say a special goodbye to Bruce, Maisie reflected later that evening. Neither had she had an opportunity to talk to him properly all day, but that had been her own decision, to keep her distance unless he chose to speak to her on her own. He had not done so, not that there had really been any opportunity...

Don't kid yourself, you silly idiot... Once again she gave herself a severe talking to. Bruce had a girlfriend, a grown-up one, and she, Maisie, would have to try and forget him. The glances that they had exchanged had probably meant... nothing at all. As for the twenty-first birthday party, Maisie had a strange feeling that it might never take place; at least, not if Bruce had anything to do with it.

# Chapter Eight

Christine Myerscough was in a reflective mood as she sat on the train which was taking her from Lincoln back to Bradford, the city of her birth. 'I'll show them,' she told herself. 'I'll show them all that I can be somebody, a real somebody, not just a mill worker or an office girl. I'm on the way; I'm going to get there, and I shall surprise everyone...'

At least she had taken the first few steps; she had pulled herself up by her bootstraps, as the saying went. She was determined that there would be no more Lumm Lane or White Abbey Road for her; no more poverty or squalor or the depravity she had seen in her early years. No more of the shady and sordid goings on that had forced her, at the age of ten, to go and live with her maternal grandmother rather than suffer any longer the immorality of her own home. What she had told Bruce Tremaine, that her parents had both been killed in a car crash, had been a lie. Myrtle and Fred Myerscough were both still very much alive and kicking. It had been a lie that was necessary, though, to assist her in her upward climb.

All the same it did not do to be too complacent. She still had not got the coveted ring upon her finger, but she hoped, once she had found a little place of her own, that it would not be very long before she achieved her aim; to marry Bruce, the squire's son from Tremaine House. She had been a little surprised and disappointed to discover that he was not the sole heir to the property and land, but that the inheritance would be shared between Bruce and his two sisters, whom, as yet, she had not had the pleasure of meeting. All the same, beggars could not be choosers, and he was well worth cultivating; besides, she was really very fond of him. She knew that his parents were worth more than a bob or two, as Yorkshire folk said; neither did Bruce ever seem to be short of a bit of brass to spend. No; there would be no more scrimping and scratching around to make ends meet for Christine Myerscough, no more saving up like mad for the occasional treat or coveted item of clothing. But she knew that she had to play her cards right. And the first step, once she arrived back in Bradford, was to find a flat, or at least a couple of rooms where she could be on her own.

She had told Bruce that when her grandmother had died she had been left all on her own, with no family and only a few friends; and that that was why she had joined the WAAF. It was true that her grandmother had died, but she had not joined up immediately. She had been invited by Sadie Gascoyne, a kind-hearted friend who worked in the office with her at the woollen mill, to go and live with her and her family.

The Gascoyne's home in the district of Heaton was a far cry from the squalid mean streets of back-to-back houses in the White Abbey Road area where Christine, until then, had spent her days. Not that her grandmother had been a feckless or slovenly sort of woman. Far from it; she had kept her windows clean and her front step had been regularly donkey-stoned. Indeed, old Lizzie Walker's house had stood out from the rest of the shabby and run-down houses in the row. Inside, too, she had always made an effort to be clean and tidy. Such furniture as she possessed had seen better days, dating mainly from the time of her marriage towards the end of the previous century; but she had dusted and polished it to within an inch of its life and had black-leaded the kitchen grate each week until you could see your face in its surface.

Lizzie had also tried to instil in her granddaughter the idea that 'cleanliness is next to godliness'. Christine had not been too sure of the godliness part, although she had gone dutifully to Sunday School each week as her gran had insisted she should do, something which her mother had never bothered about. But from an early age she had wanted to keep herself clean and tidy and as pretty as she could possibly make herself. A weekly soak in the zinc bath in front of the fire, and the washing of her fair hair, had been a ritual even when she had lived at her parents' home – no one could accuse Myrtle Myerscough of being dirty; that was not one of her failings – and it had continued all the time she had lived with her grandmother. But how she had longed for a house with a proper bathroom upstairs and an indoor lavatory, not a stinking privy at the end of the backyard. There again, Lizzie Walker had done her utmost to keep it clean, but she had been fighting a losing battle against her less particular neighbours.

Christine knew that she had had a good start as far as looks were concerned, having inherited the blonde, naturally wavy, hair and clear silver-grey eyes of her mother. Myrtle's hair had darkened considerably though, now, and maintained its brassy blonde colour only by regular treatments with the peroxide bottle.

'Yer mother's a tart,' Lizzie Walker, who did not believe in mincing her words, had told her granddaughter, when she thought she was old enough to understand. 'To think that a daughter of mine should sink so low. I'm ashamed of her; in fact I've disowned her and I don't care who knows it.' Indeed, folks did know about Myrtle Myerscough; they knew about the visitors to the house and the reason why she was able to afford silk stockings and a fox fur and flashy jewellery.

'Of course she always fancied herself did yer ma; thought she was a cut above the folks round here. Happen we spoiled her, Charlie and me, with her being the youngest, like.' Lizzie's husband had died when Christine was a small girl, and her two sons, several years older than Myrtle, had long since married and moved away. 'But the rot really set in when she married him, Fred Myerscough. We told her he was no good, but she wouldn't listen... Oh aye, I know he's yer dad, and she's yer mam and she reckons that she loves you. And if she wants to see you now and again it's not for me to say she can't. But it's a rum sort o' love to me. An' I had to get you away from it all, Chrissie love; it weren't right. It weren't right at all that a child should see such goings-on.'

Christine had been only vaguely aware, until she was eight or nine years old, of what was happening in the house where she lived on Lumm Lane, only a few streets away from her grandmother's home where, later, she was taken to live. Her mother worked at a nearby woollen mill, starting early in the morning and not returning until well after the time that Christine finished school, so the child was often left to her own devices. She let herself in with a latch key and then set about the task of peeling the potatoes and setting the table, as her mother had told her she must do, before Myrtle returned from the mill. Her father was a lorry driver, delivering machinery, sometimes to distant parts of the country, and he was often away all night. It was then that the men started to visit the house, and on the evenings that Myrtle entertained her 'gentlemen friends', as she described them to Christine, the child was sent to bed extra early.

She recalled an almighty row one night when her father had returned home unexpectedly; loud shouts and screams and the sound of crockery being thrown around, and she had hidden her head beneath the bedclothes until the furore had died down. Her mother had had a black eye the following morning, but she had gone to work as usual, and Christine had been told nothing of what had gone on. Strangely, though, the visits of the gentlemen had not stopped. Moreover, it seemed as though her father knew about them and did not say anything so long as he was away from home at the time.

Christine knew that her mother was a pretty woman, and very clean and tidy, unlike a lot of the other mill workers, some of them mothers of her schoolfriends, who looked poor and shabby and wore shawls instead of coats, something that Myrtle had never done. She was not neglected, not in the material sense; there was always enough food to eat and adequate warm clothing, mainly bought from second-hand shops or jumble sales. But the child was starved of real affection. She was an only child and, therefore, might easily have been indulged and made much of; but she had begun to realise, especially after she had left her parents and had started to work things out for herself, that she had been an unwanted child, possibly a mistake that was not intended to happen, considering the lifestyle of her mother and father.

Myrtle and Fred had moved soon after their daughter had left, leaving behind their rented property and buying a small house on the road to Shipley. Her mother no longer worked at the mill. She became a barmaid, as well as pursuing her other occupation; and Fred, as well as being a lorry driver, became known as a petty thief. He had already had one or two convictions and stretches inside. Christine, over the years, had visited them only irregularly. She had not seen them since she had joined the WAAF two years ago.

She had loved her grandmother dearly, and she had known, for the first time in her life, that she was really loved too. She remembered the row that had gone on between her mother and grandmother before she was taken away to live with Gran. She had been told to go upstairs to her bedroom, but she had been unable to help hearing some of what was being said, or rather, shouted.

'You're not fit to have a child, you shameless hussy...'

'...none of your business. I've never neglected her and neither has Fred.'

'...that good-for-nothing! You're just as bad as one another. I'm taking the child to live with me.' By this time Christine had been listening quite openly.

'Who says?'

'I say! Try to stop me an' I'll report you to the cruelty people.'

'Cruelty! You interfering old...' Her mother had let fly with such a tirade of dreadful words that Christine had seldom heard before, certainly not from her mother's lips. It was not cruelty, she raged. The child was well fed and well clothed and she was coming to no harm.

'No harm? You're harming her morally,' said her grand-mother, but Christine had not understood fully at the time what she had meant. 'What you're doing is immoral, and if that's not cruelty, then I'd like to know what is… I'm telling you, Myrtle, if you don't let her go with me, then she'll be taken away from you forcibly by them cruelty folk. And I'm not going to stand by and see that happen to a granddaughter of mine…'

It had all gone quiet then. She did not hear her mother say any more. Maybe Myrtle had decided that it was for the best after all, that she, Christine, would be happier with her gran, or maybe her mother had decided that she simply did not want her… She had never known why her mother had given in without a struggle, but it seemed as though that was what had happened. Myrtle told her the next day, quite kindly and gently, that she was going to live with her grandmother 'for a little while'. Gran was lonely and she, Myrtle, was busy working at the mill, and her father was seldom there to look after her… So the child had packed up all her belongings and walked off with her gran with scarcely a backward glance. The 'little while' had lasted more than ten years.

In some ways – material ways – life was harder now for the little girl. Lizzie Walker was by no means well off and would not accept so much as a penny from 'those two' for caring for their child. There was always enough to eat, although Lizzie had to buy the cheaper cuts of meat, and often scoured the market stalls at the end of the afternoon to purchase the leftover fruit and vegetables for a much cheaper price. There were few luxuries like shop-bought cakes – Gran did all her own baking – or ice-cream, which her mother had quite often bought. Christine was taught to save up out of her 'Saturday pennies' to buy the things she coveted. It was very seldom that her gran was able to buy her treats.

She was a clever girl, but as a grammar school education would have been out of the question – even if she had been granted a free place they would have been unable to afford the uniform and the extras – Christine had left school at the age of fourteen and had gone to work at the mill; not the one nearby where her mother had worked but one further afield which involved taking a trolley bus there and back each day.

She hated the clamour and the clatter of the machines and the boring nature of the work, but she stuck it out diligently for three years. It was then that she heard of a vacancy in the office and decided to apply for it. To her amazement – and to the gall of some of her colleagues in the weaving shed who considered she was already too big for her boots – she was told that the job of office junior would be hers provided she took lessons in shorthand and typing. Her grandmother was proud of her, and night school tuition soon brought her up to the required standard.

The girls she met in the office were more on her wavelength than her former work mates, whom she began to think of as common-or-garden mill girls. She, Christine Myerscough, was definitely a cut above them; she had always known that she was. In some ways she was her mother's daughter, but she would never be tempted to sink to the depths her mother had done to make a better life for herself. The payment for her work as a wages' clerk, which she eventually became, was quite adequate, and she was able to pay her gran a satisfactory sum each week. To her credit, she knew that the old lady more than deserved it for looking after her all those years.

Her new friends in the office, Sadie Gascoyne – her special friend – and Daphne and Vera, knew very little of her background. She had told them that she lived with her grandmother, and she supposed they knew, from the direction of the trolley bus which took her to and from the mill, that she lived in a rather less affluent area of the city than they did. But she did not see the harm in telling what she thought of as a white lie or two; and soon she almost began to convince herself that what she told them was true; that her parents had been killed when she was ten years old and that that was why she lived with her gran. And as she did not invite her friends to her home there was no likelihood that they would discover the truth. They seemed to understand the reason she gave; that her grandmother was old and frail and that company of any kind wearied her.

She had lost touch with her former schoolfriends, some of whom had known, or had guessed at, the truth about her background. But Sadie, Daphne and Vera, she was quite sure, had no idea. When she was invited to their homes she became even more aware of the difference between her circumstances and those of her friends. Their parents owned their own houses, which were in far more affluent districts. Sadie lived at Heaton and Daphne and Vera at Frizinghall, a little further away from the city centre.

It was Sadie's home that Christine visited the most. It was situated on a leafy avenue near to Lister Park, not far from the point where Manningham Lane, the long road that led out of the city centre, changed into Keighley Road. It was, in truth, quite a modest semi-detached house, but to Christine, after living in 'two-up, two-down' cottage type dwellings, first with her parents and then with her gran, in a far less salubrious area, this was luxury indeed. There was hot water whenever it was required from something called an immersion heater, even in the summer months, without having to keep the fire banked up on the hottest of days; gardens with lawns at both the front and the back; and a garage where Mr Gascoyne kept his Morris Minor car. He drove to Bradford each day to his job as an insurance clerk, and sometimes Sadie travelled with him. Christine was envious of her friend's lifestyle, although she hid her feelings very well. She was determined, however, that one day she would do even better for herself. She knew, though, that as long as her grandmother was alive it was her duty to stay with the old lady who had been so good to her, and she never flinched from it.

She was, truly, broken-hearted when her gran died suddenly, after a massive heart attack, at the age of eighty-two. She had not really been ill, apart from the odd twinge or two, which, typically, Lizzie had tried to ignore; so it had been even more of a shock to the girl, who was now left, virtually, homeless. She could have afforded the rent of the property, and she was, in effect, the sitting tenant; but she saw this as an opportunity to make her first move towards a better life. And so when Mrs Gascoyne, who had always been fond of her, invited her to share their home, she jumped at the chance. Besides, there was a family of six already waiting to move into the property that her gran had rented. Christine told the landlord that their need was far greater than her own, which was true. She soon moved her possessions, such as they were, and went to live in the district of Heaton.

There she had her own bedroom, the smallest of the three, but she preferred to have her own space rather than share with Sadie. There were comforts such as she had not known before; an interior spring mattress on her single bed, rather than the flock one she had been accustomed to; an electric fire to plug in when the weather was cold; and a bedside reading lamp. She paid Mrs Gascoyne for her board and lodgings and settled down to a comfortable existence.

But it did not last for very long. Both she and Sadie realised it was their duty to enlist and do their bit in the war, which was showing no sign of ending. They made the decision despite the fact that their mill was now manufacturing uniforms of khaki and airforce blue, and therefore their jobs could be said to be of national importance. But there were younger women ready to step into their shoes; and so, in 1943 Christine joined the WAAF and Sadie the ATS. They were good friends, but did not live in one another's pockets, and neither of them tried to persuade the other to change her mind about the choice of service.

<hr />

Now, in the September of 1945, Christine had been demobbed, whereas Sadie was not due to return home for another few weeks. But Christine knew that this would not worry her friend. Sadie was now enjoying her reunion with

Roland, her fiancé, who was an army captain. He had already been a serving officer in the Regular Army before the war began and had recently returned from Germany to the camp at Aldershot.

'Yes, I think we will soon be hearing the chime of wedding bells,' Sadie's mother told Christine, in great excitement. 'He's a lovely young man is Roland. Bill and I have really taken to him. He will be staying in the army of course; it's his chosen career. So I dare say he and Sadie will move into married quarters...'

The two of them were enjoying a chat over a cup of tea in Barbara Gascoyne's cosy kitchen, Christine having arrived back in the mid-afternoon. 'What about you, dear?' she asked. 'Have you and your young man made any plans yet?' Christine could see the older woman casting a surreptitious glance at her left hand. She felt a trifle annoyed, but she hid her vexation and smiled airily.

'No...we have no definite plans as yet. We are not officially engaged, but it won't be long before we are...' At least not if I have anything to do with it, she added to herself. 'We do have an understanding. The RAF is Bruce's chosen career as well, like Roland's in the army, although he is quite a few years younger than Roland.' She had not yet met Sadie's fiancé, who, she had been informed, was twenty-eight... A much more marriageable age, she mused; but she was determined that Bruce's lack of years should not deter him. She was convinced she would be able to bring him up to scratch if he showed any sign of hesitance.

'How old is your young man, dear?' asked Barbara. 'About the same age as you?'

'Er...he's twenty-one,' replied Christine, adding on a few months. She had not been thinking what she was saying just then, telling Barbara that he was several years younger than Roland. 'He's a little younger than me, as a matter of fact, but it doesn't matter. He's very mature for his age.'

She knew that this was not strictly true. Bruce had led quite a sheltered and a privileged life until he had joined the

RAF. The company of other men, many of them older than he was, had brought about the change from boyhood to manhood – he had told her that himself – but she knew that there was still a certain naivety and innocence about him. At twenty-two, Christine was just a little less than two years his senior. But Bruce did not know that. He believed her to be the same age as himself, although why she had deceived him she was not altogether sure. From the fear that he might have been frightened off, she supposed... But she was sure enough of him now – with her fingers tightly crossed – to risk telling him the truth.

She, Christine, was old enough to be married without the consent of a parent or guardian. Did the same rule apply to men, she wondered? Did they, too, need to be twenty-one? She guessed they did, but no matter; in a couple of months' time Bruce would be old enough to please himself. There was still that dratted coming-of-age party, though, that his parents were insisting upon. She must try her utmost to persuade him to wriggle out of it...

'...that would be nice, wouldn't it, dear?' Christine suddenly realised she was miles away, and that Barbara Gascoyne had been telling, or asking, her something.

'Sorry...sorry, Mrs Gascoyne.' She came to with a start. 'I was...daydreaming, I suppose.' She smiled sweetly, apologetically at her friend's mother. 'What was it you were saying?'

Mrs Gascoyne laughed. 'I could see your head was way up in the clouds, thinking about that nice young man of yours, I'll be bound. I know dear; you must be feeling sad leaving him behind... I was saying that you will be able to be bridesmaids for one another, won't you, you and our Sadie? Although for one of you it will be matron-of-honour, won't it? Oh, it's such a relief that that dreadful war is over and we can look forward to happy times again.'

'Have they decided on a wedding date then?' asked Christine. She felt a little peeved that her best friend had not confided in her.

'Not an exact date, no. But I think Sadie would like a springtime wedding. That would be nice... No doubt she will be full of plans when she comes home in a few weeks' time...

'That reminds me, there's something I want to say to you, Christine. You know, don't you, dear, that this is your home, for as long as you want it to be? Even after Sadie has left – and she'll probably be the first of you to get married, won't she? – you are welcome to stay, that is if you want to, of course. I've been talking it over with Bill and he agrees with me. And you'll be going back to your job at the mill quite soon, I suppose?'

'Yes, on Monday. They held it open for me; that was the understanding, although how long I stay there remains to be seen.' Christine took a deep breath, then she continued. 'It's very kind of you to say that I can stay here, and I do appreciate it, but I really think it's time that I started to look for a place of my own. Just to rent, I mean; a flat or a couple of rooms, just until such time as Bruce and I get married.'

Barbara looked a little put out. 'There's no point in paying an extortionate amount in rent when you can live here much more cheaply,' she said. 'And some landlords don't half know how to charge, believe you me.' Christine could see that she would need to be very tactful, but she would not allow herself to be dissuaded.

She nodded. 'Yes, I dare say some of them do. But maybe not all of them. I'm sure I would be able to find somewhere quite reasonable... It isn't that I want to leave – please don't think that – but I feel it's time I started to fend for myself a little more. My grandmother taught me to cook, and I did a bit when I lived with her, but not all that much. Gran always liked to be in charge...' That was true, she recalled with an unexpected stab of sadness. 'I must make an effort, and learn to run a household, even if it's only for myself. I'll soon have a husband to look after, won't I?' She crossed her fingers tightly as she said this. 'I don't want him to think that I haven't a clue when it comes to housekeeping.'

Barbara smiled. 'Most girls haven't got a clue, at least not those that have been brought up like our Sadie. Oh aye, I tried to teach her a thing or two, but it's often quicker to do it yourself than have somebody else messing about in your kitchen. Happen I've spoiled her, but she'll soon learn; I feel sure of that... Yes, I suppose I do understand what you mean, Christine, and I admire you for it. There's no rush, mind. You get yourself settled in here again, and then, if you're still set on it, Bill and I can help you to have a look around. There's ads in the evening paper sometimes about places to let, but I reckon they're snapped up pretty quickly. And I'll ask round at the local shops... I'll be sorry to see you go though, lass, especially as you've only just come back, but I know you've got your head screwed on the right way. Yes, I admire your guts...'

Would Mrs Gascoyne have been so full of admiration if she had guessed at her primary consideration – to have a place where she and Bruce could be alone, really alone, together – Christine wondered? She thought not.

There had been very little chance since their first meeting, at a dance in the Officers' Mess earlier that year, to give full rein to their feelings for one another. Christine had known at once that this young man with the deep brown eyes – so warm and at times so soulful – and dark brown hair, was attracted to her, as she was to him. He was handsome, not devastatingly so, but with clean boyish looks which seemed to set him apart from some of the other flying officers, with their waxed moustaches and braying laughs. Bruce Tremaine was a polite and modest young man, not at all the sort of man that Christine had imagined she would go for. She had always set her hopes high. She had been convinced that one day she would meet a man who could keep her in the manner not to which she had been accustomed but to which she aspired. There were other criteria as well, though. He must be passably handsome, and she must be as attracted to him, physically, as he was to her.

She had imagined someone with more verve and dash than Bruce, but she found herself coming to like him more and more for those qualities she had thought she might find wearisome; his honesty and serious approach to life – although he was not averse to a bit of fun as well – and his reliability. It was true that Christine knew a good thing when she was on to it, but it was also true that she was falling in love with him.

She soon discovered that, hidden beneath his initial shyness and the utmost respect that he always showed to her, there was a desire as passionate as her own. They danced, they visited the cinema in Lincoln, and they took walks in the country lanes near to the camp where they were both stationed. On the long balmy summer evenings, as the war was drawing to its close, they were able to find secluded spots; behind a hay barn or, once, inside it, in the lee of a hawthorn hedge, or a thickly wooded copse. But Christine guessed that Bruce found these trysting places somewhat furtive and sordid; as she did, too, if she were honest.

She guessed, also, that for Bruce it was his first experience of lovemaking, not that they had, as yet, fully consummated their love. He had told her that he had never met a girl like her. She doubted that he had known any girls at all, not in the way that he knew her. He had told her, too, several times, in moments of passion, that he loved her; and she, also had said, 'And I love you, Bruce...' feeling sure that she meant it.

Christine had had one or two boyfriends, but, until she met Bruce, not anyone with whom she had felt she would want to spend more than a few days, let alone a lifetime. There had been a young man at the mill, one of the wool buyers, whom she had gone out with a few times until he was called up into the army. Then, soon after she had joined the WAAF, there had been a flight sergeant, to whom she had lost her virginity. It had not been a rapturous experience for either or them – in fact it had left Christine feeling rather ashamed and disgusted with herself – and he had soon moved on to someone else.

At least that particular hurdle was over and done with, she told herself, but she was sure that the experience ought to be much more memorable and meaningful. She was determined to make sure that her first time with Bruce would be something to look back on with pleasure.

She was satisfied that she had made a good impression upon him. Not only had he fallen in love with her but she had managed to hide from him the truth about her background and upbringing. He had not enquired, as he might well have done, about any property or assets that her grandmother might have left. Did he not think it strange that she had been left homeless? No; his trustworthiness meant that he accepted things at face value.

Since working in the mill office, rather than the weaving shed, Christine had made an effort to lose much of the broadness of her Yorkshire accent. Oh yes, she could speak very nicely when she put her mind to it; she had always had an eye for fashion and had dressed as smartly as she could within her limited means; and her name, Christine Myerscough, she had always felt had a certain ring to it, almost as though she belonged to the upper classes. Nobody would guess that her father, nowadays, seemed to be spending as much time in prison as out of it; nor that her mother was...a member of the oldest profession. Not even to herself would Christine admit the true word.

It was not very long, only a couple of weeks, before she found suitable accommodation. A client of Mr Gascoyne was looking for someone 'nice and respectable', as he put it, to rent the premises above his ironmongery shop, and when he met Christine he decided she was eminently suitable. The fully-furnished flat – at a rent she decided she could just about afford – comprising a living room, bedroom, small kitchen and an even smaller bathroom, was on Manningham Lane, near to where it started its rise from the city centre. Her new home was only a short trolley bus ride from her place of work, and it provided the solitude that she needed. She moved in at the beginning of October.

# Chapter Nine

At the beginning of October Rebecca Tremaine sent out the invitations to Bruce's party. His twenty-first birthday would be on the 22nd of November, which fell on a Thursday; so the party was to be held on the nearest Saturday, the 24th, in the large room over the Market Hall. This room, owned by the local council, had fallen into a state of disrepair over the war years; nevertheless it had been used for children's parties and for meetings where the clientele were not too fussy about the venue.

Recently, however, it had undergone a complete overhaul. The floor had been sanded and re-polished; the blackout blinds taken down and replaced by dark green velveteen curtains to cover the once grimy – but now clean and sparkling – windows; the dais at one end of the room had been carpeted; the adjoining cloakroom and toilets spruced up and freshened; the walls distempered in cream, and the woodwork painted a glossy brown. Loaned out by the council, the Market Room was now becoming a popular venue for more sophisticated parties and gatherings. It was licensed for alcoholic drinks to be served, and if the hosts did not wish to do the catering themselves they invited a firm of professionals to do it for them.

Rebecca had been quite carried away with excitement planning her son's twenty-first party. She only wished she could have seen a comparable enthusiasm shown by Bruce, who had been home the previous weekend for a brief visit. She said so to Archie as she put the invitations into their envelopes and stuck on the stamps.

'Really, Archie, I sometimes wonder why we're bothering to go to all this trouble arranging this do. Bruce doesn't seem to be the slightest bit interested.'

Archie smiled. It was his wife who was doing all the organising and, what was more, he knew she was thoroughly enjoying it. 'Oh, come on, love,' he said. 'He's not a kid any more. You can't expect him to be bubbling over with excitement about a birthday party.'

'But it's his twenty-first, Archie...'

'Aye, I know; but he's not long ago finished fighting in a war, and happen he thinks it's all – I dunno – unimportant, irrelevant, after what he's been through.'

'But he never talks much about what he did when he was flying, does he?'

'No...happen it's as well. I dare say he tries to put it to the back of his mind. Anyway, he's got summat else to occupy his thoughts now, hasn't he? There's Christine...'

'Yes, there's Christine...' Rebecca repeated. 'And I have a feeling she might be at the bottom of all this, you know. This...disinterest in the party and everything. She's got him twisted round her little finger. He couldn't wait to get away from here and off to Bradford to see her.'

'Well, that's normal enough, isn't it? Personally, I'm glad he's got himself a lady friend at last. For years and years he never seemed interested in girls and...well, you begin to wonder...'

'Archie! What a thing to say! I certainly didn't. Anyway, he was friendly with Maisie, and with Audrey and Doris.'

'Oh aye, I know that; but they were only kids, and I think he saw himself as a sort of big brother to them.'

'Maybe...' Rachel nodded thoughtfully. 'But I've often thought that if Maisie was a few years older, then there could have been something between them. Of course I'm not suggesting that there was...'

'No; she's just a schoolgirl; Christine's much more mature. I think she'll be good for our Bruce.'

'I hope you're right, Archie... But the fact remains that he's just left it all to me, the invitations and everything. He couldn't even tell me who he wanted to invite. I was the one making all the suggestions.'

'Well, he's probably looking on it as your party, and – let's face it – that's what it is, really, isn't it? It's summat that you want to do. Bruce hasn't got any real close friends round here, with being away at school and then in the RAF. But he'll go along with it and enjoy it, you can be sure of that, provided he's got his lady friend with him. She'll be staying here, I suppose?'

'Yes, I suppose so... It's where Bruce was staying when he went off to Bradford that concerns me. He didn't say...'

'Nor can you expect him to. Give over mithering, Becky. He's a big boy now.'

'Yes...yes, I know that...' That's what I'm afraid of, she added to herself.

'Let's have a look at these invites then,' said Archie, picking up the pile of envelopes and thumbing through them. 'Maisie Jackson, Mrs Lily Jackson... What about the youngsters, Joanie and Jimmy?'

'Oh, I expect Lily will get someone to look after them for the evening; Mrs Jenner, maybe. I'm sure the last thing Bruce would want would be a tribe of children dancing around.'

'Mr Arthur Rawcliffe... Well, you'd have to invite him, wouldn't you, seeing as how he's doing the catering?'

'I would have invited him anyway, as Lily's fiancé; but, yes, you're right. He'll be there in his professional capacity. And so will his sister and brother-in-law, Harry and Florence Buttershaw, but there's an invitation for them as well. I believe they're doing very well with this new venture.'

'Aye, they seem to have backed a winner there all right. And jolly good luck to them...'

Arthur Rawcliffe and his relations, Harry and Flo, who had now gone into partnership with him, had started doing outside catering for parties and functions. They had already taken a few bookings and this one, for the squire and his wife, promised to be quite lucrative.

'The Rector and Mrs Fairchild, Audrey and Timothy Fairchild...' Archie continued. 'I reckon they'll be needing a

child-minder as well for their Johnny... The Nixons, all of
them, yes of course... How many d'you think there'll be
altogether?'

'Getting on for fifty, if they all come. And I've heard about
a trio of musicians; well, you know, the sort that the
youngsters like. They play for dancing and that sort of thing;
a pianist, a drummer and a saxophonist, and I think they
have a girl vocalist as well. So I'll get in touch with them.'

'And the cake?' asked Archie.

'Oh yes, I've thought of everything. Arthur Rawcliffe is
going to make that. And he's promised to put on a nice buffet
meal; sandwiches, meat pies, sausage rolls, trifles and
fancies; you know the sort of thing. I know we're still
rationed and we probably will be for ages, but he doesn't
think there should be any problem in getting everything he
needs. He says he'll pull out all the stops...'

And there would be no stopping his wife either, thought
Archie. She was revelling in it all despite the lukewarm
reaction of their son. He only hoped that nothing would
happen to mar her pleasure.

---

'Have you got your invitation to the party?' Audrey asked
Maisie as they boarded the school bus.

'You mean Bruce's twenty-first?' said Maisie, trying to
affect an air of nonchalance.

'Of course! What else could I mean? You'll be going, won't
you?'

'Yes, I expect so,' said Maisie, sighing a little. 'I can't think
of any reason why I shouldn't... I'm not bothered about
Bruce, you know, not any more.'

'I'm very glad to hear it.'

'I should think Doris will be going, so I'll be able to keep her
company. I don't want to play gooseberry with you and Brian.'

'Oh, go on; we're not like that!'

'But he'll be invited, won't he?'

'Yes, I should think so. Mr and Mrs Tremaine are quite

friendly with Mr and Mrs Milner.'

'It sounds to me as though it's Mrs Tremaine's party, not Bruce's,' Maisie remarked. 'I know she's been doing all the arranging. She's asked Arthur to put on a buffet, you know, and to make the cake.'

'I'm really looking forward to it,' said Audrey. 'It's ages since we went to a proper party, and it should be quite a posh do. I wonder what we should wear? D'you think it'll be long dresses an' all that? You could wear that pink one that you wore for the concert, couldn't you?'

'No,' replied Maisie, rather too quickly. 'Er...no, I don't think so,' she went on less forcibly. 'It might be just a casual sort of affair, and I don't want to be dressed up like a dog's dinner, do I?' The truth was that the pink dress brought back unhappy memories. And another truth was that she did not really want to go to the party at all...

Christine didn't want to go to the party either; in fact, she did not want the party to take place at all. She knew, though, that she would have to handle Bruce carefully if she was to persuade him to go against the wishes of his parents; well, of his mother really, she guessed. Archie Tremaine seemed to her to be a much more easy-going, relaxed sort of person, on the surface at least; quite an ordinary fellow. You would never imagine, unless you knew, that he was the local squire. He spoke with a broad Yorkshire accent and often used the vernacular of the area. Not like his wife, Rebecca. She was the one with the cut-glass accent and refined mannerisms, and Christine had known from the start that she would have to watch her Ps and Qs where Bruce's mother was concerned.

The local populace appeared to kow-tow to both of them, as they did to the rector, the Reverend Luke Fairchild. Now there was a man – a very handsome man, Christine had noted – whose eyes seemed to be looking right into your soul. Visits to the North Riding of Yorkshire would be kept to a minimum, she decided, once she had got Bruce where she wanted him.

She met him off the train at Foster Square station on Saturday afternoon; he had spent the first night of his forty-eight hour leave in Middlebeck with his parents. He greeted her rapturously, kissing her quite passionately as they stood near the platform barrier, something he had seemed self-conscious about doing in public even for a long time after they had first met. They took the trolleybus up to her flat on Manningham Lane.

'I'm dying to show you where I live, darling,' she told him. 'I couldn't believe my luck in being offered a flat so quickly. Of course, it's thanks to Bill Gascoyne, Sadie's father. He recommended me to his colleague. He told him I was a nice respectable girl,' she laughed. 'That's what he was looking for.

'By the way, talking of Sadie, she and her fiancé, Roland, are getting married quite soon.' Christine had received a letter telling her of her friend's plans not long after the conversation with Sadie's mother. 'Soon after Christmas if they can arrange it in time. Mrs Gascoyne thought that a spring wedding would be nice, but they've decided they don't want to wait so long. You can't blame them, can you, darling?' She squeezed Bruce's arm and gave him an extra loving glance, as they sat close together on the upper deck of the trolley bus. It would not do any harm, she decided, to turn his mind towards the thought of weddings.

'No, of course not; absolutely,' he replied.

'And she wants me to be her bridesmaid. Well, not just me; Daphne and Vera, our other two friends as well, but I'm to be the chief one. They're both still in the Land Army, down in Worcestershire, but they should be coming back soon.'

'That's nice for you, darling,' he replied. 'Roland – he's the army captain, isn't he?'

'Yes, that's right. Sadie's at the same camp as he is, near Aldershot. But she's being demobbed soon, and then, when they get married, they are going to move into married quarters. She's getting really excited about it, them being together for good.'

'Yes, I should imagine she is...' He turned to smile at her, and it seemed as though he was just about to say something else when Christine realised they were nearly at their stop. Damn and blast it! She had felt sure he had been going to say something significant, but the moment would have to wait. She stood up hurriedly. 'Come on, Bruce; we're there. Hurry up or he'll go past the stop.'

They dashed down the steps and jumped off the bus. The ironmonger's shop over which Christine's flat was situated was almost opposite the bus stop, on the other side of the road. Her private entrance was at the back, down a little alleyway. She led the way through the stock room, filled to capacity with cooking, household and garden utensils, and up the flight of stairs, through a small lobby and into the living room.

It was a largish room, adequately and quite comfortably furnished, with a sofa and easy chair, a sideboard – rather a monstrosity with curlicued carvings and a large mirror at the back – a small gate-legged table which folded down when not in use, and two 'utility' dining chairs. Christine had been glad of the furniture, having none of her own, save one or two small items which she had taken with her to remind her of her grandmother. She had kept a bevelled mirror which hung on a chain, which was now hanging over the tiled fireplace. She had used it whenever she was combing her hair or applying her make-up, ever since she had been interested in such things. She had also kept Gran's footstool with a petit-point floral design, somewhat worn away by the old lady's feet, and her octagonal walnut sewing table. This had been her grandmother's pride and joy, but it now stood in a corner, rarely used, as Christine herself was not much of a sewer. On top of it stood a garish vase on which was painted a childish design of a cottage and trees in vivid shades of orange, yellow and green. It had been designed by someone called Clarice Cliff and Christine had hung on to it because it had been one of the last presents that her grandfather had bought for his wife, and much treasured by the old lady. Personally, Christine thought it was hideous, but she was not without a sentimental streak and her gran had loved it.

The rest of her grandmother's furniture, shabby and old-fashioned, had been bought for just a few pounds by the family who had moved into the house. They had been grateful, and Christine had been only too happy to shake the dust of White Abbey Road from off her feet and to move on to the far more respectable district of Heaton.

She felt very much at home now in her flat – her own little place – even though the premises themselves and the furniture were only on loan. As well as Gran's bits and pieces, she had brightened it up with gaily coloured cushions and a red hearth rug, which Barbara Gascoyne had very kindly given her. And she had purchased, for a song, in Bradford Market Hall, a cut glass fruit bowl, only slightly damaged, which now stood in pride of place in the centre of the sideboard. It would not be long, she told herself, before she would be able to buy the real thing, not damaged goods. Her home would be filled with china figurines, cut glass and silverware, such as she had seen in the homes of her friends, and in particular in Tremaine House.

'So...this is it,' she said, flinging her arms wide. 'What do you think, darling? Do you like it?'

'Yes...it looks very bright and cheerful. Much better than I expected.' Bruce sounded surprised.

'You surely didn't think I would settle for any old flat, did you? I'm quite pleased with this one, for the time being. Of course, I don't really know how long I will be staying here, do I?' She glanced at Bruce, but he was taking off his greatcoat – he was still in uniform – and looking around for somewhere to put his kit-bag.

'Where shall I put these?' he asked.

'What? Oh, sling them in here for now.' She flung open the bedroom door a trifle irritably. 'Put your coat on the bed, then I'll hang it in the wardrobe later, and you can unpack your things.'

'I haven't brought much,' he said. 'Just...er, pyjamas, and a toothbrush. And... I've brought my sleeping bag as well. I didn't really know... I wasn't sure, you see...' He glanced at the bed, a double one, covered with a green silken eiderdown. 'I thought I might be sleeping on the floor, but I noticed you've got a nice big sofa. I'll be fine on there.'

'Just as you wish.' She gave a nonchalant shrug. 'But honestly, Bruce, did you really think I'd let you sleep on the floor?' She was aware that she was sounding just as crabby as she was feeling. And for no good reason, she told herself. After all, what did she expect? She knew that Bruce had to be cajoled and led along, step by step. Casting off her ill humour, she smiled at him determinedly and put a hand on his arm. 'Come along, darling. Let's go and sit down and you can tell me all your news...'

They did not talk very much when they sat down on the settee. Bruce wrapped his arms around her and they kissed longingly and passionately for several moments. His hands strayed over her body, but Christine guessed that he would go so far and no further, as he had always done in the past, even though they were, for the very first time, in a place where there was complete solitude. Where they could not be disturbed by an irate farmer, or a lowing cow or yapping dog, or made self-conscious by wakeful parents in an upstairs bedroom. These had been the anxieties, even though they had never actually materialised, that had kept Bruce from consummating fully his love and desire for Christine; that and the ingrained feeling he had that it was wrong to behave in such a way outside of marriage.

She was not surprised, therefore, when he drew their lovemaking to a halt. 'Sorry, darling,' he muttered. 'I got carried away, but you are so lovely, and I do love you so very much...' His brown eyes gazed into hers so pleadingly that she knew she would be able, at that moment, to encourage him to go further. But she decided that the time was not yet ripe. They had all evening – and all night – and she wanted it to be perfect, with no regrets, or even half regrets, on Bruce's part.

'I know you do, darling,' she said, 'and I love you too…' She eased herself away from him, then took hold of his hand. 'Now, tell me what you have been doing. How are your mother and father? And what's going on in sleepy little Middlebeck?'

As she had thought he would, he started to tell her of the arrangements for his coming-of-age party; the guest list, and the catering, and the three-piece band that would play for dancing. She was pleased to see that he did not sound enthusiastic about it.

'And…that's what you want, is it?' she asked.

'No, no I don't! I keep telling Mother that I don't want a big fuss, but she won't listen. Most of the people there will be my parents' friends… But I don't want any of my mates from the camp to be invited, or my school friends; I've lost touch with most of them anyway. Just so long as you are there, Chrissie, that's all I want.'

'Oh dear! Couldn't you ask your mother to cancel it before it's too late? I'm sure she would understand, wouldn't she, if you said that you and I just wanted a quiet celebration on our own…'

'You don't know my mother like I do,' said Bruce grimly. 'Once she sets her mind on something she hates to let go. I don't want her to be disappointed. Besides, I should imagine she's sent out the invitations by now…' He was deep in thought for a moment, then he said, 'Unless we were to make it a double celebration. It's all the fuss just for me that I don't fancy…' Christine's heart leapt. Was he going to suggest that it could be an engagement party as well? She would go along with that, even with his provincial friends and his domineering mother if she had a ring on her finger. And that would be one in the eye for that evacuee girl, Maisie Jackson, wouldn't it?

'What do you mean, darling?' she asked innocently.

'Well, it's your twenty-first soon after mine, isn't it? You said your birthday is on the fifteenth of December, didn't you? Well, what could be better? A double celebration. You haven't any relations of your own to give you a party, have you? I know my mother would be delighted if we were to share one. Now why didn't I think of it before? And you could invite your own friends, of course...'

Christine's heart had plummeted right to the soles of her feet. She had let him go on talking whilst she desperately thought of what to say. This was worse than ever. But she realised that it was time to come clean and tell him the truth. She would not be twenty-one in December as Bruce imagined. She would be twenty-three. 'Steady on, Bruce,' she began, shaking her head. 'I can't...'

She hadn't intended telling him just yet, but he would have to find out before they were married; it would need to be on the marriage certificate. 'There's something I've got to tell you. You see, I can't...'

'What? Why can't you?' He smiled disarmingly at her. 'I've told you; Mother won't mind.'

'I can't...because I won't be twenty-one. I'll be...twenty-three. I had my twenty-first two years ago... There was no party or anything,' she went on as he stared at her dumbfoundedly. 'I was in the WAAF, wasn't I? On manoeuvres, if I remember rightly.'

'But...why on earth didn't you tell me?' He shook his head in a bewildered manner. Then, 'Why did you lie to me, Christine?' he asked more sternly.

'Because... I liked you, straight away, as soon as I met you. And I didn't want to frighten you off by saying I was older than you.'

'Good grief! It's only two years.'

'All the same, I didn't want to lose you. You see, I realised that I loved you, and I didn't want you to think badly of me. And then it just went on and on, and I couldn't tell you. I'm sorry...' She looked at him with what she hoped was a pensive, remorseful kind of smile. 'Sorry, darling. Do you forgive me?'

He smiled back at her a little sadly. 'Of course I do. But… Christine, you won't ever lie to me again, will you?'

'No, of course I won't,' she said hurriedly. 'But…it was only a little lie, wasn't it? It didn't matter very much. More of a white lie really. But I know it was very silly…'

'It mattered because it was an untruth,' said Bruce, still rather solemnly. 'Big or little it was still a lie. I want to know that I can trust you. You won't do it again, will you, Chrissie, not about anything?'

'No; I've just told you I won't,' she replied, a knot of tension tightening up inside her as she recalled the other lies she had told him. 'Please don't make a fuss about it, darling. Like you say, it's only two years. I was just being silly, thinking you might mind about that… Now, you sit and look at the newspaper while I go and make us a meal. I thought it would be nicer for us to dine here than to go out…' She kissed him lightheartedly on the forehead and escaped into the small kitchen which led off the living room. It would be best, she decided, not to mention the twenty-first party again for the moment. It had caused enough trouble already.

She was determined to test her culinary skills to the utmost to show Bruce what she was capable of doing. More often than not, when she was on her own, she opened a tin or had something on toast, but she knew she could be quite proficient – her gran had told her so – when she put her mind to it.

The obliging butcher, on the same row as the ironmonger's shop, had cut her two middle-loin lamb chops which she intended to grill with tomatoes and mushrooms. Tomatoes were still hard to come by, but she had managed to get two extra large ones from the greengrocer's. She would make chips – that was easy enough and did away with the need for gravy – and open a tin of peas, as the garden variety, she found, needed a great deal of boiling if they were not to have the consistency of bullets. Her greatest problem was making sure that everything was ready, to serve up nice and hot, all at the same time.

She had made the dessert that morning. It was a trifle; sponge cake covered with custard, jelly and a precious tin of peaches, finished off with mock cream sprinkled with hundreds and thousands. She had even bought a bottle of wine; here again, the owner of the nearby off-licence shop had been just as helpful as the butcher and the greengrocer; Christine was already a popular young woman amongst the local tradesmen. The wine merchant had advised her that a red wine was considered to be correct with lamb, and he had chosen for her a bottle which he assured her was smooth and palatable and not too expensive.

But what about wine glasses? She had been in a quandary about that. Gran had never possessed any, and although there was sufficient crockery, and cooking utensils, too, for her use in the flat, there were no niceties such as glasses. But the ironmonger himself, Mr Hardacre, had come to her rescue when she had gone to him in a panic, having left it too late to take a trip to the Woolie's store in Bradford. He had unearthed a dusty box from the top shelf of his stockroom, containing six wine glasses, plain but functional, and had sold them to her at a knock-down price.

She left the kitchen door open whilst she prepared the meal, so that she could call to Bruce and, hopefully, jolly him along into a more relaxed frame of mind. She knew he was displeased with her, but it was such a little thing to make a fuss about, surely? However, she was beginning to realise what a stickler he was for honesty and truthfulness. She supposed she had known that all along, but this was the first time that she had been put to the test...and found wanting. She felt her stomach muscles tighten with anxiety again at the memory of the other untruths she had told him, but she persuaded herself that there was no way – no way at all – that he could ever find out about her past history or, rather, that of her family. Once they were married she would make sure that they settled somewhere far, far away from Bradford. Never again would she have any contact with her shameful parents.

'Are you OK, darling?' she called out to him. 'Would you like a cup of tea while I get the meal ready?'

'No, thank you,' he replied, smiling at her over the top of the *Daily Express*. 'It might spoil my appetite, and it smells delicious, whatever it is you're cooking.'

So far, so good, she thought, checking the state of the chops under the grill of the antiquated gas cooker; he seemed to be coming round. It was time to add the tomatoes and mushrooms to the grill pan, then lower the chip basket into the heated fat. There was a splutter and fizz as she did so, which told her that the fat was hot enough, thank goodness; get it too hot and it was likely to set alight, something she was scared of doing.

Oh crikey! She suddenly realised that she had forgotten to set the table, although she had found earlier, in a kitchen drawer, a white damask cloth, fortunately clean and laundered, and with only a spot or two of iron mould, and two serviettes to match. There were table mats too, with a hunting scene that had only partly worn away, and knives, forks and spoons; not silver or even EPNS, but still quite serviceable.

'I'll give you a hand,' said Bruce, as he saw her dash across to open the gate-legged table. 'Here, give those to me and I'll set the table,' he grinned. 'My mother has brought me up properly, you know. I'm not one of those men who want waiting on hand and foot, neither is my father.'

'You surprise me,' said Christine. 'I thought you would have had a housekeeper and butler and maids and all that, before the war, I mean.'

'Good heavens, no!' he laughed. 'We've never been in that league. We had a housekeeper of sorts at one time. She helped my mother with the cooking and cleaning, but that was ages ago, before the war started. Domestic servants are getting hard to come by these days. Mother still has someone to help her clean, but over the war years she got used to doing a lot of it herself, and she's a splendid cook. My father helps with little jobs around the home, and so do I when I'm there. I've told you before, the Tremaines are not nobility, not even what you might call landed gentry...' He had set the table very proficiently whilst he had been talking. 'Now, is that all? Is there anything else I can do?'

'No...thank you. Perhaps, when it's time, you could open the bottle of wine?'

'Wine, eh? My goodness, we are pushing the boat out, aren't we? I'll open it now, shall I, then it can breathe. Have you a corkscrew?'

Fortunately the kitchen drawer had held one of those as well, but she had not known about wine needing to breathe. The cork came out with a satisfying pop. 'I'll put it on the table,' said Bruce. 'Now – wine glasses?'

'Oh, yes...' She had already washed the contents of the dusty box and they were now bright and gleaming. 'We're short of nothing we've got,' she laughed, 'as my gran used to say.' She was feeling much happier again now that Bruce seemed to have set aside his former displeasure.

'Righty-ho, I'll leave you to it,' he said. 'The kitchen isn't really big enough for two and I'd only be in your way.'

Christine remembered, at almost the last minute, to put the plates to warm on the oven rack, to open the tin of peas, to turn up the heat for a final browning of the chips...and then everything was ready.

She put the chips in a separate dish in the centre of the table, having learned from meals at her friends' homes that this was the correct thing to do, but served everything else directly onto the plates. Bruce declared that it was a meal fit for His Majesty the King. 'You wouldn't get anything better at the Ritz,' he added, scraping the last of his second helping of trifle from his dish, then folding his serviette neatly and putting it to one side.

'The Ritz...in London?' asked Christine.

'Yes, of course...'

'Why? Have you been?'

'Er...no, actually I haven't,' he laughed. 'But one day we will. One day, Chrissie, you and I will dine at the Ritz.' He reached out across the table and squeezed her hand. His eyes were full of tenderness...and desire. 'Now...how about finishing this bottle of wine?'

She nodded contentedly as Bruce picked up the bottle, then they sat together on the settee each holding a full glass of wine. She began to feel totally relaxed and happy, and amorous, too, as the mellow wine slid down her throat, warming her all over. She knew that Bruce, too, felt just as she did. Before long their empty wine glasses lay discarded on the floor and they were in one another's arms. And this time Bruce did not hold back, neither from the fear of disturbance – for the very first time he knew they were completely alone – nor from the feeling that what they were doing was wrong.

'Christine... I love you,' he whispered. 'You...you know what I want, don't you? I can't help myself. But...only if you want to as well. I don't want to do anything that...'

She stopped his words with a kiss. 'Of course I want to, darling, just as much as you do. But...we would be more comfortable somewhere else, wouldn't we?'

'In...bed?' he asked. She nodded.

They crept into the bedroom hand in hand. Any embarrassment or sense of propriety on Bruce's part had been taken away by the effect of the wine. Christine, too, was in a state of euphoria, but it was what she had been aiming for all along.

They slid between the sheets and he made love to her, gently at first, then more passionately. She knew that it was his first time, but he did not show any sign of hesitance or inexperience, and neither did he appear to realise that, for her, it was not the first time. It was, in fact, only the second, and the first time, she had known straight afterwards, should not have happened. Promiscuity was not one of Christine's vices. She had been too shocked at her mother's way of life to go down that road herself. She had been determined that, for her, the time and the place, and the person, must be right. She gave a sigh of happiness. Yes, it had been...just right.

Afterwards they dressed and then, at Bruce's suggestion, they tackled together the much more prosaic occupation of washing up. The effect of the wine was beginning to wear off, but Christine still felt as though she was walking on air. Bruce had fallen quiet. She hoped he was not having regrets or feeling guilty. When they had finished their task he hung up the tea towel, then put his arms around her.

'Christine... I love you so much. You will...marry me, won't you? Not just because of...you know...because of that. I've wanted to ask you for a while; ever since I met you, really; but I thought I should wait until we had known one another a while longer.'

'Of course I will marry you, Bruce,' she replied, omitting to say that she had only been waiting for him to ask her. 'And...please don't feel that it is wrong to do...what we have done. It means that we belong to one another now, don't we?' He nodded, smiling at her with eyes full of love.

'I was always told that I should wait until I was married,' she said demurely. 'I expect you were, too. My gran used to be adamant about that. But it's hard, isn't it, when we love one another so much?'

He kissed her again. 'We'll get engaged as soon as we can,' he said. 'The next time I come we'll go and choose a ring. But...darling, we will have to be careful, won't we? You know what I mean... We don't want anything to go wrong.'

'You mean, we'll have to be careful that I don't get pregnant?'

He nodded. 'Er...yes.'

'Well, I think I'll leave that side of things to you,' she said. 'Is that all right, darling?'

'Er...yes,' he said again, swallowing hard. 'I've never... you know...bought any. But...yes.'

'Its OK just now,' she went on. 'I'm due for my period any time, so I know it's quite safe at the moment.'

He appeared embarrassed at the mention of such an intimate female matter. 'Come and sit down,' he said, leading her to the settee. 'We'll choose the ring very soon,' he went on, holding both her hands tightly between his own. 'I should be able to get over again in a couple of weeks' time. And then...shall we tell my parents? Or shall we wait until after the party?'

That blasted party! thought Christine. 'Never mind the party,' she said. 'This is more important than being twenty-one, isn't it? I feel as though I want to tell everybody right now.'

'Yes, so do I,' he replied. 'But we will know that we're engaged, won't we, you and me? And that's all that matters. My mother would be so upset if she couldn't have her party... I tell you what; we'll make a surprise announcement when I cut the cake; there's sure to be a cake. I'll tell everybody that we're going to be married, and that it's an engagement party as well as a twenty-first. How about that, darling?'

'Yes...terrific,' said Christine, not very convincingly. She thought for a moment; it might not be such a bad idea; in fact it could be quite momentous. 'It's a wonderful idea, darling,' she said. 'How clever of you!' She would be willing to suffer the celebration with his family and a crowd of people she did not know, just to see the look on Maisie Jackson's face when Bruce made the announcement. Yes, that would be well worth waiting for.

# Chapter Ten

The interview for the headship of Middlebeck School was to take place on Saturday morning, the tenth of November, at the Council offices just off the High Street. The post had been advertised immediately after the schools had returned in September, and it was hoped that the person who was appointed would be able to take up the position in January, at the start of the Spring term. It was usual to give a term's notice, but arrangements could sometimes be made between schools to fit in with staffing arrangements. There had been ten applications and a short list of four was drawn up by the end of October.

'You are on it, of course, my dear,' Charity Foster told Anne at the end of the afternoon, when they had said goodbye to the children for five days. It was the start of the half-term holiday, often referred to, colloquially, by the parents – but not by the teachers! – as 'teachers' rest'. (Teachers' rest, Mother's pest, was a frequently heard remark). But this half-term break would certainly not be a rest for Anne, because she would be moving to her new lodgings.

'I was allowed to have my say about the short list,' Charity said as they sat drinking a cup of tea, the first thing they did at the end of every afternoon, sitting by the cosy fireside, after the children had gone home and their respective classrooms had been tidied. 'But I've spoken to the other members of the interviewing panel and they all agree that you must be included. In fact, we were in agreement about all the names on the short list.'

'So...who else is there?' enquired Anne. 'Am I allowed to ask?'

'I don't see any reason why not,' said Charity. 'You will meet them all at the interview anyway, won't you? One is an army captain – ex-army, I should say – who was a deputy head in Beverley before he joined up. The other man – he is also a deputy head – is from Halifax; he is married apparently. And then there's a woman, an Infant teacher, from Doncaster; she's single, but then, of course, all women teachers were, until fairly recently.'

'I don't really stand a chance, do I?' said Anne. 'I'm sure they are all older than me, aren't they? And much more experienced.'

'They are older, certainly. The army chappie is thirty-five, and the other two are in their forties, if you must know! But age makes no difference. It's the impression you give at the interview that counts the most. So, as I've said before, no defeatist talk! You just go in there, Anne, and hold your head up high and give it your very best. Now, I suggest that we don't talk any more about it just now…

'Which day are you intending to make your move to your new place?' Charity smiled affectionately at her. Not giving her a chance to reply, she went on to say, 'Goodness me, I'm going to miss you so much, Anne. This little house won't be the same without you.'

'And I shall miss you as well, Charity,' Anne replied. 'But it's much better that I should make a move now before… well, before I'm forced to leave.'

'Unless things go your way, and then the schoolhouse would be yours…'

'You said we weren't going to talk about it.' Anne gave a wry smile. 'No, it's the sensible thing to do, to get settled in now; and then, if by some chance I do find I can stay…well, I'll move back again, that's all. It isn't as if I have a great amount of stuff to move. Monday morning; that's the time we've arranged. I told you, didn't I, that Archie Tremaine has very kindly offered to help me?'

'Yes, you did. What an obliging man he is; what would we all do without him and his shooting brake? He's always there in an emergency, is Archie. When the time comes for me to move, though, I shall need to employ a removal firm. Oh dear, it really is the end of an era, isn't it, Anne? I don't know how I shall bear to say goodbye to this little place...'

'Look at it as a new beginning and not an ending,' said Anne. 'You were quite cheerful about it all at first.'

'Yes...so I was, and I know I'm doing the right thing. But the time has actually arrived now, hasn't it?' Charity gave a deep sigh. 'And one of those four people on the list will soon be taking my place here.'

'And you will be enjoying a well-earned taste of freedom!' said Anne. 'No more being governed by the school bell, or having to suffer wet playtimes and mixed up Wellingtons...'

'And lost jumpers and irate parents,' smiled Charity. 'And dogs in the playground.' They both laughed, recalling the havoc that a stray dog could cause, running amok in a yard full of shouting children; quite a common occurrence.

'Yes, let's try to look on the bright side, Anne. It's time for both of us to adjust to the changes.'

'And we will still be seeing one another at school, until Christmas,' said Anne. 'And after that, you won't be far away, will you?'

It was the companionable evenings that they had spent together, though, that Anne knew she would miss. She looked around at the familiar room; the glowing fire, the old oak beamed ceiling, and Charity's dark furniture, gleaming with the patina of age and constant polishing; but she knew too, in truth, that it was time that she moved on. She was in too comfortable a rut, and Charity's retirement was an opportunity for her to make a change.

Charity's purchase of the little bungalow, on the estate between Middlebeck and Lowerbeck, had already been signed and sealed, but she would not be moving in there until the end of the Autumn term when her years as headmistress would come to an end. Archie Tremaine, helpful as ever, had offered to give her his advice when she was ready to choose a little car; he had even agreed to give her a few preliminary lessons in driving.

And Anne would be moving on Monday to the flat she was renting. It was two rooms, really, plus a tiny kitchenette and a shared bathroom, not a self-contained flat, but she knew she was lucky to have found it. Any property to rent was quickly snapped up nowadays by young couples setting up home together for the first time. The house, quite a modern semi-detached, was in the pleasant, tree-lined Orchard Avenue, about ten minutes' walk from the school. It was next door to the house where Anne's teaching colleague, Shirley Barker – Shirley Sylvester that was – lived with her husband and her parents. It was through Shirley that she had heard of the rooms that were to let.

'Alan and I were very tempted to take them ourselves,' Shirley had told her, 'to give us a bit more freedom. But Mum might have been hurt if we'd moved out. She and Dad have been very good, letting us have the use of the front rooms, but there's not as much privacy as we'd like, if you know what I mean. We have to share the kitchen, and there's always a mad scramble for the bathroom in the morning. Still, we shouldn't grumble, I suppose. We're paying next to nothing in rent – it would be quite a lot more, of course, if we moved next door – and we're saving up to put a deposit on a little house. And we want to start a family soon,' she added coyly.

Alan had not long been demobbed, and he and Shirley were doing what thousands of other young couples were doing in those early post-war days: living with the parents of either the girl or her husband, whilst waiting for a council house or saving up for a deposit on a modestly priced home of their own.

'You'll be OK with Mrs Smedley,' Shirley told Anne. 'She's a nice old lady; keeps herself to herself. But it makes sense, she says, to have a lodger now that she's a widow, and her family left home ages ago. Anyroad, good luck to you Anne. I'm green with envy, though – all that space, just for you! –

but it'll be nice to walk to school with you in the mornings.'

Anne got along well enough with Shirley. She had been on the staff of Middlebeck School when Anne had joined it at the start of the war, but they had never become bosom friends, just colleagues. There was not the same rapport between them that there was between Anne and Charity, the feeling that the other one was a kindred spirit. Shirley might well have been envious of her fellow teacher's friendship with the headmistress, but she did not seem to be. She was a somewhat old-fashioned country lass who did her job methodically, day by day, but without a great deal of enterprise or ambition. Anne had the impression that she could not wait to leave and become a full-time housewife and mother, looking after her beloved Alan. They had married before he was called up in 1941, and after that she had refused to go out and enjoy herself with friends, but had stayed at home night after night with only her parents for company. Now that he had returned they spent all their time together, apart from when they were working – Alan had returned to his job as foreman at the local woollen mill – and appeared to have little time for outside friends or interests. Anne, if she were honest, found her rather a dull companion.

―

Anne was shown into the waiting room in the building which housed the Council offices and realised that she was the last one to arrive. She was ten minutes early – it was still only twenty minutes past nine – but she supposed that the others had all had a train journey and had given themselves plenty of time.

She smiled and said a quiet, 'Good morning,' to the other three applicants before sitting down on one of the leather chairs with wooden arms which were arranged round the large empty table. The four of them looked at one another somewhat awkwardly, half smiling, each of them, it seemed, wondering who would be the first of them to speak.

It was the one whom Anne guessed might be the army

captain, although he was not in uniform, who spoke. He appeared though, from his stance – shoulders back and head raised enquiringly – to have a military bearing. 'I think we ought to introduce ourselves, what?' he said. 'I take it we are all here now?'

The other two looked a little unsure, so it was Anne who replied, 'Yes, we're all here.' She realised she might well be the only one with inside information. 'I believe there are four on the short list.'

'Ah, so I take it that you are local?' said the military looking man. 'On the staff already, are you?' His shrewd grey eyes looked at her questioningly.

'Yes... I am, actually,' she replied. 'I'm Anne Mellodey. I've been at Middlebeck School for six years.'

'Never mind, we won't hold that against you.' The army captain – Anne felt sure he was – laughed easily. 'They always include a local person, don't they? It's only common courtesy.' Anne felt her hackles rise, but she told herself not to react. She just smiled and nodded pleasantly. 'I'm Roger Ellison,' he went on to say.

'I'm Graham Perkins. How do, everybody,' said the other man. He looked a jovial easy-going fellow.

'And I'm Florence Wotherspoon,' said the fourth person, a quietly spoken, genteel-looking lady. 'Miss,' she added, rather unnecessarily. 'And I'll be the last one in, won't I? It's the story of my life. I'm always the last on every list.'

'Never mind, it's as good a place as any,' said Roger Ellison 'And I'll be first, if they take us alphabetically.'

'Have you always lived here, in Middlebeck?' the man called Graham Perkins asked Anne. 'I must say it seems a delightful little place.'

'On no,' she replied. Then she laughed. 'I mean – yes – it is a delightful town, but no, I wasn't born here, if that is what you mean. Actually, I was an evacuee!' She grinned. 'I came up here in 1939 with a group of children from Leeds, and I liked it so much that I stayed.'

'That's a good advert for the school and for the town,' said

Mr Perkins. 'My wife was quite enchanted with the area. We came up here to give it the once-over before I made up my mind about applying for the post. The kids are not all that keen though – we have a boy and a girl – not keen at the thought of leaving Halifax. But I mustn't count my chickens, must I?'

'No, indeed,' remarked the other lady, Miss Wotherspoon. 'That is what I am telling myself as well. I, also, think it is quite delightful up here. Such a change from Doncaster where I live. So quiet and peaceful. Do you know, it is the first time in my life I have ever ventured so far north? But now that both my parents have…passed on, I have nothing to keep me there. I've been looking out for a nice little country school.'

'It's not always as quiet as you might imagine, living up here,' said Anne. 'We have our share of excitement from time to time and the town is gradually expanding. And so is the school, of course.'

Oddly enough, Roger Ellison had not added anything to this exchange. He was just sitting there, looking from one to another of them as they spoke, his grey eyes alert and his fingers steepled together in a thoughtful manner. The conversation was brought to a halt by the arrival of a dark-suited man – one of the interviewing panel, no doubt – entering the room.

'We are taking you in alphabetical order, ladies and gentlemen,' he said. 'That seems the fairest way. So…Mr Ellison, would you come with me, please, sir?'

Anne noticed that Roger Ellison was not very tall, certainly nowhere near six foot, and that he walked with a slight limp. He was dark-haired with a small military moustache and looked every inch a soldier. They all waited until the two men were out of earshot before they spoke.

'He seems a very confident sort of bloke,' said Graham Perkins. 'At least, that's the impression I have of him.'

Anne nodded. 'As might be expected, I suppose. He's an army captain, I believe; well, ex-army.'

'Is he, by Jove?' exclaimed Mr Perkins. 'I might have guessed. He'll be used to giving orders then and making folk jump to attention. Not that I'm saying anything wrong about the fellow, you understand...' he added.

'No, of course not,' replied Anne, sincerely. They were all teachers of many years' standing and knew it would be considered unprofessional to talk about a fellow member behind his back. The same – unwritten – rule applied in staff rooms. Teachers did not run one another down to their colleagues; any opinions they formed they kept largely to themselves. 'He would make a good head, I am sure, but then...so would we all, wouldn't we?' she added with a smile.

'It all depends on what sort of a person they are looking for,' said Miss Wotherspoon. Anne guessed that she was in her late forties, possibly the oldest of the group, whereas she, Anne, was the youngest by several years. 'Some heads rule with a rod of iron, don't they? By constant use of the cane, some of them. And that's a practice I have never approved of. My present headmaster...' She paused. 'Well, I mustn't speak ill of him, even though you don't know him. But let's just say that I will be glad to get away from there.'

'And I'm sure you will,' said Anne, feeling an empathy with the woman. She, too, deplored the use of corporal punishment, and at Middlebeck School it had never been necessary, at least not whilst she had been teaching there. 'If you don't get this post, then there will be others, won't there?' She had a feeling that whoever was appointed it would not be Florence Wotherspoon.

'The present head is a woman, I believe?' said Graham Perkins. 'I'm sure she will be a hard act to follow for whoever steps into her shoes.'

'Yes, indeed she will,' said Anne. 'Miss Foster has been here for twenty-six years. She will be missed very much at school and in the town. Speaking of using the cane...Miss Foster never saw the need for it. We've had some difficult children, but they all know just how far they can go with her.

And they respect her. But she knows now that it's time for her to retire. She's seen the war through, which was what she promised herself she would do.'

'Quite so,' said Graham Perkins. 'And now we're all on the brink of a new era, aren't we? Not just the four of us here, but in the country, I mean.' They knew he was referring to the 1944 Education Act which had now been accepted as the law of the land. It would provide, it was hoped and believed, new opportunities for all students. Free secondary education was the aim, opening the grammar schools to all those who had the ability to profit from such an education, and not just those who could afford the fees.

'It all sounds very good in theory, but it remains to be seen how it will work out in practice. In my opinion...' His opinion was cut short by the opening of the door. Roger Ellison entered smiling confidently.

'Well, that seemed to go very nicely,' he remarked, nodding his head as though satisfied with his performance. 'I hope I impressed them. There's no point in hiding your light under a bushel, is there?'

'No,' agreed Graham Perkins. 'One has to try and sell oneself.'

'That's what I don't really like about interviews,' said Miss Wotherspoon. 'I've never liked talking about myself; boasting about what I can do. I suppose it's because my mother would have said I was showing off.'

'It's not boasting if you know you are good at something,' said Roger Ellison, sitting down again at the table. 'You must have confidence in yourself.' He smiled encouragingly at her and Anne found herself liking him a little more. 'You go for it, Miss Wotherspoon. Show them what you are made of.'

'Thank you... I'll try,' she said.

There was a moment's silence. Anne knew, as they all did, that it was not done for candidates to discuss the interview and the questions they had been asked. Roger Ellison would not divulge what had gone on as it would give the other three an unfair advantage, and neither would she expect him to do so. She guessed, though, that very little would faze this confident man.

'How many are there on the panel?' she enquired, an innocuous enough question to which nobody could object.

'Oh, six...no, seven,' he replied. 'I didn't actually count heads. I was too busy facing the grilling. Don't get me wrong, though. They don't bite! They are all quite pleasant. They didn't say exactly who they were, so I don't know.'

'Miss Foster will be there, the present headmistress,' said Anne.

'Yes, I picked her out; the grey-haired old lady...' She would not be pleased at that description, thought Anne. Charity prided herself on her still youthful looks, although she was not, admittedly, the height of fashion. 'She didn't say very much. She probably thought it was not her concern, what goes on after she has left. And the vicar was there; couldn't be anybody else, could he, seeing that he was wearing a dog collar.'

'He's the rector, actually,' replied Anne. 'The Reverend Luke Fairchild. He still has quite a lot of say in the running of the school.'

'Ah yes, it's rector, not vicar, isn't it, in these country parishes. I must remember...'

The door opened again and Anne's name was called. 'Miss Mellodey, would you come with me now, please?' said the man in the dark suit. She followed him along the corridor and into the room where, she assumed, the council and various committees held their meetings. Middlebeck could not boast of a Town Hall as such, but this room, which she had never seen before, was very impressive.

The members of the panel were seated around a large table, the top of which was covered in maroon leather embossed with gold, on chairs with carved backs and arms and leather seats. Anne was invited to sit on a similar chair at one of the short ends of the table. Opposite her, at the other end, was a grey-haired, grey-bearded man who she guessed would be the chairman of the proceedings; the chairman of the Education Committee, more than likely. On the wall behind him was a plaque depicting the coat of arms of the area, comprising the white rose of Yorkshire, sheep, mill chimneys and purple heather. On either side of this there were large photographs of Royalty; the present king, George the Sixth and Queen Elizabeth, and the former king, George the Fifth and Queen Mary. The one in between, who had abdicated, was not in evidence. The windows down one side of the room were of bevelled glass, with a stained-glass pattern of the flowers of the realm – the rose, shamrock, thistle and daffodil – at the top of each one. The floor length curtains were of maroon velvet, matching the leatherwork of the furniture. She did not notice all this at a glance. Like the candidate before her, she was too engrossed in answering the questions, but all the features of the elegant room, nevertheless, impinged upon her subconscious mind and she could remember it clearly afterwards.

'Good morning, Miss Mellodey,' said the chairman, and Anne replied 'Good morning,' in what she hoped was a confident voice, glancing round smilingly at all the people seated round the table. There were seven of them, three at each side and the chairman at the top. She saw Luke and Charity each give her a nod of recognition and encouragement, but she realised it would not be advisable to acknowledge them any more than she did the others.

'You are no stranger to the area, are you, or to the school?' the chairman continued. 'You have been on the staff for... six years, I believe?'

'Yes, that's right, sir,' she replied.

'Well now, would you like to tell us what you think you have achieved during your years at Middlebeck School? What do you feel you have been able to add to the life of the school?'

She swallowed hard. That was a poser. Her mind seemed to have gone a complete blank, but she knew she must have made some contribution. 'I came here with the evacuees,' she began. 'They were apprehensive, very scared, some of them, not knowing what was in store for them...and I knew that school would need to be a place where they could feel safe and cared for. I did my best to smooth over the resentment that some of the local children felt...'

'You are saying, then, that the evacuees were resented by the local children?' asked a woman in a bright red hat, who was seated next to the chairman.

'Well, yes...at first,' said Anne. 'Children can very quickly form little cliques and try to antagonise one another, and the evacuees were...different; town children as opposed to country ones. But I tried to encourage them to share their experiences and their differences. We can all learn from one another. For instance, when I came to live here I had very little idea of what it was like to live in the country. My knowledge of the flora and fauna was negligible. And so I instigated nature walks around the area, and the town children – and myself – learned a great deal that had been a mystery to us before.' She felt she was getting into her stride now.

'And I believe I have added to the life of the school by encouraging the children to take pleasure in literature and poetry. I think the most important thing any teacher can do – primary school teacher, I mean – is to ensure that the pupils can read well, and above all, enjoy what they are reading. It has always been one of my greatest pleasures in life, and I hope that I have been able to pass on something of the joy of it.' She was aware of Miss Foster nodding, but it was the woman in the red hat who spoke again.

'But what about the three Rs, Miss Mellodey? Reading, writing and arithmetic. You have talked about reading, but would you not agree that it is just as important to be able to write clearly and to have a good knowledge of mathematics, what the children call sums? Long division and multiplication, fractions, percentages, problems... These are what stimulate the mind, surely?'

'Yes, of course,' said Anne. Maths was not her forte. She had managed to get by in the subject by always being a step ahead of the children, but she had no intention of saying so. 'I believe the children at Middlebeck School have attained a reasonable standard in Mathematics as well as in English, bearing in mind the capability of each individual child, that is.'

'Yes, Miss Mellodey,' said the chairman. He smiled at her. 'From what we know of the school, I believe you are right. And I know you have played your part in keeping up the high standard set by Miss Foster.'

'Now...this is the question we will be asking all the candidates. Could you tell us, please, what would be your plans for the future, taking a long-term view, for Middlebeck School?'

This was a question that Anne had felt sure they were bound to ask, and therefore she had given it some thought. 'I think the most pressing need for the school is a hall where all the children, both Infants and Juniors, can meet together,' she began. 'Of course, I realise that there is little I can do about this. It is a matter of finance and would have to be the decision of the Education Committee. But I do know that Miss Foster has been campaigning for this for a while, and she has my support.'

'Yes, as you say, Miss Mellodey,' said the dark-suited man who had acted as usher, 'it is largely a question of finance, but it is one that is being considered quite urgently. And – should this come to pass – what use would you wish to make of a school hall, that you could not do in an ordinary classroom?'

'It is necessary, I feel, to have a focal point where all the classes can be together. The main objective would be a place where we could have a corporate act of worship each morning.' Anne could see Luke nodding approvingly. 'It is the law of the land that the school day should begin with prayers, and we do see that this is carried out in our own classrooms. But it would be so much better if it could be a shared experience, for all the children, starting with a hymn and prayers, and a reading, perhaps. The older children could be encouraged to take part themselves, in time...'

'It would take a large chunk out of the day, Miss Mellodey,' observed Mrs – or Miss – Red Hat. 'Time that could be spent on what I mentioned before; the three Rs.' Maybe she is not very religiously inclined, thought Anne, looking the woman straight in the eye before she replied.

'It need take no more than half an hour, if that,' she said. 'It works very well in the town schools... But there would be many other uses for a school hall as well as that one.'

'Go on, Miss Mellodey,' said the chairman encouragingly. 'You are doing very well,' he added, smiling at her.

She told the committee that games and what was generally called Physical Training (PT) could take place in the hall, rather than in the school yard where they were always dependent upon the weather. And for concerts, too, she went on, for occasions such as Christmas and the end of the school year. There had not been much emphasis on music and drama in the school, because there was not the room. And this was all tied in with her desire to extend the curriculum to include, to a greater extent, such things as music, drama, literature and poetry, and the appreciation of art. Education should encompass much more, she said, than learning tables by rote and lists of spellings. She would like to encourage the children to think more for themselves and to form their own ideas...although she did agree, she added, that learning to read and write and to be proficient in maths was of equal importance. She could see that Red Hat was looking somewhat put out.

'You mentioned music, Miss Mellodey,' said a rather younger woman, who had not spoken before. 'In view of your name – a very lovely name I must say – maybe it is a special interest of yours?' she smiled.

'Yes...' said Anne. 'At least... I like a good tune; a nice melody,' she added, to polite laughter. 'I am by no means an expert on the subject, although I can play the piano, after a fashion... I think children should be encouraged to find pleasure in music, as well as in the other arts.'

'They have singing lessons, surely?' asked one of the men. 'When I was at school I loved singing "The British Grenadiers" and "Hearts of Oak" and all those rousing songs.'

'Yes, they do sing,' replied Anne, thinking that the way music was taught had obviously not changed a great deal for the last forty odd years; he must be well turned fifty. She knew she must be careful, though, not to be critical of Miss Foster.

Miss Foster's idea of singing – the only music the children ever experienced – was to have all the Juniors together in one classroom, with the dividing partition drawn back. There was a piano, which badly needed tuning, in Shirley Barker's half of the room, but as Shirley was no more competent on the instrument than was Anne, Miss Foster always played for the singing lessons, with either Shirley or Anne taking charge of the Infants during this hour. The headmistress's touch was inclined to be heavy, which meant that the children had to sing loudly to compete with her, resulting in a sound which, to Anne's ears, was by no means melodious. They sang rousing songs of the type that the man on the panel had mentioned, and more plaintive ones; 'Golden Slumbers', 'Early One Morning' or 'The Ash Grove'. They read the words from well-worn red books which must have been in use ever since Miss Foster took over the school, or even earlier; at least, those who could read quite well did so, whilst the less able ones joined in as best they could. Anne had long questioned the value of such singing lessons, especially as she had heard the older boys making up their own words to songs such as 'Strawberry Fair'. 'Rifle, rifle, fol-de riddle- hi-do' – daft words to start with, she had always thought – were soon altered to 'Trifle, trifle, sock 'im in the eyeball', or some such version. Miss Foster, usually so alert, would be concentrating on the music in front of her, having no idea of what was going on.

The Infants' singing lessons took place in their own room, which was also equipped with an out-of-tune piano, and consisted solely of nursery rhymes and jingles.

'They have singing lessons, of course,' she replied to the lover of 'The British Grenadiers', 'and they enjoy them very much. But I feel we could widen the scope; by listening to records – of the more tuneful, easier to understand, classics, like Mozart or Chopin – and by teaching singing in smaller groups. Encouraging the children to sing more tunefully,' she added, hoping she was not treading on Charity's toes.

'All very commendable,' said the chairman. 'I can see you are more inclined towards the Arts subjects than the Science ones... However, let us move on from Music... What are your views on the new Education Act, Miss Mellodey?'

That was a bolt from the blue! Anne knew about it, of course, but it was of more relevance, surely, to the Senior schools – now known as Secondary Modern – rather than the Infants and Juniors, which were now being termed Primary schools. She did her best to answer coherently.

'Any act to improve Education is a step in the right direction,' she said. 'And I believe the church schools, such as Middlebeck, are to be given more financial assistance; that is good. But...it is of more significance to the older children, isn't it? And which school they go on to when they leave the Junior schools.'

'And so it must affect the Junior schools as well, Miss Mellodey.' It was Red Hat speaking again, and Anne felt herself growing tense. This woman did not like her, she thought, or, at least, was opposed to her views. 'For instance, what are your views on streaming? It will be the aim, will it not, to ensure that as many children as possible are able to go on to a Grammar school, now that the way has been opened for them?' Streaming was the grouping of children according to ability, and in village schools and other smaller schools, such as Middlebeck, it had not been considered a feasible concept.

'It is something that has never been done in this school,' replied Anne, 'because it would not be workable. Our numbers are quite small, and so the third and fourth year children are taught together as one class, but with different lessons for each group when it is necessary. As for the Scholarship exam...the ones who are the right age have sat for it, but there has never been any pressure upon them to pass, and no suggestion of failure if they are not successful. I believe it has worked very well. I dislike the word failure, and it is one that is never used at Middlebeck school.'

'But now that there are more free places, surely it is the teachers' responsibility to ensure that as many children as possible pass the exam?' said the British Grenadiers man.

'That is one view, certainly,' replied Anne, feeling she was losing control of the interview.

The Reverend Luke Fairchild came to her rescue by putting forward a suggestion that the school, as a whole, should gather together in the church, maybe once a week, for a simple service, until such time as they acquired their school hall. What did she think of the idea?

Anne agreed wholeheartedly, and soon after this the interview, which had become more and more of an ordeal, came to an end.

'Thank you very much, Miss Mellodey,' said the chairman. 'We have enjoyed listening to your views. That will be all for the moment.'

She smiled and nodded and walked from the room as sedately as she could. She felt like running away from it all as quickly as possible; she was sure she had made a complete mess of it. Looking at her watch she found she had been in the room for over half an hour.

Graham Perkins was seen next and then Florence Wotherspoon, the man's interview taking rather longer than the woman's. Then they just sat and waited.

'It's like being at the dentist's,' observed Mr Perkins.

'Do you think we are supposed to wait?' asked Miss Wotherspoon. 'Won't they inform us of their decision by post?'

'No; they come to a decision straight away,' said Anne. 'They shouldn't be long now. They've been twenty minutes already.'

'Well, may the best man win, that's all I can say,' said Roger Ellison. 'Or woman, of course,' he added.

The door opened and the man who acted as usher was there once more. He paused for a few seconds, then, 'Mr Ellison, would you come with me, please?' he said. The man stood up briskly but, to his credit, he did not smile gloatingly, as he might have done. He nodded soberly as he left the room.

'Well, so that's that,' said Graham Perkins.

'I can't say I'm surprised,' said Florence Wotherspoon with a sigh. 'What do we do now? Do we just go home?'

'No...' said Anne. 'We had better wait until they dismiss us. They'll no doubt be offering him the post. But you never know,' she grinned wryly, 'he might not accept!'

'Pigs might fly!' muttered Graham Perkins.

The usher returned after only a few moments. 'Thank you all very much,' he said. 'The post of headteacher has been offered to Mr Ellison, and he has accepted. If you send your applications for expenses to this office they will be dealt with as soon as possible.'

Graham Perkins appeared philosophical about the result. 'Well, that's that,' he said again. 'The kids didn't want to move, so they'll be pleased.'

Florence looked pensive. 'I didn't really expect to get it,' she said, 'but this is such a delightful place.' She smiled at Anne. 'I do envy you living up here, my dear.'

'Never mind,' said Anne. 'Keep on looking at the adverts. Perhaps something else will come up before long. Best of luck, anyway.'

They left the building and went their separate ways. Anne felt traumatised. She had not built her hopes up too much; nevertheless, she felt deflated. The future, suddenly, looked less hopeful. There would be changes ahead, that was certain, and she had a feeling that they would not all be to her liking.

# Chapter Eleven

'So were you very disappointed, Anne?' asked Maisie. She had come round to the new flat at Anne's request, on the Sunday afternoon following the interview, for a chat and a tea-time meal.

'A little,' replied Anne. 'Yes, I must confess I felt rather despondent for a while. I suppose it's human nature to want to win, to be the best. But I'll get over it. I keep telling myself that I've still got a job that I enjoy very much and a lovely part of the world to live in. I think the other two applicants liked the idea of living up here as much as they wanted the job. Florence Wotherspoon was very crestfallen. She was a very nice, refined, single lady. But somehow, I couldn't see her coping with a headship. It needs someone more dynamic.'

'And this chap who's got the job, you'd say he's got what it takes, would you?'

'Without a doubt. I'd picked him out straight away as a winner, and I think the other two had as well. And apparently the interviewing panel was almost unanimous in their decision. That's what I gather, at any rate, reading between the lines. Miss Foster didn't tell me everything that went on; it wouldn't be ethical. Besides, she didn't want me to feel any worse that I did already. I was convinced that I'd made a real hash of my interview, you see, but she assured me that I hadn't.'

'But Miss Foster and Luke, they would have voted for you, wouldn't they?'

'Maisie, I have no idea.' Anne shook her head. 'Maybe not; it would have smacked of favouritism, wouldn't it? And when it comes to the crunch it has to be the best person for the job, hasn't it? And that would seem to be Captain Roger Ellison. He is very forceful, and persuasive, too, I should imagine. The sort of chap who makes you sit up and take notice, and that is obviously what the committee did. I dare say he put everyone else in the shade... And I rather suspect his views on education are not the same as mine.'

'In what way?' asked Maisie.

'Oh... I don't want to go into it all now,' said Anne. 'Let's just say that I don't expect to agree with him on everything. But we'll just have to wait and see.'

'What's he like then,' asked Maisie, 'apart from being bossy and full of himself? No, I know you didn't say that, but he sounds pretty awful to me.'

Anne smiled. 'Oh dear! I shouldn't have given such an unfavourable impression of the poor chap. I didn't mean to...although I must admit I didn't exactly warm to him. He's ex-army; I told you that, didn't I? He was a captain in a Yorkshire regiment; took part in the D-Day landings, and it was then that he got a bullet in his leg and was invalided out. So that was the end of his war; apparently he was commended for bravery following the Dunkirk evacuation.'

'Did he tell you all this at the interview?'

'No; he said very little about himself. Miss Foster told me. When he was offered the position, the men on the panel wanted to know about what sort of a war he had had. It seems that when it came to talking about himself – about his war record, at any rate – he was quite reticent... Actually, Charity seemed to quite like him.'

'Is he married...or what?'

'He's a widower, apparently. His wife died suddenly, of a brain tumour, just after the start of the war. That was when he resigned from his teaching post and joined the army.' Anne paused thoughtfully. 'I suppose he's had a pretty rough time, poor fellow. I must try not to be too critical, mustn't I...? Anyway, because he has no post to resign from it means that he can start straight away in January.'

'And what does he look like?'

'Every inch the army captain, I would say.'

'Tall, dark and handsome, with a waxed moustache?'

Anne laughed. 'Not so very tall – maybe an inch or two taller than me. Dark, yes, and tolerably handsome; a little 'tache... Oh dear, the poor chap's ears must be burning... Let's forget about him, eh, and talk about something else. So...what do you think of my new abode?'

'Very nice,' said Maisie. 'This room is bigger than Miss Foster's, isn't it? And you've got all the furniture you need.'

She looked round the spacious living room, equipped with a sofa, two easy chairs, dining table and chairs, and sideboard, all in the wartime 'Utility' design, plain but functional, and she nodded approvingly. 'Yes, I like it. And you've got a nice view from the window.'

The room was at the back of the house overlooking the garden area and across the valley to the next range of hills. The front room was the bedroom, which Maisie had already seen when she took off her coat. This looked out on to the opposite row of greystone semi-detached houses, and the trees which lined the quiet avenue. They were now almost denuded of their leaves which lay in brown heaps on the grass verges.

'Yes, it's a pleasant place altogether,' said Anne. 'The kitchen is very small, but it's big enough for me, and it's got a modern electric cooker.' The kitchen was the room that had once been the small bedroom, little more than a boxroom. 'And this sofa will pull out and make a double bed; so if my parents come on a visit I'll be able to put them up. I've always gone back to Leeds to see them – they've never been up here to Middlebeck – but now that the war's over I might be able to persuade them to come. My father took the government warning, "Is your journey really necessary?" very seriously. Well, I dare say that applies to a lot of people. There hasn't been much holiday-making for several years.'

'You're not thinking of looking for another post then, Anne? Another headship, somewhere else?'

'No... I don't think so. I intend to save up like mad from now on, and then, eventually, I might be able to buy a little place of my own, like Charity has done. At least, I do have the option now, don't I? If I'd got the headship then I would have had no choice but to stay in the schoolhouse.' She laughed. 'A case of sour grapes, perhaps, but it's one way of looking at it. Anyway, I think that's enough of me and my doings... What about you, Maisie? Are you looking forward to the party? I must say, it's good to have a social occasion to look forward to; they're very few and far between at the moment. Things seem to have ground to a halt since the Victory celebrations.'

'Bruce's party? Yes, I suppose I'm quite looking forward to it,' said Maisie. 'It's only a couple of weeks away now, isn't it?'

'I was surprised that Rebecca had invited me,' Anne went on. 'I don't know Bruce very well – he's always been away at school or in the RAF – but of course I do know her and Archie quite well. He helped me when I moved in here; he's a real good sort, is Archie. They've invited Miss Foster as well, so we'll have to decide what we're going to wear. How about you, Maisie? Will you be wearing that nice pink dress that you wore for the concert? It really did suit you and it made you look very grown-up.'

'No...no, I don't think so,' said Maisie quickly. 'Actually... I'm thinking of asking Arthur if I can help with the catering. You know, serving the supper and all that sort of thing. I heard him saying to Mum that he would have to employ a couple of girls as waitresses for the evening. So I thought, Why not me? It's not as if I'm an important guest. Anyway, I want to keep well out of the limelight...if you see what I mean.'

'Yes... I see,' said Anne. 'I hope you don't mind me asking, but...you're not still upset about Bruce, are you, and his girlfriend? I thought, with you saying that you don't want to be too involved in the party...'

'Oh no,' replied Maisie, a shade too quickly. 'It's not that at all. Of course I'm not upset about Bruce. No...that's not the reason... I did get the impression, though, that Christine didn't take to me at all, and the feeling was mutual, so it's best if I keep away from her. But... I don't want to play gooseberry, you see, to Audrey, and Brian Milner.'

'Oh, so that little romance is still going on, is it?'

'Well, I don't know that you'd call it a romance,' said Maisie. 'But she likes him a lot – she doesn't say much, but I know she does – and they spend a lot of time together. He meets her out of school and they sit together on the bus, when he's not on his bike, that is.'

'He'll be going away to university though, won't he, next year?'

'Yes; he's in the upper sixth; he's two years older than Audrey and me. I suppose it might fizzle out when he goes away, although he seems pretty keen on her at the moment. I'm surprised that Aunty Patience and Luke allow her to see him so much. I know my mother thinks I'm too young to start going around with boys. She guessed about Bruce – you know, that time when I was upset – but I've never talked to her about him, like I did with you. And I know she wants me to work hard at school. I get sick of her going on about it sometimes, 'cause I always work hard without anybody nagging at me. I thought Aunty Patience might have been the same with Audrey, although I know Patience was never one to nag...'

'I'm sure she reminds Audrey of the importance of her school work,' said Anne, 'just as your mother does, Maisie. Mothers only want what is best for you, although I know they have different ways of showing it sometimes. I expect Luke and Patience know that they can trust Brian Milner to take care of Audrey. He does seem a nice sensible sort of lad, from what I know of him. He was never in my class, though. He had just gone on to grammar school when I started teaching at Middlebeck.'

'Yes...you've seen us all grow up, haven't you, Anne?'

'Yes, indeed.' Anne gave a contemplative nod and a little smile. 'It makes me feel quite old at times, I can tell you! But it's interesting to see what you all make of yourselves. And sometimes I have reason to feel very proud... What about Doris? I haven't heard you mention her much lately. She will be at Bruce's party, won't she? Has she a boyfriend in tow, as well?'

'Not that I know of,' said Maisie. 'To be honest, Audrey and I don't see her very much now, except at pantomime rehearsals. We said it wouldn't make any difference when we went to the Grammar and she went to the Senior school... But it does make a difference really, doesn't it, Anne? Since she left school she's been busy working, so I suppose we've drifted apart, just a bit. She spends a lot of time with her mother and her brothers; they're a really close family.'

'Yes, especially since Walter was killed,' said Anne. 'A very nice sort of girl, Doris Nixon; genuine and uncomplicated. You mustn't let that friendship grow cold, Maisie.'

'No, of course not!' said Maisie, sensing a note of reproof. 'It's just that we do different things, some of the time... I must tell you about the pantomime. We see Doris then, at the rehearsals, because we're all in it, me and Audrey and Doris, and Brian as well, of course.'

'Yes, I've heard that you're doing Cinderella and that you're going to be the Principal Boy, but apart from that I don't know much about it. It's a great choice – my favourite of all pantomimes – but isn't it rather ambitious?'

'You mean with the coach and horses and all that; and the transformation scene?' Maisie nodded. 'Yes, we wondered at first how we would manage it, but it's the squire to the rescue again. Mr Tremaine is going to lend us a farm truck, just a small one, and we can construct some sort of golden coach on top of it.'

'And real horses, I suppose?' joked Anne.

'Four little boys dressed in black with horses' heads,' Maisie smiled. 'Our Jimmy's going to be the leader, so he's tickled pink.'

'And what about Joanie?' asked Anne.

'She's going to be the leader of the chorus line and sing one or two bits on her own. She's quite chuffed about it. And guess what?' Maisie paused for breath. 'You know how nervous Audrey is? Well, we've actually persuaded her to have a part, instead of being in the background all the time. She's going to be the Fairy Godmother! Isn't that wonderful?'

'Yes, that's certainly an achievement,' agreed Anne. 'Audrey will make a lovely Fairy Godmother. Who is doing the producing? Is it Patience? Has she written it?'

'Oh no; we sent away for the script,' said Maisie. 'Yes, Aunty Patience is producing, with help from Mrs Hollins, of course. Quite a lot of help, actually. There's no show without Punch, you know.'

'Don't be naughty, Maisie,' scolded Anne with a smile.

'Well, you know Muriel Hollins, don't you? She has to have her say, although I must admit she has some good ideas and she's a very good pianist. And guess what?' she asked again. 'Timothy's going to play some incidental music between the acts. He couldn't be persuaded to be in it, but he's pleased that he's going to be a part of it.'

'Good for Tim,' said Anne. 'I'm pleased to see he's coming out of his shell. And who is Cinderella? Let me guess... Is it Doris?'

'Oh no,' said Maisie. 'It had to be somebody who could sing, you see, and Doris is the first to admit that she's no singer. Celia James, one of the girls from the choir, she's Cinderella.'

'Oh yes; I think I know who you mean. A dainty girl with curly hair?'

'Yes, that's right. Actually, she's two years older than me, but they wanted me to be Prince Charming because I'm quite a lot taller than Celia.'

'So...what about Doris?'

'Oh, Doris is going to be one of the Ugly Sisters.'

'Oh dear! Poor Doris,' said Anne. 'She's such a bonny girl. Why on earth have they cast her in that role?'

'Because she's such a clown as well,' laughed Maisie.

'Don't you remember her at the concert with that Matilda poem? She nearly brought the house down. She likes fooling around and she's not bothered about making herself look ridiculous. And Brian – Audrey's boyfriend – he's the other ugly sister. They're a great act. You should see them!'

'Well, hopefully, I will,' said Anne. 'I'm looking forward to it.' She would know most of the youngsters – well, teenagers, many of them were by now – who would be taking part. On occasions such as this – pantomimes and concerts – it was good to sit on the sidelines and watch their pupils and former pupils with pride; and sometimes with surprise as they saw promise of an undetected talent.

'So this will be performed in January, I take it?' she asked.

'Yes, the first week in January,' said Maisie, 'just before we all go back to school. It's on three nights; the Thursday, Friday and Saturday. I'm really glad they decided to do Cinderella. It's my favourite of all, not that I've seen all that many pantomimes. But I remember going to see Cinderella when I was a tiny little girl, with my mum and dad – my real dad I mean. When she married Sidney Bragg we didn't get any treats; at least we never went anywhere with him. I don't even know which theatre it was at – I know it was in Leeds – but I remember the shining golden coach and Cinderella's shimmering silver ballgown. I felt as though I was in Fairyland… And when we came out of the theatre it was snowing. And my dad picked me up and carried me…'

'Yes, Cinderella brings out the child in all of us,' said Anne. 'It's truly magical.' She smiled at Maisie, who appeared lost in thought, far away in that magical world with a rapt expression on her face. 'And one day, Maisie, you will meet your own Prince Charming. I feel sure of that.'

Maisie blinked and returned to reality. 'What…? Oh yes, p'raps I will. But I'm busy at the moment, aren't I, pretending to be a prince myself? My mum's busy too, making my costumes…'

Maisie reflected, as she walked home later that evening, about what Anne had said. Her Prince Charming… Well, she had given up all hope, or had tried to, that it would be Bruce. But what about Anne Mellodey and her future prospects? It bothered Maisie a little that her friend still talked about herself and Charity Foster as though they were contemporaries.

'Charity and I will have to decide what we are going to wear at the party...' she had said. What about a Prince Charming for Anne? She was still young and pretty and fun to be with. Maisie hoped that the future would hold much more for her than endless years of teaching at the village school, and memories of the young flying officer she had lost in the early years of the war.

<hr>

Arthur Rawcliffe, Lily's husband-to-be, had agreed that Maisie could be a waitress at the party; in fact, he thought it was a very good idea.

'I'll see that you don't miss all the fun,' he told her. 'I won't expect you to be on duty all evening. You must have a dance and a bit of a jive and enjoy yerself with the other young 'uns.'

'Oh, I'm not bothered about that, Arthur, honestly I'm not,' she told him. 'I'd rather be doing something useful... and you won't need to pay me, will you?'

'Don't worry; I'll see that you get a bob or two for yer trouble; a bit of spending money like... But, aye, there's summat in what you say, lass.' Arthur was a true Yorkshireman, mindful of his brass.

In the end Lily, too, had said that she would prefer to wait on, rather than be just a part of the festivities. And Doris, when she found out what Maisie had opted to do, also volunteered to help. She, also, would be happy enough, she said, with a bob or two as payment, like Maisie.

On the morning of the party day Maisie helped Arthur, and Harry and Flo, the new partners in the business, to prepare the food for the buffet supper, taking it in turns to serve in the confectioner's shop as well, which was always especially busy on a Saturday morning. Arthur had been up extremely early, at four o'clock instead of his usual five, to cope with the extra baking, and Harry had joined him soon afterwards. Lily, of course, was busy in her own draper's shop.

There were sausage rolls in flaky pastry, vol-au-vents, and pork pies – which Arthur called 'hand raised' – a speciality of his which he had reinstated since returning after the war, which folk came from far and near to buy. Admittedly, there might not be as much pork in the mixture as there had been in pre-war days, but everyone who tasted them pronounced them delicious. The open sandwiches, on freshly baked barmcakes, would be prepared later, so as to be fresh, with a variety of toppings; boiled ham, salmon, thinly sliced cucumber and tomato, and egg and cress. There were individual trifles in waxed cardboard cases, and a huge assortment of cakes; éclairs and meringues (containing mock cream which was almost as good as the fresh sort), almond tarts, jam tarts, coconut pyramids, and chocolate buns.

The pièce de résistance would be the birthday cake, large and square, seated on a silver board and iced all over in white, with blue lettering. 'Happy Birthday Bruce,' it read. '21 today'. There would be one largish candle instead of twenty-one small ones, in a silver holder, and in the centre a tiny silver aeroplane, really a child's toy, that Lily had bought from Woolworth's.

'And it's not a whited sepulchre, neither,' said Arthur, referring to the war-time bridal cakes; hollow constructions of cardboard with a tiny fruit cake hidden inside. 'It's the real thing. Not as much fruit as I'd have liked, but ne'er mind; there's even a dash of rum in it.'

'We're certainly doing Bruce proud,' said Maisie, although she had a feeling, deep down, that he would not really appreciate all the fuss and palaver. She had even had a suspicion that the party would not go ahead at all; that Christine might have persuaded him to say he didn't want it, but that had not happened. It was going to take place in just a few hours and she, Maisie, though she was putting on a show of bravado and cheerfulness, would be glad when it was all over.

—

The food, laid in large wooden trays, had been transported to the Market Room in Arthur's van. It was now ready and waiting, covered in sheets of greaseproof paper, in the small kitchen off the main room, to be served halfway through the evening. The first job that Maisie and Doris had to do, after helping to carry the trays in from the van, was to circulate amongst the guests, who were gradually arriving in ones and twos, and offer them drinks from round silver trays. There was a choice of sweet and dry sherry, and orange juice for the younger guests.

'Maisie! Good gracious, what a surprise!' exclaimed Bruce as he caught sight of her, balancing a tray full of glasses. He came towards her and she noticed that Christine quickly followed him. 'They've got you working, have they? I hope you're going to be able to enjoy yourself as well.'

'Don't worry, I will,' she replied. 'I'm just giving Arthur a hand... Happy Birthday, Bruce,' she added. She could not kiss his cheek, as she had seen some of the other guests doing, or even shake his hand, unless she put her tray down. She clung to it tightly as Bruce helped himself to a pale golden sherry of the dry variety and handed one to Christine.

'Thank you, Maisie,' he said, with a smile that could easily have filled her, once again, with longing, but she was determined not to let it. 'And thank you for your card.'

She smiled briefly and nodded. 'My mother will give you our present later,' she told him. She had decided it would be foolish and might only prove embarrassing to buy him a personal gift, so she had added her name to the book token that Lily and Arthur had bought for him. A safe present, they had thought, preferable to cufflinks and tie-pins and the like, of which he might well get an abundance. Then, because she knew she must, she turned to the girl who was hovering at his side. 'Hello, Christine,' she said brightly. 'Nice to see you again.'

'Yes...and you too, er...Maisie, isn't it?' said Christine. She smiled with her lips, but there was a tiny spark of malice in her grey eyes. *She knows perfectly well what my name is,* thought Maisie, as she nodded and walked away.

The wording on the invitation had read 'Dress Optional', but Christine had obviously decided to dress up to the nines. And it had to be admitted that she did look lovely. Her dress was ankle-length, of deep pink silken taffeta with a sweetheart neckline and cap sleeves. The skirt was covered in delicate black lace with a trimming of a black lace flower on the bodice. It looked as though it might, at one time, have been a bridesmaid's dress, updated in the 'Make do and Mend' manner that they had all got used to during the war. But if so, then it had been very skilfully done. Maisie, in her full-skirted floral cotton dress, partially covered by a frilly white apron, felt, by contrast, very young and unsophisticated; but she had been determined not to dress up too much. She was certainly glad now that she had not decided to wear her pink dress from the concert.

The evening consisted mainly of talking and dancing, or just sitting and listening to the music. The three-piece band, of piano, drums and saxophone, was called 'Civvy Street', and had been formed by three young men soon after they were demobbed. They were local lads from Lowerbeck and the girl vocalist, Belinda, was the sister of one of them. They were very accomplished, especially as they had started playing together only quite recently, and they soon had most of the guests on their feet, circling the room in waltzes, quicksteps and slow foxtrots.

Maisie, having finished serving the drinks, sat at the side with Doris, watching the dancers glide by, the women and girls all in bright colours and the men no longer in uniform. There was a feeling of relaxation, of gladness that the dreadful war was at last over and that things were normal again. She saw Bruce and Christine dance by, her arms circling his neck, to the sentimental strains of 'Long Ago and Far Away'. Don't watch, she told herself, as Bruce smiled down at his lady friend and she, starry-eyed, smiled back at him.

The dance, a smoochy foxtrot, came to an end on a discordant flourish from the saxophone, and the couples stood around and clapped. Then the trio struck up with something much more lively; and the next minute Ted Nixon, Doris's brother, was at Maisie's side.

'Are yer dancin'?' he asked with a grin. She laughed and got to her feet.

'I can do this one; it's a quickstep, isn't it?' They had been having dancing lessons that term, one afternoon each week after school ended, with the boys from the nearby grammar school; all very strictly supervised by the teachers, of course. She had not quite mastered the slow foxtrot, and the tango still had her bewildered, but a quickstep rhythm was jolly and made you feel like dancing.

'I'd like to climb an apple tree, But apples green are bad for me...' she sang quietly as she followed Ted's lead. He was surprisingly light on his feet for a farm worker, she thought. '... It's foolish but it's fun.'

'You sound happy,' he remarked, grinning at her.

'Well...yes, I suppose I am,' she replied. 'There's no point in being miserable, is there? It's a party! We're here to enjoy ourselves.'

She was forcing herself to sound more light-hearted than she was feeling, but with Ted that was not difficult. She had known him ever since she came to live in Middlebeck, as Doris's brother. Doris had two much older brothers and Ted was the younger of the two, the one who had stayed behind to take over the farm work during the war whilst his brother, Joe, and later, his father, had served in the forces. Joe was aged twenty-one, ruddy-complexioned, sturdily built and fair-haired, like his late father and his sister; he had a fiancée, a young woman called Irene from a farm near Lowerbeck, who was his partner for the evening. Ted resembled his mother, being dark-haired and dark-eyed and of a more lean and wiry build. Maisie had never given him much thought before, only seeing him as Doris's brother, but now, as he smiled down at her, she realised that he was a very nice looking young man.

'I've been waiting to have a dance with you,' he said, 'but you were busy serving t' drinks with our kid. Can I come and sit with you for a bit? I suppose you'll be helping to serve t' supper, like, won't you?'

'Yes, but not just yet,' she replied. 'About nine o'clock, Mrs Tremaine said. Yes, of course you can sit with me, if you want to.'

'You look lovely tonight, Maisie,' Ted went on, very daringly holding her a little closer. At least, it seemed daring to Maisie; she had always considered him to be a rather shy young man. 'But then you always do look lovely. I think you're a very pretty girl.'

'Well, fancy that!' she replied, a little nonplussed. 'And there's me thinking you saw me as a bit of a kid, like your sister.'

'Kid sisters grow up,' said Ted, nodding towards Doris, dancing near to them with Colin, who was Irene's brother, another farm worker. '... And so have you, Maisie. Do you think—?' His words were cut short as the dance came to an end and the compère of the group, the drummer, came to the microphone.

'And now our lovely Belinda is going to sing for you,' he said. 'Carry on dancing if you wish, ladies and gentlemen, or just sit and listen. The next dance is a foxtrot...and here is Belinda. Give her a big hand, everyone.'

A petite auburn-haired girl in an emerald green dress, sparkling with sequins, stepped up to the microphone. 'Let's sit down,' whispered Ted. 'I'm not very good at foxtrotting.'

'No, neither am I,' replied Maisie.

They sat down on the little gilt chairs, upholstered in green velvet, that had been acquired with the make-over of the room. To Maisie's surprise and slight embarrassment Ted took hold of her hand. The girl soloist, who had a pleasant, though rather tinny sounding voice, was singing about a 'Paper Doll' – it was a man's song really – about a doll that other fellows couldn't steal and who would always be faithful! Maisie had always thought it was a daft song when she had heard it on the wireless, but everyone clapped politely when she had finished.

The next one she sang, 'Swinging on a Star', was much better, a fairly recent Bing Crosby number from the film *Going My Way*; Maisie had seen it at the local cinema, the Palace, earlier that year. She sang along now – quietly though, under her breath – the words about carrying moonbeams home in a jar, and being better off than you are.

'You've got a lovely voice,' whispered Ted. 'Much better than that Belinda.'

'Shh...!' she admonished him. 'Of course I haven't.'

'Yes, you have. I've always thought so. I wanted to ask you, Maisie...would you go out with me? To the pictures or somewhere, happen next week? I've been wanting to ask you for ages. But I thought, well...you're quite a bit younger than me, aren't you? Although you look very grown-up, you do really. And...and I do like you a lot, Maisie.'

She was quite at a loss as to what to say. She liked him well enough, but had never thought of him in...that way. Not as a boyfriend. But maybe friendship was all he had in mind, not boy and girl stuff; just going out with him as she might do with his sister. But somehow, knowing that Ted was five years older than herself, she did not think so. She knew he had already had one or two girlfriends; there had been a shop assistant at Woolie's, and he had been friendly with one of the land girls staying at Tremaine House.

It would sound silly to say that her mother would disapprove; not of Ted himself, of course, but of the fact that he was several years older, and that Maisie was still at school...and only fifteen years of age. She knew very well that that was what Lily would say. She also knew that if it had been Bruce who, by some miracle, had asked her out, then she would have moved heaven and earth to persuade her mother to let her go.

'I don't know...' she began. 'Thank you for asking me, but I'm not sure. You see...'

Belinda had stopped singing and the compère was announcing the next dance. 'Now, come along, ladies and gentlemen; I want to see everybody on their feet for the... "Palais Glide"!'

'Oh...come on, Ted,' cried Maisie, pulling at his arm. 'I love this. It's great fun... I'll think about what you said, honest I will,' she added.

'Yeah, OK then...' Somewhat bemused, he followed her on to the dance floor as the band struck up with the opening chords. Then they linked arms in lines of five or six and pranced round the room, all joining in the familiar song.

> '*She was sweet sixteen, little Angeline,*
> *Always dancing on the village green;*
> *As the boys passed by you could hear them cry,*
> *Poor little Angeline...*'

Maisie felt quite carefree and merry as she stamped her feet and kicked up her legs in unison with the others in the line. It was good to be amongst friends; Audrey and Brian, Doris and Colin, who was still partnering her, and... Ted. She decided there could be no harm in telling him she would go out with him; just the once, maybe, then she would see.

The lively dance came to an end and they all took their seats again, laughing and in a jolly mood. Maisie was surprised and a little disturbed to see Bruce coming towards her, and she folded her hands in her lap, just in case Ted should reach for her hand again.

'Maisie...' Bruce began. 'I wonder if you would do me a big, big favour?' And again he smiled in the way that could so easily break her heart, if she would let it. But she wouldn't; no, she would not!

'I will if I can, Bruce,' she said easily. 'What is it? We'll be serving the supper soon, you know.'

'Yes, I know that. I wondered, just before the interval, would you sing for me? For us, all of us, I mean; that song that you sang at the concert. It's a favourite of mine, and of a lot of other people too. Would you...please, Maisie?'

'"We'll Gather Lilacs", you mean...?'

'Yes that's the one...'

'Oh...no, Bruce, I couldn't,' she said. 'It wouldn't be right, would it? They've got a vocalist – a very good one – and she might be annoyed. Oh no, I don't think so. Besides, they might not have the music and...no, no, I couldn't.'

'I've already asked them,' said Bruce, with a satisfied little smile. 'They've got the music; they sometimes play Ivor Novello numbers as requests. And the pianist will accompany you; you don't need the drums and the sax. Belinda says she doesn't mind at all. She's a really nice young woman; she says it's my party, and so I should call the tune.'

'So you've got it all arranged,' said Maisie, 'before you even asked me.' She felt a little peeved at that, but although her first instinct had been to refuse, she found herself wavering. Why not? she thought. She glanced around the room. Christine had not come with Bruce, but was sitting with his mother and father, and his two sisters and their husbands and children; it was quite a family occasion for the Tremaines. At least, Mrs Tremaine was talking, but Christine was looking fixedly and unsmilingly at Bruce.

'Yes... I'm sorry about that,' said Bruce. 'I should have asked you first perhaps. But, as you say, Belinda may well have objected...'

'Oh, go on, Maisie,' urged Ted. 'Why don't you? I remember you singing that song about lilacs at the concert. It's one of my favourites an' all.'

'All right then,' she said. She grinned at him; then, suddenly, a little spark of mischief made her say, 'OK, Ted; if you want me to sing, then I will.'

'Good for you,' he replied, putting an arm around her and giving her a hug. Only then did she look at Bruce.

'All right,' she said. 'I'll sing for you. When? Before the interval, did you say?'

'That's right,' he nodded. 'Thanks a million, Maisie. Come with me now – there seems to be a lull in the proceedings – if you're ready, that is?'

'Yes, I'm ready.' She stood up.

'Good… I'll get the compère to announce you.' He squeezed her arm briefly as they walked up to the dais. 'Thanks again, Maisie. It will make the evening…for everybody.'

After a few whispered words from Bruce, the compère stepped up to the microphone. 'Ladies and gentlemen, we have a surprise item for you tonight. Here is your very own Maisie Jackson. And she is going to sing for us that lovely song from *Perchance to Dream* – "We'll Gather Lilacs".'

She did not look at anyone as she sang; not at Ted, certainly not at Bruce, but fixed her eyes on the portrait of the King and Queen on the wall at the far end of the room.

> *'We'll gather lilacs in the spring again,*
> *And walk together down an English lane…'*

Such evocative words, and once again she thought of the country lanes around Middlebeck and the happy times she had spent there with Audrey and Tim, Doris…and Bruce. Only then did her eyes stray, but just towards her mother who was beaming at her, her smile full of pride and joy. And towards Audrey who was grinning and giving her a thumbs up sign.

There was enthusiastic applause when she had finished. She took a little bow and made to walk away, but Belinda stopped her.

'Wow! What a voice you've got,' she said, 'and I thought I could sing. You're terrific… Are you going to do it professionally, like?'

'Oh no, of course not,' replied Maisie. 'Thanks for saying that; it's real kind of you. But I'm still at school, you know. I sing in the church choir, that's all.'

'If I could sing like you I'd be after a job with the BBC,' said Belinda. She laughed. 'But I know my limitations, and I reckon Civvy Street is as far as I'll get. It makes a nice change, though, from working at t' mill.'

'You're very good,' said Maisie, 'and Civvy Street is a great little group.' What a very nice girl, she thought, as she went to join the team of caterers in the little kitchen. It was time to serve the supper, time to put on her apron and leave behind her moment of glory.

The guests helped themselves to the 'eats' arranged on a long table at the back of the room, and Maisie and Doris circulated again, with larger trays this time, holding cups of tea or coffee. Lily and Flo were responsible for making sure that everyone had another glass of sherry, at the request of Archie Tremaine. Maisie smiled and said thank you as people congratulated her on her singing, but she purposefully kept away from the family group consisting of the Tremaines...and Christine.

When everyone was served she grabbed a few savoury items and a chocolate cake from the residue of the feast and went to sit with Ted again.

'You were great!' he said, reaching for her hand, but she forestalled him.

'Let me eat my supper, Ted,' she said. 'I'm famished; I didn't have time for any tea.'

She munched away hungrily – Arthur's pies were certainly delicious – as she watched Bruce, with Christine at his side, walk over to stand at the table behind the birthday cake. Like a bride and groom, she thought, tormenting herself again, as they smiled at one another. But they were not a bride and groom; it was only a birthday cake.

Then Bruce started to speak. 'Ladies and gentlemen, all my friends and relations,' he began. 'I want to thank you for coming here tonight to help me to celebrate my birthday, and for all the lovely presents. As some of you know, I am not much of a one for parties... This was my mother's idea.' There was a ripple of quiet laughter before he went on. 'But tonight is a very special occasion, both for me and for Christine. It is not just a twenty-first party, but an engagement party as well. I have asked Christine to marry me…and to my delight, she has said yes!'

There was an outbreak of clapping, and exclamations of, 'Fancy that!' and 'Oh, how lovely!' He turned to her and they kissed, but only briefly, before he said. 'So Christine and I are going to blow out the candle, and cut the cake – our engagement cake.' Together they blew out the flame, and then with their hands clasped together they plunged the silver knife into the icing, and Archie Tremaine rose to his feet.

'This has been a surprise to Becky and me as well,' he said. 'We were only told about it today. But we are delighted, and I would like you all to raise your glasses and drink to the health and happiness of my son, Bruce, and Christine.'

'Bruce and Christine,' echoed everyone as they sipped at their sherry.

Maisie went through the motions mechanically. Although she was under age, she had been allowed a modicum of sherry, which she drank all in one gulp.

'Good for them,' said Ted. 'I've always liked Bruce. There's nowt stuck-up about him, even though he's t' squires's son and has been to a posh school an' all that. I dunno about her though. She looks a bit snooty, like, to me, but he seems well suited with her. And I must admit she's a looker… Not as pretty as you, though, Maisie, I don't mean; not by a long chalk… Hey, what's up? Has summat upset you?'

'No, of course not,' she answered. 'I'm tired, that's all. I wasn't expecting to be asked to sing and it…well, it takes a lot out of me sometimes.' Maisie suddenly realised that she was, indeed, very tired. 'But I'm OK, honestly I am.' She smiled brightly at him, hoping she had managed to blink away the stray tears.

What on earth had Bruce been thinking of, asking her to sing? She would never forgive him for that, then going on

and announcing his engagement immediately afterwards...
But if he had asked her now, instead of earlier, she most
certainly would not have been able to do it.

Ted took hold of her hand and she did not resist. 'Have
you thought any more about what I said? You know, about
going out with me? Will you, Maisie...please?'

'Yes...of course I will, Ted,' she replied gaily. 'Where shall
we go?'

# Chapter Twelve

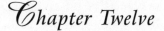

'So there will be a wedding to arrange,' said Rebecca, as she and Archie lay side by side in their double bed.

It had been a hectic sort of day, made even more so by the surprise announcement – sprung on them only that morning – of the engagement, and then the excitement of the party. Sleep was impossible at the moment, so she was making plans.

'Oh, I don't know about that,' said Archie. 'You're jumping the gun a bit, aren't you, love? Anyroad, it's up to the bride's family, isn't it, to see to everything?'

'Yes, I know,' replied Rebecca patiently, 'but aren't you forgetting that Christine doesn't have any relatives? Her parents were killed in a car crash, poor girl, and the grandmother who looked after her died a few years ago.'

'You mean...she has nobody at all?'

'It seems so, apart from friends in Bradford. So it will be up to us to make sure they have a nice wedding. It would be a shame for her to miss out. She is such a pretty girl, and I'm sure she would love a big wedding with bridesmaids and lots of guests, and our church is such a lovely setting for a wedding, isn't it?'

Archie chuckled. 'You're enjoying this already, aren't you? But it's for Bruce and Christine to decide what they want. Anyway, St Bartholomew's isn't her church, is it? And there's some regulation or other about living in the parish, isn't there?'

'Oh, Luke will sort all that out for us. I've been thinking about our Maureen's wedding, and then Angela's the year after... They were such happy occasions, weren't they, Archie? And now...well, I must admit I'm looking forward to arranging another one.'

'You've changed your tune, haven't you? Earlier today you

were saying that it was all a bit sudden, like, and that you wished they'd told us earlier; and that Bruce was still very young.'

'Yes... I know it was rather a shock at first. I suppose I still tend to think of Bruce as my little boy, with him being so much younger than the girls. But he isn't. He's a man now, and plenty old enough to be married, I suppose.' Rebecca paused for a moment. 'Sometimes I wish that he had... well...looked around a bit more. I mean, Christine's his first girlfriend, isn't she?'

'As far as we know, yes. But she's a nice enough lass, Becky. You like her, don't you? Well, you must do, or you wouldn't be thinking of arranging this big do for them.'

'Yes... I like her. She's polite and respectful to us, and quite friendly. And Bruce certainly seems to be very much in love with her. Yes, I'm sure she will be a very good wife for him.'

But there was just something about the girl that Rebecca was not sure about. She did not know herself exactly what it was, and so she had not admitted her slight misgivings to Archie. Maybe that was why she was planning an elaborate wedding, because she felt a mite guilty about the niggling little doubt that she felt concerning Bruce's new fiancée.

'Ask 'em about it in the morning,' said Archie. He leaned over and kissed her forehead. 'Goodnight, love. Get to sleep now. It'll soon be morning, and I'm tired even if you aren't.' He turned round, humping the bedclothes over him.

'Goodnight, Archie love,' she said. As it happened, she fell asleep almost at once, only to dream of Bruce running away from St Bartholomew's church, with Christine, wearing a vivid pink wedding dress and brandishing a silver cake knife, in hot pursuit of him.

—

Maureen and Angela, and their husbands and children, ranging in age from eleven to fourteen, departed soon after breakfast on the Sunday morning. They had a fair way to travel, one family to Warwickshire and the other to Norfolk.

Rebecca was a little tearful. She did not see her daughters and her grandchildren as often as she would wish, but this time they had spent a pleasant few days all together, arriving on Wednesday, well in advance of Bruce and Christine on the Friday evening. Later that day Bruce would be returning to his camp and Christine to her flat in Bradford.

There was quite a mountain of pots to be washed, which Rebecca stacked together at the side of the draining board. Christine had helped her to clear away, which was a point in the girl's favour.

'I've asked Mrs Kitson to come in and give me a hand this morning,' said Rebecca. 'She'll wash these while we're at church. She's a good worker; I've had her for years. Not usually on a Sunday, though, but this weekend has been an extra busy one.'

'Yes, of course it has, Mrs Tremaine,' said Christine. 'Thank you for making me so welcome here. I really enjoy coming up to Middlebeck. It's a lovely part of Yorkshire, much nicer than Bradford. I had never been very far from Bradford until I joined the WAAF; but it's my home, of course, and I suppose I have a soft spot for it, in spite of the grime and the smoke from the mill chimneys.'

Rebecca smiled at her. 'There's always something special about one's home town, isn't there, wherever it is? My husband and I have been thinking, dear, as you have no family of your own... Well, we're wondering if you and Bruce have made any wedding plans yet?'

'Er...no, not really,' said Christine.

'Come and sit down then, and we'll all have a little chat about it before we go to church,' said Rebecca. She led the way into the sitting room where Archie and Bruce were reading the Sunday papers.'

'Now, you two,' she began, 'put those newspapers away and listen.' She sat down on the settee and patted the cushion next to her, indicating that Christine should sit beside her. She leaned forward and smiled round at them all. 'Now... we have some sorting out to do, haven't we?'

'Have we, Mother?' said Bruce. 'What about?'

'Don't be silly, dear; about the wedding, of course,' said his mother. 'Your father and I are so pleased about your engagement. Yes... I know it was rather a surprise at first; we didn't realise your friendship had reached that stage. But we want you to know that we are happy about it. And we want to make sure that your wedding is a very happy day for both of you – well, for all of us – a day we can look back on and remember with pleasure.'

Christine and Bruce looked at one another, their expressions appearing quite blank. 'We haven't talked about it yet, Mother,' said Bruce. 'At least, not very much. We don't even know when it will be.'

'I don't want a big fuss, Mrs Tremaine,' said Christine, looking down at her hands, demurely folded in her lap. 'I am only too happy to be marrying Bruce.' She smiled sweetly at him. 'But I think we would both prefer it to be a quiet sort of occasion. As you know, I have no relatives of my own, and so...'

'And so that is why I want to help, Christine,' said Rebecca. 'I don't want you to feel that I am trying to take your mother's place. I know that nobody could take the place of your own mother, and I am so sorry about that, dear. But when you marry Bruce you will be a member of our family, won't you, and we want to make you feel welcome.'

'You already do, Mrs Tremaine,' murmured Christine.

'So...will you think about it then? We would like you to have a nice wedding here, at St Bartholomew's. Luke does a lovely service, and I'm sure you both have lots of friends you would like to invite. And we could have the Market Room again for the reception. I thought Arthur Rawcliffe catered very well...'

'Mother, will you give us time to think about it,' said Bruce. 'You have rather sprung it on us and, as Christine said, we haven't really talked much about it ourselves.'

'But you're not going to have a long engagement, are you?' asked Rebecca. 'There doesn't seem to be any point in that.

It isn't as if you need to save up, do you, like some young couples do?'

Archie spoke then for the first time. 'Becky, you must let them sort it out for themselves. It's not up to us to be making all the plans.' There were times when he could not understand that wife of his. Having been of the opinion in the beginning that Bruce was too young to be married, she now appeared to be pushing him into it, willy nilly. 'Of course we want to make sure they have a nice wedding, a real slap-up do, if they like. There's no need for those wartime economy weddings any more; thank God we're getting back to normal. But it has to be what Bruce and Christine want to do... OK?'

'Yes, of course, Archie,' said Rebecca, somewhat deflated. 'I wasn't meaning to interfere...'

To her surprise Christine leaned forward and took hold of her hand. 'Thank you very much, Mrs Tremaine,' she said. 'I appreciate what you want to do for us. Bruce and I will think about it, I promise; won't we, Bruce?'

'Er, yes...of course,' he replied, looking a little bewildered.

'We will let you know what we decide,' she went on. 'We don't want to wait too long anyway, do we, Bruce?' She smiled at him coyly.

'Er...no; definitely not,' he replied.

'It will be sometime next year anyway,' Christine went on. 'I'm sure we can promise that. A spring wedding would be nice; or June, perhaps,' she said dreamily. 'It would be lovely to be a June bride.'

'Yes, I was a June bride...' said Rebecca, equally dreamily. 'A long time ago...'

'Not all that long, love,' said Archie. 'Though I know it seems like it sometimes,' he chuckled, with a mock frown at his wife. 'Thirty-five years, isn't it?'

'Yes; fancy you remembering that, Archie,' smiled Rebecca. She turned to Christine. 'Thank you, dear. It will make me so happy if you can indulge me a little. I do so like these happy family occasions...'

'Her and her happy family occasions!' said Christine to her friend, Sadie Gascoyne, the following weekend. 'Not if I can help it. Honestly, that woman! I've never met such an interfering busy-body in all my life. He's not so bad, Archie, the squire, and he puts her in her place now and again. But she really does like to have her own way, and I just don't want it, Sadie, all that fuss and carry-on, certainly not up there in Middlebeck with all those country bumpkins.'

Sadie had recently been demobbed from the ATS and they were in Christine's flat, catching up on all the news. Sadie was due to start work again the next day, in the same mill office as her friend. 'I'm surprised at you really, Chrissie,' she said. 'I thought all girls would want to have a nice wedding now that the war's over. I'm looking forward to mine; ours, I should say; we tend to overlook the bridegroom sometimes, don't we? But I must admit that my mother is quite over the moon, arranging it all; more excited than I am, really. I expect Bruce's mother does like the idea of being in charge, but I'm sure she's only trying to please you and make it a happy occasion. With your own mother not being here, I mean; she probably feels she wants to make up for it.'

'Yes, that's what she says, and I know she's only trying to be kind. But I sometimes feel like a fish out of water up there. All those folk fussing around Bruce because he's the squire's son. And those girls that he knows; quite a harem he's got, I can tell you! They look at me as though I've come from another planet.'

Sadie laughed. 'You're exaggerating. I'm sure they don't. Haven't people made you feel welcome?'

'Ye...es,' said Christine grudgingly, knowing she was being a little unfair. 'Bruce's family are nice to me, though I feel his mother's trying a bit too hard... His father's good fun, though, and his sisters and their husbands are OK, what I've seen of them. But then there's that girl... I've told you about that Maisie girl, haven't I? If she's not in love with Bruce I'll eat my hat. But he says she's just a kid he's known for ages.'

'Well then, what are you worried about?'

'I'm not... But he only went and asked her to sing at the party, didn't he? I could've throttled him, honestly, but I didn't say anything because the next minute he announced our engagement. That took the wind out of her sails all right.' She gave a malevolent little grin, but, in truth, she hadn't noticed much of a reaction from Maisie Jackson. The girl had seemed very engrossed with the farmer's lad she had been dancing with for most of the evening. 'I wouldn't put it past him to ask her to be a bridesmaid,' she added.

'Now you're just being silly,' said Sadie.

'Yes, maybe I am...' Christine laughed. 'But I want to get right away from Yorkshire when we're married. Bruce is different, somehow, when he's up there with them. And I can't wait to leave Bradford behind.'

'I shall miss you, though,' said Sadie. 'I know I shall be leaving as well, when Roland and I get married, but we'll still be friends, won't we?'

'Of course we will,' replied Christine, and she meant it sincerely. Sadie was a good friend, one who brought the best out in her and not the worst; although there was a great deal that her friend still did not know about Christine's background. And she would never need to, once they had left Bradford; it was in that city that the danger lay. 'We will always be friends, I hope,' she said. 'Just because you and Roland are going to live in Germany, it doesn't mean we'll never see one another again, does it?'

'Goodness, I hope not,' said Sadie. 'It's not definite about Germany, yet, but there's a strong possibility that Roland will be posted there in a few months. That's why we've planned a February wedding. Rather earlier than we wanted, but you will be my bridesmaid, won't you?'

'Of course; I've said that I will.'

'I was hoping to do the same for you, but we'll probably have gone by the time you get married. Have you made any plans at all? What does Bruce say? Does he want to go along with his mother's idea?'

'No, not really... I'm working on him,' said Christine. 'A

quiet Register Office do, that's what I want. There's no harm, though, in letting his mother live in cloud cuckoo land for a little while, but I'm getting Bruce round to my way of thinking.' She gave a self-satisfied little smile.

'You're very lucky, you know,' said Sadie, 'and I hope you realise it. Bruce is a lovely young man and he thinks the world of you, doesn't he?'

'Oh yes, I do believe he does,' said Christine.

'Then maybe you could meet him – and his mother – halfway?' suggested Sadie. 'Just a small wedding, for family and a few friends, perhaps; a church wedding, I mean, here in Bradford, though, at your own church, not up in Middlebeck.'

'But I don't go to church, do I?'

'Well, at your local church then; you know what I mean. I should try not to antagonise Bruce's family, Christine. It sounds as though they're a nice family, and they have accepted you.'

'So they have,' said Christine.

But Rebecca Tremaine would certainly not have approved if she had known how much time her son and Christine were spending alone together. She was not aware, for instance, that Bruce, instead of returning directly to his camp on the Sunday afternoon, as he had intimated, had gone instead to Bradford and spent the night in Christine's flat, and in her bed, before going on to Lincolnshire the following day.

Now that they were not governed by the bureaucracy of wartime he was able to get away for at least twenty-four hours each weekend. The times they spent together were becoming increasingly passionate. Bruce was taking precautionary measures, as he had promised he would; but, unbeknown to him, Christine had other ideas.

———

Lily had been surprisingly obdurate when Maisie had asked if she could go to the pictures with Ted. She had broached the subject on the Monday evening, after Joanie and Jimmy, having been allowed to stay up to listen to *Monday Night at Eight*, had gone to bed.

'Oh, Maisie, love, I don't think so,' she said. 'You know how I feel about you going out with boys. I've told you before; you're not old enough, not until you're sixteen. If you were just a bit older...'

'But that's ridiculous, Mum,' retorted Maisie. 'What difference will it make when I'm sixteen? It's only a few months away, and everybody says I'm very grown-up for my age.'

Yes, and that is part of the problem, Lily thought to herself, but she did not voice her misgivings, except to say, 'Yes, I know, love. I know you are quite grown-up in some ways...' Lily knew that the circumstances of her life back in Leeds had forced her little girl to grow up early; that, and becoming an evacuee at the age of nine. '... But the fact remains that you are still only a child.'

'A child! Of course I'm not a child,' remonstrated Maisie. 'Joanie and Jimmy are children. I'm not! So don't treat me as though I'm a kid like them.'

'I know what you are saying, Maisie,' replied her mother, 'and of course I don't treat you like Joanie and Jimmy. But in the eyes of the law – that's what I mean – you are classed as a child until you are sixteen. Besides, Ted is so much older than you, isn't he?'

Maisie sighed. 'I thought you'd say that. What about Audrey then? She's been going around with Brian Milner for ages. I know she's sixteen now – she's older than me, worst luck! – but she doesn't look it, and she was only fifteen when she started going with him.'

'It is no concern of mine what Luke and Patience allow their adopted daughter to do,' answered Lily, 'but I'm sure they keep a strict eye on her, and Brian is still at school himself, isn't he?'

'Not like Ted, you mean? Ted's been around a bit; that's what you mean, isn't it? What d'you think he's going to do? Jump on me?'

'Maisie, really...'

'Well, if he does, I can take care of myself. I'm not a kid, and I do know what goes on. I thought you'd have realised that, Mum...' She looked at her mother steadily, and Lily lowered her eyes.

'Yes, love, I do know. I've not forgotten that awful time when you were a little girl. But that's why I want to protect you, you see.'

'From Ted?' Maisie laughed. 'But you know him, Mum, and what a decent lad he is. We've known him ever since we came to live in Middlebeck. Anyway, I don't know why you're making such a big thing of it. He's only asked me to go to the pictures. He might not ask me out again. We just got friendly, like, at Bruce's party, that's all.'

Lily nodded, a little more understandingly. She was remembering her daughter's former anguish about the squire's son, from which, fortunately, she seemed to have recovered; and she decided to relent. 'Very well then, Maisie. I suppose I will have to say yes, you can go. You were a good girl to ask me, anyway.' She might easily have told a fib about it; said she was going with a girl friend, or to something at the church. 'And I know I can trust you to behave sensibly. But you must be home by half past ten. I think that's reasonable, don't you?'

'Yes, that's great, Mum. Thanks for saying I can go.' She did not fling her arms around her mother; that had never been their way. 'Shall I go and make a cup of tea?' she asked, 'then we can listen to Valentine Dyall before we go to bed.'

'You and your ghost stories!' said Lily. 'You'll be having nightmares.' Valentine Dyall, the 'Man in Black', told spooky stories on the radio quite late at night, and Maisie liked to stay up to listen to them.

'No, I won't,' she laughed. 'It's only a story, not real life. It never disturbs my sleep.'

'That's all right then,' said Lily. 'Yes, thank you, love; we'll have a cup of tea. And there's some flapjack in the tin; Arthur brought it from the shop.'

No, it was not very likely that Maisie would be frightened

by a ghost story, thought Lily as she listened to the clatter of cups in the kitchen and the sound of her daughter's voice as she sang softly to herself. That was a good sign; she must be feeling happy. Lily felt glad that she had given in and said that she could go out with Ted Nixon. After all, she had not been all that much older herself when she had met Davey Jackson, Maisie's father; only seventeen and Davey just a year older. At least this friendship would get Maisie's thoughts away from Bruce Tremaine and his engagement. As for the ghost stories, the girl had had much more than that to frighten her in the past, and so had she, Lily.

Thank God that was all over. Lily knew she must make the most of the evenings she spent with her daughter, just the two of them, when the little 'uns had gone to bed. There had been a time when she feared that she and Maisie were growing apart, and she had been somewhat resentful of the influence that Patience Fairchild had had on the girl's life. Even during the mid-years of the war, after Lily also had come to live in Middlebeck, Maisie had remained at the Rectory, whilst Lily stayed at Tremaine House in charge of the land girls who were billetted there. It had taken a while for the mother and daughter to regain the affinity they had shared when Maisie was a tiny girl – it had been damaged almost irreparably by Sidney and Percy Bragg – but now they were once again the best of friends; notwithstanding the occasional slight dispute, such as they had had tonight.

Quite soon – early in the coming year of 1946, in fact – there would be important changes taking place which would be sure to affect, to some degree, the present closeness that the mother and daughter shared. Lily and Arthur planned to marry in early March, but before that there were changes to be made to their respective living accommodation. Mr and Mrs Jenner, the owners of the draper's shop – one day to become Lily's – had been only too pleased to give permission for the wall between the upstairs premises to be knocked down and the rooms converted into one large apartment instead of two. There would be separate bedrooms for Joanie and Jimmy, who were sharing at present, and a larger room for Maisie, if she so wished. But Lily knew that her daughter was very fond of her attic room and her bird's eye view, as from an eyrie. A larger sitting room, too, and maybe a separate dining room and a much larger, more modern kitchen. The builders were due to start work soon after Christmas and Lily was excitedly making plans.

This would be a good marriage, she was sure of it. There was no expectation of heady romance or intense passion, but she knew that Arthur loved her in a quiet, undemanding way, and that was how she loved him in return. The thought of spending the rest of her life with him filled her, if not with rapture, then with a feeling of contentment.

—

The films shown at the Palace cinema in Middlebeck were not new releases such as were seen in the Odeons and Alhambras in cities like Leeds and Bradford. A film from the previous year, *Meet me in St Louis*, starring Judy Garland, was on at the local cinema during the week in November when Maisie and Ted went out together for the first time. But as Maisie had not seen it, and as she remembered the star with a sense of nostalgia from her performance in *The Wizard of Oz*, she found herself looking forward to the outing.

The cinema had not changed very much from the time when she, with Audrey and Doris, had gone to watch the children's matinee performances during the early war years. At that time, though, the children had sat on long forms at the front of the cinema, but these had now been replaced by red plush tip-up seats like the ones at the rear. But the orange silk curtain was the same, now even more faded, and Maisie was certain that the adverts for local businesses, flashed on the screen before the performance started, had scarcely changed at all.

Before the main film was shown they sat through a nature

film about migrating swallows, a short Donald Duck cartoon, the trailer for the following week's performance – a cowboy film starring John Wayne, which Maisie did not fancy at all – and the Gaumont British News. This showed the intensive building of council houses and 'prefabs' being undertaken by the new Labour Government; the King and Queen and the two princesses strolling informally in their grounds at Sandringham; and, on a more sombre note, a brief look at the German town of Nuremberg, where the trial of Nazi war leaders had just begun.

Maisie and Ted sat at the back in the slightly more expensive seats. She was relieved that he did not attempt to put his arm round her – she could see a couple kissing quite unashamedly further along their row – but he did take hold of her hand. At the interval he bought two small cardboard tubs of ice-cream, which they ate with tiny wooden spoons.

Ted, it seemed, was not much of a one for chattering; he had said very little at all since he had called for Maisie. She had never found it hard to engage in conversation with anyone, so she was rather fazed by this.

'You're very quiet, Ted,' she said, when she had finished her ice-cream and placed the carton tidily on the floor; there was nowhere else to put it. 'Is there something the matter?' She wondered whether he was, in fact, having second thoughts about asking her out.

'No, not at all,' he replied. 'There's nothing the matter; what could there be? I'm only too pleased to be here with you.' He smiled at her fondly. 'I'm usually quiet; my sister's the chatterbox in the family, as no doubt you know, and my brother has plenty to say for himself. I suppose I take after my mother, in disposition as well as in looks. I'm not much good at conversation, I'm afraid, not unless I have something important to say.'

'That's all right then,' smiled Maisie, 'so long as there's nothing wrong. You'll find I can talk enough for two people. So...how's life on the farm?' she asked, trying to draw him out. 'Has your Joe settled down to working there again?'

'Oh aye, I think he's glad to be back home, especially with Irene, his fiancée. Her folks have a farm down Lowerbeck way.'

'So are they getting married soon?'

'I dunno; he hasn't said so. I reckon they're saving up for a place of their own. Unless he takes over our farm, of course...'

'To buy it, you mean?' asked Maisie.

'Aye, mebbe so... The squire has said he'd like to sell it and he's offered it to us, but our mam's in two minds as to what to do about it. She's getting tired, y'know. She's taken over the running of the farm since our dad died, and she works as hard as any of us. We're not right sure what's going to happen at the moment. We're having some extra help, though, so she'll be able to take it a bit easier.'

'Oh? Another farm worker, you mean?'

'Aye, sort of. We had the land girls, as you know, all through the war, but they've gone back home now. We've been told we're having some foreigners, two of 'em. Displaced persons, they're calling 'em, from Poland. Apparently they're not too happy at what's going on over there, so a lot of 'em are coming here, and they've got to be found work. So they'll be working on t' squire's land and helping us out an' all, like the land girls did.'

'And where will they live?' asked Maisie.

'I dunno for sure. Happen at Tremaine House, if Mrs Tremaine'll have them. There's plenty of room there and she's always ready to do folks a good turn... Hey up; the film's starting now; I'd best shut up...'

Maisie enjoyed the light-hearted film and the cheerful songs. She was singing the words of 'The Trolley Song' softly to herself as they left the cinema and emerged into the chilly night air.

> 'Zing, zing zing went my heartstrings,
> For the moment I saw him I fell...'

'You obviously enjoyed it,' said Ted, taking hold of her arm.

'Yes, I did, very much so,' she replied. 'Thanks for taking me, Ted.'

'Don't mench... We'll go again soon. That is, if you'd like to...?'

'Mmm...yes, I would. But not next week, if you don't mind. I'm not keen on cowboy films.'

'Nor am I for that matter. But we don't have to go to the pictures, do we? There are other places we could go.'

'Such as...?' asked Maisie.

She knew she had stumped him there. Where else was there to go in a little town like Middlebeck? Dances and social gatherings were few and far between, and although Ted went to public houses sometimes, Maisie was not old enough to go. Besides, they were not really the sort of places that well-brought-up girls frequented. During the summer time there were lots of secluded country lanes where courting couples could walk; not in the winter, though, not unless you were up to no good. Anyway, she and Ted were not officially 'courting'. She did not want to invite him to her home, nor did she expect to be invited to his, not as his girlfriend, although she had been there many times as Doris's friend.

Ted scratched his head. 'Aye, that's a problem, isn't it? Ne'er mind, I'll think of something. I tell you what, let's go and get some chips, shall we? It's a bit parky tonight and they'll warm us up.'

The fish and chip shop round the next corner was a haven of comfort and warmth, with the boiling fat sizzling away and the appetising smell of frying fish in crispy batter, and golden brown chips. They joined the short queue standing against the gleaming chrome and glass counter, and the pale blue tiled walls decorated with patterns of sea shells and seaweed and multi-coloured fish.

'Two penn'orth each, please, salt and vinegar,' said Ted when it was their turn. 'Unless you'd like a fish an' all. Would you Maisie?'

'No thanks, chips'll be fine.'

'Mushy peas?' enquired the plump fresh-faced woman in a white overall and cap.

'No thanks,' said Maisie again. 'Just chips.'

'Go on,' said Ted, 'I'll have some mushy peas, an' I'll share 'em with you, Maisie. Never let it be said that I don't know how to treat a lady.'

The woman dished out two portions of chips on to greaseproof paper, with a sheet of newspaper underneath, and Maisie and Ted added their own vinegar, and salt from a large metal container. The bright green mushy peas were in a waxed carton and the woman provided them with two wooden spoons; the chips had to be eaten with fingers.

'Thanks very much; come again,' she called as they left the shop.

Chip shop chips were a treat for Maisie as her mother did not often buy them. 'They're yummy!' she pronounced, blowing on the hot chunks of potato before savouring their delicious crispness. 'And so are these,' she added, taking a spoonful of the green gooey substance, as much liquid as solid. 'My mum never buys these.'

'No, nor does mine,' said Ted. They stood against the wall at the back entrance to Lily's shop, finishing off the remains of their snack.

'Here, give me the rubbish, and I'll put it in the dustbin,' said Maisie, making to open the back gate. 'Thanks ever so much for tonight, Ted. I've really enjoyed myself.'

'So have I,' he replied. 'I can see you again...can't I?'

'Yes, of course...' said Maisie.

'When? Next week? Or this weekend...?' asked Ted eagerly.

'I'm not sure. The thing is... I'm rather busy at the moment. There's all the practices, y'see, for the pantomime; you'll know about that, with Doris being in it. As well as choir practice, and I've...all sorts of other things to do as well.' She did not mention homework, as she thought it would make her sound like a schoolgirl, which, of course, she was... And the fact remained that she did have her homework to do. 'I'm not making excuses, honestly,' she said, realising that it sounded very much as though she was. 'I would like to see you again...'

'OK then...' said Ted. 'I understand.' He looked at her a little plaintively, then he leaned forward and kissed her gently on the lips. 'I'll get in touch with you soon, Maisie...' He nodded and smiled and then he was gone.

Maisie realised that it would be rather nice to see him again. He was an uncomplicated young man and she had enjoyed his company. She also realised that her thoughts had hardly strayed at all to Bruce Tremaine, except when Ted had mentioned the farm. She must be getting over it...

# Chapter Thirteen

'What about Christmas, darling?' asked Bruce. 'Isn't it time we were making plans?'

It was a Saturday evening in early December and he was spending the weekend with Christine, in her flat in Bradford. He found he was able to see her most weekends by careful scheming and by promising to do reciprocal favours to obliging colleagues, should the need arise. Bruce was a popular member of his squadron, relating well not only to his equals but also to senior and lower ranks.

'Christmas?' Christine raised her eyes from the pages of her *Woman's Own*, looking quizzically at Bruce in the opposite armchair. He had opted not to sit next to her because she was smoking. He smoked occasionally; it was a habit that Christine had got him into, but not one of which he was proud. He tried not to let her know, however, that her addiction – which he feared it was fast becoming – was starting to be objectionable to him. The smell which clung to her clothing, to his mind, detracted from her femininity. 'Christmas? What about it?' she asked. 'I wasn't aware that we had any plans in mind.'

'No, we haven't; that's why I'm asking you now. My mother will be expecting me home for Christmas as usual. I've managed to make it each year, even whilst I've been in the RAF. And this year, of course, she will be expecting you as well. You will be very welcome, darling; you know that, don't you? As you always are.'

'It seems to me that the plans have already been made,' observed Christine, 'without consulting me at all.' She tapped a half inch of ash from her cigarette into the glass ashtray at her side. 'You are taking it for granted that I will fall in with your arrangements...or your mother's arrangements, I suppose I should say.'

'Oh, come on, darling; it's not like that at all. It isn't as if you have anywhere else to go, have you? Obviously we will be spending Christmas together, you and me, and what else would we do except go to my parents?'

'What else indeed?' said Christine. 'Don't forget, though, that I have plenty of friends. I'm not poor little orphan Annie, all alone in a storm.'

'No; you are my fiancée now, aren't you? And soon to be a member of my family...' He looked at her concernedly. 'What's the matter, darling?'

She shook her head. 'Nothing...' she said. 'On the other hand...everything, I suppose. Yes, I'm your fiancée, Bruce, and I'm so happy about it, darling. So glad that we're going to be married. But I don't want to marry you just so that I can be a member of your family.'

'No, of course you don't. I haven't said that...have I?'

'No, but it's what you imply. Or what your mother implies, at any rate. How proud I must be to be joining the great Tremaine family...'

'Hey, steady on, darling...'

'But you must admit that she wants to organise everything, Bruce. You know how she's trying to take over the plans for our wedding. But that's not what I want. I want it to be just about you and me.'

'Well, it is, isn't it, deep down? Just you and me; nothing else really matters. Don't you understand, Chrissie, it's you that I want. I'm not bothered about anybody else.'

'That's what I want to believe,' said Christine, looking at him steadily. 'OK then; how about you and me spending Christmas on our own? We could go away somewhere, just the two of us.'

He stared at her. 'But...why? We'll have all the time in the world to be together, after we're married. It's only for a couple of days, darling. There' no point in upsetting everyone at Christmas, just because we want to be on our own.'

'No point in upsetting everyone...' repeated Christine. 'I see... But the point is this...' She paused, then, 'I'm pregnant, Bruce,' she said.

'What!' A panoply of expressions passed over his face in the few seconds following her words; shock, horror, disbelief, fright... 'But...you can't be!'

She gave a wry smile. 'Oh, but I am. I can assure you, Bruce, that I am.'

'How...how do you know?'

'How does a woman usually know?' She gave a sardonic laugh. 'I've missed a period. I'm more than two weeks overdue, and that is something that never happens to me. I'm as regular as clockwork. Anyway, I just know.'

Bruce now looked simply bewildered. 'But we've been so careful. You asked me to take care of...of that side of things, and I have done. It was something I had never done before, going in a shop and asking for them, but I did it so that we would be all right. I can't understand what has gone wrong.'

'Obviously they are not always foolproof,' said Christine. 'Don't worry, darling. It's not your fault. You've done all that you can. Besides, does it really matter?'

'What do you mean?'

'Does it really matter that I'm pregnant? Good gracious, darling; you look as though you've been handed a death sentence, not news of a birth. We'll just have to get married sooner, won't we? A lot sooner than we intended.'

'But what will we say? To my mother...and to everyone?'

'I might have known you would say that!' Christine snapped at him with what she considered righteous indignation. 'Your mother... It's always your mother, isn't it? What are you afraid of, Brucie? That Mummy will know you've been a naughty boy, not waiting until you were married?'

'No, of course not! Don't be so nasty, Christine. Mother knows we're engaged, so surely she must realise that we... But nobody needs to know just yet, do they, that you're pregnant? When will it be? Do you know?'

'Oh, I'm not sure,' she replied casually. 'The end of August, I should think.'

'Well then, what is there to worry about? We could go ahead with a spring wedding, like we had in mind...'

'Like your mother had in mind, you mean,' said Christine. 'Or was it June that she fancied? With me as big as a house side! Oh no, Bruce; that won't do at all.'

'Well then...what do you suggest?'

'I suggest that we get married first and tell them afterwards. That's why I don't want to go for Christmas, because I would have to pretend... It wouldn't be right to deceive your parents,' she said, assuming an expression of concern. 'Your mother would be full of wedding plans, and I would feel dreadful knowing that it wasn't going to happen like that.'

'So...what are we going to do then?' He seemed so utterly dumbfounded that she felt like shaking him. She wished at times that he would be more decisive and sure of himself. She knew he could be so with his comrades, and with her, too, on occasions, but when it came to his family, particularly his mother, he was always so afraid of causing offence. Now, though, in his present bewildered state, she realised he was putty in her, Christine's, hands, and that was just what she wanted.

'Tell your parents that you can't manage Christmas this year,' she said. 'You'll think of something; you're not able to get leave...or whatever. And we can go away somewhere on our own, or stay here if you like?'

'You mean...we could get married at Christmas time?'

'I was thinking about the New Year, actually. It would have to be at the Register Office, here in Bradford, I suppose. They won't need much advance warning, not like a church wedding. And then we can let your parents and everybody else know when it's all over. Tell them that that was the way we wanted it to be, without any fuss.'

'Yes, perhaps that's the best way,' replied Bruce stoically. 'It'll be an awful shock to them, but...yes, that's what we'll do.'

A couple of weeks later Bruce made the journey to Middlebeck on his own. 'It's an early Christmas visit,' he told his mother and father, forcing himself to be jovial and to act as though everything was quite normal, except, of course, that he would be unable to come home for Christmas that year.

'I suppose it's only fair,' he said ruefully, when his parents, particularly his mother, expressed their extreme disappointment. 'I've been lucky so far, haven't I? I've always managed to get home in the past; but this year it's my turn for Christmas duties.' They didn't ask what those would involve and so he didn't enlighten them. It was only a half lie, or half truth, whichever way you wanted to view it. He was hoping to get away from the camp for twenty-four hours at least, which would be spent with Christine.

'My colleagues have been very obliging recently,' he added, 'since Christine and I got engaged, so now it's time for me to return some favours.'

'This wouldn't have anything to do with Christine, would it?' His mother regarded him a mite suspiciously. 'It isn't her idea, is it, that you should stay away this year?'

'Of course not, Mother,' he replied. 'Why should it be? She's just as disappointed as I am.' He crossed his fingers tightly behind his back as protection against the lie, something he had done ever since he was a small boy. 'She is always telling me how welcome you make her feel.'

'Is she? Well then, that's good,' said his mother, with what Bruce felt to be a hint of sarcasm; or was he, in his present nervous state of mind, imagining it? 'Perhaps you will both come and see us after Christmas then? Early in the New Year, maybe?'

'Yes, of course we will.' He seized on the suggestion with a show of eagerness, although he knew that the next time he and Christine came to Middlebeck it would be as a married couple. He badly wanted to tell his mother of their plans right away and be hanged to all the secrecy; not to say that Christine was pregnant, of course, but that they wanted a quiet ceremony without any fuss. But he knew how angry his fiancée would be if he did so. 'We'll come just as soon as we can arrange a suitable weekend,' he told his mother.

'That's all right then,' said Rebecca. She smiled fondly at her son. 'I must admit though, Bruce, that it's nice to have you here on your own, for a change.'

'Yes, so it is,' he agreed, smiling back at her. He realised that his words were no less than true. Things were soon going to be very different, and he knew that what he and Christine were about to do might hurt his mother, and his father, very much indeed.

———

From her place in the choir stalls Maisie felt her heart give a jolt as she caught sight of Bruce sitting in one of the front pews with his parents. And her heart gave an extra beat when she saw that Christine was not with him. Could it possibly be that they were not together any more? No; that would be too much to hope for, after that big fuss over their engagement just a few weeks ago. She became aware that he was smiling at her a little curiously, and she realised, too, that she had stopped singing. That would never do, losing concentration and staring at him like a fool, when she should be helping to lead the worship with the rest of the choir. She smiled at him briefly, then looked away, fixing her eyes on the words and music of the Advent hymn.

'Rejoice! Rejoice, Emmanuel
Shall come to thee, O Israel...' she sang lustily.

'It was a few days later that she heard the news, through the local grapevine, that Bruce would not be home for Christmas this year, but that he and his fiancée – so it was still on then? – would be making a visit to Middlebeck early in the New Year. Would that be in time for the pantomime, she wondered? She remembered how, at one time, he had said he would be sure to come and see it. But in a way she hoped he would not be there. It would only unsettle her again, just as seeing him in the Sunday morning congregation had unsettled her. She was trying so hard to put him to the back of her mind – which she found she was now able to do, sometimes for a whole day at a time – and concentrate on her new friendship with Ted Nixon.

She was enjoying Ted's company, now that she was able to persuade him to talk a little more. They only talked about day to day happenings in the neighbourhood, however, and about how the approaching season of Christmas was making each of them busy in their own way. Maisie was occupied with her end of term activities – which she tried not to mention too much to Ted – and the forthcoming Carol Festivals at church, and the New Year pantomime; and Ted was extra busy on the farm as they harvested the Brussels sprouts and turnips, and fattened up the Christmas turkeys and chickens and the largest sow. Poor creatures, Maisie thought, not wanting to dwell on the details of the gruesome business, because she enjoyed her Christmas dinner as much as anyone.

When it came to other matters she sometimes felt that he was rather in awe of her. 'I've never been much of a one for books an' all that sort o' thing,' he told her, when he discovered that she made frequent visits to the local library; she had long been an avid reader. She told him that she too, however, read the *Daily Mirror* and *People* on a Sunday, and that as well as enjoying some classical and choral music, she also liked the popular stuff just as much as he did. They discovered that they both had the records of Glen Miller – 'Moonlight Serenade', 'In the Mood', and 'American Patrol' – played and played on their wind-up gramophones until they were quite scratchy with overuse.

She hadn't been able to see him as much as he would have wished, but he had taken to meeting her from choir and pantomime practices. They would walk slowly to her home, sometimes calling at the chip shop on the way, and say goodnight at the back gate with a few kisses. After that first time he had kissed her more lingeringly, and she had not protested.

She had not yet invited him to her home, but she had been

invited to a party at the Nixons' farm early in January. She would most likely have been invited anyway, as Doris's friend, but this time, Ted impressed upon her, she would be there because he had invited her; as his girlfriend, he implied.

Next week they were going to the cinema again, to see yet another re-run of *Holiday Inn* – with Bing Crosby singing everyone's favourite, 'White Christmas'. Lily didn't seem to mind Maisie going out with him, 'so long as it doesn't get too serious,' she kept reminding her daughter. 'You have a lot of studying to do yet, Maisie, as well as having the rest of your life ahead of you. So think on, and don't do anything silly.'

Maisie assured her that she wouldn't. She was quite happy for things to stay just the way they were. It was up to her, she knew, to set the pace and to make sure that Ted kept in line.

———

'You will come and act as a witness for us at the Register Office, won't you?' Christine asked her friend, Sadie, just before Christmas. 'It's all arranged now; eleven o'clock in the morning on the second of January.'

'Yes... I will,' agreed Sadie. She had only been told of the hastily arranged marriage a few days previously and had said that she needed time to think about her friend's request that she should be a bridesmaid; well, a sort of bridesmaid. 'And Roland will be able to stay an extra day, that is if you are still sure that you want him to be a witness as well?'

'Yes, we're sure.' Christine nodded. 'We're very grateful to you both for agreeing to do it, but there's no one else, really, that we could ask...' She paused, aware of Sadie's silence, and realised that her remark was not very tactful. 'Well, you know what I mean, don't you?' she went on. 'Of course I would want you to be my bridesmaid. We decided that long ago, didn't we, you and me? I don't want Roland to think we are just making use of him, but under the circumstances Bruce can't ask any of his mates to stand for him.'

'I don't see why not,' said Sadie. 'Hasn't he any friends at the camp? Somebody that he flew with during the war?'

'I'm sure he has friends, although I haven't met any of them yet. I know one of his best mates was killed... No; we agreed that it should be as quiet as possible, and the less people who know about it the better. They'll all find out soon enough.'

'I'm still rather unhappy about what you are doing, Chrissie,' said Sadie. 'This isn't exactly going to endear you to your in-laws, is it? And you don't want to cause a rift between Bruce and his parents, do you?'

'Oh, that won't happen. His mother thinks the sun shines out of his...his behind, to put it politely! They might be upset for a little while, but they'll get over it. I've told you; I couldn't face all the fuss and palaver up there in Middlebeck. It isn't as if we'll ever go to live up there. It'll be goodbye to Middlebeck and to Bradford.'

'Christine...are you pregnant?' asked Sadie, as though the idea had just that moment occurred to her. Christine smiled; she was surprised her friend had not asked her the question before now. She nodded.

'That's what I've told Bruce,' she answered. Sadie looked at her searchingly.

'But...are you, really? This isn't a trick, is it, to get him to the altar? Well, not the altar; to get the ring on your finger, I mean?'

'Now why ever should I do that?' asked Christine in wide-eyed innocence. 'Bruce and I are engaged, and we would have been getting married later in the year. We've just had to put it forward a few months, that's all. Bruce doesn't want to tell his folks about the baby, though, not yet. We'll have to wait and see how things work out.'

'I see...' said Sadie, raising her eyebrows and regarding her a mite distrustfully. 'And has it been decided, now, where you are going to live? Has Bruce been able to get married quarters?'

'Oh yes, of course. Quite a nice flat, from what he tells me. But we're hoping it might be only a temporary measure. He wants us to have our own house as soon as we can. There are a few quaint little villages near to the camp, and Bruce has just bought a car – a Ford Prefect, only a couple of years old – so he will be able to get around more easily.'

'He is able to drive then?'

'Of course! Bruce has piloted a plane, so driving a car is child's play to him. Yes; his father taught him to drive years ago.'

'I thought you were dead against living in quaint little villages,' Sadie remarked, with what Christine thought was a touch of asperity. 'You've had enough to say about Middlebeck, and it sounds a lovely place to me. You don't want to end up in the back of beyond with only what you call "country bumpkins" for company.'

'Oh, we'll be very near to Lincoln,' said Christine, 'and Nottingham's not all that far away. Besides, I shall be with Bruce, won't I? And that's what we want, just to be together, him and me.'

'And the baby...' Sadie reminded her.

'Well yes, of course...eventually. But that's a good while off yet. Don't tell anyone about it, will you, Sadie? I mean, we won't be broadcasting the fact that that is why we are getting married.'

'My lips are sealed,' replied Sadie. 'But you can't blame people if they draw their own conclusions.'

'Don't sound so disapproving,' said Christine, aware that she did not have her friend's wholehearted support. 'You must know what it's like. I'm sure you do, you and Roland. We love one another very much, Bruce and me. That's why... it happened.'

Sadie smiled. 'I don't disapprove; not about that, at any rate. Yes, I do know what it's like... But I hope everything works out all right for you.' She looked around the flat where the two young women had spent many companionable hours together. 'So you've told Mr Hardacre that you're leaving here, have you? And you've given in your notice at the mill?'

'Yes, to both questions,' said Christine. 'It'll be a whole

new way of life for me, living in Lincolnshire.' The biggest regret she had was about leaving Sadie behind. She was not entirely without finer feelings and she knew that her friend was genuinely concerned for her. 'I won't forget you, though,' she told her. 'I shall miss you, Sadie; we've had some good times together. And I'll still be your bridesmaid in February, that's if you still want me.'

'Of course I do...'

'Well, that's OK then. I know it'll be a grand affair...not like mine. But we're going to try and make ours as much like a proper wedding as we can, but without all the fuss. I've ordered some little sprays of flowers for you and me and buttonholes for the men. And Bruce has booked a meal for the four of us at a nice place on the road to Bingley.'

'Will Bruce be wearing his uniform?' asked Sadie. 'I could ask Roland to wear his as well. They are both still serving officers, aren't they?'

'So they are...' agreed Christine. And if she felt a pang of regret that no one else would be there to see them, it was only a fleeting thought.

There was one person Christine decided she must see before she married Bruce, not because she particularly wanted to see her or even considered it to be her duty to do so; but because she wanted her to see how little Christine Myerscough, raised in the worst area of Bradford, had bettered herself and moved up in the world.

It was on New Year's Eve that she took the trolley bus up Manningham Lane towards the suburb of Shipley, alighting at the stop near to the 'Ring o' Bells'. Her mother, she recalled, worked there as a barmaid or, rather, had used to do so. She had not heard anything about Myrtle's doings recently, neither had she bothered to try and find out. The pub was closed, however, as it was mid-afternoon, so she made her way to the semi-detached house, only a few minutes' walk from the pub, which was now the home of

Fred and Myrtle Myerscough. When they had left Lumm Lane they had lived in a small cottage-type property, then moved to their present house in the early years of the war. Christine had visited them there only a couple of times, the last one being just before she joined the WAAF.

She opened the gate with the sunray design, which denoted that the house was fairly modern, dating from the early thirties. She noticed that the green front door with the fanlight of coloured glass, also in a sunburst design, was glossy with new paint and the chromium-plated letter box and handle gleamed with recent polishing. no one could ever say that Myrtle was a slut, at least not so far as the cleanliness of her home was concerned. She had always prided herself on keeping a well scrubbed doorstep and shining windows, even when she had lived in one of the meanest streets in Bradford; one characteristic, possibly the only one, that she had inherited from her mother, Christine's beloved gran.

The door opened a few moments after Christine's knock. Her mother, clad in a red satin dressing gown stood there, staring at her with, at first, little sense of recognition. Then, 'Chrissie...' she said. 'Well, I never!' Her silver-grey eyes, so like Christine's own, lit up for a few seconds with what seemed to be a smile of welcome, but then, just as quickly, they changed. Her expression and her voice were quite hostile as she said, 'And to what do we owe this honour, may I ask? God knows how many years and we see neither hide nor hair of you, and then you turn up on the doorstep...'

'Like a bad penny, Mother,' said Christine, determined not to be cowed. 'Aren't you going to say you're pleased to see me?'

'You'd best come in, I suppose,' said Myrtle. 'It's been so long I hardly recognised you. You look older, Christine, a lot older than when I last saw you. Is the world not treating you well?'

'Very well, as a matter of fact,' answered Christine, feeling hurt and cross. 'Actually, I've got some news for you.

Stupendous news...' How dare her mother say she was looking old? It was not true; it was just that it had been... several years. And during those years it seemed to Christine that her mother had scarcely aged at all. Her hair was still the same blonde colour, too brassy and obviously dyed, but immaculately set and waved; her make-up was perfectly applied on a face that showed no hint of lines or crow's feet; and her dressing gown, clearly an expensive one, was tightly belted around a curvaceous, but still quite slim, figure.

'I'm very glad to hear it,' said Myrtle. 'Come in then, into the lounge, and you can tell me all about it, if you've a mind to...whatever it is.'

Christine followed her into the front room, which her mother called the lounge – Myrtle was a great one for the niceties – and sat down on a large red plush armchair. Everything in the room was red, of slightly differing, though complementary, tones; a cherry red three-piece suite, dark red velveteen curtains, and a red carpet, the same design as the one in the hallway, with a pattern of yellow and brown leaves. The display cabinet in the corner held an assortment of china cups and saucers decorated with red and gold roses, china figurines, and various silver – or EPNS – items. It all suggested that a fair amount of money was coming into the house, one way or another. Christine had to admit to herself that the room was cosy, with a coal fire burning brightly in the tiled hearth.

She looked appraisingly at her mother, sitting opposite her. 'Have I interrupted something?' she asked. 'Are you expecting a visitor? Or maybe one has just left?' Or is still here, she thought to herself.

Myrtle returned her level glance without any sign of discomfiture or annoyance. 'As a matter of fact, I have just been taking a bath,' she replied. 'We've got a bit of a do on tonight at the Ring o' Bells with it being New Year's Eve. And I'm expecting Fred – your father,' she added pointedly. 'He'll be home in a couple of hours if he makes good time.'

'Still long distance lorry driving, is he?' asked Christine.

'Yes,' said Myrtle abruptly. 'He's away a lot, but he gets well paid.' She didn't mention the sidelines, but Christine guessed that he would have done his share of the racketeering that had gone on during the war years with the black market. 'He'll be coming with me tonight to celebrate the New Year... It's a pity you can't join us, Chrissie,' she added. It was clear, though, that she did not want her daughter there; it was doubtful that anyone knew of Christine's existence.

'Thanks all the same,' she said. 'It's nice of you to invite me...' She paused for a moment before saying, 'but I'm far too busy. I'm getting married, you see...very soon.'

'You're getting married?' Myrtle regarded her suspiciously. 'That's a bit sudden, isn't it?'

'No, not at all,' said Christine. 'Anyway, you wouldn't know about that, would you? I know I haven't been to see you – I have been doing my bit towards winning the war – but you haven't bothered to find out what I've been doing for the last few years, have you? Actually, I've done very well for myself. My fiancé was a pilot during the war – he's still an officer in the RAF as a matter of fact – and he's the son of a squire. They own acres of land up in north Yorkshire.'

Myrtle was still looking as though she did not quite believe it. 'Where, exactly?' she asked.

'Oh, I don't suppose you will have heard of it. A little place called Middlebeck up in the northern dales. His father is the chief landowner in the area.'

'I see... And what is his name, this flying officer of yours?'

'It doesn't matter,' replied Christine. She realised, possibly too late, that the less her mother knew about it the better it might be. She couldn't divulge the name of the family in case Myrtle tried to dig them out; the Tremaines were under the impression that she was an orphan. She might have said too much already, but she had been unable to resist doing a bit of boasting. 'You don't need to know,' she went on, 'because I intend to make a fresh start, far away from Yorkshire. I doubt if our paths will cross again. You and my father have shown me all too clearly that you prefer to live your lives without me...in a way of which I can't approve. So now – well – I have my own life to live...with a man who means everything to me.'

'And what has he been told about us then, about me and your father, your disreputable parents?'

'As much as he needs to know,' Christine replied, shrugging vaguely. 'We don't talk much about what has happened in the past. It's the future that's important.'

'Yes... I see,' said Myrtle again. 'And I suppose you're having a big posh wedding, are you, up in... Middlebeck, did you say?'

'No, we're not. It's a Register Office wedding; just a very quiet affair. That's the way we both want it to be.'

Myrtle nodded, then a knowing smile spread across her face. 'Mmm...so you're up the duff, are you?' Christine cringed. Her mother's tone of voice had become more refined over the years, but she still came out with crude expressions that revealed her true background. She did not answer yes or no. 'I might have guessed you would jump to that conclusion,' she said, smiling at her mother in a superior manner. 'Some of us do have other things on our minds apart from sex.'

'Then I take it that that's a yes,' said Myrtle, grinning. She was not one to take offence. 'I can read you like a book, our Chrissie.' Christine, in spite of herself, felt a momentary pang of what could be affection at the possessive form of address. 'OK then, we'll be going our separate ways,' her mother continued, 'but there's no reason why we shouldn't have a toast to the future.' She stood up and went over to the display cabinet, the top half of which pulled down to show an array of bottles and glasses. 'What's your tipple? Whisky, brandy, or what about a gin and lime?'

'Yes...gin and lime will be fine, thank you,' said Christine, surprised and rather taken aback at her mother's gesture. She hadn't intended to get involved in any sort of social etiquette.

Myrtle handed her a crystal glass of her chosen drink,

topped with a piece of lemon. 'Well, here's to you then, Christine,' she said. 'And...to a happy marriage. I hope it brings you all that you desire.'

'Thank you,' she murmured, noticing the shrewd expression in her mother's eyes. 'I'm sure that it will.'

She did not stay long after that, declining to stay and wait for her father's return, as Myrtle suggested. What would be the point? He might be another hour at least, and she had already stayed longer than she had intended. They said goodbye without a kiss or even a handshake, but each of them was aware of something very close to regret in the other one's glance.

Myrtle watched the young woman from behind the lace curtains as she hurried away down the avenue towards the main road. That girl is far more like me than she realises, she said to herself, and she did not mean just in looks. There was a ruthless streak in her daughter, a desire to get what she wanted, whatever the cost. I hope she finds the pot of gold at the end of the rainbow, she thought. She, Myrtle, had not yet done so.

# Chapter Fourteen

It was an assorted group of people who met together on the evening of the second of January for the New Year party at the Nixons' farmhouse. Several of the guests were strangers to Maisie. She had met Irene, Joe's fiancée, several times, but it was the first time she had encountered the young woman's parents, Mr and Mrs Hindle, the farmer and his wife from Lowerbeck. Another farming couple was there as well, the aptly named Mr and Mrs Tiller from a farm on the northern side of the dale, who had been friendly with Ada Nixon since long before her husband's death.

Audrey and Brian were there as friends of Doris, and she, Maisie, had been invited this time as Ted's girlfriend. Doris did not have a boyfriend, but Maisie noticed that she was talking quite animatedly to one of the Polish immigrants. Ted had told Maisie several weeks ago about their imminent arrival, and they had made their appearance in Middlebeck a couple of weeks later; a young man by the name of Ivan Delinsky – he was the one who was talking to Doris – and a rather older man, mid-thirties or so, Maisie surmised, who was called Stefan Chevesky. It was kind of Mrs Nixon to invite them to the party, she thought; but folks on the whole had been very welcoming to these strangers who had come into their midst. 'Displaced persons' was the name for these refugees who had fled from the Communist regime, not only in Poland, but in several of the eastern European countries. It was an unfriendly, derogatory name for such men – there were, it seemed, far more men than women – who were seeking a peaceful existence after the tyranny of the war years.

Archie and Rebecca Tremaine, as was only to be expected

– they were a kindly compassionate couple – had offered them accommodation at Tremaine House, and the two men were employed on the land owned by the squire and on the Nixons' farm.

The only two guests who had not yet arrived were, in fact, the Tremaines.

'I wonder what's keeping Archie and Rebecca?' said Ada, glancing at the wooden clock on the mantelshelf, which read ten minutes to nine. 'It's not like them to be late, and I'm sure they would have let me know if they weren't coming for some reason. Have you any idea, Stefan?' She turned to the elder of the two men, who was talking to Anne Mellodey. 'Mr and Mrs Tremaine; they will be coming, will they?'

'I think so…yes,' he answered. He was dark-haired and of a slim wiry build, with bright, almost black eyes in a lean-featured, but peculiarly handsome face. 'They were talking together when Ivan and I left the house. Mrs Tremaine was a little distressed, I believe. I do not know why. But I am confident that they will arrive. Not to do so would be impolite and they are the most courteous people.' He spoke almost faultless and precise English, albeit with a guttural accent; but it was clear that he was an intelligent and probably well educated man. His colleague, Ivan, was taller and more well built, dark-eyed and dark-haired like Stefan, and they both had the gaunt, intense features that marked them out as Eastern Europeans.

'Thank you, Stefan,' said Ada. 'Like you say, they're sure to turn up sometime. Ne'er mind, there's nowt much spoiling. I'll give 'em another ten minutes or so, then we'll make a start on t' supper. They'll not mind; I'll keep a few sausage rolls and mince pies in t' oven in case they're really late… I do hope they've not had some bad news though. I know Rebecca was upset that Bruce couldn't get home for Christmas…'

Ada was talking more to herself than to anyone in particular, but Maisie was listening to what she was saying. Her thoughts, too, flew immediately to Bruce; to Bruce…

and Christine. She would bet ten pounds – at least she would if she had so much money – that it was something to do with Christine that had upset Mrs Tremaine.

'I'm feeling hungry, what about you?' said Ted, putting an arm around her. 'Mam's been busy nearly all t' day, and our Doris an' all, getting it ready. What a spread, eh?'

The table at one end of the spacious farmhouse living room was, indeed, almost groaning beneath the array of appetising food laid out on a pristine white cloth with a crocheted border. 'That there cloth was a wedding present to Mam and Dad,' Ted told Maisie. 'It only comes out on special occasions.' There were crusty loaves and pats of butter, slices of turkey, succulent pink ham, and pork with crispy brown crackling; pork pies oozing with jelly; pickled onions, beetroot and homemade picalilli; a huge trifle topped with cream and glacé cherries; fruit cake, gingerbread, shortbread and chocolate biscuits; and, as Ada had said, sausage rolls and mince pies warming in the kitchen oven. The idea would be for everyone to help themselves then find a place to eat, informally, as at a picnic.

The room was a large one, comfortably, if a little shabbily, furnished. There was an assortment of chairs; chintz covered armchairs and a matching settee, two round-backed Windsor chairs, beloved of farming folk, and several wooden ones of the ladderback type. An oak dresser on which Ada kept her day to day as well as her best china and crockery stood against one wall, and the Victorian sideboard with the mirrored back at the other side of the room was the depository for the detritus of everyday living – photographs, fruit bowl and matching biscuit barrel in a bold design of red, blue and gold; magazines and letters and unfinished knitting and sewing – but the clutter had been pushed back to accommodate the scores of Christmas cards. Others were hanging on strings fastened to the walls and, as it was not yet Twelfth Night, other evidence of the festive season still abounded. There was a pine tree, now shedding its needles, which scented the room with its tangy aromatic perfume. It was decorated with shining glass baubles and tinsel, with a lop-sided angel with a damaged wing on the top. Paper streamers of red, white and green were strung from corner to corner of the ceiling, and tissue paper bells, stars and a fat Santa Claus, which all opened out concertina fashion, adorned the walls and chimney breast. And a bunch of mistletoe, which Ted had already put to good use, hung over the doorway.

So far the guests had just mingled, forming little groups and chatting together as they sipped at their glasses of dark brown sherry or orange juice, to the background of music from the wind-up gramophone; Bing Crosby, Glenn Miller and Joe Loss and his orchestra.

It was dead on nine o'clock that there was a knock at the back door – the kitchen door, through which guests usually entered – then Ada ushered in Rebecca and Archie Tremaine.

'I'm sorry we're late,' said Rebecca. Her eyes looked extra bright; it could have been with tears, or with the frosty air. 'Oh dear! I hope you haven't been waiting for us.'

'Not at all,' said Ada. 'Nine o'clock's the time to serve supper, and it's nine o'clock now, so you're dead on time. Here, give me yer coats, and you go and have a warm by the fire. It's a bit parky out tonight, it is that.'

There was a glowing log fire burning in the stone hearth, and Archie and Rebecca stood together at one side of it. Everyone had fallen silent at the arrival of the last guests. Rebecca looked at her husband and gave a slight nod as if to say, Go on, you tell them...

'We are late,' said Archie, 'at least, later than we intended being, and we do apologise for that. The reason is... we've had some rather disturbing news today. We'd like to tell you about it now, all of you here, because you're sure to hear about it sooner or later... I suppose I shouldn't really say disturbing news, because it's supposed to be happy news, but it's been a shock to Becky and me, hasn't it, love?'

His wife smiled at him sadly, but a look of love and understanding passed between them as she said, 'Yes, a great shock...' She took a deep breath, then she grabbed hold of her husband's hand. 'Bruce rang, you see – just a couple of hours ago – to tell us that... that he and Christine are married. They got married today, at the Register Office in Bradford.'

Everyone seemed too stunned to speak. Indeed, what could they say? 'You mean...you didn't know anything about it?' asked Ada, after a silence of a few seconds. 'No, of course you didn't,' she added. 'That was a silly thing for me to say. But I mean... Oh, you poor things! I can understand how you feel. But why? Did Bruce say why?'

Maisie was shocked and bewildered, as was everyone else. But it was just as she had surmised; the Tremaine's late arrival was due to Bruce and Christine, although she wouldn't have guessed that they were married. She felt that Ada's question about the reason for the hasty wedding was rather tactless. I bet she's pregnant, she thought, and following this thought there came a stab of anguish as she envisaged Bruce and that girl together, like that.

'He said they wanted a quiet ceremony without any fuss,' said Archie. Rebecca, once again, seemed troubled and unable to say any more. 'That's all very well, I suppose; it's their wedding when all's said and done; I know our Bruce was never one for a great deal of fuss and palaver. But Becky here was looking forward to them having a nice big do. Christine hasn't any relatives of her own, you know, and we felt we wanted to do what we could for the girl and to give them a good send-off, but...' He shrugged. 'It seems that it wasn't to be. Anyroad, lets try and make the best of it; there's no point in us sitting around moping... Come on now, Ada. Let's get tucking into this 'ere supper, shall we? Becky and I have come here to enjoy ourselves.' He put a protective arm around his wife and, to everyone's relief, she gave a smile and a little laugh.

'I'll do my best,' she said.

Everyone tucked into the magnificent spread as though there were no tomorrows, several of the younger guests, including the two Polish men, returning for second helpings. It was all truly delicious. Ada Nixon was a bountiful hostess, not seeming to mind that most of the work was falling upon her, with a little help from her daughter; or that she was the only one of the gathering who did not have a partner for the evening. She seemed contented, quite happy, in fact, and Maisie was not the only one who had noticed that Ada had looked far less anxious since the death of her husband. There were several of her friends who had guessed – though they kept their own counsel – that it had not been the happiest of marriages…and that maybe she was not keen to embark on another one.

Nobody was sure whether or not it was intentional that there was an equal number of men and women there, not counting Ada. But it became obvious as the evening progressed that the single, so far unattached people, had paired off. Doris and Ivan appeared to be getting on very well together; his arm was around her as they sat with their heads close together in a corner of the room. And Anne Mellodey and Stefan, also, seemed to be enjoying one another's company, although their behaviour was more restrained than that of the younger couple.

When the carpet square had been rolled back from the wooden floor some of the couples danced together to the rather scratchy gramophone records of Joe Loss, Glen Miller and Geraldo. The two farming couples and the Tremaines were the first to take to the floor; Rebecca appeared to have brightened up considerably amidst the cheerful company, and maybe as a result of a few glasses of sherry.

The bombshell that they had dropped had not been talked about. No doubt everyone was drawing their own conclusion, rightly or wrongly; but everyone showed themselves determined to rally round and to make sure that the popular couple, their squire and his wife, had a 'reight good time of it'.

They played a few party games; they did their best to instruct Stefan and Ivan in the intricacies of 'My grandfather's cat is an amiable cat; my grandfather's cat is a beautiful cat, a crafty cat, a dangerous cat...' and so on, all through the alphabet, to the accompaniment of much stuttering and puzzled frowns and gales of good-hearted laughter. Everyone was delighted when Rebecca won the 'Pass the Parcel' prize, a half pound box of Black Magic chocolates. Ted didn't seem to mind that his record of 'In the Mood' became even more scratchy with the constant lifting and putting down of the gramophone needle.

As midnight approached all the guests began to make moves towards departing. The farming folk knew that not many more hours remained before they would need to get out of bed again, and the three girls, Maisie, Audrey and Doris, had a busy time ahead of them. The pantomime, *Cinderella*, for which they had been rehearsing for the past few months, was to be performed on the following three nights.

'Let me stay and help you with the washing up, Mrs Nixon,' said Maisie, eyeing the mountain of pots piled up by the stone sink in the kitchen.

'Bless you, no; I wouldn't dream of it,' replied Ada, 'but it's kind of you to offer, and I know that you mean it. We'll tackle it in the morning, our Doris and me. No, you get along home now; our Ted'll see you safely back. Goodnight, Maisie love, and God bless.' She kissed her affectionately on the cheek. 'It's been a grand evening, hasn't it?'

'Yes, it has. I really enjoyed it,' said Maisie, meaning it sincerely. In spite of the disturbing news, she had, indeed, enjoyed herself. 'Thank you for inviting me.'

'Of course we'd invite you,' laughed Ada. 'You're practically one of the family now, aren't you? Now, off you go. See, Ted's got your coat for you...'

The clear night air was piercingly cold and there was a covering of fresh white frost on the ground. The bare branches of the trees and bushes sparkled silver in the moonlight and a sprinkling of stars shone in the midnight blue-black sky. It was a magical sight and Maisie felt strangely moved by it all, even though she had encountered similar scenes many times before. She felt very close to Ted; not just the closeness of his arm around her as they walked along the lane, but a feeling that she was growing more fond of him. He had been an attentive and cheerful companion all evening – she had never before enjoyed herself so much in his company – and she found now that the shock of the news about Bruce's marriage had receded to the back of her mind.

She allowed him to kiss her more ardently than usual, several times, as they said goodnight at her back gate, and she felt herself responding to him more than she had ever done before. But as she felt his hand move and tentatively touch her breast – although it was only gently, on top of her clothing – she pulled away from him. She did not rebuke him, but just said cheerily, 'Goodnight, Ted. Thanks for seeing me home.'

'You know I always do...' He gave her an odd sort of look.

'Yes, I know, but thanks all the same. See you tomorrow then... No, I mean tonight actually, don't I? At the panto-mime?'

'Sure thing,' he said. 'I'll be there every night. Goodnight then, Maisie. Sleep tight...'

Lily had not waited up for her, knowing that she would be late, and knowing also that Ted would see her safely home. Her mother did not seem to mind so much about Ted now, or at least she did not say very much, engrossed as she was in the preparations for her own forthcoming marriage. Maisie knocked gently on the bedroom door, guessing that she would still not have gone to sleep.

'I'm back now, safe and sound,' she whispered. 'Goodnight, Mum...'

'Goodnight love,' said a sleepy voice. 'Have you had a nice time?'

'Yes, thank you; it was lovely.'

'Well, that's all right then. See you in the morning.'

Maisie did not fall asleep straight away. So Bruce was married... Well, that was the end of that little dream, and the best thing she could do would be to put him right out of her mind. But what of Ted? She did like him a lot. She was finding he was much more open and friendly now that they knew one another better, and she did enjoy having a boyfriend. A lot of the girls in her form at school had boyfriends, including Audrey, of course.

But her thoughts were halted sharply by the memory of what Ted's mother had said that evening. 'You're practically one of the family...' Was that how Ada Nixon regarded her already, as a future daughter-in-law? The idea of that worried Maisie. She knew that she looked older than her years; folk who did not know her sometimes took her for eighteen or so, but the fact remained that she was still not yet sixteen. Both Audrey and Doris had had their sixteenth birthdays, and probably Ada would be only too pleased if her daughter were to marry at an early age, at seventeen or eighteen, maybe. This often happened in the farming communities when girls found a suitable partner, who was usually involved in the same occupation.

But she, Maisie, was not of that ilk. Much as she was growing to like Ted, she could not see him as a future husband. Besides, that was years and years away. She had her exams to do, then sixth form, and possibly college... She must not let Ted or his mother get the wrong idea, and she must be careful that she did not get carried away by his kisses and embraces. There was a girl in her class who actually boasted that she had 'gone the whole way', although Maisie was not altogether sure that she believed her. But she knew that she must take very great care... She fell asleep eventually as her mind closed down against the maelstrom of her thoughts. She would think about it tomorrow...

As Ted watched the pantomime from the third row of the audience all he could think about was Maisie. What an absolutely stunning girl she was, and how had he, Ted Nixon, managed to persuade her to be his girlfriend?

He had felt, when he had first started seeing her, that she was in a completely different league from him; far cleverer and wittier and much more skilled in the art of conversation, and although she had come from a humble sort of background – a very disturbed and unsatisfactory one, according to his sister – she had made the most of her opportunities and seemed determined to forge ahead and really make her place in the world. And what would that be? What exactly did she want and what was she striving for? Ted did not know the answer to that; it was not something that they discussed, although they were getting along very well together in spite of their differences. But he feared that she would, one day, leave him far behind, not only in her thoughts, but in a very real sense as well. He could not imagine that the little town of Middlebeck would be big enough to contain Maisie Jackson once she achieved her aim.

Unless he could manage to make her see things differently... After all, what did most girls – nearly all girls, he guessed – really want from life? They wanted to be married; happily married if possible with two or three children. He had been brought up to believe that that was the role of a woman; to care for her husband and children and to be a helpmate and partner rather than a leader in the marriage. Apart from the more eccentric women, of course, who became doctors or judges or members of Parliament; professions that he believed rightly belonged to men. He had realised, though, as he grew older, that his parents' marriage had not always been ideally happy, but his mother had been a devoted wife, and even now, a few years after his father's death, she seemed contented with her lot in the world.

As he watched Maisie, as Prince Charming, dancing with the little fair-haired girl – Celia James, according to the programme – who was playing Cinderella, he found it hard to believe that she was still only fifteen years of age. In fact, whenever he thought about this it gave him quite a jolt. She was a vivid contrast to the girl she was partnering; inches taller and more vivacious in her sparkling prince's outfit, which had been made by her mother, she had told him, specially for this ballroom scene. The fitted tunic showed off the curves of her maturing breasts, and the short trousers revealed a pair of long and shapely legs; Ted had to force his eyes to look away.

'This is a lovely way to spend an evening...' they were singing as they twirled around the simulated ballroom, Maisie's rich melodious voice contrasting nicely with the sweet and gentle tones of Celia. She, too, was a very pretty girl, Ted realised, in her silver and white ballgown, though in a less dramatic way than Maisie. He knew that soon the dance would come to an end and that she would run away and lose her glass slipper...

A down-to-earth and commonsensical farm worker though he was, Ted was finding himself strangely fascinated by this romantic story, even though he knew it was only play-acting and that he was acquainted with most of the cast in their more workaday lives. His sister, Doris, was a scream and had had him laughing till his sides ached, as she danced and sang a riotous 'Knees up Mother Brown' number with the other 'ugly sister', the usually polite and reserved Brian Milner. They both wore huge coloured wigs, Doris's orange and Brian's yellow, blue and white striped stockings, and voluminous red bloomers showing beneath their garishly-hued dresses.

Another surprise of the evening was Audrey Fairchild, the rector and his wife's adopted daughter who, until now, could never be persuaded to show herself on the stage. She was a delightful Fairy Godmother and even managed to sing a solo, 'When You Wish Upon a Star...' which had the audience clapping and cheering like mad, to her obvious pleasure, but also to her embarrassment. Unlike Maisie and Doris she was unable to forget that she was, in reality, Audrey Fairchild, and not a Fairy Godmother who could make wishes come true.

The first evening's performance came to an end and Ted waited in the church hall for Maisie to change into her ordinary clothes to walk home.

'Well done,' he said, kissing her on her cheek when she appeared, bright-eyed and clearly euphoric with the excitement of the evening. 'You were great, but I knew you would be. I really enjoyed it, all of it.'

'Mmm…it wasn't too bad,' she admitted. 'There were one or two little things that went wrong; the transformation scene wasn't as smooth as it might have been, but we'll get better as we go on… You did say you were coming tomorrow night, didn't you, Ted? Perhaps you could help with scene shifting, if you don't mind. We could do with an extra pair of hands, especially in the ballroom scene, getting all the stuff on, the stairs and the flats and all that…'

'Flats?' he queried.

'Yes, that's what they call the big flat pieces of scenery…'

'Oh, right; I see; so long as I know. Yes, of course I'll come and help…'

They did not linger long saying their goodnights; in fact Maisie just kissed him on the cheek before he had a chance to put his arms around her. 'Ta-ra then, Ted,' she said. 'See you tomorrow.'

He realised he might have made one move too many the other night and that probably she was not yet ready to take their relationship a stage further. He was deep in thought as he walked home. Perhaps it would be wise to try and restrain himself a little, until she turned sixteen at any rate. It was not all that long to wait, only four months; he knew her birthday was on the first day of May. It was Maisie that he wanted; there was no doubt in his mind about that. But maybe he had tried to get too far too soon. In the meantime, though, there was nothing to stop him being friendly with other young folk of his own age, perhaps girls as well as lads…

———

There was a party in the church hall after the performance had finished on Saturday night, to celebrate the success of the venture. Everyone agreed that it had been a triumph, and Patience and Mrs Hollins, who had been the producers –

helped by other members of the Mothers' Union and their husbands with the costumes and props – basked in well deserved praise. They were already promising that there would be another pantomime next year.

Everyone who had been involved was invited to the party; the cast, even the little ones who had been allowed to stay up extra late, as it was a special occasion, and all the helpers including the scene shifters. Ted had pulled his weight for the last two nights and was very pleased to be invited to the party. It was really more of a 'bun fight' with hastily prepared sandwiches and cakes; non-stop chatter, as the highlights of the performances were discussed again and again; and singing – more raucously than usual – of the songs that had been performed in the pantomime.

'We'll meet again, don't know where, don't know when...' they chorused, revelling in the wartime song which seemed destined to be popular for evermore, and rejoicing in the friendships that had formed or been strengthened over the last few weeks, especially during the last three nights.

Ted had not met all of Maisie's friends, and he was rather reticent about doing so. Two of the girls whom he did know, who sung in the choir with her, were sixth-form students and he tended to feel tongue-tied and stupid when he tried to talk to them. Not that they intended to make him feel so; it was just his lack of confidence with people he thought to be cleverer than himself. But when Maisie introduced him to Celia James, the girl who had played Cinderella, he found that he was able to converse with her quite easily.

Celia was eighteen, although at first glance she did not look her age, being small and dainty with an elfin prettiness. Maisie, having introduced them, went over to chat to his sister, Doris and Ivan, who had also been roped in as a scene shifter. Celia told Ted that she had left school at fourteen and that she worked in the office of a textile mill, one of the few that were situated in the bottom of the valley. She was a sensible, down-to-earth girl, Ted decided, 'with her head screwed on the right way', as his mother would say. As he talked with her he realised that she was not as young and child-like as she appeared to be on first acquaintance; she was, in fact, quite a woman of the world and one with whom he felt completely at ease.

'I'm glad to see you two are getting on OK,' said Maisie cheerily as she joined them. 'Celia, could you come and give a hand with the clearing away, please? It isn't fair to leave all the washing up to Patience and Mrs Hollins, and all the other women seem to have disappeared; so I said we'd help. You can get off home, Ted, if you like... Thanks for coming to help; you've been great.'

'But what about you?' he asked. 'You can't walk home on your own...'

'I could if I wanted to; I'm a big girl now,' she laughed, 'but it's all right. Archie Tremaine says he'll run us all home later when we've finished. You as well, Celia, and Doris and Audrey – although she doesn't need a lift. We're all going to help.'

'OK then,' said Ted, feeling a little put out. 'I know when I'm not wanted.' He grinned to show there was no ill feeling, but he did feel, rather, as though he had been dismissed. 'I'll perhaps see you tomorrow then, Maisie? Half past seven, eh, when you come out of church?'

'Yes, all right...' she replied.

'Good night then,' he said, deciding not to kiss her, not in front of her friend and everybody else. 'Goodnight, Celia. It was nice meeting you. See you again sometime, perhaps?'

'Yes, perhaps...' she replied smiling at him.

It was just a casual remark, 'See you again', but as he walked home Ted thought to himself that he wouldn't mind at all if he were to see Celia James again...

# Chapter Fifteen

Anne Mellodey had received a letter soon after Christmas inviting her – although it was more of a demand than a request – to attend a staff meeting at Middlebeck School on the morning of the third of January. The communication was from the new headmaster, Roger Ellison, who had written – typed, to be more accurate – in somewhat pedantic tones that he wished to discuss prospective procedures and staffing arrangements for the forthcoming years.

The school, at that moment, still had only three classes; an Infant and two Junior ones, with a teaching head. Miss Foster had taken charge of the Infants, Shirley Barker of years one and two of the Juniors, and Anne of years three and four. The classes were large, but the possibility of having another teacher, or teachers, had been brought up several times and then rejected by the powers that be.

When Anne arrived at the appointed time, ten o'clock, she was surprised to see not only Roger Ellison, but the man who had acted as the usher at the interview, and another person; a woman of roughly her own age, soberly dressed in a tweed coat and hat and sensible brogues, whom she could not remember having seen before. Shirley Barker was there too, looking a little overawed, and she gave Anne what looked like a smile of relief as she entered the room. So she, Anne, was the last to arrive, of which fact Mr Ellison soon reminded her.

'Ah, so there you are Miss Mellodey. We are all here now so we can make a start. Do come in and sit down...'

'I'm not late, am I?' she asked pointedly, knowing that she was, in fact, five minutes early.

'No, no; not at all. Almost dead on time,' the headmaster

replied, looking at his wristwatch with an exaggerated gesture.

The meeting was being held in what had been Anne's classroom – she wondered if it still would be under the new regime – and the other four were already seated around her desk; it was a large table really, with drawers that locked, but it was always known as the teacher's desk. As the school dated from the mid-nineteenth century many of its features were still early Victorian. The desk sat on a little raised dais at the front of the room, the idea having been that the teacher could, thus, have a bird's eye view of what his or her pupils were doing at all times. And that was still not a bad thing, Anne had been forced to agree, although she did not approve of some of the Victorian ideas. The windows were small and quite high up; it was almost impossible for the children to see out of them. The children of a hundred years ago had not been encouraged to stare out of windows and daydream, but to concentrate on their work. Consequently the classrooms were rather dark, especially during the winter months, which meant that the lights had to be switched on for a good deal of the time. Fortunately, the lighting had been changed, some years ago, from gas to electric.

Another modern innovation that had been installed in recent years were the radiators, which ran from a coke-fired boiler. When Anne had first come to the school her room had been heated by a coal fire around which a sturdy fireguard had always to be in place. It had provided a comforting, homely touch on cold days, but the new system was much more efficient, and safer, too. Obviously the conscientious caretaker, Mr Scribbins, a man in his sixties who had done the job for years, had been at work early in the morning because the room was comfortably warm.

'Let me introduce you to Mr Fortescue,' Roger Ellison continued. 'He is a member of the Education Committee and he has kindly come here today to outline some plans that we have for Middlebeck School.'

'We have met before, Miss Mellodey,' said Mr Fortescue,

a middle-aged man whom Anne had only known as the one who had acted as usher at the interview. He smiled at her and held out his hand. 'I am very pleased to make your acquaintance again.'

'Yes...' said Anne, 'thank you...' not knowing how else to reply.

'And this is Miss Crompton,' said Mr Ellison. The woman who was a stranger to Anne half rose from her chair to shake hands. 'How do you do?' she said, and Anne replied in the same vein, wondering why she was there. 'This is Miss Mellodey,' he told the woman. 'She will be able to show you the ropes, so to speak, as will Mrs Barker. They have both been on the staff of Middlebeck for several years.' He turned to Anne.

'I am pleased to say that Miss Crompton will be joining us next week as our fourth teacher.' He beamed expansively. 'I know we will all do our best to make her welcome.'

Well, that was a surprise and no mistake, thought Anne. How on earth had he wangled that, and seemingly with no interview? And where did he intend to put another class, for goodness sake?

All was soon to be revealed. 'Now...let's get down to business,' said the new headmaster, importantly squaring the pile of papers in front of him, although Anne was to notice that he made hardly any reference to them all the time he was speaking. 'I am delighted to inform you that due to the persuasive powers of Mr Fortescue here, we have been granted a fourth teacher, and very soon – by the end of the next term, I hope – our staff will be increased to five.' He glanced around as though inviting comments, and as Shirley Barker did not speak, Anne felt obliged to do so.

'That is good news,' she said, as, indeed, it was, 'but... may I ask where we are to accommodate the two new classes?' Unless, of course, the thought struck her, that Roger Ellison intended being a non-teaching head, as was the norm in larger schools? Surely he would not be able to get away with that... But no, that was not his intention. He beamed even more fulsomely.

'Ah yes, I was coming to that. The Education Committee has informed us that we are to be given one of the new prefabricated classrooms, a double one, and it will be erected in the yard at the rear of the school. The children will still have the yard at the front in which to play and do their physical training, and it is hoped that eventually we will be able to make use of the spare land beyond the school. In the meantime though, until the new classrooms arrive, the extra class will be held in St Bartholomew's church hall. The rector has kindly agreed to this, and I believe the system worked very well in the early years of the war. It is not ideal, I know, but I am sure we will all do our utmost to make it work... And I am going to suggest, as Miss Crompton is a newcomer and will need our support, that Mrs Barker should be the one to take the class in the church hall? That is, if you wouldn't mind, Mrs Barker?'

The decisive smile, with his eyebrows raised, that he levelled at Shirley gave her no option but to murmur, 'Yes... yes, of course. I don't mind.'

Poor Shirley, thought Anne, wondering what else this 'new broom' had in store for them. Miss Foster had been asking for another teacher, and for more accommodation for the pupils, for ages, but to no avail. And now this newcomer had managed to get round the Education Committee before he had been here five minutes. Unless, on the other hand, the decisions had already been made, as the result of post-war planning. She recalled that the new Education Act had promised great things, so maybe they were already happening.

Roger Ellison steepled his hands and nodded gravely. 'Good...that is very good. In due course – I am hoping by the beginning of the next scholastic year, that is to say September, 1946 – we will have six classes, two Infant and four Junior, to keep pace with the increasing birthrate. And it is predicted that in a few years' time – by the beginning of the Fifties, if we dare look so far ahead – there will be a sizeable increase in the number of children ready to start school… Due to fathers returning from the war, of course,' he explained in confidential tones, as if they could not work out for themselves the reason for so many babies having been born. 'Goodness knows where we will put them all then…' He gave a jovial laugh, '…but let us just concern ourselves, for the moment, with the present situation, and tomorrow and its problems, I am sure, will take care of themselves.'

Anne was beginning to realise why this man had been given the post of headmaster. He certainly had what was known in the north as 'the gift of the gab', and bags of confidence to go with it. There were more surprises awaiting her and Shirley Barker, although the new teacher, Miss Crompton, had probably been informed already as to which class was to be hers. It was revealed that her Christian name was Phyllis, and that she had been granted a transfer from her school in the Huddersfield area. Her elderly parents, with whom she lived and looked after, had decided to retire to Middlebeck, and her application for a change of school had arrived, fortunately, at the time when the Education Committee had agreed to appoint another teacher.

'But even when we become a six teacher school – God willing – I still intend to be a teaching head,' Roger Ellison told them. At least that was a point in his favour, thought Anne. She had little time for the heads who directed proceedings from the comfort of their private domain – spoken of in hushed tones as the 'Headmaster's Room' – and scarcely ever set foot in the classrooms, and certainly never in the hurly-burly of the school yard. But the bombshell that he dropped next was not at all to her liking.

'As you know, the former headmistress, Miss Foster – who has done sterling work here, I must say – was in charge of the Infants. Now that is not my forte, as I am sure you will understand…' He gave a disparaging little laugh which seemed to indicate that he could, in fact, do anything if he set his mind to it. 'So I would like to suggest that Miss Mellodey should now be responsible for the Infant class. And I know she will make a very good job of it.' He looked at her, as he had looked at Shirley, with an affirmative nod which told her that it was not a suggestion, but a decision. Anne, however, was made of sterner stuff than her colleague, and although she knew she would have to submit to his plans she was determined to have her say.

'I have never taught Infants, Mr Ellison,' she replied. 'I am much more at home with children of the Junior age group, but...'

'But you are the ideal person for the task,' he interrupted her. 'That is why I am asking you to do it.' Telling you, would have been the more correct wordage, she mused. He did not say why he had chosen her for this dubious honour, rather than either of the other two women. 'I am sure you have heard the saying that if you can teach Infants then you can teach anyone?' He smiled ingratiatingly at her. 'I know it is a difficult job, but I believe you are more than capable of it.'

She nodded. She had heard the saying from the lips of Infant teachers, who believed it was, in fact, the hardest age group of all. Teachers in the Junior and Senior strata were inclined to regard it as child minding, but those who actually taught the very young children knew differently. 'Yes, of course I will go along with anything you suggest, if it is for the good of the school,' she answered. All the same, she could not help but feel that she had been demoted, moving from her Standards Three and Four, to the very bottom, as it were, of the teaching ladder.

Mr Fortescue from the Education Committee, however, soon disabused her of that notion by thanking her sincerely for agreeing to the change and by hinting that, as the school grew in numbers, there could well be promotion for the teacher in charge of the Infants. Did he mean a deputy headship, she pondered? At that moment she was bemused, knowing that the management of the school was going to be very very different in future.

Just what those differences would be was soon to be

revealed. Shirley Barker would still be teaching Standards One and Two, the seven- to nine-year-olds, but in the church hall rather than in her familiar classroom. Roger Ellison himself, as Anne had already guessed, was to be responsible for Standards Three and Four, with the new teacher, Miss Crompton, assisting him. He treated them to a lecture on the new Education Act on which, it seemed, he was an expert and a great advocate.

'It has been a beacon, lighting the way out of darkness,' he informed them, his eyes glowing with fervour. 'The abolition of fees in the municipal grammar schools is a great step forward. And it affects us right here, in our Primary school...'

That was the new word, Primary, with the sub-divisions of Infant and Junior; and Secondary instead of Senior was the name for the Grammar schools and the new Secondary Moderns. As Anne listened she realised why she had been questioned at her interview about streaming, the segregating of the children according to ability. It was the new headmaster's intention, he told them, to make sure that as many children as possible were granted these 'special' places – formerly called 'free' places – in the grammar schools. And this could only be achieved by separating the children according to their capabilities and by giving special tuition to the 'chosen ones'; although he did not actually use the phrase it was the way Anne interpreted it. The children of Standards Three and Four were to be given tests in Mathematics and English during the first few weeks of the term, and then, when they had been graded, he would teach what he termed the 'more academic' pupils and Miss Crompton the 'less able'.

Which was a far cry from the tradition of the old village school, thought Anne, as she listened in growing consternation. There had been very little rivalry between the pupils in the past. All the children had known, for instance, that Maisie and Audrey – she thought of them because they were still special to her – were at the 'top of the class' and would go on to the grammar school; whereas the majority of them, including their friend Doris, would not do so. This granting of many more special places, it seemed, would bring about divisions between the clever ones and the not so clever. Children, given half a chance, could be dreadfully cruel, and she had already heard such derogatory words as 'thickies' used on occasions. Maybe it was just as well that her destiny, for the moment, was to teach the Infants. She would make sure they did not concern themselves with such distinctions.

Anne, however, was pleased to hear Mr Fortescue refer to the suggestion that she had made, so boldly, at the interview; that the school was in need of a hall to be used as a communal meeting ground, for assemblies and concerts and for physical training; and most probably as a dining room as well, the official from the committee informed them, as the concept of school meals was now becoming more prevalent. He had obviously listened to her words and they had borne fruit, although she guessed that the decision would have been made irrespective of her request. It was on the agenda for Middlebeck School in the near future, he told the meeting. Not only would there be a hall, but also a largish staff room in which the teachers could meet, instead of the cubby hole that was an apology for one at the moment; and a staff cloakroom and up-to-date toilets and washbasins. The only toilet provision at the moment was referred to, by them, as the Black Hole of Calcutta; a dark, damp and dismal place with a cracked washbasin. Admittedly it was indoors, unlike the children's lavatories which were housed in a separate block at the far end of the playground, but it was not a place in which one would want to linger. It was hoped that eventually there would be indoor conveniences for the children as well, but that was not a priority at the moment.

A hall, a staffroom, a cloakroom and modern conveniences, and accommodation for six classes! Miss Foster would have thought that a fairy godmother had granted all her wishes at once. What a pity she could not have seen some of her dreams coming true before she retired... On the other hand, Anne guessed that Charity might well be glad to be away from it all, in her nice little bungalow at Lowerbeck.

And as for her, Anne, time would tell... Her new class would be a challenge, one that she had not foreseen and certainly would not have chosen, but she was always ready to meet problems head on. School would begin again on Monday, but before that day arrived she would need to get acquainted with her new classroom; to find out where everything lived – she was sure that Charity Foster would have left it all in apple-pie order; a place for everything and everything in its place – and to put up colourful pictures on the walls to make the place more welcoming for the children after their Christmas holiday.

On a more personal note, though, she had something else to look forward to. Stefan Chevesky, the very pleasant young man whom she had met the previous night at the Nixons' party, had asked her if she would meet him in the Green Man on Friday evening; that was tomorrow. She had accepted his invitation graciously, although not over eagerly. She had not been inside that public house – a very respectable one, near to the Market Hall – for several years, not since she had been there with her fiancé, Bill. It was not the done thing, at least not in the circles in which she moved, for women to enter pubs on their own; and until now no young man had asked her out.

She knew that she had mourned Bill for long enough. The intense ache that she had felt at first had left her heart and mind some time ago, but the memories of him remained and would always be there. But it was time now to move on. She did not foresee the young Polish immigrant as being any more than a pleasant companion, but with that friendship, as with the change in her teaching career, time would tell.

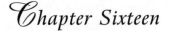

# Chapter Sixteen

It was mid-February when Christine told Bruce that she was very sorry, but she was afraid she had lost the baby. He came home to their married quarters in Lincolnshire at six o'clock one evening to find her, clad in her dressing gown, sitting on the settee and weeping uncontrollably.

'Darling, whatever is it?' he cried, putting his arms around her. 'And why...why are you in your night clothes? What has happened?'

'It's...it's the baby, Bruce,' she sobbed. 'There isn't one. I mean...there isn't going to be one. I've lost it.'

'But how...why? What do you mean?'

She explained, between her sobs, that she had felt 'all peculiar inside', as she termed it, just after lunch-time. She had gone to the toilet and then she had started bleeding; she had bled and bled, and it had all come away. 'Down the toilet, our precious baby,' she wailed. 'It's gone...'

Bruce understood very little about childbirth or labour, but this sounded rather strange to him. 'Why didn't you phone me?' he asked.

'Because I didn't know where you would be. I never know...'

'They would have found me, wherever I was... And what about the doctor? Didn't you get in touch with him? Perhaps he could have done something to...to save it.'

'He couldn't have,' she answered, rather snappily, he thought. He realised she was very upset, although she didn't appear to be weeping quite as much now. 'I was only about three months, and it's not a proper miscarriage at that stage. It's more like a very heavy period, and that's what it was like. The baby would hardly have started to form properly...but it's gone. I know it has.'

'I see...' said Bruce, frowning. 'And...are you still bleeding?' he asked rather tentatively; he was still very green about such matters.

'Of course I am, and it's painful too. Period pains are always painful – at least mine are – and this is worse. That's why I got undressed and into bed when...when the worst was over. I only got up so that I could be here when you came in. I'm sorry...and there's no meal ready.' She smiled weakly as she turned her tear-stained face up to him.

'Oh darling, as if that mattered! As if anything matters so long as you are all right. Well, you are going to have the doctor to see you right away...'

'No, Bruce...no,' she almost shouted. 'It doesn't matter...'

'But I insist,' he interrupted her. 'You can't go through all this and not see a doctor. You've signed up with the one in the village, haven't you? I'm going to phone him straight away.'

'But I've never seen him, except when I went to ask if I could be on his list. He doesn't even know me...'

'Well, he soon will. And that's another thing, darling. I kept telling you to go and see the doctor, to make sure that everything was OK.'

'It was too soon, Bruce; you can't go too soon. But I was going to see him...next week. There's no point now, though, really there isn't.'

He shook his head. 'Stop arguing; I've made up my mind. Now, you pop back into bed and I'll see to everything. Shall I warm some soup for you? I expect you're ready for something to eat, aren't you? And I'll get you a hot water bottle and how about a couple of aspirins for the pain?'

'Yes...all right,' she agreed eventually. 'Thank you...' She was looking very apprehensive, though, almost scared. He knew that she wasn't keen on going to see the doctor; in fact he didn't think that she had done so in all the time he had known her. Which time, all told, amounted to just over a year...

Just how well do you know your wife? He could hear the

niggling little voice inside his head as he busied himself in the small kitchen. Just supposing…there had never been a baby in the first place? Now where had that disloyal thought come from? he asked himself. It was obvious that Christine was far from well, and he was most certainly going to call the doctor. He could not help remembering, though, that she had not wanted anyone to know the reason for their hasty marriage. They still had not visited Middlebeck to see his parents and to tell them about the baby… He was full of guilt at the thought of his neglect of them, but quickly upon that thought there came another; there was no need now for them to know why he and Christine had married so speedily.

He recalled how she had lied to him before, about her age; he had believed she was two years younger… Were there other things that he did not know about her, matters about which she had been less than truthful? Bruce knew, however, that in spite of her failings he loved her very much; and the most important thing at the moment was to make her comfortable and then to ensure that the doctor took a look at her.

That had been a close thing, Christine told herself later that evening, although she should have realised that Bruce would insist on her having the doctor. He had arrived within the hour. She could not hear the conversation between the two of them, but she was relieved that the doctor entered the room on his own.

'Now, Mrs Tremaine, your husband tells me you have suffered a miscarriage?' He sounded a little puzzled. 'You haven't been to see me, have you? I am wondering why, if you are three months into your pregnancy? Anyway, come along, my dear, and let me examine you…'

She explained, in quiet tones that could not be overheard, that it might not be quite so much as three months, and that she had intended to come and see him very soon. She told him about the bleeding, that it had been like a heavy period…but much worse. That, in point of fact, was only a slight exaggeration. Her period had started at lunch time, as she had said. She had been waiting for it to begin so that she could get on with this fabrication – only a little lie, she told herself – and then on with the rest of her life.

The most difficult thing had been convincing Bruce that they must not make love, at least not fully, during the first three months of her pregnancy as it could bring about a miscarriage. The last thing she had wanted was to be really and truly pregnant, but Bruce had seemed to believe what she had told him. Now they would be able to start making love properly, something she had missed very much; although she would need to convince him now that it would not be wise for her to conceive again just yet. The main object in the beginning had been to make sure that they were married without any delay, and to get him away from all the distractions in Middlebeck...

She was able to wince convincingly as the doctor prodded at her stomach. She was, in truth, quite sore, as she invariably suffered from period pains; she had been forced to hide the last ones from Bruce.

'You will be fine now, I am sure,' said the doctor, smiling reassuringly at her. He did not, to her relief, seek to examine her more intimately. 'I will leave you some tablets for the pain, and if the bleeding continues for longer than five days, then let me know. Goodbye, Mrs Tremaine. It was nice to meet you, but I am sorry it was not in happier circumstances. However, there is always another time. But next time, make sure you come and see me...'

She stayed in bed for the rest of the day, enjoying the fuss that Bruce was making of her. 'Never mind, darling; we can always try again,' he assured her, forgetting, it seemed, that the child he had thought she was expecting had not been one for which they had planned.

'It was a mistake, if you remember, Bruce,' she reminded him, 'but we'd sort of got used to the idea by now, hadn't we?' She tried to sound regretful, although she did not want to cry any more; she had done quite enough of that. 'Maybe we should wait a little while, though, before we try again. It's very nice, don't you think, there just being you and me?'

'Very nice indeed,' he replied, kissing her on the forehead. She glanced at him warily, because she thought he sounded a little...odd – abrupt and suspicious, almost – but his expression was inscrutable. His next remark, though, was quite sympathetic. 'Now, you try and get to sleep, and you'll probably feel tons better in the morning.' Perhaps she had imagined it. Bruce was normally so trusting; gullible, really; and there were times – such as now – when she felt quite mean. She decided that she must never deceive him again.

She needed to recover fairly quickly because in ten days' time it would be her friend, Sadie's, wedding to Roland; and she, Christine, had arranged to go to Bradford a couple of days earlier to try on her bridesmaid's dress – or 'matron of honour', to be more correct. Sadie's mother was making the dresses, not only for the bride but for the three attendants as well. Daphne and Vera, Sadie's friends, with whom she and Christine had worked in the mill office, were to be the other two.

Christine had been relieved to board the train at Lincoln station on the Thursday morning, knowing she would have two days' respite before she saw her husband again. He had been in a strange mood, solicitous one minute, and then watching her doubtfully the next. Her 'miscarriage' had not been mentioned again – none of his colleagues, at her request, had known of her supposed pregnancy – but she knew that he was concerned about their forthcoming visit to Middlebeck, which they were to make following the wedding in Bradford. That was most likely the reason for his preoccupation, she told herself; he was feeling guilty that he had not seen his parents for so long. Although he had not admitted it, she had known that he did not want to tell them about the baby, and that was why he had kept postponing their visit. Well, now there was no need for them to know at all.

'You look a little peaky, dear,' said Barbara Gascoyne, when she and Sadie met her at the station. 'Doesn't she, Sadie? Are you all right, Christine love?'

'Yes, I'm fine now,' she replied. 'Well, more or less. But to be honest, I have been a little...unwell. I thought I was pregnant, you see...' She lowered her voice, speaking confidentially to them as they made their way to the bus stop. 'Well, I was sure I was, but then... I had a very bad period, a sort of miscarriage, I think it was, and it's left me feeling a bit worse for wear, as well as...rather disappointed.'

'Oh dear, what a shame! Still, there's always another time, isn't there, dear?' said Barbara, looking at her concernedly.

Sadie did not comment, but she and Christine exchanged glances, Sadie giving a shrewd nod and Christine raising her eyebrows and smiling ruefully. She was sure Sadie understood that she had never been pregnant at all, but she was a very good friend and would not betray her.

Sadie's wedding dress was a traditional style, in ivory satin with a fitted bodice outlining her tall slim figure, tapered sleeves and a sweetheart neckline. Everyone agreed that she looked beautiful. Most brides did, of course, but Sadie looked especially radiant on the arm of her new husband, whose quite average looks were enhanced by his army captain's uniform; they were a truly handsome couple.

The bridesmaids wore dresses of mid-blue in a similar style to that of the bride; it was a shade which suited the colouring of them all; Christine was fair-haired, Daphne very dark, and Vera somewhere in between. Another handsome couple was that of Christine and her husband, Bruce wearing the uniform of a flying officer and his pretty wife dressed in the blue which complemented it perfectly.

The reception was held at the hotel on the Bingley Road, where Bruce and Christine had enjoyed a much less grandiose affair after their own wedding. If she was regretful, or envious, or apprehensive, maybe, about the future, Christine did not let it show as she chatted and laughed and drank the health of the happy couple. There was a tear in her eye, however, as her best friend, Sadie, and Roland, drove off for their honeymoon. When they returned they would be living in married quarters in Aldershot, and there was the possibility of his being posted to Germany again, or even further afield. Goodness knew when she would see her friend again. She, Christine, had longed to leave Yorkshire and all its memories far behind, but now, suddenly, the future seemed more than a little unsure.

—

'When is it anything other than a flying visit with you?' replied Rebecca in answer to her son's announcement that he and Christine would not be able to stay very long. They had arrived early on the Saturday evening and were now enjoying the coffee and sandwiches that Rebecca had prepared in readiness for them; but they would have to leave on Sunday evening as Bruce was due back at camp on the Monday morning.

'At least we are not dependent on the trains any more, Mother,' he told her, 'now that we have the car. And Christine is learning to drive as well,' he added, smiling proudly at his wife.

'That's nice, dear,' said Rebecca, turning to look at her, but it sounded to Christine as though the words were choking her. It was she, Christine, who was being blamed for their short stay, she was sure.

'So – how are you settling down in your married quarters then?' Archie asked her. She always found him to be the much more friendly of the two. 'Don't you find it rather lonely with Bruce away a lot of the time? I believe it's a rather isolated spot, from what Bruce has told us.'

'That's why I'm learning to drive, Archie,' she replied. He had insisted she should call him by his first name and she did so quite easily; everyone called him Archie. But Rebecca had not suggested she should make free with her name, and Christine could not imagine ever doing so. 'I have felt rather cut off from civilisation, to be quite honest, although I get on reasonably well with some of the other wives.' In truth, she did not do so, finding them insular and unable to talk about anything but the airforce and their precious husbands.

'Actually, we're thinking of moving soon, aren't we, darling?' She smiled at Bruce. 'There's a house for sale in the nearby village, and we've got our eye on it, haven't we, Bruce?' Her husband frowned at her a little, but he nodded his agreement.

'Yes, that's right...' Perhaps he had thought he should be the one to tell them, but she was only trying to be friendly and chatty, the way she thought he wanted her to be.

'It's a lovely honey-coloured limestone house,' she went on. 'They all are, of course, in the villages around Lincoln. It's very pretty...' But apart from the picturesque villages she found the landscape quite flat and featureless and, to her surprise, she had found herself missing the hills and vales of her native Yorkshire. She had not been aware of it quite so much whilst she had been in the WAAF, but now she had much more time on her hands. But it was the flatness of the land that made it ideal territory for airfields, and the one in particular where she had met Bruce.

'Yes, it's a lovely part of the country,' agreed Bruce. 'Very different from Yorkshire, though, but I've got used to it now. You must come and stay with us, Mother – both of you, of course – when we are settled in our new home. I intend to make an offer for it next week.'

'Yes...thank you, we will look forward to that,' said his mother. She did not sound too enthusiastic, although she smiled fondly at her son. Christine was not granted the same loving glance and smile.

Archie, however, winked at Christine as he said, 'Aye, we'd like that, Becky and me. Let us know when you've got settled in your new place and we'll come and see you afore long. We've got to keep in touch, that's the main thing. Families have to stick together.'

Christine was gratified by his kind words. If it had not been for Archie with his ready chat and sense of humour, the day they had spent at Tremaine House would have seemed endless.

She waved cheerily to the pair of them, standing in the doorway, as Bruce started up the car and drove away early on the Sunday evening. She even blew a kiss to Archie, whom she had decided she liked very much.

'There, that wasn't too bad, was it?' said Bruce as they drove along the lane which led to the High Street. 'My father seems to have taken quite a liking to you.'

'And I like him as well,' replied Christine. 'He's a good sort; a bit set in his ways, mind you, but that's what comes of living in Middlebeck. I don't suppose he's ever travelled very far from here, has he?'

'Only during the war,' said Bruce, 'the first one, I mean. He served at the Front then as a first lieutenant, and fortunately came back more or less unscathed. He was so relieved to be safely back home again that he has never had any desire to wander far afield since then. But don't underestimate him; he's not the stick-in-the-mud that you seem to imagine.'

'What do you mean?' asked Christine. 'I thought he was all for selling the Nixons' farm and becoming a gentleman of leisure.'

'Don't you believe it,' replied Bruce. 'The sale of the farm is going through, so he told me, but he certainly doesn't intend to sit around on his backside...er, excuse me, darling,' he laughed. 'No; he was telling me on the QT that he has become very interested in politics. In fact – and there is only my mother who has been told about this so far – he has been invited to stand as a candidate at the next election.'

'General Election, do you mean? To be an MP? But there has only just been an election, last year.'

'They make plans well in advance though.'

'Well, fancy that! You do surprise me. But it's a safe Tory seat, isn't it, round here? They've already got a Conservative MP, so they won't need another one, unless the present one is thinking of retiring.'

'Oh no, no... My father would be standing against him, for the other side.'

'What! You mean... Labour?'

Bruce laughed. 'Yes; don't sound so amazed, darling. My old man is something of a Radical. I've known that for quite a while.'

'But I thought...with him being the squire and all that...'

'A title he has never really liked. He has never believed in inherited privilege. I know he sent me to boarding school, and my sisters as well; but he's always done everything he could for his workers.'

'Well, well, well; curiouser and curiouser,' said Christine. 'And what does your mother think about it?'

'I don't know. He didn't say, and I haven't asked her. She will go along with him though, I'm sure, as a good and loyal wife. Anyway, it's all a long way in the future.'

Christine nodded. 'Yes, I expect she will... We didn't get a telling-off about the wedding, did we? I thought she might have had quite a lot to say.'

'So did I, but probably my father told her to leave well alone.'

'I saw her looking at me, though; you know, sort of... curiously. She's probably still wondering if I'm pregnant.'

'Well, you're not, are you? Not any more...'

'No... I'm not. But we have the rest of our lives, darling.'

'Yes, as you say; the rest of our lives...' he repeated thoughtfully. He took his hand off the steering wheel to squeeze her hand briefly, then he fixed his eyes on the road ahead, which led into the valley and then out of Middlebeck.

# Chapter Seventeen

The wedding of Lily Jackson and Arthur Rawcliffe, which took place on the first Saturday in March, was a quietly joyful occasion. The Reverend Luke Fairchild, to their surprise, had offered to marry them at St Bartholomew's church. Second marriages – of divorcees – were very rarely performed in the Church of England, but occasionally, in special circumstances, they could be allowed to take place at the discretion of the parish priest and his bishop. Luke had considered this to be a very special circumstance, Lily being the totally innocent party in what had been a disastrous marriage.

At Lily's request, though, it was a very simple service, without a choir or a peal of bells, and with two of her family's favourite hymns rather than the traditional 'O Perfect Love'. 'All Things Bright and Beautiful' was not really a wedding hymn, and was not one of Lily's particular favourites, but as Joanie and Jimmy had suggested it she had decided to humour them. This was to be a real family occasion. The two children already looked upon Arthur as a favourite uncle and she knew he would be a loving stepfather to them, giving them the care and affection that their real father had never done, whilst Maisie, who said very little, seemed happy for her mother and had gone along agreeably with all the wedding plans, even to wearing the pink dress she had shunned since the night of the concert. This had been shortened, and the cut off material fashioned into a bolero to wear over her bare shoulders. She was the only attendant to her mother, who was elegant in a cream-coloured knee-length dress of silken crepe and a wide-brimmed straw hat. The small posy of flowers which Lily carried matched exactly the colour of her daughter's dress.

Maisie joined in with the final hymn, 'Lead us Heavenly Father, Lead us', feeling a tear come into her eye as they sang the final words,

> *'Thus provided, pardoned, guided,*
> *Nothing can our peace destroy...'*

and then listened to Luke giving the blessing. Her mother deserved some peace now, and happiness, with Arthur after all she had endured in the past. As for her, Maisie, she was surprised that she was wearing the once hated pink dress without it evoking unpleasant memories. She had heard nothing more of Bruce since the startling news of his marriage and, because she knew he must, he had faded to the far recesses of her mind.

Although it had been a quiet, rather understated, sort of ceremony, no one had been able to stop the very many folk of Middlebeck from attending. They half-filled the church, then stood on the forecourt outside, showering the couple with confetti, and shaking their hands and wishing them well.

—

The wedding meal was just a simple affair at the couple's home, prepared beforehand by Lily herself and her soon to be sister-in-law, Flo, with only a few friends and family members attending. The renovations to the upstairs rooms of the draper's shop and the bakery had been completed in good time for the wedding, and Lily was thrilled with her more spacious accommodation and especially with her modern kitchen.

Maisie had been offered a newly decorated bedroom on the lower floor, but she still preferred her attic room with its superb view over the rooftops of Middlebeck and across the valley to the distant hills. After the excitement of the wedding – for although it had been only a quiet affair the preparations had engendered a good deal of enthusiasm and pleasurable anticipation amongst all the family members – she felt that life in general seemed to have fallen flat. Everyone around her appeared so contented and sure of themselves and of what they were doing.

Her mother was very happy, singing and humming as she went about her work, and, as was only to be expected, making a good deal of fuss of her new husband. Maisie felt a little bit excluded, although she knew that that was not Lily's intention. The two of them though, mother and daughter, had grown very close since Lily had brought the family back together, and now Maisie was having to share her mother. Joanie and Jimmy were delighted with their new bedrooms – one each, instead of sharing – and neither of them seemed to have a care in the world, which was as it should be for eight- and nine-year-olds.

As for her two best friends, Audrey and Doris, their future lives appeared to be clear-cut, already mapped out for them. Audrey was still determined on her career as an Infant teacher and was looking forward with great enthusiasm to going to college, even though that was two years hence. And in the meantime she had her boyfriend, Brian. Whether he would still be around in two years' time remained to be seen, but it didn't seem to worry her.

As for Doris, who was now turned sixteen, as was Audrey, she and the Polish farm worker, Ivan, were most definitely 'courting', which was what the older folk called going out together. Maisie guessed that they would be married in a year or two, possibly still living at the Nixons' farm, or maybe even with a farm of their own, and then a couple of children as well…

But as for Maisie, she found herself viewing the years that lay ahead with uncertainty, as she wondered what the future might hold for her, not with any sense of dread but more of bewilderment. She had never had any wish to go to college or university, although she knew she was capable of doing so. Her teachers at school were taking it for granted that she would, but she certainly did not want to be a teacher…or a doctor, or solicitor, or barrister, professions which were being undertaken more and more by women. She did not want to sit at a typewriter all day, or work in an office or a shop. She enjoyed her little job in her mother's shop and in the bakery next door from time to time, but those were only temporary occupations. At the moment there was nothing that appealed to her, but she did not like admitting to this if anyone asked her, as they so often did, 'What are you going to do when you leave school, Maisie?' And even when she had been so madly in love with Bruce, her thoughts had never really gone so far as to contemplate marriage.

Nor did she think about that possibility with Ted Nixon. Things had cooled off between them, although she was still 'going out' with him, as far as she and everyone else were concerned. She had seen, though, what might lie ahead if she had allowed the friendship to develop, as it seemed to have been doing at Christmastime. Ted would become more and more serious about her, they would 'go further', and she might – God forbid! – even become pregnant, or else he would want an engagement or an early marriage. That was what often happened to couples in a little town like Middlebeck. But such things were not for Maisie, at least not for a very long time.

And so she had told Ted that she was studying very hard – which was true – and could not see him quite so frequently; and Ted, surprisingly, had accepted what she had said without arguing.

—

'Well, thank goodness that lot's over!' said Audrey to Maisie, one afternoon towards the end of June. It was the final day of their School Certificate exams and they had just completed their eight subjects with the History paper that afternoon. They were travelling home together on the bus as Brian, Audrey's boyfriend with whom she sometimes cycled home, was away on a field trip with other members of the Upper Sixth, after completing their Higher School Certificate exams. 'I can't believe it's come to an end, can you? Freedom at last, glorious freedom... What did you think of the History paper then? I expect you thought it was a doddle, didn't you?'

'No, did I heck as like!' retorted Maisie, although History, in fact, was one of her favourite subjects. 'I haven't thought that about any of the papers. It all depends on whether you have swotted up the right subjects, doesn't it? I'm glad there was a question about the French Revolution – Miss Green said there most likely would be, didn't she? – because I felt I knew that inside out. Especially with us having to read *A Tale of Two Cities* for the English Lit course.'

'Yes, I chose that one as well,' replied Audrey. 'The French Revolution; the Unification of Austria; and the policies of Pitt the Younger... How boring it is, though. How can that be of any relevance to us, all those ancient prime ministers?'

'Oh, I don't know. Clement Attlee'll be history in a hundred years' time, won't he? Some poor fifth formers'll be learning all about him and Winston Churchill...'

'Oh give over, Maisie! That is so-oo depressing... Let's think about something nice. Actually, we've got a surprise for you, Mum and Dad and me; that's why Mum's asked you to come to tea today.'

'Have you?' Maisie turned to her eagerly. 'That sounds exciting. What is it?'

'It will be exciting,' said Audrey mysteriously, 'but I'll let Mum tell you about it; it was her idea.'

---

The surprise turned out to be a holiday in London for all the Fairchild family – Luke and Patience, Audrey and Timothy, and little Johnnie who would be five in September – and on which Maisie was invited to accompany them. The very idea of leaving Maisie out of such an exciting event would have been unthinkable, Patience told her.

Maisie was so thrilled when she heard the news that she was rendered speechless for at least a minute, especially as

Luke had added that he would be footing the bill for all of them, including Maisie, and that they would be staying at a big hotel, the Regent Palace, which was situated in the very centre of London, right next to Piccadilly Circus.

'An' we're going to see the soldiers, an' the horses, an' the big palace where the King lives, aren't we, Daddy?' said Johnnie, jumping up and down on his seat with excitement.

'And Westminster Abbey and St Paul's Cathedral,' Timothy informed her, rather more studiously. 'And Dad says we'll be able to travel on the Tube, Maisie. There are trains, you see, that run under the ground, even under the river, and it's called the Underground, but most people refer to it as the Tube.'

'That's right, Tim,' said Luke, smiling a little at the precise way in which the boy expressed himself, but feeling very proud of his adopted son and the way he was shaping up towards manhood; he was thirteen now and showed signs of early maturity and academic prowess. 'You've been reading up all about London, haven't you? And we shall expect you to be our own personal guide. If we rely on your mum and me we are quite likely to get lost.'

'The Underground is very simple, Dad,' said Tim. 'Each line has a different colour, you see, and where they cross, that is where you have to change to a different line. The Central Line is red, and the Circle Line is yellow...'

'Well, it's good to know that one of us will know the way around,' laughed Patience. 'It's years and years since I was in London. As a matter of fact, I've only been there once, and Luke has been twice, haven't you, dear? We thought it would be a nice treat for all of us. You girls have been working so hard with your exams, and so has Timothy. And Johnnie will be starting school in September, won't you, love? Anyway, we thought a visit to our capital city would be a very good idea. Apparently the city is just beginning to get on its feet again, after the war. The Londoners have been so very brave and they deserve our support.'

'Thank you ever so much for inviting me, Aunty Patience,'

said Maisie, finding her voice at last. 'When are we going? Is it soon?'

'Yes; just as soon as you break up from school in July. I know it will be hot in London at this time of the year, but never mind; I know we will enjoy every minute of it. We're going by train, of course. Change at Leeds, and then it's straight through to London.'

'To King's Cross,' added Timothy. 'That's the station we will arrive at.'

The first adventure in an exciting week was to travel in a taxi from the station through the busy streets of London. But busy was not really the word for it, thought Maisie. It was much more than busy; it was hectic, tumultuous, with the noise of taxi horns blaring, the revving of engines and the screech of brakes, and all around were hordes of people, thronging the pavements and taking their lives in their hands as they dashed across the roads. She had never seen so many people or so much traffic. It was far busier than Leeds, which city she had not visited for several years. Living in sleepy Middlebeck for so long she had forgotten about the hubbub of city life. To be catapulted into it so suddenly was a shock, but she knew it was all going to be so thrilling.

They found that finding their way around London was not really difficult, provided that you had a good map with all the main streets and the places of interest clearly marked; and it was easier, they soon discovered, to walk rather than use the buses or the underground. To appease Timothy, however, they did take a few journeys on the Tube, so that he could show off his prowess with the multi-coloured map. And he was as good as his word; not once did he get them lost, or get on a train going the wrong way which, apparently, was a common mistake made by strangers to the city.

And to please Johnnie they had a ride on one of the big red buses. He had a Dinky bus in his toy box at home, but it could not compare with the real thing. He sat on the front seat of the upper deck staring our delightedly at Nelson's Column in the middle of Trafalgar Square, where hundreds of pigeons were pecking at the nuts thrown to them by tourists. Timothy tried to give a running commentary to his little brother, but he eventually gave up when he realised his words were going in one ear and out of the other. He, too, just stared, taking in the wonderful sights and storing the memories in his mind to be mulled over later.

Every evening when they had finished their sightseeing and returned to the hotel, Tim retired to the bedroom he was sharing with Luke, Patience and Johnnie, to write up his diary. When they got back home he would make a journal, he had decided, including the postcards he had bought and some of the snapshots that Luke had taken.

Maisie and Audrey had no such good intentions. They had already done quite enough writing during the exam fortnight. But the memories of this holiday would be lasting and very precious ones, they were sure of that. The two of them were sharing a bedroom and they lay awake for hours each night, discussing the events of the day. As Patience had predicted, it was hot in London, very hot; and the hotel, tucked away in a corner of one of the busiest parts of the city and surrounded by tall buildings, retained the heat of the day, even with the windows flung wide open. And when the girls finally fell asleep they were often awakened in the early hours of the next day by the dustcart collecting the refuse from the hotel and the others nearby. Their window overlooked a back alley, but even the dinginess of the view or the clang of dustbins and smashing of bottles at two o'clock in the morning could not detract from their delight in all the new experiences they were enjoying.

'What have you enjoyed the best of all?' asked Maisie as they lay in bed on the very last night. They had returned rather later than usual after having a final meal at what had become their favourite eating place: Lyon's Corner House on the Strand. They had had a slap-up meal of steak and chips that evening, followed by apple pie and cream. Maisie had, again, been fascinated by the Nippies, as they were called, in their neat white aprons and caps, dashing hither and thither with their laden silver trays held high aloft.

'Oh... I don't know,' replied Audrey. 'What a difficult question. There's so much to remember, isn't there? I enjoyed the trip on the river boat, seeing all the sights from a different angle. St Paul's dome – d' you remember how it shone in the sunlight? And going under Tower Bridge and seeing all the cargo boats unloading in the Pool of London. And the Angel Inn; I thought it was amazing to think that it was there in Tudor times and that it's still here. Just think, perhaps even William Shakespeare had a drink there.' The captain of the boat had given a running commentary and had told them that the Angel Inn in Bermondsey was the oldest inn on that bank of the Thames. They had learned all sorts of gems of information this last week.

'And the Changing of the Guard,' Audrey continued. 'I know it's put on for tourists, for folk like us who want to stare, but it's exciting all the same. And wasn't Johnnie thrilled?'

The little boy had stared, mesmerised, at the troop of Life Guards with their helmets shining in the sun and their gleaming bayonets pointing upwards at their side. Their red tunics had glowed as brightly as the geraniums in the flower beds near to Buckingham Palace, and the regimental music had made them feel 'so proud to be British', as Patience had remarked. Timothy had informed them that the Royal Standard flying – somewhat limply on that very hot day – from the palace flagpole meant that the King was at home. And how thrilling that was, to feel that King George the Sixth was actually so near to them.

'I enjoyed the view from the Monument,' said Maisie. 'It was a bit scary at first, looking down all that way...'

'Scary! I was terrified!' said Audrey. It had taken a while for Maisie to persuade her to take in the view, and she had kept her arm around her all the time. It had been a breathtaking view; the dome of St Paul's was the focal point, then, further away, the Tower and the River Thames, like a broad greyish-blue ribbon running under its myriad bridges towards Westminster, an endless panorama of roofs, chimneys, spires, towers and domes. It was like that poem by Wordsworth, written on Westminster Bridge, Maisie had thought.

Timothy had reminded them, when they returned to terra firma, that the Monument was Sir Christopher Wren's memorial to the Great Fire of London, and that the view that they had seen from the top that day was almost exactly the same as the one seen by Samuel Pepys and those who had lived in the city at that time, apart from the rebuilding of St Paul's. For not only were some of the well-known sights visible from the Monument, but also a scene of destruction, the legacy of the Blitz; a scene such as would have been viewed following the devastating fire three hundred years before.

'What a miracle it was that St Paul's was not bombed,' Luke had remarked when they had paid a visit to the cathedral, and had seen how it stood like a sentinel amidst the vast areas of rubbish and rubble which still surrounded it. In the patches of earth the rose-bay willow herb plant had grown up and flourished, covering stretches of ground with its bright pinky-purplish flowers. It had come to be known as London Pride by the inhabitants of the city.

'Perhaps the next time we go they might have rebuilt the area around St Paul's,' said Maisie, recalling Luke's words. 'It's said that London was rebuilt within three years of the Great Fire, but I don't believe that, do you? It looks as though it may take much longer this time. War is dreadful, isn't it, Audrey? I hope there will never, ever be another one.'

She stopped suddenly, realising that Audrey might find her remark tactless, considering that the girl had lost both her parents during the war. But Audrey did not appear to be affected by her friend's words.

'Yes...' she agreed. 'It is dreadful... But we have to look to the future now, as my father is always reminding us.' It was amazing, really, how Audrey could refer to Luke as her father in such a forthright way. It had not always been so, certainly not at first, when she had been adopted by the rector and his wife, but now she seemed very proud of the fact. 'And the future for you and me, Maisie, is exams and more exams,' she went on. 'We'll start studying for our Higher in September.'

'For goodness sake, give it a rest!' retorted Maisie, laughing. 'It's ages and ages till September. Let's try and think of something more cheerful... Are you looking forward to seeing Brian again? Have you missed him?'

'Mmm...sort of,' said Audrey. 'Yes, it'll be nice to see him again. Actually, I've hardly thought about him at all; we've been so busy. What about you...and Ted?'

'Same here,' replied Maisie. 'I must admit I've hardly given him a thought all week.' She surprised herself by her admission, but it was true. 'I sent him a card, but it seems as though out of sight has been out of mind as well. Isn't that awful?'

'Not really,' said Audrey. 'Middlebeck seems a long away away, doesn't it? But I expect we'll settle down again.'

'We will have to, I suppose...' said Maisie thoughtfully. 'Anyway, we'd better try and go to sleep. Goodnight, love. Sleep tight...'

'Goodnight, Maisie...' her friend replied.

Maisie did not go to sleep for a while. Middlebeck did, indeed, seem to be a very long way away from London, not only in distance but in its way of life; the steady day to day existence endured – or maybe even enjoyed – by its inhabitants, who had no desire to live elsewhere or to seek a different kind of lifestyle. She had realised this past week that there was a whole world waiting for her away from the northern dales, not only in Britain but much further afield. She had never before been out of her native Yorkshire, and London was only the start. There were other parts of the British Isles to explore; Scotland, Ireland, Wales, the Lake District, the Cotswolds, or the far western counties of Devon and Cornwall. She had seen pictures in the windows of travel agencies they had passed, and these yet unseen places had beckoned to her enticingly.

In the windows of the airline agencies in the Strand or Regent Street – BOAC, KLM, or Pan American Airways, names which were starting to sound familiar, even to ordinary untravelled folk – there were models of aeroplanes with great silver wings, advertising flights to Paris, Rome, Amsterdam, or the United States of America.

And in the windows of the Cunard Company were models of the two great British ocean going liners, the Queen Elizabeth and her sister ship, the Queen Mary, which were now making the journey each week between Southampton and New York. There were adverts for cruise ships, too, visiting such wondrous places as the Mediterranean ports, the Norwegian fjords, or the islands of the South Seas.

Only for the rich, of course, excursions such as these, but that did not stop Maisie from wishing and hoping.

———

They arrived back in Middlebeck on Thursday afternoon, and the same evening Maisie had a surprise visit from Ted. Lily and Arthur, tactfully, left them alone in the living room to talk. Lily had noticed the rather hangdog expression on the young man's face, she had told Maisie later, and had guessed that he might want to speak to her privately.

'This is a surprise,' said Maisie. 'I wasn't expecting to see you till after choir practice. I thought you might meet me out tomorrow night, like you sometimes do.'

'Er, well…that's why I wanted to see you now,' said Ted, staring down at his feet and wiping his clammy hands on his trousers before he raised his head and looked at her. 'Before you see Celia at choir practice, I mean. I've got summat to tell you, Maisie… I'm awful sorry, but…'

'But you've started seeing Celia, haven't you?' she interrupted. He nodded silently. If she were honest with herself she was not surprised, although it had given her rather a start all the same. She had noticed, on the odd occasions that the three of them had been together, that the other two seemed to get on very well. She gave a slight shrug. 'Well then, that's OK, if it's what you want. Thanks for telling me and not leaving me to just...find out.'

'I'm sorry, Maisie,' he said again. 'I don't want to hurt you, honest I don't, and neither does Celia. I haven't taken her out whilst I've been seeing you, only this week while you've been away. And she said I had to tell you before I saw her again. I do think a lot about you. And I know I could easily get to – you know – be even more fond of you. But it's no use... You've got all your studying to do, your sixth form an' college an' all that. An' I'm just an ordinary bloke. Nowhere near good enough for you, Maisie...'

'You mustn't say that, Ted,' she replied. 'Never, not about me nor about anybody else, because it's not true. We're just different, that's all... But I suppose it wouldn't have worked in the long run, with you and me. Anyway... I hope you and Celia get on OK. She's a nice girl and she's probably better for you than I was.' She stopped speaking because she didn't know what else to say and she was beginning to flounder; besides, even though what she was saying to him was true, it still hurt to think that he didn't want to go out with her anymore. She blinked hard.

Fortunately he stood up then. 'Well, I'll go now... There's no reason why we can't still be friends, Maisie. You'll still... talk to me, won't you? And Celia...she feels quite bad about it.'

'Yes, Ted...it's OK,' she said briefly. 'Thanks for coming. See you soon then...'

'Ta-ra, Maisie. Be seeing you...'

'He's dumped me, Mum,' she said when her mother came into the room a few moments later. 'And he's started going out with Celia James from the choir; you know, the girl who was Cinderella.'

'Oh dear!' said Lily, sitting on the settee and putting an arm around her. 'I guessed it might be something like that; he was looking a bit shifty. Well, never mind. You can't really call it dumping you, love, because you weren't really much more than friends, were you?'

'Er, no... I suppose not.'

'And he wasn't right for you. I never thought he was. He's a nice enough lad and all that, but he's not the one for you, Maisie.'

'Why? Because he's got a Yorkshire accent and he works on a farm and gets his clothes mucky?' Maisie's hurt was making her feel that she wanted to strike out at somebody, although she knew, deep down, that her mother's words were true. Ted was not the one for her, and she had known that their friendship could not have continued for much longer.

'Now, now, I didn't say that,' replied Lily. 'I know you're upset, but you'll get over it, really you will. Anyway you are only sixteen, and you're going into the sixth form soon, remember. You have years and years ahead of you before you need to start thinking seriously about boyfriends.'

'You didn't say that when you met my dad, did you? How old were you? Seventeen?'

'Yes...but that was different. I was just a mill worker and so was he. I could never have gone to college an' all that even if I'd wanted to. But I want you to make the most of your opportunities, Maisie. Times are so very different now...'

———

As had been expected, both Maisie and Audrey's School Certificate results were very good. They had both passed in all their subjects, Maisie gaining distinctions in English Language, English Literature and History, and credits in most of the other papers; apart from General Science, which had never been of great interest to her and in which she had scraped through with only a pass mark. Audrey's results were equally gratifying. She, too, had excelled in the English papers and also in Mathematics. Her prowess in this subject she had inherited from her real father, who had been a bank manager in Leeds.

They were both well qualified to enter the Sixth Form and start studying for their 'Higher'. Maisie chose English Literature, Geography and History as her main subjects, and Audrey, English, Geography and Art; she would need to be proficient in this last subject if she were to succeed as an Infant teacher, and she already had a flair for painting and drawing.

Audrey, therefore, was not one of the group of twelve girls, plus two teachers, who journeyed to York during the first week of December on a History trip. It was known educationally as an Environmental Visit, to provide an insight into the subject they were studying, and also, it must be admitted, to be a little holiday as well, one of the perks of being a sixth form student.

They alighted from the train at York Station, said to have been the largest railway station in the world when it was completed in 1877. With its high arched glass roof, supported by an iron framework, it was an impressive sight. Maisie had visited the city before on a couple of occasions, but mainly to look at the shops and to take a cursory look at some of the well known sights. But for the next few days they were to make a detailed study of the city and, inevitably, write a thesis on returning as part of their course work.

The place was steeped in history, and it was not difficult to imagine themselves back in Victorian, or even Medieval, times as they wandered through the narrow twisting streets with their jettied houses practically meeting across the cobbled roadways. Their quaint, old-fashioned hotel was in a black and white building in Low Petergate, which street, they were told, had originally been part of the Roman fort's main road.

Maisie had known that York – Eboracum, as it was then called – had been an important city, second only to London, fortified by the Romans, but she had had no idea that Constantine the Great had been proclaimed Emperor there in AD 306.

And after the Romans came the Vikings from Denmark

and Norway. They had captured Anglo-Saxon York in AD 867 and settled there. They called the town Yorvik and made it their main base in England; until they were driven out by King Edward of the Saxons in 954...

All too long ago and too far away to be of much consequence to us today, thought Maisie. All the same, she was captivated by stories such as these, and enthralled by their in-depth studies of such places as the Minster, the Treasure House and the Mansion House, Clifford's Tower, and the many old churches, tucked away in corners of the cobbled streets.

They walked through the streets in a crocodile, more or less, and for most of the time they were expected to wear their school uniform of navy and pale blue. But the teachers trusted them to behave as sensible young women, and provided they were all back at the hotel at five o'clock – by which time it was dark – in readiness for their early evening meal at six, they did not do too much counting of heads.

Maisie had palled up that week with a girl called Jill, with whom she was sharing a room along with two other girls, Hilary and Sheila. On the third day of the holiday the girls were told they could make their own way back to the hotel – they had been visiting the Minster and the hotel was only a few streets away – provided they kept in twos or threes and promised, on no account, to be late. Maisie and Jill, who had been together all afternoon, looked at one another and grinned.

'There's a shop I want to look at in Stonegate,' said Jill. 'We passed it the other day, but there wasn't time to stop. I noticed a gorgeous teddy bear that my little sister would love...'

'OK,' said Maisie. 'Let's go then. And I'll see if there's anything I can get for my brother and sister...'

York was a magical sight at that time of the year, only a few weeks prior to Christmas. Already a dazzling Christmas tree was shining out into the darkness surrounding the Minster, and the shop windows were gay with toys and gifts, glittering baubles and streamers and artificial snow; such a contrast to the gloom of only two years before, when blackout restrictions had made all such light and gaiety impossible. Fairy lights were strung across Stonegate, a somewhat broader road than many of the others, and here there was a variety of shops; high class ladies and gents' outfitters, hatter's, and exclusive shoe shops such as only the rich could afford to patronise, cheek by jowl with toy and gift shops; tobacconists, tea rooms, from which there drifted an appetising aroma of roasting coffee, even a butcher's and a grocer's shop.

The little shop that Jill had sought was a veritable treasure house, and both girls felt like tiny tots again as they admired the exquisitely dressed dolls and cuddly animals, wind-up trains and cars and boats, the jigsaws, games, coloured balls and skipping ropes... Jill had known all along what she wanted. The little teddy bear was no more than six inches tall, dressed in a blue coat and woolly hat. Maisie, after much deliberation, decided to buy an identical one for Joanie, but dressed in red instead of blue. She did not play very much with her dolls now, but Maisie knew she would love him. And for Jimmy a Chinese Chequers game and a pack of Happy Family cards. The gifts were not as expensive as they might have imagined for such a prestigious area of the city, and the lady shop assistant thanked them profusely for their custom and invited them to 'Come again'.

'Okey dokey,' said Jill. 'That was great, wasn't it? Let's get back to the hotel. I'm starving, aren't you?'

Maisie agreed that she was, and was looking forward to their evening meal. The food was well cooked and filling rather than 'posh'; such things as shepherd's pie, toad-in-the-hole, or battered fish and chips, suitable for hungry girls and no doubt offered at a special rate, distinct from the hotel's usual pricey menu.

'Hey, wait a minute...' she said, grabbing hold of her friend's arm as they passed by a shop that she had not noticed before. It was a Travel Agency; there was a model of a green and cream coloured coach in the centre of the window, and all around it were large photographs of scenes of the British Isles; Trafalgar Square, the Scottish Highlands, Blackpool Tower, Windermere, the Welsh Mountains... 'Galaxy Travel' read the sign over the door, and on the pile of brochures displayed in the window.

'So what?' said Jill. 'We're not thinking of booking a holiday, are we? Come on; there's nothing here of interest to us... What's up?' For Maisie was showing no sign of moving. She was staring at the coloured pictures longingly, as she had done at those in the London travel agencies, and at something else she had noticed; an advert fastened to the window...

'WANTED; INTELLIGENT AND ENTERPRISING YOUNG WOMAN TO ASSIST AS A BOOKING CLERK, AND ALSO WITH THE PLANNING OF TOURS AND EXCURSIONS FOR GALAXY TRAVEL. GREAT TRAVEL OPPORTUNITIES FOR SUITABLE APPLICANT. ENQUIRE WITHIN.'

'Look at that...' She pointed to the notice. 'Read it...' Jill read it while Maisie watched her. Then she shrugged.

'So what?' she said again.

'That's what I want to do,' said Maisie. 'I didn't know it before, but that's just the sort of job I want. Look what it says... Great travel opportunities...'

Jill stared at her. 'Are you bonkers or what? You're in the sixth form. They're expecting you to go to university. You can't go and work in an office like that...'

'Who says I can't?' retorted Maisie. 'Be blowed to university! I've never wanted to go there, and I only stayed on at school to please my mum and because I didn't know what else I wanted to do. But now I do. Oh Jill, I'm so excited...'

Jill took in her shining eyes and the elation in her voice. 'Gosh!' she said. 'You really mean it, don't you?'

'You bet your life I do...'

'Well then, go in and enquire about it, like it says...'

'Shall I?' Maisie took a step towards the door, then she stopped. 'No, not in my school uniform. They'll think I'm a bit of a kid... Just a minute; I know... They've said we can have tomorrow afternoon to ourselves, haven't they? To do Christmas shopping or whatever we want, and that we don't need to wear our school uniform. That's what I'll do; I'll come back tomorrow...'

'Gosh, Maisie! I wish I had your courage and that I was as sure of what I wanted to do,' said Jill as they headed off back to the hotel. 'My parents want me to be a History teacher, like my dad is, and I suppose I will. I never really dare to argue with them...'

'Don't tell any of the others, will you?' said Maisie. 'This is just between you and me. Anyway, p'raps nothing'll come of it; it might be just pie in the sky.'

'No, I won't say anything, I promise. Cross my heart and hope to die...'

---

Maisie knew she looked older than her sixteen and a half years – she was always being told so – especially when she wore clothes of her own choice and not her school uniform. She was glad she had brought her beige wrap-around tweed coat with her. It was a couple of years old and had been lengthened by her mother with fur fabric trimming at the hem, and also at the collar and cuffs, but it was still quite smart. With it she wore her best wedge-heeled brown leather shoes and shoulder bag, and a red felt beret which sat jauntily at an angle on her dark curly hair.

She felt that she looked her best and was determined to appear confident. All the same she could not ignore the stab of apprehension and a small voice inside her saying, 'What on earth do you think you are doing?', as she opened the door and stepped inside. The shop – or was it termed an office? – was empty apart from a middle-aged man with grey hair and dark-rimmed spectacles who was standing behind the counter.

'And how may I help you?' he asked politely; the sincerity of his voice and the look of interest in his sharp grey eyes put her at her ease at once.

'I've come about the advert in the window,' she replied. 'You are wanting an assistant...and I am wondering if I might be considered for the post?'

He looked at her appraisingly for a moment before he nodded and held out his hand. 'Let's introduce ourselves first, shall we? How do you do? I am Henry Galloway, and you are...?'

'Maisie Jackson,' she replied as she felt his firm handshake. 'How do you do? Er... I expect you have had a lot of enquiries, haven't you?'

'No, not yet,' he said. 'There may well be, but the notice has been in the window for only two days. And the two young women who have enquired about it so far were not at all suitable. Now... Miss Jackson, would you like to tell me a little about yourself, and why you think this particular job would suit you? Do sit down, my dear...' He motioned to a leather-seated chair with arms on her side of the counter, then sat down himself on the other side. 'What is your position at the moment?'

'I am still at school, actually,' she replied. There was no way she could be anything but honest. 'In the sixth form – I am nearly seventeen...' Well, she would be in a few months' time. 'Not here in York, though. I live in Middlebeck, up in the northern dales... I don't know whether you will have heard of it?'

'Of course...' His eyes twinkled. 'I am a travel agent. Middlebeck is a delightful little town. Do go on...'

She told him that she was on a school visit and that the advert in the window had seemed to shout out to her; she had known at once that she had to come and at least find out about it. Yes, she was studying for her Higher School Certificate, she told him, and – yes – her family had great hopes that she would continue with her education but...

'But you feel that this might be your true vocation?' enquired Henry Galloway, understandingly. 'I must agree that education is important,' he went on, 'but sometimes the education that life has to offer can be just as worthwhile as years spent at college or university; and it is vital that you should feel happy and secure about the choices that you make. Now, I must tell you all about our new enterprise here...'

She learned that the name 'Galaxy' was partly a derivation of his surname and that of his wife, Trixie, but had been chosen as well for the suggestion of far-away worlds which it conjured up. It was a family owned business, started only the previous year – just after the end of the war – when his wife had come into 'quite a tidy inheritance'. As their home was in York he and his wife managed the York branch, and there was another office on the Headrow in Leeds. They hoped, eventually, to expand and open branches in other northern cities, maybe even across the border in Manchester and Liverpool.

They were concentrating mainly on coach tours and presently owned a fleet of six, which travelled to most parts of the British Isles. After six long years of war and austerity folks were starting to think again about holidays. They did day trips, too, to nearby beauty spots and places of interest, and tours of their own city, York, for those who wanted to learn about the history of the place. And who would be better equipped to act as a guide than me? thought Maisie, feeling a surge of excitement.

'And we deal with all sorts of travel enquiries,' said Mr Galloway. 'I was a booking clerk on the railway before we opened up here, so I have the railway network at my fingertips, so to speak. We have not yet ventured abroad with our coach tours, but we hope to do so within the next few years. Starting with France, most probably, as it is our nearest neighbour. Do you speak French, by the way?'

'*Oui...mais un peu, seulement,*' she said, grinning. 'But I can improve, I know. I passed it with a credit.'

'Very good. I admire your enthusiasm.' He smiled at her. 'Now, Maisie...if I may call you Maisie?'

She nodded. 'Of course.'

'Well, I feel already that you would be eminently suitable for the post. I have a sort of sixth sense about it. But I do

have a few reservations, as I am sure you will understand?'
She nodded again.

'You see, I would want to know that your mother and
your…stepfather, you said, didn't you? I would want them to
be happy about this. You are not just wanting to get away
from home, are you?' He looked at her shrewdly.

'Oh no, not at all,' she replied. 'Arthur – that's my mum's
husband – and me, we get on famously, and I have a feeling
he would support me. But I admit that my mother might
need a bit of persuading.'

'And your school? You have just started your sixth form
course?'

'We are not very far into it, though. And girls do leave…'
Oh dear, so many problems, she thought.

'And I would need references, of course, from your
headmistress perhaps, and your vicar? People who can vouch
for your suitability. And a copy of your birth certificate. I
know it sounds like a lot of red tape, but provided you can
satisfy me that everything is in order, I don't think I would
need to look any further. And I know my wife will agree.' He
beamed at her. 'She has taken the afternoon off to do her
shopping as there is always a lull before Christmas, apart from
people booking train tickets. So, my dear, I will take the notice
out of the window and when I receive your references and the
OK from your mother, we will consider that the job is yours.'

Maisie was starting to feel bemused; it was all happening
so quickly. 'Thank you…' she gasped. She shook her head
bewilderedly. 'I can't quite believe it…' A thought struck her;
how stupid she was not to have thought of it before. 'I don't
know anybody here, though. I would have to find
somewhere to live…'

'Don't worry about that. Trixie and I could sort that out
for you. Comfortable digs that are not too expensive, eh?'

'Yes, that's right. Thank you…' The enormity of it all was
just starting to sink in. 'And when…when would you want
me to start?'

'Oh, should we say early in January?' He consulted a

calendar. 'Monday, the seventh of January; how does that sound? It would give you time to sort things out at home.'

A customer entered the shop and stood at the counter awaiting assistance, the first one there had been apart from a couple of women who had taken brochures from the pile and then gone out again. Maisie stood up and held out her hand. 'Thank you so much, Mr Galloway. I'll be in touch with you soon...and thank you for being so helpful.'

'Not at all. It's been a pleasure to meet you... See you soon, I hope; the best of luck! Goodbye for now, Maisie...'

She dashed along Stonegate to the little tea room where she had arranged to meet Jill. Her friend was already tucking into a toasted teacake.

'You'll never guess!' cried Maisie, her excited voice causing the customers at the other tables to turn and look at her. 'I've got it! Can you believe it? He says I can have the job...'

—

'Maisie, what on earth are you talking about?' said her mother. 'Of course you can't go and work in a travel agency in York. What an idea! You don't know anybody there. Where would you live? No, no...' Lily lifted her hand in a gesture of dismissal. 'Let's hear no more about it. It's a silly idea, and you'll come to realise it yourself when you've thought about it properly.'

'But I have thought about it, Mum, really I have. Just like I've thought before about what I wanted to do...and you know that I hadn't any idea. That's the only reason I went into the sixth form, to see if anything might appeal to me later, and now it has...'

Lily sighed. 'You're not thinking straight, Maisie. It would be a waste of your education, all those good marks you got in your School Cert. I wanted so much more for you than just working in an office.'

'But it's not just working in an office,' Maisie argued. 'I would have a chance to travel; Mr Galloway said so. And I could study French and learn to speak it properly and...and all sorts of things,' she ended, a little lamely. She had been trying ever since her brother and sister had gone to bed to win her mother round to her point of view. She noticed Arthur giving her a sympathetic smile now, and then he winked at her, almost imperceptibly.

'It might not be such a bad idea, Lily,' he said, turning to his wife. 'And I believe that Maisie has thought it through, haven't you, love? You can tell me that it's none of my business if you like, and maybe it isn't. But it's the first time the lass has shown enthusiasm for any sort of a career. And I think she could go far.'

Maisie smiled at him. 'Thank you, Arthur,' she said.

'Education isn't just to do with book learning,' he went on, 'as I know very well. She'll happen learn more by experiencing things in the real world.'

'That's just what Mr Galloway said,' added Maisie.

'I can see I'm being got at from all sides,' said Lily with a frown, although from the look she gave her husband Maisie surmised that she was not terribly annoyed. 'But you must try and see it from my point of view. We know nothing about this man, and Maisie is very young to be thinking of going to live in another city... This has nothing to do with you splitting up with Ted Nixon, has it?' She looked sharply at her daughter. 'I know you were quite hurt when he started going out with Celia.'

'Of course not, Mum! That's a ridiculous idea,' scoffed Maisie. 'And it's ages ago...'

'All right then,' said Lily. 'You win...the first round, perhaps,' she added, seeing Maisie's elated expression, 'but the battle is not over yet. I'll phone this Mr Galloway and have a chat with him, but I'm not promising anything at the moment, mind...'

'I wish you could try to persuade my mother to let me go,' said Maisie the next day to Anne Mellodey. She had felt that she must go and talk the matter over with her friend who was several years older, not only in age but in wisdom and experience too. Anne might well think it was a foolish notion. But, to Maisie's delight she encouraged her.

'I can tell you are somewhat restless here, Maisie,' she said, 'and you do have a maturity beyond your years. Compared with you, Audrey is still quite a child, in spite of her having a boyfriend; but don't tell her that I said so.'

'No, I won't,' smiled Maisie, 'but I think that friendship might have fizzled out now that Brian has gone to university. So...you don't think I'm completely round the bend?'

'No, not at all. I think it would be worthwhile to give this travel agency a try, to find out if it is your "cup of tea". But I don't want to stick my oar in and talk to your mother; it has nothing to do with me and I wouldn't blame her if she told me so. But if she does decide to let you go, then I might be able to help... Do you remember Jean Bolton? She was one of the teachers up here when we all came in 1939.'

'Yes... Miss Bolton; I remember her.'

'Well, she got married, you know, a few years ago and went to live in York. I still hear from her now and again. She gave up teaching, and after the war she and her husband took over a small guest house, just outside the city walls. I know they take long-term lodgers, and I'm sure their prices would be reasonable. It would set your mum's mind at rest, wouldn't it, if you were to stay there? It's just a suggestion, of course.'

'A very good one, Anne,' said Maisie. 'Thanks ever so much. Let's just see how things go, shall we; but I rather think I might be winning... Now, what about you? How are things at school? And how about Stefan? Are you still seeing him?'

'Nosey!' replied Anne, tapping her forefinger on her nose and blushing a little. 'Yes... I am still seeing Stefan. We are just good friends, though...'

'I've heard that before,' laughed Maisie.

'No, it's true...but we do have a lot in common. He is a very well read man and there is always something to talk about. But he doesn't say much about his life in Poland, and I don't ask.'

'And what about your esteemed headmaster? Are you and he still daggers drawn?'

'No, of course not. We never were really; I'm sorry if I gave that impression. We had different ideas, that was all, and we just had to agree to differ. Actually, Roger is mellowing, and I never thought I would be able to say that. I think he was determined to make his mark at first, but he wasn't used to the set up in a village school, which was what ours was, virtually.'

'I heard that a lot of parents objected to the streaming; to their children being classed as "dunces", as they put it.'

'Yes, there were a few heated arguments, and he was forced to climb down, to a certain extent, although Roger would never admit that that was what he had done. So now we have four Junior classes, one for each year group – unstreamed, theoretically; although the teachers, of course, do know the sheep from the goats – and two Infant classes... And yours truly has been granted the post of Deputy Head, in charge of the Infants, coming into effect in January,' said Anne with a smile of quiet pride.

'Gosh! That's great; congratulations!' said Maisie

'So you might say that everything is hunky-dory, especially as they are getting on well with the new building plans. You won't know the place when you come back to visit us, Maisie.'

'Oh, I mustn't count my chickens. Mum might still say no...'

'Look on the bright side,' Anne told her. 'I have a feeling that everything is going to turn out just fine.'

—

And so it did. As Maisie walked over Lendal Bridge on the seventh of January, 1947, on her way to her new post at 'Galaxy Travel' she felt that never in her life had she been so happy...

# Chapter Eighteen

Bruce was puzzled as to why Christine was not yet pregnant. They had been married for a year and a half and there was still no sign of what his mother liked to call 'a happy event'. In one sense there was all the time in the world because he was only twenty-two and a half years of age, and his wife was twenty-four; the fact of her seniority still niggled at him sometimes when he thought about her deception. At first, after her miscarriage – and that was another thing which he continued to find puzzling – they had been careful to avoid conception. But for the last year or so he had stopped making his weekly visits to the chemist's or the barber's shop, and Christine had appeared as willing as he was to start a family.

He knew that she had not settled down to life as an RAF wife as well as he might have wished. She had been more contented, though, since they had moved from their married quarters at the camp and bought a house in the nearby village, which was fast developing into a small town. She had shown the housewifely skills, then, to which he had been looking forward, making the pretty honey-coloured stone house into a comfortable home, to which he enjoyed returning at the end of each day. But the monotony of the chores had proved to be not enough to keep Christine happy, and before long she had taken a part-time job.

The main street of the village, at one time, had contained – in addition to the long row of houses – only the church, the pub, and a few shops; a post office, a general store and a bakery. It was now expanding and some of the houses which opened directly on to the pavement had been converted into shops. One of the first of these to open was a high-class ladies' gown shop, soon to he followed by a gents' outfitters, a chemist's, and a 'boutique' selling baby linen and fancy goods. Christine had been employed at the shop which sold ladies' clothing for several months and, gradually, her working hours had increased from part-time to what amounted now to almost full-time employment. With the appropriate payment, of course, but to Bruce that was of minor importance. He would have liked to have his wife with him when he had his time off, rather than see her working on a Saturday which, she insisted, was the shop's busiest day. Tourists and day trippers were now finding their way to the quaint little Lincolnshire town and she could not be spared, or so she told him. But he guessed that she was enjoying being indispensable, especially when it meant, as it had done last weekend, that she was unable to accompany him to see his parents in Middlebeck.

—

It had been good to see Bruce at the weekend, thought Rebecca... She paused from her task of dead-heading for a moment to sniff at a particularly fragrant rose, the pale pink of its petals merging almost to a salmon colour at the centre. The rose beds at the front of Tremaine House had been particularly lovely this summer, and what a joy it was to grow flowers again after so many years of 'Digging for Victory'; although she had insisted on keeping one or two flower beds to cheer and console them through the depressing war days.

And, though she knew it was wrong of her to admit to the thought, it had been good to see Bruce on his own. He was much more like her own dear son again when he was away from Christine, but Rebecca had not shared her feelings with Archie. He got on quite well with his daughter-in-law and never talked disparagingly about her. Well, men looked at these things differently, she supposed, especially where a pretty girl was concerned.

Bruce appeared to be happy, however, in his marriage. He

assured her that he was, and on the one occasion when she and Archie had visited them in their new home she had been able to find no cause for alarm, or even for a slight criticism. Christine had shown herself to be a dutiful and contented wife, unless she had been on her best behaviour in front of his parents.

Rebecca wondered now, though, why the young woman needed to go out to work. She certainly did not need to do so for the money; Bruce was able to provide for her quite adequately, which Rebecca had always believed it was a husband's place to do. She had always found interest and fulfilment enough in her own home without seeking diversions elsewhere. She could not understand why Christine did not feel the same.

But it was unkind of her to criticise the girl, she rebuked herself. Maybe she was really wanting to start a family and only working until such time as that might happen. Rebecca was surprised that it had not happened already. When the two of them had got married in such a hurry she had waited then for what she had thought would be the inevitable news. But she had been wrong... She had felt remorseful then about the suspicions she had harboured concerning Christine – it was sure to have been her fault, she had decided, for leading him on – and then, in her more realistic moments, about her son as well, because it did take two after all...

The truth, of course, was that she did not like her daughter-in-law very much. It was something she tried to hide because she could not give a logical reason for her dislike. It was a question of

> 'I do not like thee, Doctor Fell,
> The reason why I cannot tell...'

to quote the old rhyme.

She was distracted from her thoughts by the click of the garden gate, and she turned round to see a woman coming up the path. She gave a start... It must be that she had just been thinking about the girl, because for a moment she thought that the person coming towards her was Christine. She was older, though, she could tell as the figure came nearer, but she was most definitely the image of her daughter-in-law. She blinked rapidly and took a deep breath. Pull yourself together, Rebecca, she told herself. You're imagining things.

The woman was dressed in a black suit, despite the heat of the July sun, with a tiny black hat with an eye veil perched on her platinum blonde hair. 'Excuse me,' she said, 'I'm sorry to trouble you. I don't know whether I've come to the right place, but I'm trying to find a young woman called Christine. Christine Myerscough, she used to be called, but I'm afraid I don't know her married name.' Her voice sounded quite refined, but with underlying broad Yorkshire vowels.

'Christine Myerscough, yes... She is married to my son,' said Rebecca. 'She's called Christine Tremaine now.' She looked at the woman, who met her gaze unflinchingly; her clear silver-grey eyes were so like those of Christine. 'May I ask, though, why you want to find her? She isn't here. They live in Lincolnshire, but I would like to know why...'

'Why do I want to find her?' said the woman. 'Because she's my daughter, that's why, and because I have some news for her.'

'Your...daughter?' gasped Rebecca. 'But I understood... That is to say, we thought...' How could she tell this woman that they had believed her to be dead? Clearly Christine had deceived them – and Bruce as well? – because this person, most obviously, was who she said she was, Christine's mother.

'I'm Myrtle Myerscough,' said the stranger, holding out her hand.

'How do you do?' replied Rebecca, rather belatedly. 'I'm Rebecca Tremaine.'

'What has that daughter of mine been telling you?' asked Myrtle. 'A pack of lies no doubt.' She gave a sorrowful smile. 'Happen she told you we were both dead and gone, is that it? I wouldn't put it past her. Well, as a matter of fact that's what I've come to tell her. Fred, my husband – that's her father whether she likes it or not – he was killed in a road accident last weekend, and I thought she should know.'

'Oh, my dear, I am so sorry,' said Rebecca, instinctively putting an arm around the woman, to whom she found herself warming. 'Do come in and sit down for a while. I'll make us a pot of tea, and then you can tell me...whatever you think I should know.'

Myrtle Myerscough did not need much persuading, and she followed Rebecca through the spacious hallway and into the elegant drawing room. 'Nice place you've got here,' she said, looking around with an appreciative glance. 'Oh aye, that daughter of mine knew what she was doing all right, didn't she? Had her eye on the main chance, I don't doubt... I suppose you might say she's her mother's daughter,' she added, almost to herself, 'but she went about things differently from what I did. I suppose they've got a bairn by now an' all, haven't they, our Christine and...what did you say your son is called?'

'I don't think I did,' said Rebecca, 'but he's called Bruce. No...there is no baby.'

'Well, blow me down! I was wrong then...'

'Look, why don't you sit down and make yourself comfortable, and I'll go and make the tea, then we can have a chat. I can see there is quite a lot we need to talk about.' Rebecca quite literally pinched herself as she went into the kitchen. Could she be dreaming this? She had always known, though, that there was something odd about Christine...

'She told us she was brought up by her grandmother,' said Rebecca, over a cup of tea, 'and that when her gran died she was quite alone, and that was why she joined the WAAF.' Better not to dwell on what Christine had said about being an orphan... But why on earth should she say so when it was a downright lie? Because she was ashamed of them for some reason, Rebecca intuited, as she listened to the tale; ashamed of both her mother and her father. Her sympathy, though, was for Myrtle, who, she guessed, was a rough diamond maybe, but not without some finer feelings.

'Aye, I'm reading between the lines here, and I can see that Lady Muck was ashamed of us,' said Myrtle, reverting to a more pronounced Yorkshire accent. 'Well, I suppose I always knew she was. I was nobbut a mill girl, you see, Mrs Tremaine, but I discovered there were other ways of earning a few bob, if you know what I mean. I was always quite a good looking lass...' Rebecca thought she understood, although it was hard to take in. 'And my hubby, too, he didn't always keep to the right side of the law. Anyroad, my mother took the child away from us to live with her, said we were a bad influence on her, so I reckon if she's grown up despising us we've only got ourselves to blame. But as for Fred, well, he's dead now and the funeral's on Friday, so I thought I'd best come and tell her.' A tear glistened in the corner of her eye and Rebecca's heart went out to her.

'How far have you travelled, Mrs Myerscough?' she asked. 'And how did you know where to come? You said Christine didn't tell you her husband's name?'

'I've come from Bradford this morning, and I'll be going back there tonight. And if you tell me where I can find our Chrissie I'll try again tomorrow. She came to see me just before she got wed – boasting, of course – but all she let slip was that her fiancé's folks lived in Middlebeck and that his father was the squire. So when I got here I made some enquiries and Bob's yer uncle. You're very well known round here, of course.'

'Yes, we have been here a long time,' replied Rebecca. 'But "squire" is only a courtesy title, I can assure you. It doesn't mean very much now... My husband should be back shortly, and when you have had a meal with us – yes, I insist that you should – then he can run you back to the station. And of course I will tell you where you can find Christine...' Rebecca had mixed feelings about this astonishing revelation. She was angry, and sad too, about the way her son – and she and Archie as well – had been deceived. Christine was about to get her come-uppance. But she reminded herself that the girl was about to hear of her father's death. She, Rebecca, must try to be a little more charitable.

'They are living in Lincolnshire,' she told Myrtle. 'In a village not far from Lincoln...' She wrote out the address for her on a piece of paper. 'I believe they are quite happy. Anyway, you will be able to see for yourself. What a shock it must have been for you, my dear, losing your husband so suddenly.'

Myrtle told her, bravely fighting back the tears, that he had been in a head-on collision with another lorry on the main road, returning from Middlesbrough to Bradford. Nobody had really been to blame as the wheels had skidded in the heavy rain. 'Mind you, he was always in a tearing hurry, dashing to get home on a Saturday night... He wasn't a bad sort of bloke, all told...'

When Archie returned he insisted that Myrtle should not only stay for a meal but for the night as well, and then make the journey to Lincoln and onwards the following morning. She had no luggage with her, but Rebecca could lend her such personal items as she might require. Whatever the woman's failings, Rebecca could see that she was as fastidious in her dress and appearance as was her daughter.

Archie was just as shocked and dumbfounded as Rebecca was by the revelations. 'Aye, it's a rum do and no mistake,' he commented, when he returned from running Myrtle to the station on the Wednesday morning. 'And you reckon she might be a prostitute? I can't really see that.'

'I think that is what she was hinting at,' said Rebecca. 'But what I can't get over is the girl deceiving us like that. When all's said and done they are her parents, no matter what they might have done. It was a wicked thing to do, to tell us they were dead.'

'Oh well, I dare say Christine had her reasons,' replied Archie, still unwilling even now to criticise his daughter-in-law. 'I only hope it doesn't harm their marriage. They seemed to be getting on very well.'

'Mmm...yes, of course,' said Rebecca. 'They'll just have to sort things out, won't they? It'll put the cat among the pigeons, though, that's for sure.' But her hopes for the outcome of this crisis were not the same as her husband's.

———

Wednesday afternoon was the only time during the week that 'Alma's Fashions', the shop at which Christine worked, was closed, apart, of course, from all day Sunday. Wednesday was the day when she tidied around and set her little home to rights, and the day on which Bruce tried to get home a little earlier. She would cook a more special meal than usual, then they would go out to the village pub and have a few drinks

Their house, just off the main street, was only five minutes' walk from her place of work. It was situated in a secluded little area named Cherry Tree Close. Cherry trees, which in the springtime were a mass of pinkish-white blossoms, lined the pavements. Even now, in the height of summer, they were a pleasant sight with their slender trunks and browny-gold leaves, through which the sun cast dappled shadows on the grass verges.

Altogether, this was an agreeable place in which to live, thought Christine, as she stood at her lounge window, adjusting the curtains of floral chintz and replacing the ornaments she had dusted; her gran's vase, a cut-glass ashtray, and a posy bowl of china flowers. She was in one of her happier moods that day. She was enjoying working with Alma Copeland in the shop; the woman, some ten years older than herself, was fast becoming a friend as well as her employer. Christine felt, if she played her cards right, that she might before long be offered a partnership in the business, or at least a share of the profits, rather than a weekly wage. One of the perks of working there was that she was able to buy garments at a reduced rate. Only that morning, with Alma's permission, she had put aside for herself one of the prettiest of their range of summer dresses, which she would pay for at the weekend. Another reason for Christine's feeling of elation was that she had managed to wriggle out of the visit to Middlebeck the previous weekend, and Bruce would not be pestering her to go there for another month at least. At the moment she was trying to persuade him to take her on a holiday to the south coast. Torquay appeared to be a very nice place from what she had seen in the brochures; an elegant and refined sort of resort; they called it the English Riviera. She felt that Bruce was showing more interest now; she could usually get him round to her way of thinking if she used her most persuasive charms.

She stood still for a few moments, smiling to herself, lost in her reverie. Then she saw a woman coming up the garden path. She gave a start, and the posy bowl slipped out of her fingers and landed on the carpet. Unconsciously, she noticed that one of the flower heads had broken off – hell and damnation! She had paid quite a lot for that piece of china – but there was no time to worry about it now. The woman coming up the path was...her mother! She dodged back behind the curtain, but it was too late; Myrtle had seen her and was raising her hand in greeting. There was nothing she could do. But would she really have pretended there was nobody at home if her mother had not seen her? she wondered.

Trying desperately to compose herself, she went to the door where her mother was waiting. She knew there was no point in being rude to her and telling her to go away, that she wasn't welcome. She just hoped that Myrtle would say what she had to say and then go, before Bruce returned home. Oh hell, no! That was not very likely; he would be coming home early today. She took a deep breath and opened the door.

'Hello...' she said. 'This is a surprise.' Her fixed smile did not hold any warmth, neither did her mother's.

'Surprise?' repeated Myrtle. 'From what I gather it's more of a bloody great shock than a surprise! It certainly was to your mother-in-law when I turned up on her doorstep. She thought I was pushing up the daisies, didn't she, me and your

dad? Well, that's what I've come to tell you... Aren't you
going to ask me in?'

'Yes, come in,' said Christine automatically. Oh, damn and
blast and bloody hell! This was dreadful. She must have been
to Tremaine House... How else could her mother have found
her whereabouts except by seeking out the Tremaines? She
was desperately trying to think what she had said.
Middlebeck...yes, she had probably mentioned Middlebeck,
and her mother, who was no fool, had sorted the rest out for
herself. Well, the cat was out of the bag now, and even if
Myrtle went away again before Bruce returned there was no
way she would he able to prevent him from learning the truth.

Her mother followed her into the lounge and they both sat
down on the pink plush armchairs. Myrtle was all in black,
Christine noticed, and her eyes looked sad and vacant.

'You father's dead,' she said suddenly, without any
preamble. 'So what you told them posh in-laws of yours is
partly true now; that's one of us gone...'

Christine felt herself blanch and a spasm of remorse
grabbed at her. 'Oh no!' she gasped. 'That's dreadful! I know
it was wrong, what I said, but I thought it was for the best.
I didn't mean to... How did it happen, my dad...?'

'Road accident,' said Myrtle, 'a head-on collision; he was
killed outright, or so I believe. The police came to tell me on
Saturday night. The funeral's on Friday, if you want to come.
You'll please yerself, of course, you always do, but if you
want to show your respects...' She gave a cynical laugh.
'That's a joke, isn't it? You never had any respect for him
while he was alive, did you? Nor for me, neither, so I can't
expect you to show any now.'

'Don't be like that, please... Mum,' said Christine. For the
first time for years she felt genuine tears of regret filling her
eyes. 'I am sorry, really I am... But you know as well as I do
that we drifted apart ages ago, and I wanted to make a fresh
start, that was all.'

'And so you have, haven't you?' Myrtle nodded. 'You've
done very well for yerself, our Chrissie. I'm very impressed

with your in-laws. She's a bit lah-di-dah, mind, but she's a kind-hearted woman, and that Archie's as nice a chap as you could wish to meet. Treated me like royalty, they did. I even stayed the night with them. What d'you think about that, eh? You wouldn't find him, the squire, treating folk as though they're summat the cat's dragged in. He's a proper gentleman.'

'Yes, so he is,' agreed Christine. 'He's been very kind to me.'

'And she hasn't, I take it? Well, if the lady of the manor has been less than welcoming to you it's no more than you deserve. Happen she can see you for what you are; there's no flies on Rebecca Tremaine, I'm sure o' that. Well, she won't be very delighted with you now, will she, trying to pull the wool over their eyes, the way you've done.'

'I wanted them to think that I came from a nice respectable background...'

'Respectable, eh? You know what? I think that woman would have admired you more if you'd told the truth, well, some of it at any rate. Did you really think you could fool her that you were out o' t' top drawer? That's the difference between you and me, Chrissie. I don't pretend to be what I'm not. Oh aye, I've tried to better meself and climb a bit higher up the ladder, y'might say. I like having nice clothes and a nice home to live in, same as other folks have. OK, yer father's been inside a few times, and I've earned me money in a way you don't approve of. But I've never lied about meself. I can't say that folk respect me – happen they don't – but at least I know that some of 'em genuinely like me. Maybe I don't look up to folks as I should, but I don't look down on 'em neither.'

Myrtle was silent for a few moments and so was Christine. She did not know how to answer; all that her mother was saying was painfully true. 'If this marriage of yours is what you want,' she went on, 'then I'm glad for you. If it continues to be what you want, of course. How is your husband going to react when he finds out about the lies you've told? I reckon he must have been a gullible young fool in the first place, not to see what you were up to.'

'He's not a fool!' retorted Christine. 'He's very trusting, though, I must admit.' At least he used to be, she thought; too trusting; but she was not so sure that he was always taken in by her now. 'But I didn't really mean to deceive him, or his parents. We fell in love, Bruce and me; we really love one another. And I wanted it to work out, that's all.'

'And so you tricked him into an early marriage by pretending you were up the duff, is that it?'

'How did you...? I wasn't! All I told you when I came to see you was that we were getting married. If you imagine that Bruce had to marry me, then you're barking up the wrong tree. I've told you; he loves me...'

'Shut up, Chrissie,' said her mother, not unkindly. 'I can read you like a book. Well, he sounds worth hanging on to, this fellow of yours. I just hope it keeps fine for you. Am I going to meet him then? Are you expecting him home soon? I can smell summat good cooking in the oven.'

'It's a chicken,' Christine replied tonelessly. 'He comes home early on a Wednesday.' She had decided that she must bow to the inevitable. Her mother was not showing any sign of departing and she could not throw her bodily out of the door. Even if she did go, there was no way she could stop Bruce from finding out. She might as well be hung for a sheep as a lamb, she supposed... 'Would you like a cup of tea?' she asked meekly. 'I'm sorry; I should have asked you sooner...'

'Better late then never,' said her mother. 'Thank you, Christine; that would be lovely.'

And that was how Bruce found them when he arrived home some twenty minutes later, sipping tea from the best china cups as though they were bosom pals.

'Hello, darling,' he called as he opened the front door. 'Something smells good...' He stopped dead on the threshold of the lounge. 'Oh... I'm sorry; I didn't realise you had company... How do you do?' He held out his hand to the woman who was a stranger to him, but Christine could tell from his half smile, half frown that he was puzzled. 'I don't think I have had the pleasure...' he said.

'Bruce,' said his wife. 'This is my mother...'

'Your...mother?' He let go of the woman's hand, but he was still looking at her intently. 'Yes; I can see... But I don't understand... I thought... You told me...'

'Yes, you thought I was dead, didn't you, lad?' said Myrtle, 'and my husband an' all. Well, as you can see, I'm very much alive and kicking, but my husband died last weekend; killed in a road accident. So I've come to tell our Chrissie. Such a job I had to find her, though, but I got here in the end, thanks to your mam and dad. She'll have a lot of explaining to do, won't she?' She nodded towards Christine. 'But you'd perhaps better leave it till later. I'm sure she had her reasons.'

Christine did not know whether she was being sincere, or just vindictive. What she was most aware of was Bruce's look of horror, not aimed at her mother but at her, Christine.

'Mrs Myerscough...' he began. 'It is Mrs Myerscough, is it?'

'Yes, that's right, but I'd rather you called me Myrtle.'

'Very well then... Myrtle.' He smiled uncertainly at her, then almost collapsed into the opposite armchair. 'I am very sorry to hear about your husband; what a dreadful shock it must have been for you... This has been a great shock to me, as you can see, but at least I am glad to see that my wife...' he gave her a withering glance, 'has made you welcome now. You are, indeed, very welcome here. Have you come all the way from Yorkshire today?'

'Yes, I have... I went up to Middlebeck yesterday, to find out what I could. I knew your father was the squire, you see. Christine told me that bit.'

'Yes, I can imagine...' said Bruce thoughtfully.

'Anyway, your parents very kindly invited me to stay the night; lovely folk they are, Bruce. So I set off again this morning, and I'll get a train back from Lincoln in a little while. There's one in the early evening, I've been told.'

'So how did you get up here?'

'On the bus. I was lucky enough to just catch one. I don't suppose they run very frequently.'

'You're right; they don't. But don't worry... Myrtle; I will run you back to Lincoln in the car. But before that you are going to stay and have a meal with Christine and me. She always cooks something special on a Wednesday, don't you?' Again, the look he gave her held no sympathy or affection. 'There will be plenty to go round; isn't that right, Christine?'

'Yes,' she said briefly. 'I'll go and see to the vegetables, if you will excuse me.'

'Thank you very much, Bruce,' she heard her mother say, as she gladly made her escape. 'You are a very kind young man. I can quite see why Christine was so taken with you...'

<hr>

'But why, Christine, why did you lie to me?' Bruce asked repeatedly that evening when he had returned from taking her mother to Lincoln station. 'It wasn't just a white lie, either. It was downright wicked to tell me that your parents were dead.'

'One thing led to another, Bruce, and when I'd said it I couldn't go back. I didn't want you to think badly of me. I wanted you to think I was from a nice respectable background. I knew your father was somebody important and well thought of...'

'Yes, you knew my father was the squire and so you decided to latch on to me? I can see it all now.'

'No, no... It wasn't like that at all. I loved you, Bruce. I still love you; you know I do...'

'And so you deceived me time and time again? That's a strange kind of love, Christine. Telling me you were only twenty when you were twenty-two, and then pretending you were pregnant... Oh yes, I came to my senses about that little ruse a while ago, and I have a pretty good idea as well about why you are not getting pregnant now. But this lie about your parents is the worst of all. How could you imagine I would think badly of you because of what your parents had done? You are not responsible for their actions. I understand that you had a good upbringing with your grandmother? I'm sure she didn't encourage you to cheat and lie.'

'I wanted something better,' she answered sullenly. 'You have no idea what it was like, living in a hovel like I did, with an outside lav and a zinc bath in the kitchen, and wearing clothes bought from a jumble sale. And I was determined not to go the way my parents had gone to get a bit of extra money; stealing and living off immoral earnings.'

'What you have done is just as bad, Christine; in fact, in my view it is worse. At least your mother has her own code of honesty. She told me something of her life, and that of your father. Not everything, I don't suppose, but I can read between the lines. And I can understand, I suppose, why you broke away from them. But you should have told me, right at the start, at least some of the truth. I feel now that I will never trust you again.'

'Bruce, please don't say that...'

But for the next two days he scarcely spoke to her.

'Your father's funeral is tomorrow,' he said the next day. 'You will be going, I take it? I think you should.'

'Yes,' she replied. 'I almost promised that I would.'

'Then try and keep your word, for once in your life.'

'Would you...would you care to go with me, Bruce?' she asked tentatively.

'No.' His reply was curt. 'You will have to do this on your own.'

He did at least run her to the station on Friday morning; the funeral was to take place in the afternoon. She hoped that by the time she came back on Saturday she might be able to work round to a reconciliation with him.

But when she returned home, after spending Friday night in a small hotel near the centre of Bradford, she found that Bruce was not there. He had left a note...

'*Dear Christine, I think it might be as well if we parted company for a while. As I have told you, I feel that I can no longer trust you. I wonder, in fact, if I ever really knew you at all. I will be staying in staff quarters at the camp. For the time being, you may remain in the house.  Bruce.*'

She screwed up the letter, holding it in a tight ball in her hand. She felt tears of anger and frustration, and of sadness, too, come into her eyes. She had lost him; she supposed she had known all along that Bruce was a man of high principles. Whatever was she going to do now?

# PART TWO

# Chapter Nineteen

**M**aisie took off her tweed coat, unzipped her fleecy-lined boots, then slipped her feet into her court shoes. She was rather fed-up by now with the snow, which had lingered well into February; but it seemed, at last, that a thaw might be setting in. She had slushed her way through icy puddles on the walk from the tram stop and it looked now as though it was beginning to rain. One good downpour might clear it away properly, until the next time. You could never be sure of the weather in Yorkshire or of how long the winter might last.

It had felt odd at first to be back in Leeds, the town of her birth. She had been in two minds at first whether or not to accept Henry Galloway's offer of the managership of the office in the Headrow. But her common sense had told her it was too good an opportunity to miss. She was still a few months away from her twentieth birthday, and here she was, the youngest manageress by far in the string of offices that were springing up in the cities of Yorkshire and Lancashire. In addition to York and Leeds, the first two to be opened, there were now branches of Galaxy Travel in Bradford, Sheffield, Manchester and Liverpool.

She had been determined not to live anywhere near Armley as the place held too many unhappy memories for her. She had been fortunate, however, to find a small two-roomed flat, with a kitchenette and shared bathroom, at Woodhouse, near to the moor and not far from the University buildings. She had been living there ever since she had moved to the Leeds branch the previous year, in the summer of 1949.

'You mean to say you will be living on your own?' her

mother had asked, in some trepidation. 'I'm not sure that that's a good idea, Maisie love.' Her mother had been happy enough – once she had got over the fact that her daughter was leaving home to work in a travel agency in York – about her lodging with Jean Bolton, Jean Mullins as she was now, and her husband in their guest house. Lily remembered Jean – Miss Bolton – as a teacher at Middlebeck School, so she was sure that Maisie could come to no harm there.

'It's an excellent idea, Mum,' Maisie had assured her. She had already procured the flat on a previous visit to Leeds and only told her mother about it when the deal was signed and settled. 'I'm a big girl now, you know, in charge of an office – what do you think about that then? – and it's time I had my own place. It's only small, but in a year or two I might be able to afford somewhere bigger.'

'Don't try to run before you can walk, Maisie,' her mother had said. 'But I must admit that I'm proud of you. I had my doubts when you said you wanted to leave school – well, you know I was dead against it – but I realise now it was probably for the best. I know you're happy and you're doing what you want to do. You must be careful, though, living on your own…'

Looking after herself had not, at first, been as easy as Maisie had blithely imagined, after living in digs with everything provided for her, for two years. Doing her own cooking and cleaning, washing and ironing, had been a rude awakening, although, thankfully, the flat had the luxury of central heating. From an antiquated coke boiler, to be sure, but at least it functioned and was taken care of by the man who owned the property. Her flat was at the very top of the Victorian house, up several flights of steep stairs, but once she had got used to living on her own she had come to enjoy it.

Thank goodness the office was centrally heated, too, she thought, wriggling her cold toes and warming her hands on the radiator. The warmth was just coming through, as she had switched it on when she arrived. She was always the first to arrive, to unlock and to make sure all was ready for the early clients. She had two assistants working with her; Barry, a trainee who was sixteen and had not long left school, and a mature woman, Olwen, who worked part-time, usually in the afternoons. Maisie had felt embarrassed at first, being in charge of someone who was so much older, but Olwen did not mind at all. She was only working for the extra money, she told Maisie, and had no intention of making a career of it. She showed keen interest, though, in her work, as did most people who were employed in travel agencies. It was fascinating work, dealing with far-away places and helping people to plan their journeys and their holidays. Next year, 1951, Henry Galloway planned to introduce European coach tours for the very first time, and he hoped, eventually, to branch out into their own tours incorporating air travel.

He had proved to be a great inspiration to Maisie, ever since she had set foot in his shop on that chilly December day in 1946. She had learned about all aspects of the business, mainly as a booking clerk at first. Then, during the winter months, Trixie Galloway had taken her on the 'recces' that she did to holiday resorts all over Britain; preliminary visits to hotels that had been recommended to them, to see whether they came up to the standard expected by Galaxy Travel and by their clients. Good food, plentiful and well-cooked; comfortable bedrooms with running water; an adequate number of bathrooms and WCs for the use of guests; and a comfortable lounge area where the guests could relax, if they so wished, of an evening. Bournemouth, Torquay, Eastbourne, Brighton, Llandudno…places which had only been a spot on a map to her before, or a coloured picture in a brochure, she had visited all these and more during her time with Galaxy.

They ran conducted tours of the city, too, for visitors who were spending a few days, maybe, in York, and wished to learn more of its history. Maisie had been entranced by the place ever since the school visit, which had been the start of it all. It was a great joy to her to be actually living there; to explore the little cobbled streets and alleyways and discover hidden squares that she had never found before. She never tired of visiting the Minster, and the Castle Museum and Railway Museum, all with their atmosphere of a long bygone age.

When she had been working at Galaxy for over a year she persuaded Henry Galloway to allow her to act as guide on one of the city tours. They ran both coach tours and walking tours, usually employing qualified guides. Maisie, however, having been on a couple of the tours, was convinced that she would be able to do just as well. With Trixie's prompting, he agreed to give her a try. The guides, on the whole, were elderly, and Maisie had her youth and a winning personality on her side. He insisted, though, that Trixie should accompany her at first; after all, she was only eighteen. But Trixie soon realised that she was very competent and sure of herself. Besides, she looked several years older than she really was, well able to deal with clients' questions or with any 'awkward customers'. There were very few of those, though, all the tourists seeming happy to lap up the information handed out to them.

The city coach tour was easy. The driver knew his way around and Maisie, standing at the front with her microphone, pointed out the various places of interest. 'Here, ladies and gentlemen, we can see Micklegate Bar, and this is where, in olden times, they used to hang the heads of traitors... The bars are really fortified gateways into the city, as you can see, but in York the gates are called bars, and so we have Fishergate Bar, Monk Bar, Bootham Bar... And the streets, contrarily, are known as gates, and so we have Stonegate, Ousegate, Coppergate...

'And now we are crossing the River Foss. This was dammed by William the Conqueror – I mean to say that he built a dam, not that he condemned it...' and she would wait for the polite laughter, '...to protect his castle, provide power for his corn mills, and to create a fishpond for his personal use...

'And over that wall, if you look quickly to your left now, you can see the gravestone of Dick Turpin...and here, on Petergate, is the house in which Guy Fawkes, York's most infamous citizen, was born...'

Such titbits of information, the more ghoulish the better, she found pleased the customers and as time went by she grew more confident and revised her spiel accordingly.

Walking tours could be a little more difficult as some people – usually the middle-aged women – tended to loiter behind, looking in shop windows. Maisie led them through the old streets of York; the Shambles, originally known as Fleshammels, the street of the butchers; Swinegate, once called Swynegaill, dating from the thirteenth century when pigs were kept there; Stonegate, Petergate, Deangate... ending at the Minster with a tour of the 'largest medieval Gothic church in England'. She held a small Union Jack flag aloft as she led the way through the streets, and then around the hallowed aisles and transepts of the church, which her little crowd was meant to follow. She was relieved that she had never yet lost anyone.

Her work was flexible and that was what made it the more interesting. And so she was delighted when, soon after her nineteenth birthday, Henry asked her if she would act as courier on a five-day coach tour to London. The regular courier had fallen ill and Henry knew that she would be a very capable replacement. Part-time staff would be only too pleased to take over her office work in her absence. There was never any shortage of these as Galaxy had earned a reputation for fairness and reasonable wages.

It was great, she had enthused to Henry after her return, and she had enjoyed every minute of it. She had stayed with the clients at a small hotel in South Kensington, and as the driver knew the city like the back of his hand, it had all been plain-sailing. Please could she go again, she begged, if a stand-in was required? She did two more tours that year, one more to London and another to Edinburgh. This was foreign territory to her, but she swotted up the facts before she went.

And the capital city of Scotland proved to be another fascinating old city.

Galaxy was unusual in that they provided couriers as well as drivers on some – though by no means all – of their tours, especially those which were advertised as 'cultural tours'. It was Henry's view that drivers had enough to do to keep their eyes on the road without, at the same time, trying to give a running commentary. This was common practice with many firms, but Henry had been determined never to cut corners at the expense of the customers' safety.

He reminded Maisie, however, that she had been employed first and foremost as a booking clerk, at which job she was proving most efficient. No more tours came her way for the rest of the year, apart from the York excursions which she did once a week. And then, six months ago, had come her transfer to Leeds...

She knew that she had to buckle down and concentrate on her position as manageress. She could not leave her post to go swanning off to the other end of the country. Maybe one day...she often mused. They had recently started booking air tickets for independent travellers, to Paris, Rome, Amsterdam, Athens, even New York...although they did not, as yet, organise air tours on behalf of Galaxy Travel. Maisie made up her mind that one day she, too, would visit such places. In the meantime she would do the very best job she could in the place where Fate had placed her.

Middlebeck seemed not only miles but light years away at times; although when she went home, every six weeks or so, she soon picked up the threads again with her friends and family. Audrey was in her second year at a college not far from Leeds and would leave there in the summer of this year. She hoped to obtain a teaching appointment somewhere in the north of Yorkshire. Audrey was still very much a home bird and Maisie wondered if she had ever really settled down to college life; she certainly did not say very much about it. Audrey was still not inclined to give much away about her private life and thoughts. Maisie met her now and again in the city centre, to look at the shops or to enjoy a snack together, and their friendship was still as firm as ever.

Doris was married to Ivan Delinsky, the Polish farmer. Maisie and Audrey had been bridesmaids in the summer of 1948, when Doris was a young bride of eighteen. The couple now had a nine-month-old baby boy and lived in their own little cottage, near to Nixon' farm where Ivan still worked. The farm was now a family concern, owned and worked by Ada, Joe and his wife, Irene, who also lived there; and Doris and Ivan.

Ted, also, was married to Celia, and they were expecting their first child in the summer... Maisie held no hard feelings towards the pair. She knew that Celia was far more suitable as a wife for Ted than she would ever have been. They, too, had their own little place, and Ted worked the remainder of the land which still belonged to Archie Tremaine. There was talk of Ted buying it eventually, as Archie was set on following a political career.

He had thrown in his weight – and considerable funding – with the local Labour party, and had been selected as the candidate for the forthcoming election; which would take place very soon, towards the end of the present month, on the twenty-third of February. The last time Maisie had visited Middlebeck there had been posters a-plenty in evidence. 'Vote for Archie Tremaine, your local Labour candidate', decorated in the party colours of red and yellow. The title 'squire' was not used at all. Archie was now, 'One of us; a man of the people'. It did not mean much to Maisie as she would not be able to vote until the next but one election, by which time she would have reached the age of majority, twenty-one. She had not really sorted out her own political persuasion, but she hoped that Archie, for his own sake, would be successful.

And what of her love life? Thinking of Archie led her thoughts automatically to Bruce. She knew that his marriage had come to grief, but that news, strangely enough, had not caused her to indulge in wild imaginings. She had scarcely seen him over the past few years. Their visits home had rarely coincided, and when they did they had not sought each other's company, except to say hello and exchange a few pleasantries. Her infatuation with Bruce, which she had convinced herself it must have been, now seemed 'long ago and far away', as the words of the song said.

'Have you got a boyfriend down there in York? (or Leeds),' people asked her whenever she went back home. Or 'Are you courting yet?'

'No...' she would answer. 'I'm far too busy...'

She had been out with one or two young men. Olwen's son, Mike, had taken her to the pictures recently and was anxious for another date. He was nice enough, but she was not sure about him. And in York she had been friendly with one of the tour drivers, until she had discovered he was married; and she had had a 'fling' with another booking clerk who had joined the staff for six months. But there had been nobody so far who had ignited a spark of anything but friendship and liking; certainly not love or the feeling that, 'This is right; he is the one for me.'

She was young and happy and fulfilled in her work and, as her mother kept reminding her, she had 'all the time in the world to think about marriage.' Her mother, in fact, was very proud of Maisie's achievements. She had not reached the scholastic heights that she could have attained, but she had worked hard and made great progress in the career she had chosen, and that was enough for Lily, and enough for Maisie, too, at the moment.

⬤

By mid-morning a pale sun had followed the early rain and the last vestiges of grubby slush and snow were fast melting in the gutters. It had been a quiet sort of morning in the office with no more than a handful of customers. Olwen had gone through to the little kitchen at the back to make the coffee, and Barry was busy sorting out a pile of invoices, so it was Maisie's turn to attend to the couple who had just entered the shop.

The woman was quite young and very smartly dressed; what Maisie still in her own mind termed as 'posh', a favourite word from her childhood when the difference between herself and 'posh' folk had been very marked. She was wearing a fur coat – rich brown fur, though of which kind Maisie was not sure; she was not well up in furs, but she did not think it was mink – and a small red hat with a long feather sticking through it. Her long and slender legs were clothed in the sheerest nylon stockings, and her red leather shoes had pointed toes and ridiculously high heels for such inclement weather. Or maybe they had parked their Rolls or some such car not far away, Maisie wondered?

As for the man, he looked as though he might be what was known as a 'spiv'. His grey pin-striped suit, reminiscent of the old demob suits, but of a much better quality, had a long narrow-lapelled jacket with broad shoulders, after the American style. He wore a trilby hat perched on the back of his longish dark hair. All this Maisie noticed in the first minute or so as the couple approached her. Then she looked at the woman's face, at her golden-blonde hair, beautifully coiffured, her red lips – painted, but not gaudily – and her silvery-grey eyes. It was the eyes that Maisie remembered...

She and the woman both spoke at the same time.

'Christine! It is Christine, isn't it?'

'Maisie...well, fancy that! You are Maisie, aren't you?'

'Yes, I'm Maisie,' she replied, smiling a little uncertainly at the woman she had thought of, at one time, as her adversary. But there was no look of hostility there now in Christine's lovely grey eyes, only friendliness and surprise. 'It's...it's good to see you again, Christine. It's been a long time...'

'It certainly has. It must be – what? – about five years since I last saw you. But you haven't changed very much; you're a lot more grown-up, of course.' She turned to the man at her side. 'Darling, this is Maisie... Jackson, isn't it? She used to live up in Middlebeck, and what a surprise it is to find her down here. Maisie, this is Clive; Clive Broadbent, my fiancé.'

Maisie shook hands with the man and they exchanged 'How do you dos?' He was quite good-looking, she thought, in a flashy sort of way, but considerably older than Christine, she guessed...or Bruce, of course. His close-set eyes reminded her of Stewart Granger.

'So...what are you doing here, Maisie?' asked Christine. 'Working, obviously, I can see that... Have you been down here long?'

'I've been in Leeds for six months,' replied Maisie. 'Before that I was in York, working for Galaxy Travel. Actually... I'm the manageress here,' she added, unable to hide the touch of pride in her voice.

'Are you, by Jove? Good for you,' said the man, Clive. And Christine, too, to give her her due, did not stint with her praise.

'Well done, Maisie! That's a great achievement, isn't it, at your age? You can't be more than... How old are you now? Let me see; eighteen, nineteen...?'

'I'll be twenty in May,' said Maisie, a little abruptly. Was there a slightly patronising tone in Christine's words? Or maybe she had just imagined it... 'So, what can I do for you, Christine? Did you want to make a booking, or is it just an enquiry?' she asked in a businesslike voice. Bruce had not been mentioned, and she saw no reason to bring him into the conversation if Christine did not do so. She surreptitiously glanced at the young woman's left hand when she removed her gloves. Her ring was a huge solitaire diamond; much grander, no doubt, than the ring that Bruce had once bought for her. Maisie had never seen that one, though; she had not wanted to know.

It was Clive Broadbent who answered. 'Yes, we would like to book train tickets to London, if you please, Miss Jackson. We could go to the station, of course, but I happened to notice when I was passing the other day that there was a travel agency here.'

'We haven't been living in Leeds very long, you see,'

Christine added. 'Only a couple of weeks, which is why we haven't seen this place before. We have just moved into a new house at Headingley, haven't we, darling? And Clive has recently opened a new warehouse here. He's in the retail business, you see...'

Maisie nodded. She had guessed at something of the sort, but she mustn't misjudge the fellow; his dealings were probably all above board.

'And Christine and I are going to tie the knot,' said Clive, grinning at his fiancée. 'Aren't we, darling? I'm going to make an honest woman of her. The last Saturday in February, that's the time; Leeds Register Office, that's the place... And then we're off to London for our honeymoon.' They looked at one another lovingly.

It was as though there had never been any Bruce, thought Maisie. But she was startled to realise that that fact meant very little to her any more.

'Very nice, congratulations,' she said. 'Of course I can book the tickets for you. What time of day do you want to travel...?' She checked the times and the dates and issued the appropriate travel vouchers. Clive paid with a crisp five pound note.

'How about your accommodation?' she enquired. 'Or has that already been arranged?'

'Yes, it has for sure,' replied Clive. 'We've booked in at the Strand Palace. Honeymoon suite, no less, for five nights. We always stay there when we go to the city, don't we, darling?'

'Yes...' she replied, smiling coyly at him, 'but this will be the first time in the honeymoon suite.'

'We will know where to come now for any travel arrangements we need,' said Clive. 'Thank you, my dear, for all your help.'

'Yes, thank you,' added Christine. 'And all the best for the future, Maisie dear. I'm sure you will continue to do well... You found that Middlebeck was too small for you, did you? There's not much scope there, is there, for a bright girl like you?'

Maisie felt a little miffed. 'I didn't exactly outgrow it,' she answered, 'if that's what you mean, but this opportunity came along and so I took it. But Middlebeck is still home to me.'

'Yes, of course; there's no place like home, is there?' Christine's smile was friendly enough, but Maisie was not sure whether or not it was wholly sincere. Was there still a trace of resentment there, she wondered, a harking back to the rivalry of a few years ago? She decided it would be best to bring matters to a close. She nodded.

'As you say; there's no place like home... Well, it's been nice to see you again.' She held out her hand. 'Goodbye, Christine... Mr Broadbent; and I wish you both every happiness.' They all shook hands cordially and the couple left the shop.

Maisie watched them as they closed the door behind them and then walked up the street arm in arm, their heads close together. She gave a deep sigh, shaking her head in a bewildered manner.

'What's up, Maisie?' asked Olwen, as she entered with a laden tray. 'You look as though you've seen a ghost.'

Maisie smiled wryly. 'You could say that; a ghost from the recent past, but this one's still very much alive.'

'She's quite a looker, that woman,' observed Barry. 'Friend of yours, is she?'

'No... I never considered her to be a friend,' replied Maisie. 'More of an enemy,' she added, but under her breath and not intended to be heard. 'I must say, though, that the years seem to have improved her, in disposition, I mean. She was always good-looking, as you say, Barry.'

'That fellow she was with looked like one o' them spivs,' he remarked. 'Her husband, is he?'

'No; her fiancé,' she replied. Clearly he had formed the same impression of Clive Broadbent as she had. 'Never mind them now, they're not important.' She doubted that she would see them in the shop again, in spite of what the man had said. 'Come on now, it's coffee time. Ooh, my favourite choccy biccies! Thanks, Olwen.'

'I won't be working this afternoon,' Olwen reminded her.

'I'm doing the morning instead because I've got a dental appointment this afternoon.'

'Yes, that's OK; I've remembered,' Maisie nodded.

'But our Michael said he might pop in and see you this afternoon.' Olwen gave her a meaningful glance. 'If you don't want to see him again, Maisie, then tell him, please, would you...?' She did not sound annoyed, just concerned. 'He's a sensitive sort of lad, and I'd rather he was disappointed sooner, rather than later, if you see what I mean.'

'Yes, I do,' replied Maisie thoughtfully. 'Don't worry, Olwen; I won't play fast and loose with him... It's just that I don't feel ready yet for a serious relationship.' And Mike Palmer, she could tell, might soon start to get too intense.

'No, neither is our Michael, but he does take himself so seriously. You don't mind me mentioning it, do you, Maisie?'

'No, of course I don't. I like Mike very much. I will go out with him again, but I'll try to make him see that I just want to be friends, and nothing else.'

Olwen nodded. 'Yes, it'd be best if he could see it that way. He still has a long way to go. Another year and a half at university, and he hasn't decided yet what he wants to do afterwards.'

Mike Palmer, Olwen's only son – only child, in fact – was in his second year at Leeds University. He had opted to live at home rather than go to a college in another part of the country, which would have meant staying in digs or a hall of residence. Maisie thought it was a mistake and that he needed to break away from the apron strings.

When he came into the office later in the day she agreed to go with him to see the big movie, *Samson and Delilah*, which was showing at the Odeon. And then, perhaps, they could have a bite to eat later? he suggested tentatively. With his college scarf of maroon, green and white stripes slung round his neck and his short sandy hair standing on end, he looked younger than his twenty years. She was touched by the look of delight in his limpid brown eyes when she said yes to his plans. Oh dear, she thought; as his mother had warned her, she must be careful not to hurt him.

Thoughts of Christine – and of Bruce – kept invading her mind for the rest of the day. She tried to remember what she had been told about their marriage. Rebecca Tremaine had been rather guarded about the whole affair, but Maisie had gathered that Christine's mother, who they had all believed to be dead, had surfaced, searching for her daughter. Christine, it appeared, was not all she had seemed to be. Maisie had felt from the start that there was something odd about the girl, although she had to admit that her judgment had been biased by her feelings for Bruce. Her present fiancé seemed much more suited to her, Maisie mused.

But what of Bruce? Where was he living now and what was he doing? Was he still in the RAF? Since she had left Middlebeck she had not bothered to enquire. She did not know his whereabouts, but, although she might try to deny it, it would not be true to say that she did not care.

# Chapter Twenty

Maisie had arranged to meet Audrey on the first Saturday afternoon in March. They usually met in the arcade near to Schofield's department store before going up to the café on the third floor to have a cup of tea or coffee and a toasted teacake. She was surprised, therefore, to receive a phone call from her friend at the office on Friday morning. She sounded anxious and in a hurry.

'Maisie...' she began breathlessly, 'can you meet me this afternoon instead of tomorrow? Please, it's very important. I've got something to tell you...'

'Er...yes, I think so,' replied Maisie. 'Yes – of course I can.' She was, of course, in charge of the office – the 'boss' – which she tended to forget. 'Whatever's the matter, Audrey? You don't sound like yourself at all.'

'I can't tell you now. And I've got to go; I'm due at a lecture. I'll see you later then... You will come, won't you? Three o'clock at the usual place.'

'Yes, don't worry; I'll be there,' she promised.

She arranged for Olwen and Barry to look after the office, saying that she would not be long; not much more than an hour, she hoped, although Audrey did sound to be in quite a state about something or other.

When she met her friend, who was already waiting at the arcade, she was surprised to see that she was not wearing her college scarf. University and training college students, of whom there were many in and around the city of Leeds, were proud of their colleges' colours and usually took every opportunity to display them. Audrey was dressed in a smart tweed coat – she was always smartly turned out – and she was carrying a small weekend bag as well as her shoulder bag.

'Oh, Maisie... I'm so glad to see you.' She flung her arms around her friend, and Maisie was dismayed to see the glint of a tear in the corner of one eye.

'So am I,' she replied, giving her a hug. 'Come on, let's get inside out of the cold.'

They passed through the beauty department with its fragrant aroma of perfume and powder, and the haberdashery department, and went upstairs to the café. They managed to find an empty table for two, although the place was fast filling up with shoppers.

'This is on me,' said Maisie. 'Coffee and a toasted teacake; OK?'

'Yes...anything,' replied Audrey, but she sounded quite disinterested.

'All right; I'll go and order, then you can tell me what's the matter.' Maisie went to the counter, then returned to find her friend staring down at her hands, agitatedly plucking at the loose skin around her nails; a habit she had had since childhood, especially in troubled times.

'Now, what is it?' asked Maisie, getting hold of her hands to stop the frenzied plucking. 'You've got me worried... Are you going somewhere?' She glanced at the travel bag at the side of Audrey's chair.

'To stay with you tonight...if you'll have me,' said Audrey, looking at her with frightened eyes. 'I've told them at college that I've got a dental appointment this afternoon, and that afterwards I'm going home for the weekend. We're allowed two weekends a term. But it's not true, none of it...' She stared at Maisie, her blue eyes brimming now with tears. 'Maisie... I'm pregnant. I'm...I'm going to have a baby.' Her shoulders began to shake, but she was crying silently and her voice, to Maisie's relief, was the merest whisper. The next table was well within hearing distance, but the two middle-aged ladies seemed very busy with their own concerns and were chattering away twenty to the dozen.

Maisie could not take it in at first. 'You're...pregnant?' she whispered. 'Oh, Audrey, are you sure?' Her friend was so naive, or so Maisie believed, that she may well have not known, exactly, what led to pregnancy.

'Of course I'm sure. I've missed two periods now,' said Audrey. She took a deep breath, seeming to take more control of herself. 'But I'm not going to have it. I've arranged to have an abortion...and I want you to help me.'

'What!' Maisie's cry was much louder than she intended and the women on the nearby table looked across at her. 'But...but you can't!' She leaned over the table. 'You're probably just late...but even if you are...having a baby... you can't do that, what you've just said.'

Audrey did not answer, but kept looking at her, quite impassively now. The waitress, arriving with the coffee and teacakes, halted any conversation for a few moments. Then Maisie said, 'Come on, tell me about it...if you want to, of course. Who was it...and how did it happen?'

Audrey gave a weak smile then. 'In the usual way, I suppose. It doesn't really matter who it is, because he will never know about it; but I suppose I'd better tell you... You remember I told you about that girl I know at college? Jennifer, the one that lives near Roundhay Park; she's not a close friend, but we're in the same division sometimes for lectures. Well, it's her brother... But he's engaged to be married... Oh, Maisie, it's such a mess!'

A mess? It was a catastrophe, thought Maisie. And that it should happen to Audrey, of all people. Maisie felt as though she was in a dream, or a nightmare to be more correct. Innocent little Audrey? She just couldn't take it in. 'Go on; tell me about it,' she said.

'There was a party at Jennifer's home, just after New Year. They're quite well off, they've got a big house near the park. She invited quite a few of us, and I went back a day early, you see, to go to this party, and I stayed the night there. And her brother and me...well we got quite friendly. And I suppose I had too much to drink, and his girlfriend wasn't there, she'd got the flu and...well, it sort of just happened. I don't suppose he's thought any more about it...'

'But what about their parents? Where were they while all this was going on?'

'Oh, they'd gone away for a long weekend. Jennifer and Joel – that's his name – they seem to do pretty much as they like.'

'And what about Jennifer? Have you told her about it?'

'No, of course I haven't. I've told you, she's not a close friend. Nobody knows but you and...well, there's another girl at college that I told, to find out about what I could do. I was desperate, you see, and she's generally reckoned to be – well, you know – quite genned up about...about contraceptives and abortions and things.'

Maisie blinked. She couldn't believe what she was hearing. She sighed. 'Eat your teacake,' she said. 'It's getting cold...'

Audrey cut her teacake in half and started to eat it and drink her coffee. They both munched in silence for a few moments, and Maisie was surprised to see that her friend appeared to be enjoying it. She guessed she had not had anything to eat since breakfast time. As for herself, she chewed automatically, not tasting what she was eating, her mind full of the awful thing Audrey had said she was going to do. Surely she couldn't mean it? Finally she could contain herself no longer.

'Audrey...' she said, leaning towards her and whispering urgently. 'You can't do it. It would be very wrong, and dangerous, too.'

'But I've no choice, have I?' Audrey looked at her blankly.

'Of course you have. Girls have got pregnant before. You're not the first and you certainly won't be the last.'

'Not a daughter of the rector, though... I can't tell them, Maisie. How can I? They'd be so ashamed of me. I'm telling you, it's the only way.'

Maisie shook her head despairingly. 'You say...you've arranged it? What, exactly, have you done?'

'It's a place near Woodhouse Moor, a bit further on from where you live.'

'What do you mean, "a place"? A back street abortionist?'

'No, no; it's not like that at all! It's a nice house, a detached one with a garden, and it's quite posh inside. And the woman who saw me was wearing a white coat and everything. She was very nice and helpful and she said they could take me tomorrow. Ten o'clock, that's when I've got to be there. So I wondered if I could stay with you tonight? And then...would you come with me in the morning... please, Maisie.'

Audrey's eyes were filling up with tears again and her pleading expression tore at Maisie's heartstrings. 'But it's wrong!' she said. 'You must know it is. It's illegal, and they could be prosecuted for doing something like that. Is he a doctor...he or she or whoever?'

'Yes, I think so. I think it's the woman's husband, the one who saw me. I've told you, she was very kind and friendly and she said I'd nothing to worry about.'

No doubt she did, thought Maisie, feeling sick with fear and anxiety and wondering what on earth she could do to stop her friend from taking this disastrous step. 'And...what would it cost? Did she say?'

'Yes...ten pounds,' said Audrey. 'I've already paid. She said that was what clients usually did. So I can't back out of it now, Maisie. I've got to go through with it, but I can't go on my own. Please say you'll come with me... You're my best friend, aren't you, and I couldn't possibly ask anybody else.'

Ten pounds... That was more than a fortnight's wages to Maisie, and Audrey was only a student. But she supposed that Patience and Luke did not leave her short of money. They would be horrified, though, if they knew what it was being used for. She shook her head again. 'It's a lot of money,' she said, 'but it's not the money that's important, is it? It's you that matters. Oh, come on, Audrey; just think sensibly about it. It's not the end of the world. Luke and Patience are not ogres. They're understanding people and...'

'No, no, no!' cried Audrey. 'I can't possibly tell them.' Luckily the two women at the next table had gone and there was something of a lull in the restaurant. 'This time tomorrow it will all be over. I keep telling myself that, but I can't go through with it on my own. Please, Maisie…' She looked at her so imploringly that Maisie felt herself beginning to relent, but only a little.

'Well… I'll see,' she said. 'But you can certainly stay with me tonight.' She hoped that by the next morning she might have persuaded her friend to change her mind. She smiled sympathetically at her. 'I do understand, honestly, how you feel. And it's such hard luck, isn't it, to get caught the first time? But it seems to happen like that with a lot of girls.'

Audrey hung her head. She was silent for a moment. Then, 'It wasn't the first time,' she said, so quietly that Maisie could scarcely hear her.

'What did you say?' she asked. 'For a moment I thought you said it wasn't the first time…'

Audrey nodded. 'Yes, that's what I said…' She looked up at her friend. 'I can't lie to you, Maisie. It wasn't the first time I'd…done that. You remember when I went out with Brian? We'd been going out together for a long time and… well, you know how it is, don't you? You must do…'

Maisie looked at her in horror. 'You what? Indeed I don't know how it is! Do you mean to say that you and Brian Milner, that you…?'

'Yes, we did,' said Audrey, in quite a matter-of-fact voice. 'Oh, come on, Maisie. Don't pretend to me that you're all that innocent. You went out with Ted Nixon, and he was years older than you, and I know he was dead keen on you…'

'Yes, maybe he was, but we never did…that!'

Audrey frowned, looking at her in some surprise. 'And you told me you went out with that coach driver, and he was married…'

'Yes, and that was when I told him, No, ta very much. I don't go out with married men…'

'And there was that fellow who came to work in your office in York. You went out with him for quite a while; I remember you telling me that you had quite a fling.'

'Yes, Colin... But when I said we'd had a fling I only meant that he used to take me to pubs and nightclubs and places like that. Not that we'd...' She shook her head. 'I was an innocent little girl from the country when I first went to live in York, you know. I'd never set foot inside a pub – I wasn't old enough anyway – and doing that sort of thing was a real eye-opener to me. But I have never done...that, not with Ted or Colin or anyone.'

'You mean to say that you're still...a virgin?'

'Good God, yes!' exclaimed Maisie, forgetting herself for a moment. 'I mean...yes, of course I am. And I will be until I meet the person that I know is right for me. And even then, we've always been told that we should wait until after we're married, haven't we?'

'You're shocked at me, aren't you?' said Audrey, looking soulfully at her friend. 'Honestly, Maisie, I really thought... You're so grown up in your ways. You were always so much more mature than me... I'm sorry if I've shocked you.'

'No... I'm not really shocked,' she replied. 'Just surprised, that's all.' But she was shocked; she had found herself deeply shocked by Audrey's revelations. This was the girl she had befriended and taken care of when they had been sent to Middlebeck as evacuees; the girl who had always seemed so shy and insecure, and so prim and proper too, at times. She remembered how she had raised her eyebrows at Maisie's dress with the bare shoulders. And above all, Audrey was the daughter of the rector...

'I'm surprised at Brian Milner,' she said. She decided to give her friend the benefit of the doubt and to believe that Brian had led her on. 'I always thought you were just good friends; well, possibly a little bit more than that, but you decided to end it, didn't you, when he went away to university?'

'It was getting too intense,' replied Audrey. 'I was only sixteen, and I knew I shouldn't have...you know. But I really liked Brian a lot. And since then there's been nobody, honestly, until I got involved with Joel.'

'It's a wonder you didn't get caught before,' observed Maisie, a little self-righteously, because she couldn't help how she was feeling. 'With Brian...'

'Oh no, he was careful,' said Audrey. 'He took precautions...you know.'

Maisie nodded. She didn't know, but she guessed what Audrey meant. She was being made, regrettably, to change her view of her friend, and she didn't like it. But Audrey, come what may, was still her best friend and she knew that she had to help her now. But she prayed, how she prayed deep inside her, that she would change her mind about what she intended to do tomorrow.

'We'll go when you're ready,' she said. 'I promised I wouldn't be too long away from the office. It sometimes gets quite busy on a Friday afternoon, and I'm supposed to be in charge.'

'Yes, I'm ready,' said Audrey. 'What shall I do? Shall I meet you when you've finished for the day? I can have a look round the shops, not that I feel much like shopping at the moment.'

'No,' said Maisie. 'I'll give you the key, then you can get the tram back to my place and make yourself at home. I'll be back as soon as I can; OK?'

'Yes, thank you... You're being very kind to me,' Audrey said as they made their way down to the ground floor. 'What about tomorrow? Will you be able to take the time off?' She looked pleadingly at Maisie once again. 'I do need you to be with me...'

'Mmm...yes,' she replied. 'We close at twelve o'clock on Saturdays, so I'm sure Olwen and Barry can manage on their own for half a day. Don't worry; I'll be there for you, Audrey...' Her friend would need her to be there to give her moral support, whatever might happen.

Olwen and Barry were very willing to run the office on their own for the three hours on Saturday morning. Barry, as the other full-time member of staff, had a key of his own and Maisie knew he would feel quite important being left in charge. He was shaping up well in all aspects of the work, but this would be the first time he had opened up the shop. She explained to them that her friend was quite poorly and was relying on her, Maisie, to go with her for an urgent doctor's appointment. She did not go into details and they did not enquire.

She arrived home to find Audrey ensconced in an armchair reading a magazine; she appeared to be much calmer. At least she had set the table for tea – she had visited Maisie several times and knew where everything lived – but it was up to Maisie to set to and make a meal. Bacon and eggs with fried bread would be quick and tasty, she decided, and she was pleased to see that Audrey ate it with enjoyment. Maisie guessed she was trying – and succeeding, it seemed – to put tomorrow's ordeal out of her mind; as though, having unburdened herself to her friend, she was now able to turn her thoughts to other matters.

She did not mention the thing that was uppermost in her mind, and surely must be in Audrey's too, although she was managing to conceal it very well. But she knew that before they retired to bed she would have to broach the subject again. They talked instead about events that were taking place back home in Middlebeck…

At the end of the previous month Archie Tremaine had been elected as the Labour Member of Parliament for the district of Middlebeck and Lowerbeck, unseating the Conservative businessman who had held the seat for many years. Not, however, by a tremendous majority. The election, throughout the country, had been something of a cliff-hanger, and although a Labour government had been returned to power, with Clement Attlee still at the helm, it was with a considerably reduced majority.

'My father said that Archie was very lucky really to be elected,' observed Audrey. 'Apparently it was a close run thing.'

'Still, he got there, didn't he?' said Maisie. 'I'm glad for his sake, and I'm sure he'll do a lot of good work for the constituency. He will have to live down in London though, won't he, for a lot of the time? I wonder if Rebecca will go with him? It will be a big change for them.'

'Have you heard anything of Bruce lately?' asked Audrey. 'I heard that he was thinking of leaving the RAF.'

'No, I haven't heard anything,' replied Maisie. 'Not a dicky-bird... Oh, that reminds me, I must tell you something. You'll never guess who came into the shop a couple of weeks ago...'

'Go on, who was it? Not Bruce, obviously.'

'No... Christine with her new chap! They'll be married by now...' She told Audrey the tale of her encounter with them, with full details of what Christine had been wearing, and her flashy engagement ring. 'She was as nice as pie, actually; I was really surprised.'

'So Bruce is divorced now. He's footloose and fancy free again...' said Audrey, looking keenly at her friend.

'Obviously...' said Maisie, but she did not rise to the bait.

Later that evening they went on to talk about the plans that were afoot at the High Street premises owned by Arthur and Lily Rawcliffe. Lily had come into full ownership of the draper's shop early in the previous year, when Cyril and Eliza Jenner had both died quite suddenly. Cyril had succumbed to the flu in the January, and Eliza had died only two months later. Of a broken heart, folks said; at all events she had lost her will to live. They had been a devoted couple and life without Cyril must have seemed meaningless to her.

Lily was devastated by her death as she had been a very good friend over the years, and the fact that she was now the owner of quite a substantial property had meant very little to her at first.

The drapery business had not been doing too well. It had always been a somewhat old-fashioned shop, especially when Eliza Jenner had been in charge. Since Lily had taken over the management she had tried to bring their merchandise more up to date, but she had found as the years went by that she was up against more and more competition.

Since the end of the war there were more ready-made clothes on the market; synthetic fibres were all the rage and garments could be bought reasonably cheaply. She realised that many of her customers were now shopping further afield, making expeditions to the larger towns and cities now that goods were more readily available.

On the other hand, Arthur's bakery business next door had been going from strength to strength, as had his outside catering business. The same idea had occurred, it seemed, to both Lily and Arthur at the same time; but it was Lily who first made the suggestion that she might close the draper's shop, and that the premises could be made into a restaurant... Only to find that Arthur had been considering exactly the same thing for quite a while, but had not wanted Lily to think that he was seeking to take over her own little enterprise.

Consequently, they had contacted a firm of builders, and work was now going on apace to convert the draper's shop into a tearoom.

'Well, rather more than a tearoom,' Maisie told Audrey now. 'It'll be a restaurant really, but only quite a small one because it's not a very big area. Mum thinks it'll be popular with shoppers who want to pop in for morning coffee or afternoon tea, but Arthur is rather more ambitious. He want to do lunches, and evening dinners sometimes, if they're booked in advance. He's got all sorts of plans, but they'll just have to see how it goes.'

'So when is it going to open?'

'In a few weeks' time, all being well. Arthur wants to open in time for Easter, certainly. They're trying to think of a name for it at the moment. "Rawcliffe's Restaurant" is OK, but I think they need something a bit more catchy...'

Maisie noticed that her friend was not listening as intently now. She had finished her drink of chocolate and was staring down at her beaker, twisting it round and round in her hands. It was ten o'clock, and if she was going to raise the dreaded subject again that night, Maisie decided she had better do it at once.

'Audrey...' she began. 'How are you feeling now? I mean...are you still in the same mind, or are you beginning to realise that it would be a foolish thing to do? Not only foolish, but very wrong as well. You must realise that...'

'I do, I do!' Audrey turned an anguished face towards her. It was clear she was still in a state of great torment. 'I know all about that; I know it's wrong. But I'd rather go through with it than have to tell my parents what I've done; that I'm pregnant... I couldn't tell them, never, not in a thousand years. I couldn't do that to them. They've been such wonderful parents to me, Luke and Patience, since my real mum and dad died. In fact, they are my real parents now, and I just can't hurt them like that, Maisie... Don't you understand?'

'I think so,' said Maisie. She went over to her and took the mug out of her hands, then put an arm around her. 'I'll be there for you, Audrey, I promise... Now, I think it would be a good idea if we went to bed, don't you? You must have my bed – no, I won't listen to any arguments – and I'll sleep on the settee. And you're going to take some aspirins to help you to get to sleep...'

'Come on now, there's a good girl,' she said, returning with the pill bottle and a glass of water. 'In fact I'm going to take two myself to settle me down. Off you go now and use the bathroom; it's free at the moment, and the woman on the next floor sometimes takes ages. I've put a hot water bottle in your bed. See you in the morning...'

Audrey clung to her for a moment, then silently went off to prepare herself for bed. Maisie knew it was doubtful that her friend would sleep very much. She, too, lay awake for a long time, despite the dose of aspirin, but eventually her agitated thoughts diminished and she slept until the alarm clock wakened her.

———

She decided that there was no point in harrassing her friend any more. She had done all that she could. Maybe a night's rest – if Audrey had been able to sleep – would have helped her to view things differently. At all events, it was up to Audrey now to make the decision.

It soon became clear that there would be no moving her from her resolve to go through with her plan. Audrey would drink only a cup of tea, with nothing to eat. She had been told to make sure she had an empty stomach. She seemed calm; too calm. At just after half past nine they boarded the tram and travelled the two stops to the other end of Woodhouse Moor, then walked to the house that Audrey had visited before.

Maisie was feeling sick at heart, and sick in her stomach too, so she could imagine that Audrey must be feeling ten times worse. She was slightly encouraged, however, when she saw the house. It was, as her friend had said, quite posh, both inside and out; and clean, too, which was far more important.

The door was opened by a woman in a white coat, the same woman, Maisie guessed, that Audrey had met previously. 'Ah yes, Miss Dennison,' she said. 'We were expecting you.'

Maisie was a little surprised to hear Audrey give the name that she had had as a child, before she had been adopted by the Fairchilds; presumably because she wanted to safeguard her identity and, maybe, not to connect the name of the rector and his wife with the sordid operation she was about to undergo.

'And this is…?' The woman looked enquiringly at Maisie.

'I'm Audrey's friend,' she said unsmilingly. 'I'll wait for her, if that's all right with you?'

'Yes, quite all right.' The woman gave a nod and the briefest of smiles. 'Come along in…' She ushered them into a room at the front of the house which was furnished quite comfortably, but not lavishly, with easy chairs and low tables on which were copies of magazines: *Ideal Home*, *Yorkshire Life*, and *Amateur Gardening* amongst others. 'I'll leave you here for a little while, then I'll come and tell you when my husband is ready for you, Miss Dennison.'

They both sat down uncomfortably on the edge of the armchair seats. There was an eloquent silence for a few moments, and then Maisie spoke. 'Audrey...' she whispered urgently. 'It's not too late, you know, to change your mind.'

Audrey shook her head. 'No...' she whispered back. 'I've come this far, and it'll soon be over. So long as I know that you'll be here waiting for me.' Her voice broke on a sob and she looked away, blinking rapidly. She clenched her hands together tightly. 'I've got to get a grip of myself. It'll soon be over...' she said again.

After only a few minutes the door opened and the woman – Maisie had never discovered her name – was there again. 'Miss Dennison, if you would come with me, please...'

Audrey walked from the room without a glance at her friend. If she had looked at her Maisie was sure she would have cried out, 'Audrey, don't! You mustn't...' But it had to be her own decision when all was said and done.

Maisie sat and waited, not knowing how long the wait would be. She was not sure, in fact, just what would be happening to Audrey. Would she have an anaesthetic, or would she be conscious of all that was going on? She shuddered, staring at the clock on the mantelshelf and watching the hands move round, so very lowly. It had a loud tick and it sounded, to Maisie's ears, like a solemn harbinger of doom.

Nine-forty...nine-forty-two, nine-forty-three... When the hands of the clock had almost reached a quarter to ten the door burst open and Audrey dashed in. 'Maisie...oh, Maisie!' she cried, flinging herself at her friend. 'I can't do it! I can't, I can't... Take me home, please, Maisie. I want to go home...' She burst into tears.

Maisie felt a great weight lift from her mind. Thank goodness... No, more than that. Thank God! she said silently inside her head. She held her friend close. 'Of course I'll take you home,' she said. 'Let's get away from here, right now.'

The woman was hovering in the doorway. 'Miss Dennison

will lose her money, of course,' she said. 'We can't be responsible for people changing their minds.'

'Money!' Maisie almost spat at her. 'What does the money matter compared with my friend's life? You might have killed her.'

'Now just you look here,' the woman expostulated. 'We run a reputable business, and I'll have you know that we have never lost anyone...'

'There's always a first time,' retorted Maisie, 'and when it happens I hope you are found out and punished. Come along, Audrey; let's go...' She took hold of her arm and guided her out of the door and down the path.

'I'm sorry...' whimpered Audrey, 'but I just couldn't do it, Maisie. Not when I saw the bed and all the instruments on the table. And he told me to...to take off my underwear and to lie down. And I just panicked. I'm sorry...'

Maisie put an arm around her. 'Why do you keep saying you're sorry? I'm not sorry... I'm glad, really really glad, and I'm sure you must be too. You know it was wrong... What did you mean when you said you wanted to go home? Did you mean...to Middlebeck?'

Audrey nodded. 'Yes...' she whispered tearfully. 'I need my mum, and my dad. They've been so good to me, and I know they'll understand. Luke and Patience always understand, and they always make everything come right...'

# Chapter Twenty-One

Before they made the journey to Middlebeck – for Maisie knew that she would have to go with Audrey – they went back to the flat.

'Breakfast, first of all,' she said. 'You'll feel tons better when you've got some food inside you.' She made several slices of toast which Audrey ate, spread lavishly with butter and marmalade, finishing off with a banana.

'You'll come with me, won't you?' asked Audrey. She seemed much, much calmer, as though a colossal weight had been lifted from her. 'I don't know how on earth I'm going to tell them, but I want you with me, Maisie... We won't tell them, though, about – you know – what I was going to do. I feel ashamed of it now, more ashamed than I am about being pregnant. That's our secret, isn't it, for ever and ever?'

'Of course it is,' replied Maisie. 'And you know I'll come with you; you didn't need to ask. I told you I would be there for you, whatever happened; but I'm so relieved you changed your mind. I would have gone along with you and supported you, whatever you had done, even though I didn't agree with you. But now that you've come to your senses everything will be just fine, you'll see.'

'They'll be shocked,' said Audrey. 'And so disappointed in me, so ashamed... Oh dear, whatever have I done?'

'You made a mistake,' said Maisie, 'just like thousands of other girls have done before you. But I should imagine Luke and Patience are pretty shock proof by now, don't you?'

'I suppose so... Come on, Maisie; let's get moving, or I shall change my mind again about telling them.'

'OK... I'll fling a few things into a bag, then I'm ready. I shall have to come back tomorrow, though, to open the office on Monday. I can't leave them in the lurch any longer.'

'And I suppose I will have to go back to college...' said Audrey. 'Do you think so? Or will I have to leave...?'

'Don't let's think about it now,' replied Maisie. 'But no – I'm sure you won't need to leave. You finish your course in June, don't you? It's not very long... Now, could you clear these few pots away for me, there's a love, while I get ready...'

They caught a train in the early afternoon after lunching at a snack bar near to the station.

'Do you remember the first time we made this journey?' asked Audrey, when they had left the city centre and the outer suburbs of Leeds behind and were passing through the wide Vale of York.

'Could we ever forget?' smiled Maisie. 'Saturday, the second of September, wasn't it? 1939 – the day before war broke out.'

Audrey giggled. 'You sound like Rob Wilton,' she said. 'The day war broke out, my missus said to me...'

Maisie joined in with the comedian's catchphrase, glad that her friend was actually starting to laugh again. 'Yes, off we went into the wide blue yonder. I don't suppose we gave a thought to how long we might be away from Leeds...' And, subsequently, the little town of Middlebeck had become home to both of them, although Maisie did not wish to remind Audrey of the circumstances that had led to her staying there.

'And now we're both back again in Leeds,' observed Audrey. 'At least you are, right in the city centre, and I'm not so far away.'

'But I still think of Middlebeck as home,' said Maisie. 'I was eager to get away, but it's always nice to come back.'

'You took care of me on that day, all those years ago,' said Audrey. 'And you're still taking care of me, aren't you? I don't know what I'd do without you, Maisie, honestly I don't.'

'Now don't start getting maudlin on me.' Maisie grinned

at her and nudged her elbow. 'Here...' She held out a paper bag. 'Suck a barley sugar and shut up! Or else we'll be so far down memory lane we'll never get back.'

Audrey smiled. 'We had barley sugars on that day as well. I remember...but they were mine, not yours. My mum used to say they were very good when you were travelling, to stop you from feeling sick.'

'Well, there you are then... Let's be quiet, shall we, and read our magazines?' The other folk in the carriage were a silent lot and Maisie did not want them to overhear any unwise confidences; the woman sitting opposite, pretending to read a book, looked as though her ears were out on stalks. She closed her eyes, lulled by the rhythm of the train, and dozed for a while, the sleep she had lost the night before finally catching up with her.

Audrey dozed too, and when they awoke they were travelling through the hills and valleys of the dales country. They smiled at one another, then looked out of the window at the familiar scene as the train approached Middlebeck. The ruins of the castle on a distant hill; the river, and a little waterfall cascading down a gully; greystone cottages with spring flowers just beginning to peep through the earth... and then they had arrived.

They lifted their bags from the luggage rack and alighted. There was no one to meet them because no one knew they were coming. Audrey was starting to look a mite apprehensive again. She glanced uncertainly at Maisie, biting her lip, which was beginning to quiver a little.

'Come on, best foot forward,' said Maisie. 'It's not far and our bags aren't heavy.'

They made their way up the gentle slope of the High Street. Halfway up, the road widened out into the Market Square and, as it was Saturday, the market was in full swing. Maisie wondered if their friend, Doris, might be serving on Nixons' dairy produce stall, but it would not be wise to linger at that moment.

She glanced to the right as they drew near the property

owned by her mother and Arthur. Through the window of the baker's shop she could see Flo, Arthur's sister, serving a customer, but the other window, once the draper's, was boarded up. There were signs, however, that the work was progressing satisfactorily.

'Are you going to call in and see your mum?' asked Audrey.

'No, not yet,' Maisie replied. 'I'm coming with you; first things first. That is, if you really want me to be with you when you see your parents...?'

'When I tell them, you mean? Yes, I want you there, please, Maisie. You said you would...' Audrey's blue eyes looked tearful again and Maisie took hold of her arm.

'OK then, off we go... Gosh, it's good to be back.'

'Yes, so it is,' agreed Audrey. 'At least it will be, when I've got this over...'

—

She had her own house key, but she decided it might be better to ring the bell. After all, they were not expecting her.

Patience opened the door. She looked amazed, and then delighted. 'Audrey, what a surprise! And you too, Maisie! Well I never!' She put her arms around Audrey, hugging her and kissing her cheek, then she greeted Maisie in the same way. 'What brings you here? I'm delighted to see you of course...but there's nothing wrong, I hope?' She looked anxiously first at Audrey and then at Maisie. Although Maisie had said 'Hello', Audrey had not yet spoken.

'No, not really,' replied Maisie, 'at least...'

'I've got something to tell you, Mum,' Audrey broke in without preamble, and Maisie thought she was going to blurt it out there and then.

'Let's take our coats off first,' she said. 'And we'd love a cup of tea, Aunty Patience, if you don't mind? Where's Luke?'

'He's in his study,' said Patience. 'I'll go and tell him, if he hasn't already heard you. Timothy's gone for his piano lesson and Johnnie's gone to play with a friend from school...' She was looking puzzled. 'There is something the matter, isn't there?' She looked concernedly but very lovingly at Audrey. Her keen eyes could see that her adopted daughter was certainly very worried about something. 'Well, whatever it is, I'm sure we can cope with it... Nobody has died, have they?'

Maisie shook her head. 'No, nobody has died, Aunty Patience.'

'Well then... I'll go and make the tea first,' she said. She knocked on the study door as she passed. 'Luke, you'll never guess who's here...'

Luke came out of his study almost at once and went into the sitting room. Audrey and Maisie were standing there looking at one another uncertainly.

'Hello, you two,' he said, kissing Audrey on the cheek, and then Maisie. 'This is a nice surprise. I didn't hear you arrive.' He laughed. 'Patience thinks I'm busy with my sermon, but I've finished it in good time, so I was listening to the wireless. The football results will be on soon...'

He looked at them enquiringly. 'There's nothing the matter, is there?' he asked, just as Patience had asked. 'You're both looking rather lost and forlorn... Take your coats off, for goodness sake, and sit down.' Obediently, they did so. 'Now tell me...what's the matter? Have you heard some bad news?'

'Oh no, it's nothing like that...' It was Maisie who spoke. 'At least, Audrey is rather worried about something and she wanted me to come with her. She'll tell you both in a minute, won't you, Audrey?'

Audrey nodded. 'I'm sorry... Dad. I'm in a bit of a mess. I'll tell you about it in a little while. Mum's gone to make a cup of tea because we were gasping for one. We've travelled from Leeds just now.'

'I see; a spur of the moment decision, was it?'

'Sort of,' said Maisie. 'Audrey wanted to come home.'

'Well, I'm pleased about that at any rate,' said Luke. 'Home is the best place to be if you're worried about something. Ah, here's Patience... Where would we be, I wonder, without our cups of tea whenever there's a problem?'

Patience was looking a little less anxious now and she busied herself setting out the china cups and saucers on a little table and pouring out the tea. 'There now,' she said, 'the cup that cheers. It really is lovely to see you, girls, whatever it is you want to tell us. Have a drink of your tea first...'

Audrey accepted the cup gratefully. She drank deeply, even though the liquid was hot, then placed her hands around the cup as though to steady her nerves. There was an emotive silence for a few moments. Patience and Luke glanced at one another guardedly and then at Audrey.

She put her cup and saucer down on the table, looking first at one and then the other of her adopted parents. Then she took a deep breath and, 'I'm going to have a baby...' she began, in what was quite a clear and resolute voice. 'That was what I wanted to tell you...' Then she hung her head, staring down at her hands clasped in her lap. 'I'm sorry, I'm really sorry...'

There was a sort of gasp from Patience which she tried to cover up, and Maisie noticed that Luke closed his eyes, shaking his head in sorrow or disbelief, or some of both, maybe. She felt sure, though, that they would rally round and support her friend once they had recovered from the shock. She was not disappointed.

After several seconds Patience dashed across and knelt on the floor by Audrey's chair. 'Oh, my darling,' she said, putting her arms around her, 'Never mind; you're here with us now. What an awful shock it must have been for you, but I'm so glad you had the courage to come and tell us. It's very brave of you.' She glanced across at her husband. 'Isn't it, Luke?'

'Yes...yes it is,' he replied, looking and sounding more than a little dumbfounded. 'I'm surprised, though; very surprised, Audrey...' He looked at her quite sternly, and Maisie could see her friend's eyes filling up with tears again.

'But there is no point in recriminations. What is done is done,' he continued. 'I'm sure you never intended it to happen, and Patience and I will stand by you, you can depend on that.'

'Thank you...' whispered Audrey. 'Maisie said that you would. I was scared to tell you at first, you see, that's why I went to tell Maisie, and she's been ever so good to me.'

'I feel dreadful that I knew about it before you,' said Maisie. 'But with me being there in Leeds Audrey decided to come and tell me. And I persuaded her to come home.'

'That was sensible,' replied Patience. 'Thank you, Maisie, for looking after her. You've always been such a sensible and reliable girl.' She smiled warmly at her before glancing, rather more uncertainly, at the other girl, the one they had adopted. It seemed to Maisie as though Patience was wishing that Audrey had shown a little more common sense.

She realised that it was probably time for her to take her leave of them and go home to see her own mother and family. Patience and Luke would need time on their own with Audrey, to come to terms with the situation and to decide what was to be done about everything. She stood up. 'Well, I'm going to love you and leave you now. Mum still has no idea that I'm here. I'll see you sometime tomorrow, Audrey, before I go back to Leeds; OK? Thanks for the tea, Aunty Patience... Bye, Luke, see you soon...'

Patience came to the door with her. 'My goodness, what a shock!' she whispered. 'Thank you ever so much Maisie; you're such a good friend to our little girl. That's what she still is in some ways, I'm afraid...' She lowered her voice even more. 'Who is it? Do you know? Has she got a steady boyfriend then?'

Maisie shook her head. 'No; I gather it was...just one of those things. Don't be cross with her, Aunty Patience. It wasn't her fault.'

Patience smiled. 'Fair enough. You're a good girl, Maisie; one of the best.' She kissed her cheek. 'Goodbye, dear, and God bless...'

'We will say no more about...all this until after we have had our meal,' said Patience, returning to the lounge where Luke and Audrey were sitting in silence, not looking at one another. 'Timothy will be back soon from his lesson; I thought he would have been in before now, but he's probably called to see a friend; and Johnnie's staying for tea at Gary's house... So we will have a talk tonight when Johnnie's gone to bed... Won't we, Luke?' She looked at her husband who appeared to be in a brown study.

'Yes, of course we will...' he answered, a trifle absent-mindedly. 'I don't want you to think I'm angry with you, Audrey. I'm surprised, as I've said, and it takes a bit of getting used to. But I've been around long enough to know that such things do happen, often to the most unlikely people; and Patience and I have dealt with worse problems in our time, haven't we, love?' They smiled affectionately at one another. 'Off you go now...' He smiled at Audrey, 'and help your mum with the tea... Oh, here's Tim at last,' he added as they heard the front door open and then close.

'Hello – what are you doing here?' asked Tim as he entered the room, unwinding his school scarf from around his neck and putting down his music case. He was seventeen now and in the sixth form at the Grammar School at Lowerbeck.

'Well, that's a nice greeting, I must say!' retorted Audrey. 'Aren't you pleased to see me?'

'Of course! I wasn't expecting you, that's all. Mum didn't say anything about you coming home.'

'That's because she didn't know. Maisie was coming up to see her mother,' Audrey invented hurriedly, 'and so I decided to come with her. I'll be going back tomorrow... I expect,' she added, a little uncertainly.

'What d'you mean? You'll have to go back. You've got lectures on Monday, haven't you?' said Tim. He didn't wait for her to answer. 'What's for tea, Mum? I'm starving!'

'As usual,' smiled Patience. 'It's toad-in-the-hole, one of your favourites. Audrey's just going to set the table, aren't you, love?'

Audrey nodded, following Patience into the kitchen. Tim could occasionally be coerced into doing the odd chore; but, by and large, it was the sort of household where the menfolk were content to leave it all to the women.

—

'Now...lets get down to brass tacks,' said Luke later that evening, when Johnnie was in bed and Tim had gone to the Youth Club at the church. 'We don't intend to give you the third degree, Audrey. It would serve no purpose, and we don't want you to feel any worse than you do already.'

'Thanks, Dad,' murmured Audrey. 'Actually, I feel tons better since I've told you both. I was frantic; I didn't know what to do...until Maisie talked some sense into me.'

'Yes, she's a good lass; she always was,' observed Luke, 'but it's you that we are concerned with now, my dear, and we are going to be with you, Patience and I, every step of the way.'

'Thank you,' said Audrey again. 'I know you must be cross with me really, even though you're being so nice about it. I mean...it's awful for you, isn't it, with you being the rector? Much worse than it would be if you were just... ordinary.'

Luke smiled. 'That's how I've always thought of myself; just an ordinary man who happens to wear his collar back to front.'

'You know what I mean,' said Audrey. 'And you're not ordinary, at least I don't think you are. But what are people going to...?'

'What are people going to say?' Luke finished the sentence for her. 'What does it matter what anybody says or thinks? We will have to live through that, you and your mother and I.' He looked at her quite sternly for a moment, and she could almost hear his unspoken words, You have brought it on yourself... 'But from what I know of the people of this parish – the majority of them, at any rate – you will get a lot of support and understanding.'

'Audrey, love...' Patience broke in. 'There's no chance of you marrying this young man, is there? Whoever he is... Does he know about it?'

'Good gracious me, no!' answered Audrey. 'No, to both questions.' She sighed, a deep rending sigh, partly of relief that she was able to talk about it at last with such sympathetic parents, and partly because she knew she was, still, in a hell of a mess. 'I'll tell you about it...and after that I want to forget the circumstances, if I can...

'You know I went back early after Christmas to go to that party at Jennifer's? Well, it was then...that it happened. I'm afraid I had too much to drink, and I got talking to Jennifer's brother. He was nice to me and we had a laugh together, and we got on really well and...that's what happened. He's probably never given it another thought, and I don't want him to find out. He's got a steady girlfriend, you see, but she wasn't there... I'd drunk too much, I know I had; I've done a lot of silly things since I went to college...' Her voice had been getting more and more agitated, then she began to sob as the tension of the last few days and weeks drained away from her. 'I'm sorry; I'm so very sorry; I've hurt you both so much...'

'Come along now, darling.' Patience, sitting close to her on the settee, put her arms around her. 'Have a good cry and you'll feel better. Everything is going to be all right, I promise.'

Eventually her sobs lessened and she dried her eyes and smiled at them. 'You're so good to me... What do you think I should do? I mean...there's college. I won't be able to go back, will I? And the baby...and I won't be able to get a job, because I won't be a proper teacher. I couldn't anyway, because of the baby...'

'Let's deal with one thing at a time, shall we?' said Patience, taking hold of her hand. 'At least I'm glad you're talking about the baby as though it's yours, which it will be. You mustn't consider adoption; I know some girls do in your position, because they have no choice.'

'No; no, of course I wouldn't,' said Audrey, remembering, with a pang of guilt, how she had considered doing something much worse. She was realising now, and had been ever since her flight from that dreadful house, that she really did want to have this baby, and to keep it. But there were still many, many complications.

'And we are not going to tell any silly stories about it either,' Patience went on, 'pretending that it's mine, for instance. I've known of cases where the family has been so ashamed that they've kept the daughter out of sight – and the mother too, presumably – and then said that the child belonged to the mother, the one who is really the grandmother. This happens quite a lot.'

'I think you are rather too old to get away with that, aren't you, darling?' said Luke with a twinkle in his eye.

'No, why should I be?' his wife retorted. 'I won't be fifty till the end of the year...' She laughed. 'I suppose you're quite right, though. I certainly wouldn't want to pass it off as mine, but I won't be too old to do my share.' She shook her head bemusedly. 'Do you know, Audrey, there was a time when Luke and I longed for children, and it seemed as though there would never be any.' Audrey had heard all this before, but she smiled and listened attentively.

'And then you came along, my dear, and we were so pleased to be able to adopt you; and then Timothy. We really thought that this was God's answer for us, to adopt, rather than to have any children of our own. And then, just like a miracle, little Johnnie arrived. I still think of him as being a miracle child... And now there's going to be another baby. Oh, Audrey, love – we mustn't be ashamed. We'll hold our heads up high, all of us, and I'm sure that God will bless us.'

'What about Tim, and Johnnie?' asked Audrey. 'Are you going to tell them?'

'All in good time.' It was Luke who answered. 'Tim is old enough to understand, and Johnnie...well, as I said, all in good time. And did you say something about not going back to college, Audrey?'

'Well, I can't, can I? I'm pregnant, and they might find out. Well, they're sure to...'

'Patience has just said that we'll hold our heads up high, and that is just what we are going to do. There is no reason at all why you shouldn't finish your college course. It would be such a waste to give up now. March, April, May, June... you have only four months left to do, and then you will have your teaching certificate.'

'And what use will that be to me, with a baby? Anyway, by the end of June everybody would know.'

'When is the baby due, dear?' asked Patience. 'Do you know?'

'The beginning of October, I think,' said Audrey. 'Of course I've not seen a doctor yet...' She shuddered inwardly, thinking of the one that she had seen, 'but I'm sure about it, about being pregnant, I mean. I've been feeling sick and... I just know.'

Luke appeared to be deep in thought. He looked concernedly at Audrey. 'I do understand how you must feel about people knowing, but we have decided not to be ashamed, haven't we? By the end of June, yes, I suppose you will be...er... showing, but probably not too much. You are only slightly built.'

'But won't that make it worse, if I put a lot of weight on?'

'I don't know. I am really quite vague about such matters,' replied Luke. 'But I am going to help you as much as I can. I shall drive you back to college tomorrow and have a word with your principal, Miss Montague, isn't it?'

'Oh, Dad, she's an ogre! She'll eat you alive!'

'I doubt it,' laughed Luke. 'I've dealt with plenty of ogres in my time. Besides, it's amazing what a clerical collar can do for calming down ogres. I shall explain the situation to her.'

'Oh no, don't! Please don't! She'll probably expel me.'

'That she won't! You can't tell me that a woman of her experience has not dealt with similar situations before. And you've never crossed her in any way, have you?'

'No... She takes our group for RE, and I get on quite well with her really. She seems to like me, I think. But everybody's a bit scared of her.'

'Religious Education, eh? Couldn't be better,' said Luke. 'We should get on like a house on fire. I'll see if we can come to some arrangement about your... Physical Education you call it, don't you? We don't want you overdoing things in the early stages.'

'And there's Greek dancing as well,' said Audrey. 'Prancing around in those silly tunics. But that's better than PE. I must admit I'd be quite glad to get out of that. But what would I say to the tutor who takes us, Miss Peabody?'

'The truth would be best,' said Luke, 'but don't worry; I'm sure we will be able to sort things out for you. Be a brave girl, and all will be well, I'm sure.'

—

Luke and Patience sat on their own for more than an hour after Audrey, and then Tim, had gone to bed. It was just turned midnight when they eventually retired, far later than usual on a Saturday night, considering that Sunday was Luke's busiest day of the week; but there had been so much on their minds, so much that they needed to talk about on their own.

'I'm stunned,' Patience had said several times. 'I'm finding it so hard to believe. Audrey, of all people! She was always such a shy, timid sort of girl.'

'But isn't that the sort that it often happens to?' observed Luke. 'And she told us she'd been drinking; I find that hard to take in as well, but I suppose they get up to all sorts when they get away from home.'

'We tried to bring her up well, didn't we, Luke? As though she was our own daughter. She always seemed to know right from wrong; I can't understand it.'

'There is no point in beating ourselves black and blue about it now, though, is there? What is done can't be undone, and we will have to try and be positive about it. She needs us more than ever now, Patience.'

'And we weren't too strict with her either, were we, darling? I mean, it wasn't as if she felt she had to kick over the traces when she left home. We never said too much when she was friendly with Brian Milner, because we felt we could trust her, and him as well, of course. He was – well, is – a very nice boy. Now if it had been him, Brian, I suppose it wouldn't have been quite so bad. At least he was her boyfriend.'

'But she was only a youngster at that time, Patience; it was before she left school. And then it all fizzled out when he went to university. Very sensible, really, although I'm sure they were never much more than good friends.'

'You don't think that she and Brian might have...?' asked Patience. 'I'm wondering now if we might have given them too much leeway.'

'No, I don't think so for one moment,' replied Luke. 'Brian was a very sensible lad. No; I think Audrey has just been unlucky; she has been caught the first time and, as I've said, that can happen to the nicest of girls.'

'Or to the ones who haven't as much nous...' said Patience thoughtfully. 'I can't imagine it happening to Maisie, can you?'

'No, I suppose not,' agreed Luke. 'She's always had her head screwed on the right way, has Maisie. Still, you never can tell...'

'Audrey is our daughter now, and we love her dearly,' said Patience, 'but Maisie was always the one who had the confidence and the common sense, God bless her... She will always be special to us, won't she?' Maisie had been their first evacuee, before Audrey and then Tim had joined the Rectory family, and she had a special place in both their hearts.

'Yes, indeed,' said Luke. 'But it's Audrey who needs our love and support and our prayers. She has made a mistake, and she knows it, but mistakes can be rectified.'

'Yes...all things work together for good,' said Patience.

'For those who love God,' added Luke, finishing the verse. 'But I'm sure He tries to help those who never think about Him, as well... Come along, my dear. it's tomorrow already, if you know what I mean...'

Hand in hand they climbed up the stairs.

# Chapter Twenty-Two

M aisie joined Patience, Audrey and Johnnie in their pew near the front of the church on Sunday morning. Timothy was in the choir and Johnnie was a somewhat reluctant churchgoer at the moment, but he had no choice in the matter.

'I thought you might be singing in the choir,' whispered Audrey.

'Oh no; that wouldn't be fair,' replied Maisie. 'I haven't been to any of the practices and I don't really belong to it now. Anyway, it's nice to listen for a change. What about you? How are you feeling now?'

Audrey grimaced. 'If you mean physically, not too good. I felt awful sick this morning. I've only had a piece of toast; I couldn't face the rest of the stuff that the others were tucking into. Tim noticed...but I told him I'd got out of the habit of eating big breakfasts. He doesn't know yet, you see.'

'But how are you otherwise...you know? They were OK with you, were they, after I'd gone?' Maisie spoke very quietly, although it was doubtful that Patience could hear her, or, to give her her due, would be listening. Johnnie was between her and the girls and she was talking to the lady on her other side, one of the members of the Mothers' Union.

'Yes, of course they were. They've been great, Maisie, like you said they would be. So understanding; I don't really deserve it.'

Maisie squeezed her arm. 'Yes you do. I knew it would be all right. You seem much happier about...things.'

'Yes, so I am. They've persuaded me to go back to college and face the music!' She grimaced again. 'I'm dreading that, but Dad says he'll go with me. Oh yes; I've got something to tell you... Luke says he'll take you back to Leeds at the same time, but we won't be able to set off until after the evening service. Is that OK with you?'

'Of course it is. I was thinking I would have to catch an afternoon train, but now I can have a bit longer here. That's really kind of Luke...' It was odd, she thought, or maybe it was understandable, that Audrey alternated between the names of 'Dad' and 'Luke' when speaking of the rector. He had been a loving father to her over the years, but there must be times when she thought about her real father, Alf Dennison, who had been killed when she was ten years old.

'Shh... He's here now, your dad,' said Maisie, as the choir, followed by Luke, progressed out of the vestry. 'We'd better shut up!'

They all stood to sing the opening hymn, 'For the Beauty of the Earth'. The words were poignant, thought Maisie, when they came to the third verse.

> 'For *the joy of human love; brother sister parent,*
>    *child...*
> Lord *of all, to Thee we raise, this, our grateful hymn*
>    *of praise.'*

She wondered if Luke had chosen the hymn specially.

—

After the service Maisie was pleased to see Anne Mellodey waiting for her on the pathway. Anne was just saying goodbye to Charity Foster, her old headmistress and friend, whom she often accompanied to church on a Sunday morning.

'Maisie, how lovely to see you, dear!' said Charity, still Miss Foster, of course, to Maisie.

'And you too,' she replied. 'It's only a flying visit though. I'm going back later today.'

'And I must fly as well,' said Miss Foster. 'I've left a little lamb joint in the oven and I don't want to find it burnt to a cinder. Cheerio for now...'

'Fly is the right word,' smiled Anne as the still sprightly lady hurried off down the path. 'You should see her in that little car of hers, flying along the High Street. To be quite honest, I don't accept a lift from her if I can help it. I make the excuse that I prefer to walk, which is quite true, of course.'

'You have never learned to drive then, Anne?'

'No; there's never been any need to. I live near enough to school.'

'You have to admire Miss Foster, though, learning to drive at her age. It couldn't have been easy.'

'She thought it was. She says she's taken to it like a duck to water,' laughed Anne. 'But not everybody is of the same opinion.'

'She's not had any accidents though, has she?'

'No, fingers crossed... Anyway, Maisie, I'm so pleased to see you. I've got some news for you! If I hadn't seen you soon I was going to write. I'm sorry I haven't written for a while, but all sorts of things have been happening.'

'That's OK. I've been rather negligent, too, with my letter writing lately. So, what do you want to tell me?'

'I can't tell you right now.' Anne gave a secretive sort of smile. 'Could you come round this afternoon? Come and have tea with me, or are you going back early?'

'No, not until this evening. Luke is taking me back at the same time as he takes Audrey to college.' Audrey was standing with Patience, chatting to two of Patience's friends. Maisie felt somewhat relieved that she had not come to join in the conversation with herself and Anne. A little selfish of her, perhaps, she thought, guiltily. But there were times when she liked to have Anne all to herself.

'That's lovely then,' said Anne. Her bright blue eyes were glowing with animation, and Maisie thought she could guess what the news might be. 'See you later then, about half past two?'

'Yes, I'll look forward to it...'

Lily had been pleased to see her daughter, but not over surprised at her sudden arrival, or over curious about the reason for the visit. Maisie explained that it had seemed like a good opportunity to pay a brief visit because Audrey had felt it was time she came to see her family. She gave no hint of Audrey's real reason for coming. No doubt when the news broke, as it most surely would, there would be talk enough, although Lily, having suffered more than enough traumas of her own, would not be one to condemn.

Both she and Arthur were preoccupied with their plans for the new restaurant. The work was progressing well, according to schedule, and they were still hoping to open at the Easter weekend, in a few weeks' time.

'We've decided on a name,' Lily told Maisie as they ate their Sunday lunch. 'It's going to be called "Arthur's Place". That's all, just "Arthur's Place". Short and to the point and easy to remember.'

'It wasn't my idea,' said Arthur. 'It's not just my place, is it? It's Lily's as well, and our Flo's and Harry's. But they seemed unanimous, the rest of 'em, so I'm not going to argue.'

'Sounds OK to me,' said Maisie. 'I'm sure it'll catch on. It was your bakery in the first place, wasn't it, Arthur, and your idea to do the outside catering? "Arthur's Place"… Yes, I like it. I must certainly try to be here for the grand opening. Yes, I'm sure I'll be able to come. Our office will be closed Easter Monday…'

———

'So you're still here, Anne,' Maisie remarked after she had settled down in one of her friend's easy chairs, in the upstairs flat she had lived in for quite a few years. 'You did talk about moving at one time, didn't you? About buying a little place of your own…'

'Instead of paying rent? Yes, I did, but I was nicely settled in here and near to school, so I never made the effort. And now… I won't need to!' Anne's eyes were shining more brightly than ever as she put out her left hand, displaying the ring on the third finger; a cross-over style of an emerald and two diamonds. 'I'm getting married, Maisie! Quite soon actually, although we've only just got engaged. I wanted you to be one of the first to know. I've told Charity, of course, and my parents.'

'Gosh, that's wonderful news!' exclaimed Maisie, going over to give her friend a quick hug. 'I did guess, though, that that might be what you wanted to tell me. You've been friendly for a good while, haven't you, you and Stefan? Although nobody was very sure whether you would...'

'Whether we would make it to the altar?' smiled Anne. 'I wasn't sure either and...no, we didn't make it, not Stefan and me.' She laughed at Maisie's incredulous face. 'I'm not marrying Stefan Chevesky – I thought you would have known all about that. No, I'm marrying Roger – Roger Ellison.'

'Roger Ellison? The army captain? Your...headmaster?' To say that Maisie was surprised was not the half of it; she was flabbergasted. She stared at Anne in astonishment whilst her friend smiled back at her, clearly delighted that her news had made such an impact. 'But...you didn't like him. You said you were daggers drawn; in fact I was surprised you'd stayed at that school...so long.' Her voice petered out. 'I reckon you must have...changed your mind?'

'You could say so,' laughed Anne. 'More than a bit. Roger and I have been friendly – very friendly, you might say – for about a year, although, before that we had been coming round to accepting one another's point of view and realising we were not so very different after all. We always had the children's interests at heart, deep down, both of us.'

'Never mind about the children,' said Maisie. 'Tell me about you and Roger. How did it happen? And...what about Stefan Chevesky?'

'I'm really surprised you didn't know the tale about Stefan,' said Anne. 'I thought it was the talk of the village. I know you're not living here now, but I thought your mother might have said something.'

'Mum and Arthur are very busy with their own concerns at the moment, and she's not one to gossip. She probably forgot she hadn't told me, whatever it is. Do tell...'

'Well, to put it in a nutshell, Stefan had a wife and son, back in Poland.'

'No! Of all the deceitful cheating so-and-sos...'

Anne gave a wry smile. 'I can't really say that, Maisie. In spite of what a lot of people thought, we were never anything but good friends, and he never gave me any reason to think it might be otherwise.'

'But he should have told you he was married, shouldn't he? You must have wondered why...'

'Why he didn't take things further? Yes, maybe I did...but we enjoyed one another's company and that seemed to be all that mattered. We had a lot in common; love of books and music and the countryside. And I suppose he was glad to meet a "kindred spirit", as you might say, so far from home. He didn't tell me he was married, for reasons best known to himself, and as the time went on I expect it became more and more difficult to tell me. But I'd started to get more friendly with Roger, so finding out about Stefan wasn't the shock that it might have been.'

'What happened to him, Stefan, I mean? Has he gone back to Poland?'

'Oh no; his wife and son – he's eight years old – have come over here. He's working at a farm Lowerbeck way, and they're living in a little cottage owned by the farmer. But he's got his own workshop there, so I'm told, and in his spare time he's working at the occupation he had back in Poland before the war.'

'And what was that? I thought he was just a farm labourer. Although he always seemed to be worth a bit more than that, if you know what I mean.'

'Yes, he was.' Anne nodded. 'He had to take just a menial job when he came over here, as they all did. He had been brought up on his father's farm, but then he became a skilled craftsman – a wood carver. He made all sorts of objects, useful as well as decorative ones, and he had a thriving business until the war started. He joined the Polish army... and afterwards he found that he had lost everything. So he came to Britain... And I suppose he was saving up to bring his family over here.'

'And he told you all this, did he? But forgot to mention his wife and child?'

'He told me a little at a time... They had a hard time with the regime in Poland and he knew he had to get away. Apparently his wife and son went back to live with her parents, although I didn't know that, of course, not at first. He told me in the end...when they were due to arrive. But by that time Roger and I had become friendly, as I've said, so I wasn't as hurt as I might have been.'

'I still think it was a rotten thing to do,' said Anne. 'So... you've been keeping your friendship with the headmaster a secret, have you? You dark horse, Anne! Well, I hope you're going to tell me all about it now.'

'Of course I am. I know you'll like Roger when you get to know him better. You don't really know him at all, do you, Maisie?'

'No, only as Joanie's and Jimmy's teacher at one time... And I've got to admit he worked wonders for them.' To the surprise of many folk, certainly with regard to Jimmy, both children were now attending the Grammar schools in Lowerbeck. 'I shall certainly look forward to getting to know him better. He must be OK if you like him, Anne.'

'I do...very much.' She blushed a little. 'We've kept it quiet, mainly because of the children. You know what kids are like if they get hold of an idea. So we behave very circumspectly at school. It's always Mr Ellison and Miss Mellodey, although I think the rest of the staff must have guessed. We have six teachers now, you know, including Roger, who still takes a class.' Maisie had noticed how the once small village school had gradually mushroomed in size, part of the playground now having been taken over for the new buildings.

'You really are one of the first to know,' Anne went on. 'Roger gave me the ring on Friday evening, so I've only been wearing it for two days. We'll break the news to the staff tomorrow, although I don't think it will be any great surprise, and as for the children, I suppose they will get to know by degrees. We don't want to make a big thing of it, but they'll be sure to know by the end of the summer term. That's when we plan to get married; the first Saturday in August, soon after school has finished.'

'Gosh! You don't let the grass grow under your feet, do you? So you'll be back living in the schoolhouse. Well, just imagine that!

'So I will... But Roger intends that we should buy our own house as well. A schoolhouse is all very well, but it's only yours as long as you have the post. We've realised we have to plan for the future.'

'I'm amazed at your news, Anne. But I'm really pleased for you. I can tell you think a lot about this... Roger.'

'Mmm... First impressions cannot always be relied upon. I must admit I thought he was self-opinionated, too sure of himself...but I've realised it was a front. He wanted to appear confident at the interview; he badly needed to be offered that job, to get back his nerve and his self-confidence, so he's told me since. And he might have overdone it...' She laughed. 'The rest of us candidates didn't get a very favourable impression, but fortunately the committee could see his worth. And, of course, they were probably swayed at that time – just after the war – by his war record. He was commended for bravery at Dunkirk; that's when he was injured and invalided out. He is really a very kind and unpretentious sort of man, although he does have quite strong opinions about some things.'

'So where is he now? Shouldn't he be with you on a Sunday afternoon?'

'We had lunch together at the schoolhouse after I left you. We haven't attended church together yet... And I told him I was seeing you this afternoon. He's heard a lot about you,

Maisie, I can assure you. I want to ask you, you see, if you will be my bridesmaid?'

Maisie gasped with surprise, and with delight. 'Me? Of course I will! I'd love to... But why me, of all people?'

'Why not?' smiled Anne. 'I've no sisters or close relations. I can't very well ask Charity, can I?' Maisie giggled quietly, thinking of the former headmistress in a pink satin dress or something of the sort, carrying a bouquet. 'I have one or two friends at school and a college friend I've kept in touch with. But who would I ask but you, Maisie? We've shared such a lot, you and I, since we came up to Middlebeck together.'

'I would be delighted,' said Maisie. 'I do feel honoured. Thank you so much for asking me.'

'We don't want a big "do",' Anne continued. 'I mean, we don't want lots of little bridesmaids and pageboys and so on. I was in two minds as to whether to have a conventional white dress – I shall be thirty-six by the time we get married – but Roger says I must. So I want you to be my sole attendant. I thought about asking Audrey and Doris as well, and then I decided against it. Anyway, Doris is pregnant again. I don't know whether you knew?'

'No, I didn't actually.'

'Yes, their second child is due in September. So that rules her out, doesn't it? And I haven't really kept in touch with Audrey lately, not since she went to college.'

And Audrey, too, would be very pregnant by the beginning of August, thought Maisie. But she knew that now was not the time to tell Anne of her friend's dilemma.

'And we were wondering, Roger and I, whether Arthur would put on a meal for us after the ceremony? Wedding breakfast they call it, don't they, although it will be lunch time, of course. Possibly about one o'clock if the wedding is at twelve, but we will have to make arrangements with Luke first.'

'Do you mean in the new restaurant?' asked Maisie.

Anne nodded. 'Yes, that's right...'

'I'm sure he will; he'll be delighted. It won't be a very big place though, you know. I don't know how many they will be able to accommodate, but you'll have to sort that out with Arthur.'

'I'm not sure yet how many there will be. As I said, we don't want a big "do", but it's amazing how the numbers add up when you start to count. If you ask so-and-so, then you have to ask so-and-so as well...'

'I can imagine,' said Maisie. She had never seen her friend so elated – at least not since Bill, her fiancé, had been killed all those years ago – and she had a special radiance about her. It was obvious that she was very much in love with Roger Ellison; and Maisie hoped that the marriage would bring her all the happiness and fulfilment that she deserved. 'I'll leave it to you to tell Arthur what sort of a meal you will require and the numbers and everything. In fact, I won't even mention it to them. It's up to you to spread the good news; I'm sure everybody will be delighted.'

'I hope so,' said Anne, 'but I am delighted, so that is all that matters.'

'May I tell Audrey, though?' asked Maisie. 'Luke's driving us both back to Leeds later tonight, and she might think it's odd that I've not told her. She's sure to find out about me being your bridesmaid; so, if you don't mind...'

'Of course you can tell her. She'll be on the guest list; so will all the Rectory family. Do you think she'll understand about me having just you as a bridesmaid? She won't feel left out?'

'No, I'm quite sure she won't,' replied Maisie confidently. 'Audrey has quite enough to think about... Her exams will be coming up soon, and her final school practice, so she tells me. I reckon she'll be fully occupied, one way and another...'

---

'How is Miss Thomson going on?' asked Audrey as she and Patience were washing up after their Sunday lunch. 'I noticed her in church, and when she was going down the path I saw that she was walking with a stick.'

'She's as well as can be expected for a lady of her age,' replied Patience. 'Nobody is quite sure how old she is. Amelia considers that her age is nobody's business but her own, but she must be getting on for eighty, if not more.'

'And she still lives alone over there, does she? She was on her own in church. Or does she have a live-in maid, like she used to have?'

'No, not any more. She hasn't had anyone living there since the land girls left at the end of the war. People keep telling her she should have a companion, but she's as stubborn as a mule.'

'So what's changed?' smiled Audrey.

'Oh, she's nothing like as crotchety as she used to be. Quite mellow in fact, in some ways. Having the land girls living with her did her a world of good, and she still gives your father a run for his money on the church council! It's difficult to get live-in maids these days. Girls have become much more independent since the war and they're looking for other kinds of jobs; they don't want to go into service any more. Daisy, of course, was one of the last of a dying breed.'

'Yes, she was a treasure,' agreed Audrey. 'Miss Thomson didn't realise just how valuable Daisy was until she left to join the ATS, did she?'

Audrey was remembering how the maid-of-all-work, Daisy Kitson, had taken her under her wing and mothered her when she had gone as an evacuee to live at Miss Thomson's house. She had been scared out of her wits at first by the draconian old woman, but Daisy had made it all so much better... Until the time when the two of them, the maid and the evacuee, had displeased 'Old Amelia', resulting in Audrey going to live at the Rectory and Daisy joining the ATS. But that was all a long time ago, and Audrey felt sorry for the old lady now, living alone in that big house on the other side of the village green.

'I think I'll go across and see her this afternoon,' she said. 'What do you think, Mum? Or...does she not like having visitors?'

'I think that would be very nice indeed,' said Patience. 'That's very kind and thoughtful of you, Audrey. She will be pleased to see you, I'm sure. She has quite a few visitors. People don't mind going now because she's not the cantankerous old woman she used to be. I'll give you a pot of my raspberry jam to take to her, and a ginger cake I made yesterday...'

—

A few moments passed after Audrey knocked at the door, but she waited, feeling sure that Miss Thomson would not have gone out. Sure enough, the door opened eventually and the elderly woman peered out questioningly. 'Yes...who is it?' Her beady, almost black, eyes behind the rimless spectacles appeared as sharp as ever, but Audrey guessed that she probably did not see everything as clearly as she had used to do.

'It's me, Miss Thomson,' she said. 'Audrey... You know, Audrey Fairchild, from the Rectory.'

'Audrey! Yes, of course it is.' Miss Thomson smiled and her eyes softened as she looked closely at her visitor. 'Come along in, my dear. How nice it is to see you. I noticed you in church this morning with your mother, and that friend of yours was there too, wasn't she?'

'Yes... Maisie,' replied Audrey, following her into the lounge, which did not appear to have changed at all since the early days of the war. The old-fashioned furniture and the patterned carpet were the same, as were the velour curtains, partly drawn to keep out the sun, although there was little sun to be seen. It smelled musty, and Audrey remembered that fires were very rarely lit in that room, although it was the one into which visitors were always shown. Miss Thomson stopped to switch on an electric fire, and two bars started to glow, which made the atmosphere a little more cheerful.

'Maisie and I both decided to come home for the weekend,' she said, sitting down on what was called an easy chair; it was anything but, being stuffed with horsehair.

'We're going back later today. My father is driving us to Leeds. Maisie works there now, you know, and I'm at college near Leeds.'

'Maisie...yes, I remember.' Miss Thomson sniffed, a little disapprovingly. She and Maisie had crossed swords right at the beginning of the war when the little girl had stood up for her friend and, Audrey recalled, had referred to her as a 'nasty old woman'. And after that, 'Old Amelia' had never really warmed to Maisie as everyone else had seemed to do, believing that the child was cheeky and too forward by half. 'She's working in a travel agency, isn't she? In charge of it, so I've heard.' There was clearly not much wrong with the woman's grasp of the facts. 'That should suit her down to the ground; she always had a lot to say for herself, that one... And what about you, Audrey? You're still at that college are you, training to be a teacher?'

'Yes, that's right. I finish though, at the end of June.'

'So you'll be coming to teach here, I suppose, at the village school?'

'Oh no, I don't think so,' replied Audrey. The possibility of that had not occurred to her; she was not sure that she would want to teach in her own town. And under the circumstances it would be impossible. Just for the moment she had almost forgotten her predicament, at least it had receded to the back of her mind; but now the awfulness of it all was taking hold of her again. 'No...' she said. 'That wouldn't be a good idea. I'm not sure what I shall do. I'll probably get a post...somewhere else.'

Amelia was looking at her keenly. 'I can see you in charge of our village school one of these days.' She nodded sagely and smiled. 'You were always such a clever little girl, and so sensible...'

Audrey began to feel confused and anxious again. Whatever would the old lady say when she discovered the truth? What would they all say? The enormity of it was threatening to overwhelm her, and she had thought she was coping so well after unburdening herself to her parents. She could feel her hands starting to tremble and she clasped them together, staring down at the carpet. Change the subject, please, please...she said silently. You don't know what I'm like; I'm not sensible at all...

Her eyes lit on the bag at the side of her chair and she grabbed hold of it. 'My mum has sent you some jam,' she said, 'and a cake. She says she hopes you'll enjoy them.'

'Thank you, dear; how very kind of her,' said Miss Thomson. 'I don't bake any more now, so that will be a real treat. Mrs Kitson does some baking for me now and again. You remember Mrs Kitson, don't you, Audrey; Daisy's mother? She cleans for me a few mornings a week and does my washing and ironing, and the baking occasionally. People keep telling me I should have somebody to live with me, but I like my independence. I do my own shopping, although it takes me longer than it used to do.'

Audrey recalled that it was always Daisy who had done the shopping, along with all the other jobs, but the war had forced everyone, even genteel old ladies like Miss Thomson, to do more for themselves.

'How is Daisy?' she asked now. 'Do you hear from her?' Her moment of panic was passing, but she knew she must steer the conversation to other people and away from herself. She might have realised, though, that Miss Thomson would ask questions about what she was doing; old ladies were always nosey.

'Oh yes, Daisy keeps in touch with me now and again. She and her husband – Andy, isn't it? – they went to manage a farm in Worcestershire. They have two children, a boy and girl. She always sends me a Christmas card...'

Audrey refused the offer of a cup of tea, knowing that that would force her to stay a good deal longer. For the next half hour or so they chatted about this and that; about the work that was going on at Arthur Rawcliffe's new restaurant; the numerous market stalls that had sprung up in the last year or so, all selling the same sort of produce; 'new brooms' on the church council who wanted to change everything...

When there was a lull in the conversation Audrey decided to take her leave. What would be Miss Thomson's reaction to her the next time they met, she wondered? Luke had said she must hold her head up high, but it was not going to be easy.

She was glad of Maisie's company on the journey back to Leeds. They chattered away in the back of the car – although it was Maisie who was doing most of the talking – leaving Luke to concentrate on the road ahead. He had acquired the second-hand Ford Anglia a couple of years before, to assist him in his parish work and his visits to his bishop and rural dean.

They stopped at Maisie's flat, and she departed with a cheery smile and a wave. 'Good luck,' she said. 'It'll all be OK, you'll see. Thanks for the lift, Luke, Be seeing you...'

How confident she always is, thought Audrey; she could not imagine her friend getting into this sort of a predicament. She was starting to feel nervous again; scared stiff, in fact. However would she be able to face Miss Montague and Miss Peabody and everybody?

'Come and sit at the front with me now,' said Luke. He looked at her anxious face and smiled confidently at her. 'Be strong and of a good courage,' he said. 'All will be well. We'll face this together, you and I...'

The words of one of Luke's favourite hymns flashed into her mind.

'No *lion can him fright,*
*He'll with a giant fight...'*

Yes, it would be all right. Luke had always been able to make things right...

'Sit yourself down and I'll tell you what I've got in mind, Maisie. You don't have to say yes, but I'd like you to at least consider it, as a temporary measure...'

'You're transferring me to Timbuktu,' she laughed.

'No...no, not quite; we haven't got so far yet. But we will, one of these days, we will...' He nodded, steepling his fingers and tapping them together. 'What I was wondering is this... Would you act as a courier for us for the next few weeks? On what we call the "cultural" tours; you know, of course, you've done them before. The fact is, Thelma has been forced to give up much sooner than we expected. She's pregnant – you probably know that – and she would be leaving us at the end of the summer anyway, but she's been suffering with high blood pressure and she has to stop work immediately...'

'So you want me to take over...? Mmm...yes, of course I'd love to.' Maisie knew without any hesitation that she wanted to do so. 'But...what about my position here? I'm not suggesting I can't be replaced; I know I can, but I thought that this was what you wanted me to concentrate on; running an office rather than doing the courier's job. I used to love doing it, of course, but I thought you wanted me to stay here.'

'The thing is, Maisie, that you are a veritable Jack of all trades...'

'And master of none?' she smiled.

'Oh no, not at all. You are the master of whatever you set your mind to... Thank you, Olwen.' Henry broke off as the tea arrived. 'Come and have a cup with us, Olwen, and you too, Barry. I don't think you will have any more customers today.' He checked his watch. 'Five minutes off closing time. You have my permission to turn the sign round to Closed. Then you can listen to what I have to say to Maisie. It will affect you both, of course...'

Galaxy ran three cultural tours now for the 'more discerning travellers', those who wanted to learn something of the history, environment and culture of the places they were visiting. These were a five-day tour to London; another

# Chapter Twenty-Three

M aisie was surprised to see Henry Galloway entering the Leeds office late one afternoon, towards the end of May. She smiled and nodded at him, then carried on with the booking she was engaged upon whilst he spoke to Barry and Olwen. They were not in awe of their boss, knowing that he trusted them all to run the office competently.

Galaxy was still primarily a family firm with Henry as the managing director, but there were now other shareholders as well as family members, and Maisie was proud to be one of them. Henry had presented her with the shares as a reward for her loyalty and ability, and for the hard work she had done for the company. And when she turned twenty-one in the May of next year he intended to give her a place on the board.

'Hello there, Henry,' she said when the wealthy lady, one of their best clients who had been booking an airline ticket to New York, had departed. 'Checking up on us, are you? She grinned at him. 'It's a while since we saw you in our of the woods.'

'No, I know I don't need to do that.' He looke appreciatively. 'Everything appears to be run smoothly. No problems?'

'No, none at all. And we are having a Bookings are well up on this time last year.'

'Good, good... Actually, Maisie, I've big favour. I would have rung you, but best if I talked with you, face to fa make us a cup of tea, please, there'

'Certainly, Mr Galloway...' C room behind the office, and Hen.

five-day tour to Stratford-upon-Avon; and a seven-day tour visiting the city of Edinburgh for three nights, followed by three nights in Callander. These tours ran alternately, each one taking place every three weeks or so. Galaxy's fleet of coaches was gradually being enlarged, but was insufficient to run every tour on a weekly basis, as some of the larger coach companies did. The tours to seaside resorts, which required only a driver and not a courier, had been extended to include places further afield, in Cornwall and the Isle of Wight, in addition to the old favourites such as Bournemouth, Torquay and Eastbourne.

'Believe me, you are the best person for the job,' said Henry. 'We don't employ many couriers, just Thelma and Sheila; she only started this year and is still learning the job. We know we will have to advertise Thelma's post, and maybe we will be able to replace her quite soon...but in the meantime, if you could see your way to helping us out, Maisie?'

She smiled. 'You have twisted my arm...' Although she had not needed much persuasion. 'When do you want me to start?'

'The next tour – it's the Scottish one – goes on Sunday, the fourth of June. Is that OK?'

'And now it's... May the thirtieth. Less than a week! Not much time... I'll have to swot up on my history of Edinburgh; and Stirling Castle as well now, and Callander...' The last time she had done the Scottish tour it had been only five days to Edinburgh, but now it included the resort of Callander, near to Loch Katrine, the setting for 'The Lady of the Lake'. 'And I'd better take a look at Sir Walter Scott again...' Already she could feel the excitement starting to bubble up inside her.

'You'll be fine, I know you will.' Henry smiled confidently at her. 'You'll be back from Scotland on the Saturday, so you will be able to have the weekend at home before the next five-day tour starts; that's on Monday, June the twelfth. That's the one to Stratford-upon-Avon, so you had better start brushing up on your Shakespeare as well!'

'What! I thought it was just Edinburgh you wanted me to do...'

'No... I did say for the next few weeks; Edinburgh, Stratford, and then – possibly – the five days to London. By that time we might have found a full-time replacement for Thelma. And in the meantime Colin will be coming to take over here in your absence. You worked with Colin in the York office, didn't you, Maisie?'

'Yes...so I did.'

'He's a good bloke, is Colin. He's working as a relief manager at the moment, but I hope to be able to fix him up with a permanent position before long. Now, Maisie, when you've locked up we'll go and have a bite to eat, you and I, before I head off back to York. There's a Hagenbach's café not far from here, isn't there?'

'Yes, that will be lovely, thank you...'

'And I can give you all the gen about the tours. You will have stayed at the Edinburgh hotel before, and the London one, but the hotel in Callander will be new to you – a very comfortable hospitable place from all the reports we've had – and the one in Stratford is new as well. But you don't find it difficult to fit in anywhere, do you, Maisie...?'

The central starting-off point for the tours was in Leeds, at the bus station on Wellington Street, so Maisie did not have far to travel on the following Sunday morning. She took a taxi in order to arrive there well before the appointed tour departure time of ten forty-five. This was to allow time for passengers from York, Manchester, Liverpool and the other northern towns and cities to arrive, brought there by a team of part-time relief drivers. The coach drivers who were taking out tours that morning – to Torquay, Bournemouth, Weymouth and the Scottish tour – were already congregated in the snack-bar enjoying mugs of strong tea and toast, and in one case, bacon and egg. His breakfast? wondered Maisie, or maybe it was his second one of the morning.

'Hi there,' she said, joining them after collecting a mug of coffee from the counter. She had met them all before, some only briefly, but they greeted her warmly.

'You're with me, I believe,' said Bob, a cheerful round-faced man – the one who was tucking into the bacon and egg. It was well known that Bob enjoyed his food, as his ample waistline proved. 'Well, I know you're with me, 'cause I'm the only one with a courier, aren't I?' The other three tours, to the south of England, were simply holidays with excursions that did not require a courier's special knowledge, although the drivers were expected to find out a few facts and interesting points about the places they were visiting.

'Good tour this one, Maisie,' he went on. 'You'll enjoy it. And the food! By the heck, I'll bet you've never tasted such roast beef as they serve up there in Callander. It's making me mouth water just thinking about it!'

'D'you ever think of 'owt else but yer belly?' quipped one of his mates. 'Trust you to land the Scottish tour again!'

'Aye, an' I'm not likely to let go of it neither,' laughed Bob. 'It's a pity it's only once every three weeks.'

By and large, the coach drivers kept to their own tours, possibly alternating between two or three, as none of the tours left every single week. But as Galaxy had a reputation for comfortable hotels and good food none of them ever complained about their diet whilst they were away from home. Indeed, Bob was not the only one who was more than a little corpulent. Long hours behind the wheel, which resulted in a sedentary lifestyle, plus a three-course cooked meal every evening was an occupational hazard!

The drivers were all smartly attired in their regulation dark green blazers with a green and white striped tie. Maisie's blazer was bright red, so that she could be spotted easily in a crowd, and she wore a red and white candy-striped blouse and a badge which stated, MAISIE, GALAXY COURIER. They did not bother overmuch with surnames, but the Christian names of both the courier and the driver would be one of the first things the customers would learn, and would then use endlessly for the rest of the week!

The coaches were painted in dark green with GALAXY TOURS written boldly in white. At first their insignia had sported only the white rose of Yorkshire, but it had recently been altered to include the red rose of Lancashire, as many of their clients were from across the Pennine border. This symbol was on the pockets of the drivers' blazers, and on Maisie's as well.

By ten-thirty all the travellers had assembled and Maisie helped many of them, not just her own passengers, to locate the right coach. She felt excited; it was always so at the beginning of a tour; the anticipation of the pleasures – and sometimes the worries, too – of the week that lay ahead. Thirty-six new people to get to know; that was always the hardest job. You had to get a mental picture of each one firmly fixed in your mind as soon as possible just in case – God forbid! – one of them should stray away and get lost.

As soon as they had left the city of Leeds behind and were heading through the open countryside she stood at the front of the coach, her microphone in her hand.

'Good morning, everyone...' she said brightly and, she hoped, confidently.

There was a murmured response of 'Good morning...' from some of the seats, but Maisie did not exhort them to 'Speak up; I can't hear you!', as some jolly couriers were wont to do. She knew they would lose their inhibitions before they had been very long on the road. 'My name is Maisie and I am your courier, and this is Bob, our very competent and experienced driver. It is our job to look after you all this week, and I can assure you we are going to have a most enjoyable time together. Anything at all you want to know, any problems, be sure to come and ask me. I will tell you more as the day goes on, but for now...just enjoy the scenery, or catch up with your beauty sleep if you wish!'

There was polite laughter, and she was gratified to see

nearly all smiling faces looking back at her. They were mostly middle-aged couples, husbands and wives or, in some cases, two ladies sitting together. They appeared quite elderly, very few under forty...or so it seemed at a first glance. But that was usually the case. They were quite subdued now, but after a day or two in one another's company they would be talking and laughing together as though they had known one another for ages.

They stopped soon after midday at the little town of Moffat in the centre of the Lowland sheep-farming area. Lunch had been pre-booked at an hotel on the main street as it was difficult to find places open on a Sunday. It was when they left the town behind and were heading northwards through the lovely scenery of Annandale that Maisie was able to impart to her captive audience her first gem of information.

'The hollow in the hills we will shortly be coming to, ladies and gentlemen, is known as the Devil's Beef Tub. It is said to have been a hiding place for stolen cattle...'

But the fish and chip lunch was lying heavily on several stomachs, and Maisie's words, in some cases, fell on deaf ears, or were even answered by snores. She decided to leave them in peace for a while.

—

The Edinburgh hotel was situated on Princes Street, almost opposite the memorial to Sir Walter Scott, a soot-blackened edifice with a Gothic spire reaching up two hundred feet. It had been erected in 1844 as what was considered to be a fitting tribute to the famous son of the city, but its architectural merit had been argued about ever since.

Maisie had stayed at the hotel before and knew that she and the passengers would enjoy the comfortable rooms and the appetising food during their three-night stay. The two days, Monday and Tuesday, would be fully occupied with sightseeing; and she had been burning the midnight oil for the past few nights, genning up on all the facts and anecdotes, so that she could relate many of them without continual reference to a guide book.

The castle, parts of it dating back to 1100, dominated the Edinburgh skyline, perched high on Castle Rock. Monday morning found them there, bright and early, exploring the apartments of Mary, Queen of Scots (including the chamber where James VI, later James I of England, was born); the Scottish Crown Jewels; the tiny chapel of St Margaret; and the Castle Esplanade, before breaking for lunch. They would reassemble, Maisie told her eager followers, at the foot of the castle steps at two o'clock, ready to begin their exploration of the Royal Mile.

Bob, after driving them to the castle, had spent the time on his own, having no wish to visit the place yet again. He had arranged to meet Maisie, though, for lunch. They found a snack bar that was not too crowded in a little street near to St Giles' Cathedral.

She glanced around. 'Good... None of my folk seem to have found this place. I must admit it's nice to get away from them for a little while. I've had my work cut out this morning, trying to keep up with all their questions. They're a lively lot, and the thirst for knowledge of some of them – mostly the elderly ones – is quite amazing.'

Bob grinned. 'Isn't it always the same on these – what d'you call 'em? – cultural tours. Me, I just drive 'em here. If you've seen one castle you've seen 'em all in my book. Edinburgh's a bonny city though, I must admit. Are you going to be doing this tour regular, like, Maisie?'

'No, I don't think so,' she replied. 'It's supposed to be just for the next few weeks – alternating with London and Stratford – until they get a replacement for Thelma.'

'Oh aye; she's expecting, isn't she? Nice lass, Thelma. But I reckon she'll have her hands full before long, once the bairn arrives.'

'It's not due just yet, Bob. She's had to give up because of high blood pressure.'

'Oh, I see; poor lass... She'll be OK though, if she takes it easy. The same thing happened to my wife when she was carrying our second one, our Eddie, but she was as right as rain once she stopped dashing around. Your family has to come first, that's what me and Mavis have always said...'

They broke off to place their order with the waitress: cheese omelettes and a pot of tea for two. 'We shan't need much,' said Bob. 'There'll be the usual hearty meal tonight... But it's Callander that's the one for food, Maisie. By Jove, you're in for a treat there all right...'

Maisie liked Bob. She had worked with him before on a couple of occasions and had felt very safe in his company. He was a family man through and through and, as he had just said, they came first with him. But it could not always be easy, she was sure, being away from home for several days at a time.

'How do you manage to cope with your home and family commitments?' she asked him. 'I'm sure you must miss your wife and children, and they will miss you.'

'So they do,' he nodded. 'But look at it this way; it's like another honeymoon for me and Mavis every time I go home.' He winked at her. 'Well, sort of, you know what I mean,' he added quickly, as though he might have shocked her. 'We've adjusted to being apart because the pay's quite good; Henry Galloway's one of the best when it comes to bosses, and then there's the tips. My Mavis is a very competent woman and the kids are well-behaved, though I say it meself. But if ever she said she couldn't manage on her own any more, I'd give it up. I'm home most weekends of course, and we have a few days off every three months or so. And I can take the wife along an' all for a free holiday at the end of the season. There's a few perks, y'see.'

'It's seasonal work though, isn't it? What do you do in the winter months?'

'Taxiing mostly. We get by, and I catch up with all the odd jobs at home. I do all my own painting and decorating...'

The meal arrived and they ate for a while without talking. Yes, Bob was a real family man, thought Maisie. She could not see him playing away from home as some of the other drivers did, flirting with the young unmarried women on the coach, sometimes doing more than just flirt, from what she had heard. There were certain drivers who would consider that to be one of the perks of the job.

'You'll not catch me larking around,' said Bob suddenly, as though he had read her thoughts. 'Not with the grand little wife I've got at home. It's disgraceful the way some of my mates carry on while they're away. But I don't say 'owt; I mind me own business. If they want to risk their marriage it's up to them... Not that there's much chance of any crumpet anyway on this tour, eh Maisie?' His eyes twinkled with merriment and she laughed out loud.

'Apart from your good self, of course,' he added, grinning at her. 'No offence intended...'

'And none taken,' she said smiling. 'To be honest, I went out with Eric once or twice – quite a while ago – until I found out he was married. He hadn't said...'

'No, he wouldn't. He's a wily devil is Eric; you want to steer well clear of him. Er...you won't think I'm propositioning you, will you, Maisie, if I invite you to go for a drink with me this evening?'

'No, of course I won't; I'd love to,' she replied. 'Come on, Bob; let's get this bill paid. My eager beavers will be waiting for me in fifteen minutes' time. Do you want to come with us this afternoon? The Royal Mile and Holyrood? You're very welcome...'

'Nah...thanks all the same. I'll have a mooch around the old alleyways by meself, then I'll find a quiet spot and read me book till it's time to pick you lot up again. Four-thirty you said, didn't you? See you later, Maisie...'

By the time she had 'powdered her nose' and walked back to the steps, most of the company was assembled, and the others arrived on the dot of two o'clock.

The first stop of the afternoon was at the nearby Greyfriars Church.

'Are we going to see Greyfriars Bobby?' she had already

been asked several times. The group was nothing if not predictable. They stood around, agog with interest – or somewhat blasé if they already knew the story – whilst she recounted the tale of the terrier whose statue crowned the fountain near to the church. Bobby's owner was Jock Gray, a shepherd who had died in 1858 and been buried in the churchyard. The faithful Bobby had watched over the grave of his master for the remainder of his life, fed by the people of Edinburgh. When he died, in 1872, he was buried at the side of his master.

There were suitable exclamations of 'Aah...' and 'What a lovely story...' as they went on to explore the rest of the Royal Mile, the network of ancient streets running from Castle Hill to the gates of Holyroodhouse. The Lawnmarket; St Giles Cathedral, from the pulpit of which John Knox had preached his fiery Calvinism; the house where, it was reputed, he had lived; Canongate...leading eventually to the Palace of Holyroodhouse, the former home of the kings and queens of Scotland.

As Maisie had anticipated, the story which fascinated the group the most was the one of the murder of David Rizzio, the favourite of Mary, Queen of Scots. She imbued her voice with as much feeling as she could as she recounted how, on a night in March, 1566, a gang of nobles, led by the Queen's husband, Lord Darnley, entered the Queen's room by a private staircase and stabbed to death, in her presence, her friend and secretary, David Rizzio. There was even the bloodstain remaining on the carpet. Maisie pointed it out, although adding to herself, If you believe that you will believe anything... The murder of Rizzio, though, was one of the best-documented murders in history.

The evening meal was hearty, as Bob had predicted, and Maisie was glad of the walk along Princes Street and through the gardens to work off the effects of the mulligatawny soup, steak and kidney pie, and butterscotch tart. The hands of the floral clock, said to be the oldest one in the world, stood at a quarter past nine, and dusk was just beginning to fall as

they strolled out of the gardens and across the road to a little
pub that Bob had visited before.

Maisie looked around warily. She was not sure whether or
not women in pubs were frowned on, north of the border.
She had heard that they were looked on askance in County
Durham and Northumberland, but as Edinburgh was a city
frequented by tourists they might have become more
accustomed to Sassenach ways. A quick glance told her that
this was probably so. There were a lot more men than
women, but there were several ladies accompanied by men;
none, however, who appeared to be without a male escort.

'You won't report me for having the odd half of bitter, will
you?' laughed Bob.

'No, of course not; why should I? Er...how strict is the
rule about the drivers' drinking?'

'Pretty strict. We're forbidden to drink at all while we're
on the road, and it's only an idiot who would disobey. We've
got everyone else's lives in our hands as well as our own. You
might get the occasional bloody fool – pardon me! – who
thinks he can do as he likes, but just one report of 'owt of the
sort an' he'd be out on his ear.'

'I've always found the driving exemplary on our tours,'
said Maisie, 'yourself included. You'll have slept off the
effects of half a pint by morning, won't you?'

'Aye, so I will. What'll you have then?'

'Oh...a small gin and lime, please...'

'Okey doke; coming up...'

She watched him as he stood at the bar. An ordinary sort
of chap; medium-height, sandy hair just starting to fade at
the temples, mid-forties, she guessed, old enough to be her
father at any rate. He was so nice and comfortable to be
with. She knew already that his company on the tour this
week would add to its pleasure. She had, if she were honest,
been a mite apprehensive, as well as excited, at her new
venture. Until now she had done only the occasional tour,
but she had committed herself now for a few weeks at least.
But this tour was going to be a memorable one. She could

feel it in her bones. She smiled at Bob as he returned with the drinks.

'I'll have a ciggy an' all, if you don't mind,' he said, sitting down and reaching into his pocket for a rather battered silver case. He handed it to Maisie.

'No, thanks... I don't. But you go ahead; it doesn't bother me.' The air in the far corner though, she noticed, was blue with smoke.

'Good girl. I shouldn't start neither, if I were you. It's not a good habit to get into, but it helps us drivers to unwind, the occasional ciggy. Not that I'd ever smoke at the wheel; that's forbidden an' all, and rightly so.'

'And passengers who smoke are supposed to keep to the back few rows,' said Maisie. 'On the whole they do as they're told. But you might get the odd awkward customer who likes to stick up for his rights.'

'Aye, and there's summat to be said for that, I suppose. You can't interfere too much with folks' liberty... Now, Maisie love, tell me a bit about yerself. You're a Yorkshire lass, I know that; from the dales up north, I've heard tell?'

They discovered that they had both been born in Leeds, Maisie in Armley, and Bob in the Sheepscar district, where he still lived. She told him about her evacuation to the northern dales and how she had come to look upon Middlebeck as her true home. But her desire to travel, to 'spread her wings', as she put it, had led her back to Leeds.

'Sometimes I can't believe how lucky I am,' she told him. 'My promotion to manageress, and now this chance to be a courier for a while...'

She learned that Bob had worked for Galaxy ever since Henry Galloway had started the company. Before that he had been a bus driver for the Leeds City Transport company.

At ten-thirty they strolled back up Princes Street to their hotel. The lounge was almost deserted, apart from a group in a corner playing a game of cards.

'Not much in the way of entertainment in this hotel,' remarked Bob. 'You have to amuse yourselves, but most folks are tired out with tramping round Edinburgh all day. Wait till we get to Callander though. They put on a Scottish night, Scottish dancing an' all that. And there's a young fellow that sings all them well-known songs, "Annie Laurie" and "Loch Lomond"... Real talented he is.'

'Good; I'll look forward to that...' Maisie stifled a yawn. 'Goodnight, Bob. Thanks for looking after me. See you in the morning...'

There was only a half-day excursion the following morning, after which the clients had a free afternoon in which to shop or do their own sightseeing. Bob drove the coach around the countryside on the outskirts of Edinburgh, as far as the Royal Botanical Gardens, and then back to Arthur's Seat. The eager tourists scrambled up the lower slopes of the extinct volcano, exclaiming at the magnificent views over the city, and standing in groups, or singly, to have their photographs taken. Maisie lost count of the number of times she was snapped, on her own, or with her arm around one or another of the passengers. Possibly some of the snaps would find their way back to Galaxy's head office, as promised, and would certainly be passed around friends and relations back home.

'And that's Maisie, our courier. A lovely girl she was; nothing was too much trouble...' At least she hoped that was what they would say...

Maisie and Bob stayed in the lounge after the evening meal, chatting with some of the guests, mainly passengers from the coach, although there were a few private guests there as well. Bob was keen to show off the items he had bought that afternoon as presents for his family. His wife, Mavis, and his children, ten-year-old Susan and eight-year-old Eddie, featured a lot in his conversation. He had bought a large box of Edinburgh rock in several pastel colours. Maisie had tried it once and had found it to be a sickly sweet confection, not a patch on the proper Blackpool rock, the bright pink minty sort that you could buy at all the seaside resorts.

'And this is for our Susan...' A Scottish girl doll, complete with kilt, sporran, tam o' shanter and frilly white blouse, scores of which were to be seen in the shop windows of Princes Street and the surrounding area. 'And a red tartan tie for Eddie; Royal Stuart, it is... And this is for the wife, my Mavis...' He opened a small box to reveal a Celtic brooch; stones of various muted colours in a silver setting in the shape of a round shield. It was only costume jewellery to be sure, but quite beautiful and chosen with love and care, as were the other items. Just tourist souvenirs, but Maisie knew that the recipients would love them.

'D'you think she'll like it?' he asked, a little anxiously.

'Of course she will,' replied Maisie. 'There's no doubt about that... She's a very lucky lady,' she added.

They said goodbye to Edinburgh the following morning. The journey to Callander would not be a long one, so they made a midday break at Stirling to visit the castle high above the Firth of Forth. After she had finished her talk – the first time she had done that particular one – about the castle... 'It was lived in by the various King Jameses, but turned into the luxurious dwelling place you see today by King James the Sixth, or James the First for us Sassenachs...' the passengers were given ample free time for lunch.

She did not mind too much when a few of them were five minutes' late returning to the coach, the first time that this had happened. She didn't think they could get lost here, and now that they had left Edinburgh there was a more free and easy atmosphere to the holiday. It may be a holiday for them, but it's not for you! she reminded herself. All the same, she was conscious of a certain gaiety, a lifting of her spirits in anticipation as they took the road north-west towards Callander.

The Cameron Hotel was a greystone building in its own grounds on the outskirts of the busy little town. No sooner had Bob pulled into the car park than a grey-haired man, holding a clip-board, came on board.

'Hello there, Bob.' He shook hands with him. 'Nice to see you again. You've made good time. And good afternoon, ladies and gentlemen...'

There was a rousing greeting of 'Good afternoon...' from the travellers; they were all finding their feet now.

'And good afternoon to you too... Maisie.' He glanced at her badge. 'You must be our new courier. A very special welcome to you...

'Now, ladies and gentlemen, my name is Gordon Cameron – yes, you've guessed; I'm Scottish! – and I am the manager of the Cameron Hotel. My family and I will do our best to make sure you all have a happy and comfortable stay with us. I will read out the numbers of your rooms, then you can go to the desk and collect your keys from Moira, our receptionist. It won't take long. Don't worry about your luggage. Bob and I, and my son, will see that it is brought to your rooms as soon as possible...'

Maisie looked around the spacious foyer. It was rather dark – she guessed the building dated from the mid-Victorian era – but it was not gloomy. The windows were quite small and mullioned, although one of them was of stained glass depicting Bonny Prince Charlie in his Stuart tartan kilt. The carpet was a serviceable green and black tartan and several green leather armchairs were grouped around two low tables. On the walls there were prints of Highland cattle and animal scenes that she thought were copies of Landseer. A stag's head looked down from the alcove above the door, which was not really to her liking.

She stood to one side, waiting till the end to claim her key. There was a young fair-haired man as well as the receptionist behind the desk, giving out the keys and welcoming the guests. Bob was already busy, heaving suitcases, one in each hand, from the boot of the coach into the foyer. He paused for a moment, putting the cases down and wiping his brow.

'Here, Maisie... I want you to meet somebody. This is Andy Cameron, the young fellow I was telling you about, the one that sings so nicely. And not only that, he's the chef an' all! Andy...this is Maisie, our new courier.'

She stepped towards the desk, reaching for the young man's oustretched hand.

'Hello there, Maisie,' he said. 'I'm very pleased to make your acquaintance. You are, indeed...very welcome.'

She found herself looking into the pair of bluest eyes she had ever seen, shining with pleasure and good humour, and a wide smiling mouth.

'Hello...' she said, and her voice was almost a whisper. 'I'm very pleased to meet you, too.'

# Chapter Twenty-Four

Andrew Cameron was the son of Gordon Cameron, the owner and manager of the hotel and, as Bob had said, the chef of whom she had already heard such glowing reports. After a few seconds, during which she felt as though she was drowning in his intense blue gaze, she pulled herself together and smiled.

'Bob has been singing your praises ever since we left Leeds,' she told him. 'I'm sure we are in for a veritable feast.'

'Aye, I've one or two wee surprises up my sleeve,' he grinned. 'I like to ring the changes and try out new ideas. And on Friday night we have our special Scottish banquet...'

'Let me guess... Haggis, followed by roast venison?'

'Wait and see...! You'll be here for the rest of the season will you, Maisie? Every three weeks, I mean, when the tour is here?'

'I'm...not sure,' she replied. 'There will be a permanent replacement for Thelma eventually, but it's not quite decided yet.' It was intended, in fact, that she should fill in only for the next three weeks or so, but she was beginning to think that it might not be a bad idea to extend her time as courier...

Andy nodded and smiled. 'You'll see how you like us first, eh? Aye, well, that's no' a bad idea.' His voice was easy on the ear, a gentle Scottish burr, not too pronounced, and with a friendly and sincere tone. She guessed he was in his mid-twenties, quite tall and reasonably handsome in a craggy sort of way; a younger edition of his father, with the same firm jawline and crinkly hair, the colour of pale corn.

'Now – I mustn't take up any more of your time. Here's the key to your room, Maisie. It's on the second floor. We've no lift, but the stairs are quite shallow and manageable for the older guests. Is that your bag? Very good; I'll carry it up for you…'

She followed him up the stairs, carpeted, like the foyer, in the green and black tartan. The sun was shining through a stained-glass window on the first landing, depicting a Scottish warrior, casting shimmering lozenges of red, yellow and purple on the dark carpet.

'That's Rob Roy Macgregor,' said Andy, following her gaze. 'Somewhat stylised, no doubt, but he's quite a hero round these parts, so he is. I hope you've been brushing up on your Sir Walter Scott?'

'I have indeed,' replied Maisie. '"The Lady of the Lake" and all that…'

'Aye, and we've a likeness of her as well on the next landing… There she is,' he said, when they had climbed the remainder of the stairs. 'Lady Ellen Douglas, the original Lady of the Lake. I say a likeness, but no one really knows, do they, what she looked like?' The stained glass portrayed her in a blue gown looking out from the battlements of a castle.

Maisie's room was just two steps away. 'There you are,' said Andy. 'Bathroom and all the necessities down the corridor… We'll be serving a cup of tea for the guests in about half an hour or so, in the downstairs lounge. So I'll leave you in peace now, Maisie. See you later…'

The room, quite small but adequate, was at the back of the hotel, overlooking a pleasant garden area. There was a paved terrace and steps leading down to a lawn, and beyond that a stream and a wooded area. She stood there for a few moments, drinking in the view across to the distant hills. These mountains of the Trossachs were not particularly high, but impressive for all that, bathed in the sunlight of the late afternoon. It was all so lovely, so peaceful… Maisie felt an inexplicable surge of happiness seize hold of her.

She turned away from the window, flopping down on the bed and shaking her head in bewilderment. If she were honest with herself she knew only too well the reason for the feeling of joy and light-heartedness that had come over her. A smile from a pair of blue eyes...

Eyes as blue as the bluebells in the woods in springtime, beyond Nixons' farm; the blue of a summer sky; or cornflowers in the Rectory garden... Stop it, you silly fool! she admonished herself as all kinds of similes, the sort that you read in romantic stories, came into her mind. Whatever was she thinking about, allowing her head to be turned by a winning smile?

He was a good-looking young man, to be sure, very friendly and personable, but to be so suddenly smitten, as she felt she had been... It was ages since a member of the opposite sex had had that sort of effect on her. Not since... Bruce. The thought of Bruce Tremaine, coming into her mind unexpectedly – she didn't often, consciously, think about him now – gave her a jolt; she wondered momentarily, how he was faring. Had he married again, or was he engaged? She did not think so, or word would have reached her via the Middlebeck grapevine. The other young men with whom she had spent some time over the past few years – Ted, Colin, Mike Palmer, who was still waiting and hoping that she might have a change of heart – had been pleasant enough companions. Occasionally she had felt the stirrings of what she supposed was desire; it was good to be cherished and made a fuss of, and she had returned their kisses and embraces, but she had never felt, with any of them, that the friendship could ever develop into something more lasting.

You silly fool, Maisie Jackson! she told herself again. He will probably turn out to be married. He might even have a couple of kids; he was plenty old enough. Or, at the very least, a young man as attractive and agreeable as Andy Cameron was sure to have a fiancée or a steady girlfriend.

She had a quick 'wash and brush-up' in the bedroom washbasin, after locating the necessary little room down the corridor. Very few hotels had bedrooms with their own private baths and toilets, certainly not the hotels that Galaxy used on their tours. The cost of these rooms would be too expensive a price for clients to pay at the moment; but these 'en suite' facilities, as they were called, were gradually creeping into the larger, 'posher' establishments. It would be nice to have your own lav and bath, thought Maisie, but she could not see that happening in the near future.

She applied a fresh coating of cherry-red lipstick, the same colour as the stripes on her blouse, but did not change out of that and her navy skirt. She was still officially on duty, although it was customary to change later, for evening dinner. Then she went downstairs and located the lounge which opened off the entrance hall. It was a large room, much lighter and brighter than the foyer, with a red tartan carpet around the sides and a polished wooden square in the centre which she guessed would be the dance floor. There was a baby grand piano on a small stage at one end of the room and all around the carpeted area there were groups of comfortable chairs and low glass-topped tables. Most of the guests, it seemed, were already assembled, drinking the tea being poured out by a couple of waitresses with gay tartan pinnies over their black skirts.

Maisie sat down at a table with two middle-aged ladies she had met earlier in the week. She had met and spoken to everyone, of course, but these two were nice and friendly without being too effusive. Some clients could be rather demanding and over-friendly, thinking it gave them a certain amount of kudos, being well in with the courier.

'Have a shortbread biscuit,' said Beattie, one of the ladies, pushing a doily-covered plate towards her. 'They're delicious, aren't they, Gladys?'

'Mmm... I'm on my second one already,' said that lady. 'But we shouldn't really, not if we want to do justice to our meal tonight... Oh look – I think Mr Cameron is going to talk to us.'

Gordon Cameron stood at the end of the room on the little dais to address them. 'Once again, ladies and gentlemen, good afternoon to you. I hope you have all settled into your rooms. Any problems – extra pillows required, or if you would like an early morning wake-up knock at the door – just come and see us at reception. As I said before, we will do all we can to make your stay here a very happy one.

'This is a family concern...' He pronounced it as 'concairn' with the Scottish intonation that Maisie was finding so pleasant to listen to. '...myself, my wife, Jeanette, and my son, Andrew. Then there is Moira, our receptionist, and our small team of waiters and waitresses, plus the two assistant chefs who help my son. We all work together as a happy family...'

Maisie glanced around unobtrusively as he was speaking. There was no sign of Andy, but she assumed he would already be hard at work in the kitchen; nor, as yet, of the wife that Gordon had mentioned. She noted, too, with interest, that there was no mention of any daughter-in-law...unless, of course, she reminded herself, there was one elsewhere who played no part in the running of the hotel.

Gordon Cameron was telling them that the Cameron Hotel had been in the family for several generations, handed down from father to son. 'Aye, once we'd settled down and stopped fighting one another we decided on the more peaceful occupation of looking after tourists. The Camerons of old belonged to a warrior clan, you ken. Aye, we were loyal to the Stuart cause. No doubt you'll have seen our window to Bonnie Prince Charlie. But I can assure you that we are now loyal subjects of His Majesty King George the Sixth, God bless him. There he is, to prove there's no ill feeling...'

On the wall opposite the windows there were three large pictures; a portrait of King George and Queen Elizabeth in ceremonial dress; a photograph of Princess Elizabeth and the Duke of Edinburgh on their wedding day; and a painting of Balmoral Castle, Queen Victoria's favourite Highland retreat.

They were informed of the times of breakfast and dinner and of the events that were planned for the evenings when they returned from their tours. This evening there would be an informal get-together in the lounge; Scottish dancing would take place on Thursday; and, to end the week, there would be a banquet on the Friday evening, followed by an entertainment of singing and dancing.

—

Maisie leaned back in her comfortable chair, sipping her orange juice and listening contentedly to the voices around her, all joining in heartily with the familiar Scottish songs and ballads. Andy was leading the singing, strolling round from table to table with a microphone in his hand, inviting people here and there to join in or sing a line or two on their own. Many were too inhibited to do so, but those who did were rewarded with a cheer from the folk sitting near them.

Jeanette, Gordon Cameron's wife, was seated at the piano, and she seemed to be able to play anything that was requested. She was a bonny, plumpish woman with merry brown eyes, and hair as dark as her husband's and son's was fair. Both of them, Mr and Mrs Cameron, appeared to be in their late rather than early fifties, putting them at well turned thirty, Maisie surmised, when their only son Andy was born.

Maisie joined in with the songs she knew, but not too enthusiastically at first. She didn't want people to think she was showing off; although she knew she had a good voice and, what was more, that voice was longing to be heard. Singing was a pleasure she had not had much time or opportunity to indulge in of late. Oddly enough, as she heard the Scottish songs she had not heard for years, she was transported back in memory to the schoolroom in Middlebeck and the singing lessons with the headmistress.

Charity Foster had not been much of a pianist, but she had done her best. The children had sung along lustily from their little red books of words, their voices getting louder and louder to compete with Miss Foster's heavy chords on the piano.

*'Oh ye'll tak the high road, and I'll tak the low road,*
*And I'll be in Scotland afore ye...'*

they had chorused, having little idea of what the words
meant, but it was a good tune.

Or 'Charlie is me darling...' Maisie remembered the sly
glances of the little girls to one another, as there had been a
handsome lad in their class called Charlie, and he had
blushed crimson each time it was sung. And another
favourite had been 'The Bluebells of Scotland'...

*'Oh where, tell me where has my Highland laddie gone?...*
*'He's gone to fight the foe for King George upon*
*   the throne...'*

Those must have been the warriors who had not supported
the Stuart cause, she pondered now. But they had been given
no inkling as children as to the history behind the words; she
had picked that up much later through her own reading. But
why was Andy singing it, she wondered, if his clan had
supported the Stuarts? Probably because it was just a jolly
good song, now, as it had been in the schoolroom.

Andy was into the songs from the Hebrides now, which
were not quite so familiar to most of the guests.

'Westering home and a song in the air,' he sang in his
pleasant tenor voice as he came near to Maisie's table. She
returned his smile, then decided to throw caution to the
winds as she joined in with the next verse.

*'Tell me o' lands of the Orient gay,*
*Speak o' the riches and joys of Cathay;*
*Aye, but it's grand to be waking at day*
*At haem with my ain folk in Islay...'*

He smiled his approval at her when they came to the end of
the song. 'And a round of applause, please, ladies and
gentlemen, for our charming courier, Maisie.' He nodded

confidently. 'And we haven't heard the last of that lovely voice, I can promise you that… I'll see you later,' he said quietly, leaning down to speak to her. 'I didn't realise you could sing. Would you sing for us, please, tomorrow night, or Friday. Or why not both nights?'

'I'll… I'll think about it,' she replied, finding herself blushing a little. 'Yes…probably I will.'

He nodded his approval at her again before addressing the audience. 'Thank you, Maisie… And now, ladies and gentlemen, my mother, Jeanette, will entertain you on the piano. Just background music whilst you chat to one another. Thank you all for being such a nice friendly crowd. I can see we are going to have a grand time together these next few days.'

Maisie was sitting with Bob the driver, the two ladies, Beattie and Gladys, whom she found comfortable and easy to get along with, and another married couple whom she had spoken to rather more than the others, as they occupied the front seat on the coach, next to her courier's seat.

'My goodness, Maisie; you've been hiding your light under a bushel,' said Hilda, the lady from the front seat. 'Hasn't she, Jim?'

'Aye, you've got a grand voice,' said Jim. 'And you mustn't be shy, lass. We'd love to hear you sing for us. Of course you're not shy, are you, not really? You couldn't be, not in the job you've got.'

'No, that's true,' replied Maisie. 'I must admit that shyness has never been one of my problems. When I was a little girl I had far too much to say,' she laughed. 'I was a bit dropped on, though, when Andy asked me to sing tomorrow. I've no music with me, but I expect Mrs Cameron – Jeanette – will be able to play whatever I choose. She's a lovely pianist, isn't she?'

'She is that,' replied Bob as they listened, with one ear, whilst they were talking together, to the gentle lilting piano music. Jeanette had a touch which made the keys sing as she played the familiar tunes – not Scottish ones now – from well known musical shows, 'The Desert Song', 'Bitter Sweet', 'The Maid of the Mountains', and, more up to date, 'Oklahoma'.

'They're a talented family altogether,' Bob continued. 'Mr Cameron, the boss, he plays the bagpipes. I dare say he'll give us a tune – if you can call it a tune,' he grimaced, 'on Friday night when we have the banquet. Not much in my line, bagpipes; it sounds more like cats yowling, but he's good, I've got to give him that. And I told you about Andy and his singing, didn't I?' It was Maisie that he was talking to. The other four were now engaged in a discussion of previous coach holidays they had enjoyed, always a favourite topic of conversation.

'Yes, you did,' said Maisie, 'but I didn't realise he was also the chef. As you say, he's...very talented.'

'You enjoyed the meal then? Well, I could tell you did,' Bob chuckled. He and Maisie had sat at a little table for two, where they would take all their meals. Hotel managers realised that enough was enough; when you had been with the passengers all day you enjoyed a little privacy at meal times.

'It was superb,' she replied. The mushroom soup, tender lamb steaks baked with potatoes and leeks, and the light lemon sponge to finish with, had all been delicious. 'I shall have to watch my waistline, though. I think I'd better ask for a small portion tomorrow night, especially if I've to sing afterwards.'

'If you've got the will power,' laughed Bob. 'I'm afraid I haven't when it comes to food. My wife's complaining that I've got what she calls a beer belly, but I tell her it's certainly not the beer. Ne'er mind, eh? I shall have a jolly good walk around on Friday, when it's my free day, to get rid of some of these extra pounds.'

'Is that what you usually do? I suppose you have quite a lot of time to kill, don't you, on these tours?'

'Aye, there's all the waiting around while you're visiting your castles and what-have-you; and Henry Galloway insists that we have one day off on each tour. That's the rule, of course, with all coach companies, but whether they all keep to it is another matter. I'm not easily bored, though. I can always find summat to do to pass the time. I don't get fed up with my own company. If you find your own company boring, then other folks will as well, that's what I always think.'

'That's true,' agreed Maisie. 'But nobody could find you boring, Bob, that's for sure... Tell me – Andy Cameron, is he married?' She spoke in a matter-of-fact voice, or so she hoped, determined not to reveal that she was really the slightest bit interested. But Bob's humorous grey eyes twinkled and he gave a chuckle.

'I thought it wouldn't be long before you asked me that.' She raised her eyebrows in a casual manner.

'No reason, Bob, honestly. I just wondered, that's all.'

'No, he's not married, Maisie,' he replied, quite seriously, 'and he's not got a lady friend at the moment, at least not as far as I know...  I wouldn't blame you, lass, if you fancied your chances there,' he whispered. 'He's a grand lad; not just good-looking, he's a really nice bloke an' all.'

'Yes, he does seem...very nice,' agreed Maisie. She and Bob exchanged a conspiratorial smile before she went on to change the subject.

'So...we're off to the Trossachs tomorrow, Bob, and Loch Katrine. It's all new country to me, so I will be relying on you to find the way around. I've got my spiel ready, but it's more of a relaxing day tomorrow, isn't it? I must be careful not to overdo the talking... The highlight will be the steamer trip round the loch, won't it? Then we stop for lunch at Balquhidder, don't we?'

'Aye, that's right...'

Jeanette Cameron was playing Ivor Novello melodies now; 'Perchance to Dream'... Maisie stopped talking and listened as she heard the familiar strains of 'We'll Gather Lilacs', the song she had thought of as 'my song'. Bruce had asked her to sing it at his twenty-first birthday party, which had turned out to be his engagement party. And so it had never become 'our song', hers and Bruce's, as she had hoped at one time that it might. Perhaps she could sing it tomorrow night...

But as the memories came flooding back she knew it would not be a good idea. She was remembering the English lane of the song which had always been, in her mind, a lane way beyond Tremaine House and Nixons' farm. A lane that was white and fragrant with blossom in springtime; gold and brown and russet in the autumn, with ruby red berries glistening in the hedgerows; and sparkling silvery white when the first frosts and snow arrived. A lane she had wandered along with Bruce...and Audrey and Doris as well, of course. But that was all a long time ago, or so it seemed to her now. It was time to move on and, maybe, to start gathering new experiences, the memories of the future. 'We'll Gather Lilacs' was part of the past...

She was pensive for a few moments, lost in her thoughts and memories... Jeanette was playing something different now; tunes that were not quite so familiar. She listened carefully, frowning to herself a little. Then she recognised the music. It was from *Brigadoon*. Of course it would be; the Scottish musical show that had been performed on Broadway and later on the London stage, about a village that only appeared – what was it? – once every hundred years?

'It's almost like being in love...' she hummed along to the melody. No, she couldn't sing that one. People might start to get the wrong idea! Jeanette moved on to a different melody, one that Maisie had always thought was a charming song. She had sung it along with the radio many times, but she had never sung it as a solo. It was a long time, in fact, since she had sung a solo at all.

'And all I want to do is wander, through the heather on the hill...' She mouthed the words, singing them softly to herself. Yes, that's the song she would sing; 'The Heather on the Hill'.

'A penny for them,' said Bob suddenly. She gave a start.

'Sorry, Bob; were you saying something?'

'No, not really, but you were miles away,' he laughed. 'I reckon they're worth more than a penny, eh Maisie, your thoughts?'

'They might be...' she answered. 'As a matter of fact, I was thinking about what I'm going to sing tomorrow night. And now I've decided. Would you excuse me please, Bob? I'll just go and have a word with Mrs Cameron.' That lady was now taking a well-earned rest from the piano, and was drinking an orange juice that someone had bought for her. 'And then I think I'll turn in. It's been a long day and I want to be fresh for tomorrow.'

'Aye, all right, love,' said Bob. 'That's very wise. I shan't be long after you. Goodnight, Maisie...'

'Goodnight, Maisie,' echoed the group of passengers. 'See you in the morning...'

Jeanette said she would be delighted to accompany Maisie the following evening, and she lent her a copy of the music. Maisie wanted to be sure she knew the words off by heart; it was so unprofessional to sing from a copy. She had been hoping that Andy might reappear to discuss it with her, but he was nowhere to be seen. He had said, 'See you later...' but perhaps that meant tomorrow...

Breakfast the following morning had a Scottish flavour. Maisie said no to the oatmeal porridge and the potato cakes, but was unable to resist the finnan haddock – which the Scots called Finnan Haddie – poached in milk and butter. It was a pleasant change from bacon and eggs, in fact she had never tasted such delicious fish.

Andy, she presumed, would be busy in the kitchen. She guessed he would be not merely busy but rushed off his feet, cooking breakfasts not only for the coach party, but for several private guests as well, about fifty people in all. And the breakfast menu was quite extensive, with eggs cooked in a variety of ways – boiled, fried, poached or scrambled – as well as sausages, mushrooms, tomatoes and black pudding, in addition to the bacon.

They were all assembled in the foyer by nine-thirty ready to start their day's tour, waiting for Bob to bring the coach round from the parking spot at the back of the hotel. It was then that Andy appeared at Maisie's side. She felt a sudden surge of happiness, and an excitement which she knew she must not reveal too openly. In fact she must try not to show at all the effect that his sudden presence had on her; she was not some silly teenager.

'Maisie...' He put his hand on her arm and she felt a tingle right through her. 'I wanted to catch you before you set off.'

'Oh...hello, Andy,' she said easily. 'You want to know about my song, do you? Yes; I've decided I'd quite like to sing for you all, but don't expect too much, will you? I'm rather rusty; it's ages since I sang in public.'

'Och, you'll be fine; I know you will. My mother has already told me what you've chosen, and very nice too. That musical is a particular favourite of mine. Have another one up your sleeve, though, won't you? They're sure to want an encore... Ah, here's Bob now, raring to go.' The driver was sitting at the wheel with the engine running. 'Enjoy your day, Maisie... Have a good time everyone,' Andy called to the rest of the crowd as they went out of the door and started to mount the steps of the coach. 'See you all later...'

'Goodbye, Andy...' they chorused. And after Bob's cheery good morning to them all they were quickly on their way.

The area known as the Trossachs was a stretch of country some five miles wide which was often known as 'the Highlands in miniature'. It was a most beautiful region of craggy hills and sparkling lochs, birch-covered mountains, tumbling streams, moorland and glen, all contained in a smallish area. Maisie told her passengers how tourists had started to come to the Trossachs at the beginning of the nineteenth century when Sir Walter Scott wrote his novel, *Rob Roy* and his epic poem, 'The Lady of the Lake'. She told them the tale of Rob Roy Macgregor who stole sheep from the Lowland pastures to feed his clansmen. He was a fierce Jacobite follower, and his reputation was similar to that of England's Robin Hood, one who stole from the rich to give to the poor. Strangely enough, he did not suffer a violent death, and after being pardoned he spent the rest of his days in freedom in the little village of Balquhidder.

'We will be visiting his grave later today,' said Maisie, 'but now, ladies and gentlemen, I am going to stop talking and let you enjoy this beautiful scenery in peace.' That was what she wanted to do herself. It was her first visit to the Scotland north of Edinburgh, and she had not imagined anything quite so awe-inspiring.

It proved to be a memorable day, with a memorable evening to follow. After the meal – which included the roast beef that Bob had been looking forward to all week! – a troupe of Scottish dancers came in to entertain the guests, dressed, of course, in their kilts of various tartans. The Cameron men, Gordon and Andy, were also wearing their kilts in the Cameron tartan of their ancient clan. This was a bold red and black, complete with sporran and worn with black velvet jackets and lace jabots.

Maisie's eyes, try as she might to prevent them, kept straying towards Andy's striking figure as he sat nodding his head in time to the rhythm of the dancing. 'The Eightsome Reel', 'The 'Dashing White Sergeant', 'Strip the Willow', 'The Duke of Perth'... The troop performed them all so expertly, their kilts swirling, their feet darting in and out, the men just as light and graceful in their movements as the women. And then the audience was invited to join in an eightsome reel. It was tremendous fun, and although some of the guests appeared to have two left feet, it was obvious that Bob had done it before. Maisie, too, felt she acquitted herself very well; she had had a little experience of Scottish dancing at the school lessons they had shared with the boys. Towards the end of the dance she partnered Andy, and he smiled and gave her a friendly wink before he whirled her round so fast that her feet scarcely touched the ground.

'That's enough, I think,' he laughed as the dance came to an end. 'I mustna exhaust you. You must get your breath back before you sing. And so must I. Come along now and I'll buy you a drink.'

The dancing had finished and it was time for a break before the second half of the evening's entertainment began. There was a small bar area, licensed only to serve drinks to guests who were staying there and not open to the general public.

'I'll stick to orange juice,' said Maisie. 'I must keep a clear head while I'm singing. I don't drink much apart from fruit juice anyway when I'm doing this job, although the passengers are continually asking me, 'What will you have?''

'Aye, so I can imagine,' said Andy, who had also decided to drink orange juice. 'They're always asking me if I'd like "a wee dram"! But I'm no' a true Scot, at least as far as the whisky is concairned. I can take it or leave it... Now, Maisie Jackson, tell me all about yourself...'

She suddenly felt shy, an unusual state of affairs for her, and a little confused. She could feel herself drowning in the intense blue of his eyes; it was the way he was smiling at her so eagerly and encouragingly. She gave a little laugh. 'What do you want to know?' she asked.

'Anything, everything...' he shrugged.

Once she had started she found it easy to talk to him, but then Maisie had never found it difficult to talk; and Andy was a good listener, joining in with his own comments and repartee. He very soon knew the outline, if not all the details, of her life story. Her time as an evacuee and eventual settling down in Middlebeck; her decision to leave school early and work at a travel agency rather than go to college as her mother had wanted her to do.

'But I think she's realised now that I made the right decision,' she said. 'Mum only wanted what she thought was best for me.'

'Parents always do,' said Andy. 'Mine were the same. It was more or less taken for granted, of course, that I should go into the family business, but they wouldna have insisted if I'd been dead against it. At least, I dunna think so... But as it happened I never wanted anything else but to be a chef, like my father. He was the chef before me, you ken, but he made sure I had the proper training, and not just what I learned from him. I did my training at Gleneagles; and now...here I am, and here's where I'll stay, I suppose. But you can't always see what's round the corner, can you?' She could not fathom, at that moment, his enigmatic smile.

'So, Maisie...you're not really a courier? But you obviously enjoy it. You're good at it too, and I can tell that the clients like you. Is there no a chance you might decide to carry on with it? Won't you find office work rather tedious after you've been on the road?'

Yes, so I will; I know I will...said a small voice inside Maisie's head. How on earth would she settle down to routine after all this? But another voice was warning her not to read too much into what Andy was saying. He was just being nice and friendly; he was not begging her to stay...

'I really can't say,' she answered. 'There is a lot to consider, and this job – the courier's job – is not as permanent as being in charge of an office. Anyway, I've promised to fill in for the next few weeks, and then...well, I will have to see. But I may well be back in three weeks' time...' she added quietly.

'I certainly hope so,' he replied, smiling at her in the way that made her heart turn a somersault. 'Now, Maisie...are you ready? I think we'll start with your solo, then you won't have time to get nervous. OK?'

'Yes... OK, Andy,' she replied.

He jumped up and moved over to the stage. 'And now, ladies and gentlemen,' he began, when the noise had hushed a little, 'we have had the dancing, and so...on with the singing. And this is the moment you have all been waiting for. Here is Maisie, your courier, and she is going to sing for us one of the lovely songs from *Brigadoon*. Here she is – Maisie Jackson.'

She could feel the warmth of their applause even before

she started to sing, and the slight fluttering of nerves that she had been experiencing vanished completely. She smiled across at Jeanette who played the opening bars. The she began.

> *'The mist of May is in the gloamin', and all the*
> *    clouds are holdin' still,*
> *So take my hand and let's go roamin' through the*
> *    heather on the hill...'*

It was a most evocative song and she was aware, from their smiling faces, of the emotional response of the audience. She sang it through twice, as she had agreed with Jeanette. When she reached the last line of the song she realised that Andy had come onto the stage and was standing next to her. He gently took hold of her hand and joined in the last line with her,

> *'...If you're not there I won't go roamin' through*
> *    the heather on the hill,*
> *The heather on the hill...'*

Then they smiled at one another as the audience clapped and cheered.

# Chapter Twenty-Five

B ack home in her flat on Saturday evening, after she had said goodbye to her passengers and to Bob, Maisie felt as though she was just awakening from a dream. The last few days had been filled with such out of this world experiences, and now it was time to return to reality.

Harsh reality, she thought to herself, wryly, as she made a cup of tea and prepared a simple meal of beans on toast; a far cry from the lavish Scottish banquet of the last evening. She now had a day and a half in which to adjust and to get her thoughts in order before embarking, on Monday morning, on her next tour to Stratford-upon-Avon. She felt tempted to ring Henry Galloway at once, to tell him that she would like to take on the job of courier on a full-time basis; but she was forcing herself to exercise a little commonsense and self-control. It would be sensible, she knew, to do the next two tours and – possibly – the next Scottish one and then to take stock of the situation.

She ate her meal and washed up, tried but failed to get interested in a book, then retired to bed early. But not to sleep; a host of memories were chasing round and round in her mind. Eventually she gave up trying to sleep and allowed herself to wallow in them...

The skirl of the bagpipes as Gordon Cameron played the haunting Scottish airs; her first taste of venison – tender and surprisingly sweet, roasted to a pleasant brownish-pinkness, but not oozing with blood, so as not to offend the Sassenach taste; the sparkling blue waters of Loch Katrine on what had been a perfect summer's day; the multi-coloured tartans and nimble feet of the dancers; but, above all, her memories of Andy Cameron were the ones that kept returning.

Surely she could not have imagined the tender look in his
eyes as he had sung along with her of wandering 'through the
heather on the hill'? And when he had sung, on the last
night, 'Will ye no' come back again...?' he had looked
straight at her. When they had left on Saturday morning –
was it really only today? – he had kissed her lightly on the
cheek.

'It's been good to meet you, Maisie. So...all being well, we
will see you in three weeks' time?' His voice had held a
question and he had seemed eager to hear her answer.

'I hope so, Andy...'

'And so do I...'

But am I imagining all this, she thought, or am I falling in
love with him? Could it just be, though, that she felt that the
time was ripe; that it really was time that she fell in love with
someone? And Andy was the only one who had made her
feel this way since... Bruce. The thought of him intruded
momentarily, but she pushed it away. Bruce was in the past.

Andy had made her feel more alive, more vital and aware
of the sights and sounds going on around her. But was it just
she, Maisie, who felt that way, or had she had a similar effect
upon him as well? She could not be sure. But time would
tell... She had already decided that she would do the next
tour to Callander; but as far as the months – and years? –
beyond that date, she did not dare to look so far ahead, not
yet.

Monday morning brought the start of a new five-day tour;
different faces, a different driver and a different venue. The
countryside of the South Midlands, around the River Avon,
was an area she had not visited before, just as the Scottish
Lowlands had been. But one again she had swotted up about
all the places they were to visit. That had filled up her
Sunday very nicely and had stopped her from doing too
much day-dreaming.

Stratford-upon-Avon and all the buildings connected with
Shakespeare; Anne Hathaway's cottage; the castles of
Kenilworth and Warwick; and the nearby towns of Coventry

and Royal Leamington Spa all added up to make an extremely busy and interesting week for Maisie, as well as for her passengers. And once again they were full of praise for her when the five days came to an end.

She called in the Galaxy office on Saturday morning as she had promised to do, to see if all was well and if there were any messages for her. She found Colin Mather very obviously in charge – looking a little suspiciously at Maisie, in fact – and Barry busily occupied. Olwen was not there as it was her Saturday morning off.

'There's a message for you from the boss,' said Barry. 'He's coming over to Leeds today...'

The note said that Henry Galloway wished to meet her at Hagenbach's café for lunch, to talk to her about how things were going.

'Fine thanks, Henry. Everything's just fine,' she told him over the hearty meal of fish and chips that he had insisted on. 'I am really enjoying myself.' She decided to make no special mention of Scotland, but he forestalled her.

'Yes...we have already had a few letters from satisfied customers – very satisfied, I may say – from the Scottish tour. They praise you very highly, Maisie and, what is more, they said how much they enjoyed your singing!'

'Oh, how nice of them,' she said, feeling most gratified. She had sung on the last evening in Callander as well, but the Stratford tour had been a much more sober one with no singing or dancing. 'Yes, it did seem to go down rather well...'

'In fact I am wondering, Maisie, if you would like to carry on in that capacity – as courier – for the rest of the season? And beyond, if you wish... Please don't think that I am trying to get rid of you from the Leeds office. That isn't my intention at all, and if you want to go back there straight away, then you must do so. It is, after all, your office, and you have a very good reputation there...'

'But Colin is managing just as well as I ever could,' said Maisie. She smiled. 'Actually, Henry, you have solved a problem for me. I was in two minds as to whether to ask you if I could continue as courier for the rest of the season. I had decided to do the next two tours and then to take stock. But now – well – you seem to have made the decision for me...'

'Only if it is really what you want to do, Maisie...'

'Oh, it is! I can assure you that it is...' She could feel an upsurge of joy and excitement, but she knew that there must be no mention to Henry, at least for now, of the personable young man at the Cameron Hotel.

'And if you are concerned about the salary,' he went on, 'we will make it right with you. You will be paid the same rate as you have been getting as manager. A courier is not normally paid as much as an office manager, of course...'

'But there are the tips,' said Maisie smiling. 'Some people are very generous. To be honest, I hadn't really thought about that aspect of it.'

'But we have, Trixie and I,' said Henry. 'You are invaluable to us, Maisie, and you must certainly not be out of pocket. Now, this is what we have in mind, with your agreement, of course...'

He suggested that she should continue as courier for the three 'cultural' tours until the end of the season, that would be towards the end of September. After that, during the winter months, her work would be flexible. She might be asked to fill in as office manager at any of the various branches, if so required; and also to go on preliminary visits, to appraise the facilities and the general aspect of prospective new hotels, both in Great Britain and in Europe.

'We are already getting excited about next year,' Henry told her. 'In 1951 we will be extending our programme to include trips abroad; Belgium, the Netherlands and France to start with; not too far across the channel. We have a list of possible hotels and we are hoping that you and Trixie will go and give them the once-over. We will be using the cross-channel ferries for the tours; Dover to Calais, that's the shortest route and the most economical way to do it. But for you and Trixie I think we could run to air travel. Red Rose

Airlines; they're quite reasonable and efficient.'

It all sounded tremendously exciting. Maisie had never flown; in fact she had never been abroad, nor had the majority of young women of her age.

'It sounds wonderful,' she said. 'I can't quite take it in. One minute I'm quietly going about my business in Leeds, and the next minute... I'm going to travel the world!'

'Well, not quite the world,' smiled Henry. 'I don't think Galaxy will be venturing as far as the USA or Australia for some time to come! But there are certainly a couple of hotels in Paris to be reccied, and others in Brussels, Ostend, Amsterdam... These are priorities, so I would like you and Trixie to get cracking as soon as you've finished your tours. We want to get our new brochure out as soon as we can in the New Year. As a matter of fact, Trixie and I have already made a few preliminary visits. A tour to the Loire Valley, that's almost completed, and another one to Brittany, that is in the late planning stages...'

'And you will be wanting couriers for these Continental tours as well, I suppose?' asked Maisie.

'Yes, so we will... And you will be one of the first to be considered, Maisie, if you decide that is what you would like. But for the moment, let's take one step at a time, shall we? Let's not try to run before we can walk. Next week you will be in London, and the week after it will be Scotland again. And if you are agreeable I would like you to continue with your singing. Our singing courier... That is something we hadn't even thought of and it's certainly going down well with the guests. I take it that the Cameron family have no objection to you singing? I know they provide their own entertainment.'

'Oh no, they don't mind. In fact it was Andy – he's the son, I don't know if you know him?' she asked casually, 'it was Andy who invited me to sing.'

'Yes, I've met him just the once when I went up there. An excellent chef, of course; that's one of the main reasons for us going there...' Maisie stared down at her plate, hoping that her interest in that young man was not at all obvious. She had been unable to resist mentioning his name, but she must not divulge her secret feelings for him by any unguarded word or glance.

'So you have four months, more or less, Maisie, to establish yourself as a courier. Although I think you have managed to do that already, haven't you? We are very grateful to you, and I know that Colin Mather will be very pleased when we offer him the permanent post in the Leeds office. Now...you are quite sure, are you, that this is what you want? It's not too late if you feel at all undecided...'

'I'm quite sure, Henry,' she replied. 'This is definitely what I want.'

—

Bob did not seem surprised to see her nine days later when she joined him in the snack-bar at the bus station, to start their second tour together. In the meantime she had spent five hectic days in London, and the Scottish tour would seem quite peaceful and relaxing by contrast.

'Hello there, Maisie.' He grinned broadly and winked at her. 'I had a feeling, somehow, that you would be back.'

'Yes, you're stuck with me all summer, Bob,' she laughed. 'Like it or lump it!'

'Oh, I like it all right. You and me, we get on famously, don't we, love?' He smiled at her and then at his fellow drivers.

'Some chaps have all the luck, don't they?' retorted one of them. 'Goodness knows how you put up with him, Maisie love. If ever you want a change, you know where I am.'

'I'll bear it in mind, Jack...' she laughed.

Thirty-six different faces to remember once again, but she was getting quite used to that now. She devised little tricks – quirks of personality, unusual clothing or headgear, or tone of voice – to distinguish one from the other. They appreciated it when you remembered their names. She never used their Christian names, however, unless she was invited to do so, whereas she was 'Maisie' all the time.

She had worked out that she had six more Scottish tours to do before the end of the season, and about the same number to London or Stratford; although Sheila, the courier who had started that year might be asked to do a couple of those; at the moment Sheila did mainly day trips and the city tours of York. Maisie knew there was a possibility that visiting the same places every few weeks might become tedious, but it was up to her not to let any hint of boredom show in her voice or in her association with the passengers. She was continually reading up interesting new facts and anecdotes to relate, and taking notes, also, of things that members of her party told her. Sometimes they were more knowledgeable than she was.

The weather was a little inclement in Edinburgh and raincoats and umbrellas were the order of the day. When they visited Stirling Castle it bucketed down and they were forced to take what shelter they could. But by the time they arrived at Callander in the mid-afternoon the rain had almost ceased, and a fitful sun was trying its hardest to shine out from behind the grey clouds.

Gordon Cameron came onto the coach to welcome them to the hotel, as he had done before; and Andy, once again, was in the entrance hall assisting Moira in giving out the keys and then carrying the luggage.

'Hello again, Maisie,' he greeted her cheerily. 'It's good to see you. You decided to give us another try then, did you?'

'Oh, more than that, Andy,' she replied. 'I'll definitely be here for the rest of the season; well, every three weeks. We've been doing some shuffling around of jobs and I'm a full-time courier for the moment. By order of Henry Galloway, of course.' She did not want to make it too obvious that it had, in truth, been just as much her idea.

'Well, that's great; couldna' be better.' He handed her the key. 'Same room as before, Maisie. Come along noo, and we'll get your luggage upstairs.'

He paused at the bedroom door, putting down her bag and

small case. 'And I've been thinking to myself, how would it be if we were to sing a duet or two this time, you and me? Only if you're agreeable, you ken...' His blue eyes regarded her intently.

As if I could possibly refuse, she thought. Her heart gave a leap as she looked back at him, then quickly looked away before she should flounder or begin to blush. 'Of course I will,' she replied. 'That's a very good idea. "The Heather on the Hill", do you think? The audience seemed to enjoy that one.'

'Aye, so they did. We'll sing that tonight, if that's OK with you? And I have one or two others in mind... We'll get together with my mother, shall we, later tonight and see what we can sort out? It makes a nice change to sing duets instead of solos, and it's a wee while since I had someone to partner me. Cheerio then, Maisie; see you later...'

Who else had he sung with? she wondered as, once more, she started to unpack her belongings. And did he sing at other times and in other places, as well as to entertain the guests at the hotel? In a church choir, maybe, or an amateur operatic group? She knew so very little about him...

They discovered that they both liked the songs of Ivor Novello and Jerome Kern, and they tried a few later that evening; much later, in fact, when most of the guests had left the lounge or were having a last drink at the bar at the other end of the room. Maisie sang the melody line most of the time, whilst Andy harmonised above or below her. She soon realised he was quite an expert musician. He could read music perfectly, having learned to play the piano as a child, he informed her; whereas she, Maisie, had acquired her knowledge by degrees, mainly through her involvement with the church choir. Jeanette accompanied them most proficiently and was generous with her praise.

'Your voices blend beautifully,' she told them. 'Anyone would think you'd been singing together for ages. Well done, Maisie...and you too, Andy,' she laughed. 'It makes a nice change, though, to hear a different voice.'

'Very well, then; Ivor Novello tomorrow night, after the Scottish dancing, and Jerome Kern on Friday. Is that OK with you, Maisie?' asked Andy.

She nodded. 'Yes, that's fine with me...' She was feeling quite dazed and more than a little tired. It had been a long and exhausting day – but then most of them were – but pleasantly so. She knew it was time for her to retire to bed. She drank the remainder of her fruit juice, then she stood up. 'If you'll excuse me I really must go now. I have a few things to sort out before the excursion tomorrow. Thank you for playing for us, Jeanette... And thank you too, Andy; I've enjoyed it.'

'Goodnight, my dear,' said Jeanette. 'I'm sure you must be very tired. Sleep well; see you tomorrow...'

'Yes...goodnight, Maisie, and thank you too,' said Andy.

She smiled at them and left. It was not quite true that she had things to sort out for the following day. All was in order, but she knew that she must get to bed now and try to sleep. Her head was buzzing with tunes and full of jumbled impressions of the day and, most of all, of thoughts of Andy. They were getting on well together, she and Andy, she mused as she lay down between the crisp white sheets. They had decided to sing 'Waltz of my Heart' and 'Fold Your Wings' by Ivor Novello the following night. She was glad that 'We'll Gather Lilacs' had not been mentioned... In a surprisingly short time her mind closed down and she slept until the morning.

The weather during the last week of June was not nearly as sunny as the first week of the month had been. Their views of the Trossachs and Loch Katrine were somewhat obscured by the low-lying mist and drizzle. But the passengers, on the whole, were cheerful, taking the weather in their stride as they knew they had to do in Scotland. It was unusual to go a full week without rain.

And so they enjoyed even more the comforting warmth of the hotel in the evenings; the good food and pleasant company and the masterly entertainment by the singers and dancers.

Maisie's and Andy's duets were received with great enthusiasm. 'You make a lovely couple,' several of the coach passengers told her confidingly. One of them, a middle-aged spinsterish lady, surprised her by asking, in a whisper, when she returned to her seat, 'Is there something between you and that young Andy, my dear? Is he your young man?'

'Oh no,' replied Maisie, feeling her cheeks turn a little red. 'Nothing like that. I only met him a few weeks' ago. We just decided it might be nice to sing together, that's all.'

'Mmm, I see...' the curious lady replied. 'If you say so, dear; but you're a bonny lass and he's a lovely young man.' She smiled coyly at Maisie, who just laughed and shook her head.

That was on the last night after she and Andy had sung the Jerome Kern songs, 'I'm Old-fashioned' and 'The Folks who live on the Hill', both chosen because of their appeal to a rather mature audience.

Then, later on, Maisie sang her solo, 'How are Things in Glocca Morra?'... 'with apologies, ladies and gentlemen, for choosing a song that is not Scottish, but Irish, simply because it happens to be one of my favourites.'

She followed it with 'Wish upon a Star' from one of her all-time favourite films, *Pinocchio*.

*'When you wish upon a star, your dreams come true...'*

Would they come true? she wondered, when she was home again at the end of the tour. Andy had once again kissed her lightly on the cheek and said, 'See you in three weeks' time, Maisie? And you'll be thinking up some fresh songs, eh?'

'Yes, Andy, I will...' she had replied.

⌒

Once again her mind was full of the memories of her three days at the Cameron Hotel. Whilst she was there she felt joyful, filled with an exhilaration for life and kindliness towards the world at large, and especially to her coach passengers. She knew only too well the reason she felt that way, but she was trying to warn herself to be sensible, to proceed with caution. She had been careful not to smile too effusively at Andy, or to allow her eyes to linger too long when he looked at her in a tender way when they sang together. It was the way all duettists glanced at one another when they were singing a song full of sentiment and passion. It didn't mean there was anything special between them... did it?

Had she imagined, though, the look he cast in her direction when he sang, on his own, the Jerome Kern song, one that they had both agreed was one of their favourites?

> '...I will feel a glow just thinking of you,
> And the way you look tonight...'

She had felt, indeed, that she had looked her best that night, in her full-skirted summer dress of pale green with a dazzling white collar, and with her dark hair freshly shampooed to bring out the highlights. Her mirror had told her that she was attractive – it wasn't conceited to think that way, was it? – as she had applied her coral lipstick and a touch of green eye-shadow to her eyelids. She had needed no face powder as the summer sun – on the days that it had decided to shine – had brought a rosy bloom to her cheeks.

She was cautious, though, possibly too cautious, about wearing her heart on her sleeve. She knew she had been guilty of doing so before, over Bruce. Others had noticed how she felt; Anne and Audrey and her mother... And she suspected that Christine, also, had guessed at her feelings for the man she was going to marry; that was why the young woman had been so cool and unfriendly towards her. But had Bruce himself known of her feelings, she wondered? No matter, though; Bruce was in the past. She had fallen in love with Andy now; she was sure after her second meeting with him that it was so. But it was up to the man to make the first move in what was known as the mating game, and the girl must wait for him to do so. That, she had always been told, was what nice respectable girls did...and so she would wait and hope.

There were other matters, however, to occupy her mind. In five weeks' time it would be Anne Mellodey's wedding, and Maisie had made arrangements to have the week prior to that at home, first in Leeds and then in Middlebeck. Sheila, the other courier, would do the London tour that week.

She and Anne had visited Schofield's store in Leeds ages ago, soon after Anne had told her about the engagement, and had chosen their dresses; an elegant bridal gown of ivory silk brocade, and a bridesmaid's dress of pale blue silken taffeta.

There remained just one more visit to Scotland, in the middle of July, before the early August wedding. By that time the trees would be in full leaf – spring, and therefore summer, came somewhat later north of the border – and the hedgerows burgeoning with blossom. Maisie found herself looking forward to it with an intensity she had not known before.

Andy asked her to go out with him that week. On the Friday morning, Maisie's free day, they set out soon after breakfast, taking the road northwards. They travelled beyond the Trossachs to Loch Tay, and then onwards to Loch Tummel and Loch Rannoch, his red MG Midget eating up the miles.

'I remember singing about these places at school,' said Maisie. 'Loch Tummel and Loch Rannoch... How does it go? I don't think I've heard you sing that one, Andy.'

'Aye, "TheRoad to the Isles",' he nodded. 'I could include that one tonight.' He started to sing...

*'Sure by Tummel and Loch Rannoch and Loch Aber*
  *I will go,*
*By heather tracks wi' heaven in their wiles;*
*If it's thinkin' in your inner hairt there's braggarts in*
  *my step,*
*You've never felt the tangle o' the isles...'*

Maisie joined in the last line with him thinking that never in her life had she felt quite so happy.

They stopped for a midday picnic by the shores of Loch Tummel. 'They call this Queen's View,' he told her, 'because Queen Victoria was so impressed by the view that they named it after her.'

'Yes, I can imagine why,' replied Maisie. 'It really is breathtaking.'

The mountains were higher here, the tops obscured by a capping of cloud, but the lower slopes already purpling with the first blooming of the heather. The Heather on the Hill... she mused. She had sung about it and now she was seeing it for real.

They picnicked on chicken sandwiches, meat pie, crisp apples and shortbread, with a mellow white wine to add the finishing touch. 'Just one wee glass for me, though,' he said. 'I must get you back safely.'

He talked to her of his plans, one day, to own more than just the one hotel; a cluster of Cameron Hotels, say four or five, stretching from Edinburgh to as far northwards as Dundee and westwards towards Oban. But it was only a pipe dream. Besides, his father was still in control and that was the way Andy wanted it to continue at the moment. Maisie listened and they chatted together easily, but she said nothing of her own dreams. How could she?

When they had finished their meal he leaned forward and kissed her gently on the lips, just once. 'Thank you, Maisie,' he said. 'You are a lovely girl, and a great companion... But we must awa',' he laughed, springing to his feet. 'Duty calls and my colleagues will be baying for my blood if I'm no' back by three-thairty. There's a banquet to prepare...'

They packed the basket and travelling rug into the back of the car and set off back to Callander. For the rest of the day Maisie thought about that kiss, so fleeting that there had not been a chance for her to respond to it, to kiss him back... But it was a kiss all the same.

When they said goodbye the following day he kissed her on the cheek, as he had done before. But that was because Bob was there, she told herself, and all the coach passengers. Andy, as she did, realised the wisdom in being circumspect.

# Chapter Twenty-Six

At nine-thirty on Saturday morning – Saturday, the fifth of August, Anne and Roger's wedding day – there was a queue as always at Arthur's Place. The confectioner's shop had been in existence for many years, before being known by its new name, and was still as popular as ever. Arthur Rawcliffe's home-baked bread, cakes and pies had a well deserved reputation in Middlebeck and Lowerbeck and queues formed especially early on a Saturday, and on Wednesday too, those being market days in the little town.

The restaurant which had now been open for more than three months was flourishing as well. As Arthur and Lily, and Flo and Harry, had hoped, it had proved to be a popular rendezvous for shoppers taking mid-morning tea or coffee, and also for lunch-time meals. They had done a few evening functions, too, but these required advance notice; and today, of course, it would be their very first wedding. The shop part of the business would stay open only until eleven o'clock, the customers having been given due warning of this, and the café would be closed all morning whilst the room was prepared for the wedding breakfast, a three-course meal for thirty guests, at one-thirty.

Lily paused for a moment after serving one of their regular customers with a freshly-baked loaf, still warm from the oven, wrapped in tissue paper, and an assortment of 'fancies' which she had put into one of their special cardboard boxes with 'Arthur's Place' printed on the top.

'Yes, it's a lovely day, isn't it, Mrs Harrison? Like you say, real bride's weather. You're coming to the church, are you, to watch them come out? Yes, I know it's right on dinner-time, but even so I think there'll be a good crowd there... Yes,

Anne has been at the school for a good while, ever since the start of the war; a very popular teacher... No, we don't know him quite as well, but from all accounts he has made quite an impact there. You have to speak as you find, don't you, and I must say Mr Ellison has done very well for my two children... Ta-ra then...'

Arthur's Place was almost opposite the market square and Lily, as she stood looking out of the window for a moment, had a good view of the crowds of people – women in the main – thronging the stalls, buying their fruit and vegetables, cheese and eggs and farm produce, sweets and sixpenny toys for the children. It was a scene she never tired of watching; the market was such a happy friendly place.

The road that ran between the market and the shops on the opposite side was always extra busy on a Saturday morning. There was a Belisha beacon with a flashing orange light a few yards away from the confectioner's shop, which was supposed to make it easier for pedestrians, but special care was still needed when crossing the road. Children in particular were always being warned to 'Look both ways'; the number of cars on the road had increased dramatically since the end of the war.

Lily noticed a familiar figure coming away from the market stalls. It was Miss Thomson, 'Old Amelia', with a shopping basket over one arm and her other hand clutching a big black handbag. She was dressed in her tweed coat and felt hat although the day was already quite warm; but it was possible that she felt the cold keenly. She looked very frail; Lily had thought so for a while. She walked with a stoop, her head looking down at the pavement rather than ahead at the approaching traffic. A couple of cars passed whilst the old lady stood uncertainly at the kerbside; she was attempting to cross, it appeared, some yards away from the Belisha beacon. Why wasn't anyone trying to help her, thought Lily? Because nobody had noticed her; they were all engrossed in their own affairs. Lily decided she would go herself and assist the old lady. She came out from behind the counter.

'Excuse me...' she said edging round the small queue of people. 'I won't be a minute. I must go and help Miss Thomson to get across the road.'

At that moment a small green car appeared from the direction of the station and the lower end of the High Street. It was not travelling quickly at all – Lily was relieved, later, that she was able to swear to that – but Miss Thomson was either tired of waiting or, more than likely, had not seen it... Whatever the reason, she stepped off the kerb before Lily had a chance to reach her, right into the path of the oncoming vehicle. There was a sickening thud and then a screech of brakes as the bonnet of the car made contact with her small figure. The next moment Miss Thomson was lying spreadeagled on the road, her spectacles askew and shattered, her shopping basket on its side, spilling out apples and oranges and a small cabbage.

Lily gave a cry. 'Oh no, no...' and the folk on the pavement, only too well aware now of what had happened, gasped in horror. At the same moment the driver's door of the little green car opened, and Charity Foster got out. Her face was white and she was already trembling with shock and fright.

'I couldn't stop! There wasn't time; I couldn't do anything... She stepped right in front of me, so suddenly. The poor old lady... Oh no... Oh dear God! It's Miss Thomson...'

Lily hurried to Miss Foster's side and put her arm around her. 'I saw what happened; I saw it all. You didn't have time to stop. She stepped right in front of the wheels, like you said. Oh dear, are you all right? No, you're not, are you?' Miss Foster was trembling visibly now and beginning to sob, tears of shock, no doubt, for nobody had ever seen the previous headmistress lose control. She was such a sensible, level-headed person, always knowing how to cope in an emergency; but this one, it seemed, was too much for her. She was no spring chicken herself, thought Lily.

The figure on the ground was motionless and one of the few men on the scene knelt at her side. He put his head to her chest and felt at her wrist.

'I can't hear her heart, and I can't feel 'owt neither, but I can't be sure...'

'For God's sake, somebody get an ambulance,' cried another man. 'And don't move the old lady; best not to touch her. Let the ambulance men do it.'

A woman had already gone into the nearest shop, a newsagent's, and an ambulance and the police had been called. By this time quite a crowd had gathered and the traffic from both directions was at a standstill.

'I think she's dead, isn't she?' whispered Charity Foster. 'Look at her...she's not moving at all. Oh...oh dear, oh God, whatever have I done? People are always telling me that I drive too fast...'

'Shh...!' Lily admonished her. 'You mustn't say that!' Miss Foster was speaking in a quiet voice, almost inaudible with the shock, and no one except Lily could have heard what she said; but Lily realised the danger there might be in admitting to anything at all. 'Listen to me, Miss Foster... You were not driving fast at all; I can vouch for that. And when the police arrive, which they will, you must not even hint at what you have just said to me. She stepped out right in front of the car, and all these people will say so as well.'

'The police...' murmured Charity. 'Oh dear, I don't think I can stand it...'

'Come along now,' said Lily, 'come into our shop. You must sit down and rest. It's been a dreadful shock.'

'It weren't your fault, love...'

'You couldn't have avoided her; nobody could...'

'Don't you worry; we'll stick up for yer...'

Members of the crowd were quite vociferous in their support of Charity.

'Take her inside, Lily, and give her a tot of brandy,' said Arthur, who had just arrived on the scene. 'I'll wait here until t'police come, an' th' ambulance... Looks to me as though it might be too late though,' he added in a whisper. 'Poor old lass...'

The ambulance arrived quite quickly, within ten minutes, and the police at roughly the same time. Miss Thomson's seemingly lifeless body was lifted gently on to a stretcher and then into the back of the ambulance. One of the men was seen to shake his head despairingly, but they did not say whether she was alive or dead.

The policemen asked questions of the people at the scene, who were unanimous in their insistence that the driver of the car had not stood 'a snowball in hell's chance' of avoiding her. And when they went into the confectioner's shop to talk to Miss Foster, Lily told them the same thing.

'Miss Thomson's sight is not very good, officer. I don't think she is really fit to be out shopping on her own, but she lives alone and she is fiercely independent. Miss Foster here is dreadfully upset about what has happened, as you can see. She wasn't to blame...'

'So everyone says,' replied the police sergeant, 'but we have to make our enquiries, you understand...' He took a statement from Charity and her name and address.

'Yes, of course,' he said, 'I remember you. Both of my kiddies were in your class, and very well they did an' all. Now don't you worry, Miss Foster. This is just routine...' He turned to Lily. 'You know her then, the old lady who was knocked down?'

'Yes, of course. Miss Thomson; she lives next door to the school, facing the village green.'

'And...who are her next of kin, do you know?'

'Well...there is nobody really, as far as I know. She had a sister, but I believe she died some years ago. There may be nephews or nieces, but there is nobody in this area. There are plenty of people, though, who are concerned about her; the rector and his wife, and the people at the church.'

'Yes... I see. Well, thank you; that will be all for now. We will contact the hospital with regard to Miss Thomson, but it didn't look too good for her... We will let you know.

Goodbye then, and thank you for your cooperation.'

The crowd had dispersed and Arthur came back in the shop and into the room at the rear where Lily had taken Miss Foster. 'Now, Miss Foster, what can we do for you? Would you like me to run you home? Your car...'

'Yes, my car...' she said. 'I've abandoned it, haven't I? And to be quite honest, I feel at the moment as though I will never drive again.' She put her hands to her head. 'It's like a nightmare; to think that I was responsible for killing that poor old lady...'

'Now now, we don't know that yet, do we?' said Arthur. 'She may come round. Any road, you heard what everybody said. You were not to blame; it was just an accident...'

'Oh, why couldn't I have stayed at home?' said Miss Foster. 'I didn't really need to go out. I only wanted a few things from the market, so I thought I'd go early and then get back in plenty of time to get ready for Anne's wedding. Oh dear... Anne's wedding! And we were all looking forward to it so much. This couldn't have happened at a worse time. And for you as well; you must be terribly busy.' She shook her head. 'You haven't time to be bothering with me. Oh dear, I feel so confused and woolly-headed, and that's not like me at all.'

'Happen it's the effect of the brandy,' said Arthur with a wry smile. 'Now, you just sit there for a few more minutes, Miss Foster, and Lily and me, we'll decide what's the best thing to do. Aye, I know we're busy, but not so busy that we can't help a good friend. We'll be shutting t'shop quite soon anyroad...' Flo and the young girl who came to help on Saturdays had been dealing with the queue in Lily's absence.

It was decided that Harry, Arthur's brother-in-law, should run Miss Foster back home to Lowerbeck. She insisted that she would be all right when she had had a sit down and a cup of tea in her own home. As for the shopping she had intended to do, there was nothing that she required too urgently apart from the bread and cakes she always bought at the weekend. Lily wrapped these up for her, and added one of their special meat pies and two sausage rolls, free of charge. When it was time for her to depart for the wedding, which was to take place at twelve o'clock, Anne had very kindly promised to send a car for her. Arthur promised to move her car from the main road to his own parking place at the back of the shop, although Miss Foster was still vowing that she would never set foot inside the vehicle again.

'Poor old lass!' said Harry, when he returned from taking her home. 'Miss Foster, I mean, not the one as was knocked down. She's still blaming herself. I hope to God the old woman comes round... Aye, Miss Foster'll be OK, though, I'm sure. She's a tough little body, isn't she, and strong-willed an' all. She's determined to pull herself round and go to the wedding...

'And we'd better get our skates on, hadn't we; shut up the shop and get on wi' the meal? I know most of it's been prepared, but we've no time to waste. Eh, dear! What a bloomin' awful time for it to happen...'

They felt even less like preparing a wedding feast when the police sergeant came round a couple of hours later, with the news that Miss Thomson had died. She had, in fact, been found to be dead on arrival at the hospital.

'It's just as well our Maisie's not here,' said Lily. 'I know she had one or two spats with Miss Thomson when she was a little girl, but she'll be upset, I know...'

Maisie had gone round to Anne's flat earlier that morning so that the two of them could prepare for the wedding. It was decided that they should not be told about the tragic accident until the wedding celebrations were over. It would not be necessary to tell Anne and Roger at all until they returned from their honeymoon. It would not be right to cast a blight on such a happy occasion.

And it was, indeed, a joyful ceremony, followed by a happy and convivial reception at Arthur's Place. Luke and Patience, of course, had been informed of the accident and its outcome, but agreed that the bridal couple should not be told. It was Patience, rather than Luke, who said she would tell the white lie that they decided was necessary, although it went against the conscience of both of them. Miss Thomson, who had always lived next door to the school, had been invited to the wedding. Patience would explain to Anne, who would be sure to notice the old lady's absence, that Amelia was in bed with a sudden attack of what was thought to be flu; and – no – it would not be a good idea to visit her as she was probably highly infectious...

'Please forgive me, Lord...' prayed Patience. Anne and Roger looked so blissfully happy...

⌒

Maisie had gradually warmed to the 'headmaster', which was how she had used to think of him, after she had met him a few times. He and Anne seemed very compatible and were very good friends as well as being – she was sure – very much in love.

Anne looked regally beautiful in her high-necked slim-fitting gown, with a pearl-trimmed headdress and long silken tulle veil. Roger was only a couple of inches taller than his bride, a dapper figure in his dark grey suit with a contrasting pale grey waistcoat. His dark hair was now silvering a little at the temples, and since shaving off his military moustache he seemed, to Maisie, to look kindlier and less bombastic. His grey eyes smiled lovingly at Anne as they stood on the church steps after the ceremony, posing for the photographer and laughing as the onlookers, many of them their own schoolchildren, showered them with confetti.

It was a smallish gathering at the restaurant, but the largest one, so far, that Arthur's Place had accommodated. The guests who had not been there before looked round admiringly at the white and gold Regency striped walls, on which were displayed water colour pictures of Yorkshire scenes, the matching gold curtains, the dazzlingly white tablecloths and the pure white china plates and dishes, bordered in gold. Maisie, of course, was the only bridesmaid, and Roger's best man was his brother, Gerald, whose wife, Mildred, and two teenage children were also present. Roger's parents were dead; but Anne's mother and father had come from Leeds, and Maisie, meeting them for the first time earlier that day, had liked them very much.

Apart from these few family members the guests were all friends; many of them Anne's friends of many years standing in Middlebeck, all of whom had now taken Roger to their hearts as well. There were the teachers from the school, and Miss Foster, looking a little preoccupied; the Rectory family, including Audrey, whose rapidly increasing figure was well concealed by her floating summer dress of pink georgette. Maisie thought she looked well and appeared quite serene, her predicament having been accepted, by and large, by her father's congregation, with very little comment. Doris, too, there with her husband, Ivan, was quite obviously pregnant, but she was not trying to disguise it. She looked the picture of health, every inch the typical farmer's wife with her rosy cheeks, ample waistline and beaming smile. Maisie was pleased to see how happy she looked.

Archie and Rebecca Tremaine were there, but Maisie had been surprised to see that Bruce, also, was with them. She had caught sight of him for the first time as they all stood outside the church. Their glances had met and they had smiled and waved to one another. She had not felt an upsurge of euphoria and excitement, as she once would have experienced on seeing him; more a feeling of gladness and delight at seeing an old friend. She realised that she must, at last, be well and truly over him, in 'that way'. Her heart and mind were elsewhere, in the heather-clad hills of 'Bonnie Scotland'. And next Wednesday, in only four days' time, she would see Andy again. She felt a glow of pleasure at the thought and she gave an unconscious smile.

Bruce, sitting at a nearby table, must have thought the smile was for him, because he was looking in her direction with a bemused half-smile on his face. Well, maybe it was, in part. She waved to him cheerily. 'See you later...' she mouthed, and he nodded, raising his thumb in assent.

Everyone agreed after the meal and the speeches were over that Arthur and his team of workers had surpassed themselves with the excellent meal. The piping hot chicken soup, made from fresh ingredients, was obviously not from a Heinz tin; the tender slices of spring lamb served with new potatoes and a variety of vegetables, fresh from the market; and the sherry trifle, in which the vital ingredient had not been stinted; followed by full-flavoured coffee; a banquet, indeed, 'fit for the King and Queen'.

The small crowd of guests milled around, and Maisie found herself face to face with Bruce. He leaned towards her and kissed her cheek. 'It's lovely to see you again, Maisie. I can't say it's a surprise, because my mother had told me, of course, that you were to be Anne's bridesmaid.'

'But it's a surprise for me to see you,' said Maisie. 'I thought you would be far away in foreign parts. I know you don't often get home these days, do you?'

Bruce smiled. 'Home...yes. I still think of Middlebeck as home, but my home – well, the place that I give as my permanent address – is in Altrincham, near Manchester. I have a flat there; it's handy for the airport, you see. A lot of our flights depart from Ringway as well as Leeds airport.'

'Yes, I heard that you were a pilot for Red Rose Airlines. Galaxy do quite a lot of business with them now. At the moment, though, I'm not working in the Leeds office. I'm acting as a courier for the season; well, probably for longer than that...'

'Yes, my mother was telling me about it... I wasn't actually invited to the wedding, you know. I'm not exactly a gate-crasher, but when Mother told Anne that I would be home this weekend – quite unexpectedly – Anne said of course I must come along. So here I am...' he laughed. 'Maisie, it really is great to see you... How about coming out with me tonight, then we can catch up with all our news? We could have a drive out somewhere and a drink and a bite to eat maybe... What do you think?'

'That would be lovely, Bruce; but we certainly won't need much to eat, will we? I'm supposed to be on tour again tomorrow, up in Scotland. The tour sets off in the morning from Leeds, but I've got permission to start a day later. So I shall catch a train to Edinburgh tomorrow afternoon and join the tour in the evening.'

'That sounds sensible. You do a conducted tour of Edinburgh, do you?'

'Yes; three days in Edinburgh, and then up to Callander, in the Trossachs, for the rest of the week. Have you ever been there, Bruce? It's a lovely part of the country.'

'Yes, I went touring in Scotland with my parents, when I was much younger. As you say, it's a beautiful area...' They smiled at one another, and then Bruce took hold of her arm. 'Oh look; the bride and groom are ready to go. Come on; let's see them on their way.'

Anne had changed from her bridal gown into a two-piece summer suit in a pretty shade of turquoise blue, with a tiny hat made of matching feathers. Roger's car was waiting at the kerbside where Arthur had parked it ready for them, as promised. But well-wishers had been at work and the Morris Minor was now festooned with streamers, and a placard on the back declared 'Just Married'.

Anne was carrying her bridal bouquet and, keeping to the tradition, she threw it high in the air in the direction of the guests. Eager hands reached out to grasp it, but it was Maisie who caught it amidst laughter and cheers. Probably that had been Anne's intention as the flowers had been heading straight towards her.

After a final flurry of confetti and waves and smiles, and kisses for their relations and closest friends, Roger started the car and they drove off down the High Street in a southerly direction. Maisie knew that they intended to tour the Cotswold area.

'Well, what d'you know?' she laughed, brandishing the bouquet. 'Actually, I couldn't avoid it.'

'It didn't look as though you wanted to avoid it,' said

Bruce. 'The question is, who do you know?'

'Ah, that would be telling!' she replied, and then seeing his puzzled smile, 'Well, to be honest, not a lot,' she added. 'Not yet at any rate. But who can tell what is round the corner...'

---

Bruce had arranged to call for her at seven o'clock that evening, and they drove through the country lanes, northwards to a tiny village by the name of Kilbeck, consisting of little more than an ancient church and a cluster of greystone houses, with a stream running by the side of the road. And an old inn, the 'Adam and Eve', which was popular with the customers who knew it well, but which never became too crowded as it was well off the beaten track.

The inn appeared almost as old as its name, with whitewashed walls inside and out, an oak-beamed ceiling and a flagged floor. There was a huge inglenook fireplace in which a log fire burned in the colder months, and this was now filled with an arrangement of fir cones and colourful dried leaves and flowers. The chintz-covered chairs and the matching curtains at the diamond-paned windows, and the highly polished round tables helped to relieve the otherwise stark surroundings.

Bruce ordered a beer for himself and a gin and lime for Maisie whilst they studied the menu. Their mood was more subdued than it had been earlier in the day, because when the bride and groom had departed the news had soon got round about the tragic accident of the morning. Miss Foster, of course, had been particularly upset. Archie and Rebecca had taken her home with them to Tremaine House and, according to Bruce, had invited her to stay for the night as it would not be good for her to be on her own at the moment.

'I never knew Miss Foster as well as you did,' Bruce said now, 'because I was never at the village school. I rather wish I had been...at the village school and then at the grammar school. I'm not sure that I approve of children being sent away to be educated. Speaking for myself, I was still very naive when I left school. And I rather think that my father is coming round to the same belief, now that he is having to toe the Labour party line. It's a changing world, Maisie, but not before time.

'As for Miss Thomson, I never really got to knew her well. She had a reputation for being a fearsome old dragon, didn't she?'

Maisie smiled. 'She certainly did, but she mellowed, somewhat, as time went on. Audrey got on quite well with her in the end, but I don't think Miss T ever really forgave me for being rude to her when I was a kiddie. I was a cheeky little kid, wasn't I? But I had to stick up for Audrey, or so I thought.'

'Yes, you were a little terror at times,' laughed Bruce. 'You gave me a run for my money as well, when we first met.'

'Yes, I remember; when Prince knocked Audrey down in the lane...'

'That's right. Dear old Prince; he was a faithful friend.' The Tremaine's collie dog, who had been a constant companion to Bruce during the school holidays and afterwards, had died only a couple of years ago. 'Rusty's a good dog, too, but I don't know him as well as I knew Prince. Rusty's my mother's dog really; she has the most to do with him with my father being away so much... Have you decided what you want, Maisie?' The waitress was hovering with her notebook and pencil.

'A ham salad, please,' said Maisie. 'After the wedding meal I felt I would never be able to eat again. A ham salad would be just about right.'

'And I will have the same,' said Bruce. 'And some of your nice crusty bread, please,' he said to the waitress.

'You mentioned Audrey,' he continued, when the waitress had left. 'I was very surprised... My mother told me about it, of course. Apparently everyone is rallying round her, which is good, and she seems to be quite in control of herself. You are her closest friend, aren't you, so I suppose you knew?'

'Yes, I was the first one she told. She was in a terrible state, as you can imagine. She was frightened to tell her parents, but I managed to convince her that she must...' Maisie knew that the fact that Audrey had considered abortion must never ever be mentioned to anyone... 'And Luke and Patience have been wonderful, as you can imagine.'

Audrey had told her when they had met together earlier in the week that she had managed to complete her teacher training course. Several people, inevitably, had guessed at her condition, but had been very understanding towards her. Jennifer, however, Joel's sister, had started to ignore her and the two of them had not spoken for several months; no doubt Jennifer had guessed at the truth and chose not to know about it. The exam results would be out later that month, and so whatever might happen in the future, Audrey would – hopefully – have her teaching qualifications.

'And who was it...do you know?' asked Bruce, to Maisie's surprise. She would not have thought he would ask such a question.

'Yes, I do know...but it's irrelevant,' she replied. 'There could never be any question of them getting together. It was at a party, the brother of somebody she knew... But Audrey never talks about it now, so please forget about it, Bruce.'

She must have sounded a little sharp because Bruce was immediately apologetic. 'I'm sorry, Maisie. I wasn't being nosey, although I know it sounded like it. It's just that... well...my mother wondered if it might be Brian Milner. My parents are friendly with the Milners, you know, and Brian, apparently, has been down to see Audrey a couple of times since she came home from college. He has been working for a firm in Durham for the last year or so; he's an industrial chemist, you know.'

'I didn't know that!' replied Maisie. 'Well, I knew about his job, of course, but I didn't know he had been to see Audrey. Fancy her not saying...but she can be a dark horse at times, can Audrey. But he is definitely not the father, I can assure you of that.'

'No...so Mrs Milner said, and Brian too. But be that as it may, he seems to be getting friendly with Audrey again. Ah, here comes our food...'

The thick slices of home-cured ham with a plentiful side salad, and crusty bread spread with butter was a more than ample meal, and the glasses of mellow golden Chardonnay added the finishing touch.

'Just one glass for me,' said Bruce. 'I must get you back safely.' Maisie remembered Andy saying the self-same thing when they had picnicked by Loch Tummel...

'We have talked about everybody but you and me,' said Bruce. 'Tell me about yourself, Maisie. You are enjoying your new job, are you?'

'Yes...' she replied, but she felt suddenly at a loss for words. She did not want to say too much about her work as a courier or...anything. 'I enjoy it very much. But...won't you tell me about your job, first? You are seeing a lot of the world, aren't you? It must be very exciting.'

'When I get to stop over, yes,' said Bruce. 'But sometimes we turn round and come straight back.' But he had seen Paris, Brussels, Rome, Venice, Amsterdam, Copenhagen... he told her. And they hoped, soon, that Red Rose Airlines would do transatlantic flights. 'So... New York, possibly, in the not too distant future.'

She nodded, and there was a few second's silence. Then, 'I was sorry about your marriage, Bruce,' she said, knowing that she would have to mention it sooner or later. It was not strictly true; she was not sorry, but it was the polite thing to say in these circumstances. 'I saw Christine, by the way. She came into the office – oh, several months ago now, in the winter – with...a man. They were booking tickets.'

'Yes, Clive Broadbent. She married him,' said Bruce. 'I did know about it. Of course I had to know; she wanted the divorce...'

'I'm sorry; perhaps I shouldn't have mentioned it...'

'Of course you should. I am glad you did.' He smiled wistfully at her. 'Christine and I were never really right for one another. I was too young, Maisie, far too young and naive to be married, especially to someone like Christine. But she dazzled me. She was pretty and witty and fun to be with, and so I told myself that she was what I wanted.'

'I thought she seemed much nicer when I met her this year,' said Maisie. 'You know; softer, kinder, less...er... abrasive. I was glad to see there was a nice side to her as well, because I hadn't liked her very much before...' Now, where did that come from? she asked herself. Maisie, why on earth don't you learn to think before you speak? 'Sorry...' she said. 'Me and my big mouth!'

He laughed. 'She was a chameleon-person all right, was Christine. Yes, there were certainly two sides to her, and I saw what I wanted to see. We were happy for a while, I must admit though, and then I found out she had lied to me, in all sorts of ways. I would have understood if she had told me at the start about her background; but no...she pretended she was something that she wasn't; and the worst thing of all was telling me that her parents were dead. I found it hard to forgive her for that. I suppose I have forgiven her now, though. In the long run it would never have worked out for Christine and me.'

'You didn't need to tell me about it, Bruce...'

'But I wanted to, Maisie...' He was looking at her intently across the little round table. 'You and me...well, the time was never quite right for us, was it? When I first met you, you were just a little girl – a cheeky little kid, as you said.' He laughed. 'But you were quite grown-up for your age, even then.'

'I had to be,' replied Maisie, wondering where this conversation was leading. 'My childhood back in Armley, that had made me grow up fast, certainly much more so than Audrey.'

'But you were – what? – only nine years old, and I was fourteen. As I told you, I was rather naive, and I enjoyed being a sort of big brother to you and Audrey, and Doris; of course I had always known Doris.'

She nodded, not knowing quite what to say.

'You were just a little girl ...' he said musingly, 'and then, suddenly – or it seemed very sudden to me – I noticed that you had grown up...into a lovely young woman. But I knew that you were still only fifteen years old, far too young for me, Maisie. I was twenty, and I had already met Christine and...oh, damn it all, Maisie, what I am trying to say is that the timing was all wrong for you and me...wasn't it? You know what I mean, don't you?'

'Yes, I know,' she said gently. 'Bruce... I was crazy about you.' There, she had said it. 'And I was so jealous of Christine; that was why I didn't like her. Everybody – well, the ones that had guessed – tried to tell me I would get over it, and so I did...eventually.' She felt a trifle embarrassed, but Bruce was smiling at her in a very friendly and understanding way.

'But we will always be friends, won't we, Bruce? It's great, being here with you tonight.'

'Yes, I certainly hope we'll always be friends, Maisie...' He took hold of her hand. 'And it has been a really lovely evening. But now – well – it's too late for us, isn't it? You have met somebody, haven't you, that you...like a lot?'

'Yes, I have,' she nodded. 'He hasn't said anything, not yet, but I know that he will...soon, I think.'

'Mmm... I knew by the look on your face when you caught Anne's bouquet. I hope he truly deserves you, Maisie.'

'And what about you, Bruce?' she asked. 'Is there... someone?'

'Oh, there have been a few...' His eyes twinkled.

'A girl in every port, eh? Or every airport?'

'Not exactly, but we do quite frequent trips to Paris. There is a young lady who works in a hotel near to the Tuileries Gardens; she is the receptionist. I have stayed there several times and we have become...quite friendly.'

'I see,' Maisie smiled. 'A French girl?'

'No, actually she is English, but she has worked in Paris for a few years. We get on very well together.'

'Then I hope it all works out well for you, Bruce... She's a very lucky girl,' she added shyly.

'Thank you,' he said. 'And so is your young man, very lucky indeed... I take it he lives north of the border?'

'Yes; how did you know?'

'By the look in your eyes when you talked about Scotland... Be happy, Maisie.' He squeezed her hand. 'And... be very sure, won't you?'

'I am sure...' she replied, as Bruce let go of her hand.

# Chapter Twenty-Seven

So she hadn't been mistaken about Bruce's feelings for her, she thought, as she headed towards Edinburgh in the late afternoon of the following day. Five years ago, when she was fifteen and he was twenty, he had known, if the timing had been different, that they could, and probably would, have come together as rather more than friends. But that age gap of five years between fifteen and twenty was insurmountable. At fifteen one was, technically, still a child, and twenty was on the verge of adulthood. And Christine had already been there.

And now, five years later, when that five years' difference in age would not matter in the slightest, it was too late. Bruce was obviously very interested in the young lady in Paris, and she, Maisie, would be seeing the young man with whom she had fallen in love in just a few days' time. She thought of Bruce fondly, and, she had to admit, with a slight feeling of regret; but they had promised one another that they would always be friends. And now, she was looking to the future. Her heart gave a leap and her spirits soared at the thought of seeing Andy again.

The two days in Edinburgh had, by now, become very familiar to Maisie. The only differences were the weather; one day it could be boiling hot and the next bitterly cold, even in August, with a chilly wind blowing in from the Firth of Forth. And the passengers: different faces, different personalities each week, but the questions they asked were pretty much the same, their favourite ones being about the ill-fated Mary, Queen of Scots, and the bandit, otherwise Scottish hero, Rob Roy Macgregor.

Wednesday afternoon found them once again at the
Cameron Hotel, being greeted by Gordon on the coach, and
then by Andy and Moira as they handed out the room keys.

'Hello again, Maisie,' he said. 'Good to see you. I'm
looking forward to our duets; I've thought of one or two new
ones, with your approval, of course...'

'Yes, of course...' She didn't have time to say more as a
rather fussy lady, one who had already made her presence
felt on the coach, had interrupted and was asking Andy
something about her room; it was not next door to that of
her brother and sister-in-law, as she had requested. Maisie
smiled at him and then carried her own bags up the flights of
stairs to her room.

Andy was never present for the welcoming cup of tea,
served when they had all had time to sort themselves out, as
he was by then hard at work in the kitchen. But it was then
that Maisie noticed the strange young woman assisting
Moira with handing round the tea and shortbread biscuits.
Not strange in the sense that there was anything odd about
her; far from it; she was a very pretty fair-haired girl and she
seemed to have a pleasing manner with the guests. But she
was strange in the sense that Maisie had not seen her before.
A new waitress, maybe, although she was not dressed as one.
Maisie felt a chill strike through her and a feeling of
impending heartache, although she could not have said why.

This was the time when she found it good to mingle with
the guests, to move around and chat to one little group and
then another, asking if they were enjoying the tour and
whether they had any problems. She did not find out
anything about the newcomer until dinner-time when she
and Bob sat at their own table, a little removed from those
of the coach passengers and private guests. The young
woman in question was not helping to serve the meal, as
Maisie had thought she might have been, but was sitting at
a table with three other people, two women and a man, who
were not on the Galaxy tour.

'Who is that? Do you know?' Maisie asked Bob, nodding

discreetly in their direction. 'That young woman; I noticed her earlier, at tea-time...'

'Oh aye; I was wondering that meself,' replied Bob. 'So I asked Moira; you know me, of course, dead nosey.'

'And...who is she?'

'Well...it seems, like, that she's a friend of Andy,' replied Bob, looking at her a little guardedly. 'She's been working away at a hotel up in Inverness – she's a receptionist, I believe, same as Moira – but she's come back to Callander for a week's holiday. She lives here, Moira said; in the town, I mean...'

'Then why is she staying here, at the hotel? She is, isn't she?'

'Oh goodness, Maisie! I don't know the ins and outs of it all, only what Moira told me...'

'She's Andy's girlfriend, isn't she?' Maisie felt her heart plummet right to the soles of her feet. 'Go on, you can tell me. I'd rather you did, then it'll save me making an even bigger fool of myself.'

'Now, now, steady on,' said Bob, reaching out and patting her hand. 'Nowt o' t' sort. I asked Moira if she was his girlfriend, 'cause, like I said, I'm nosey. Any road, I know how you feel about that young fellow...'

'You didn't tell Moira that, did you?'

'No, of course I didn't. Cross my heart, Maisie, I haven't said 'owt to anybody. But I can't help noticing meself that you're...rather fond of him.'

'I've fallen in love with him,' said Maisie, flatly. She stared unseeingly into space for a few seconds, before she said, more vehemently, 'Oh Bob, why do I never learn? I've done this before, worn my heart on my sleeve, and it all came to nothing.' She thought of her recent farewell to Bruce. 'And now I've gone and done it again.'

'Hey, hang on a minute,' said Bob. 'I've been watching the pair of you, you and Andy – on the QT, like – and from what I can see of that young chap he feels just the same way about you. And what's that you said about wearing yer heart on yer sleeve? You've done nowt o' t' sort. Many a lass would have thrown herself at him, but you've been – what's the word? – circumspect; aye, that's it, circumspect, like the well-brought-up girl that you are. Happen a bit too much so. It's time you and him said what you feel instead of singing about it.'

Maisie actually smiled then. 'What's she called? Do you know? And is she – was she – his girlfriend? Tell me, Bob. I have to know.'

'She's called Laura; I don't know what else. Aye, it seems they were friendly at one time. She was the receptionist here before Moira. I reckon he's known her since they were at school; she was a local lass and then she came to work here. But summat went wrong and she disappeared up to Inverness. And that's all I know. Now…eat up yer roast pork – nice bit o' crackling, this – and start planning yer strategy. Aye, that's what you need; a plan of action.'

Maisie did not agree, although she did not say so to Bob. Dear Bob; what a good friend he had proved to be during the four tours she had worked with him. He liked to know what was going on around him, certainly, but she knew he would not divulge anything she had told him in confidence. And what she had said in an unguarded moment, that she had fallen in love with Andy, she could trust him not to repeat to anyone.

But she did not think it would be a good idea to 'set her cap' at him, which was what Bob seemed to be suggesting. If Andy did still have feelings for this girl, Laura, then Maisie would only end up looking a bigger fool than she was already considering herself to be. After all, how long had she known Andy? For two months, she might say, and that was not long; but in reality it was only nine days, three days out of each tour, that was all. It had been long enough for her to know that she had fallen in love with him. But what about Andy? He had kissed her, very gently, once or twice; he had looked at her tenderly when they sang together; and he obviously enjoyed her company. If he really cared about her, though, cared enough to want to take their friendship a stage further, then he would make it clear to her.

This Laura suddenly appearing had complicated matters, at least to Maisie's way of thinking, but she would not be seen to compete for his attentions. She remembered how Christine had disliked her on sight, and the feeling had been mutual. As a fifteen-year-old girl she had made it obvious how she felt about Bruce. Now, at the much greater age of twenty, she hoped she had learned wisdom. She would not exactly 'play hard to get', but she would not do any running either; and she would be very friendly and charming to Laura when she made her acquaintance, which she was sure to do quite soon.

—

Wednesday evening was always an informal time for the guests to relax and chat together, but Maisie took her time in going down to the lounge. She lay on her bed for a while, trying to interest herself in the latest Agatha Christie, but she could not stop her mind from wandering. Besides, hadn't Andy said something about some new duets? She should go and find out what he had in mind, but tonight they would no doubt sing something they were familiar with, and she would sing a song with no romantic connotations whatsoever.

As she had predicted – and feared and dreaded, too – Andy was sitting chatting to Laura when she entered the lounge. Not on their own, though; it was a table for six and there was an empty chair. Maisie smiled and would have walked past, but Andy raised his hand in greeting and patted the chair next to him. 'Maisie, won't you come and join us?'

'I'd be pleased to,' she said, smiling not only at Andy, but at the girl at his side and the three people from the coach.

'I thought mebbe you didn't feel like singing tonight,' said Andy. 'You don't have to, of course, but the guests do enjoy it. You are OK, are you, for later on?'

'Sure I am,' she said. 'I was engrossed in my book, that's all, and I hadn't noticed the time. Then I suddenly realised I was neglecting my duties.'

'Not a bit of it,' said Laura. 'You are entitled to a wee bit of time to yourself.' She had a pleasant Scottish lilt to her voice and she spoke quietly. 'You're the new courier, aren't you?'

'Not so new now, eh, Maisie?' said Andy. 'This is your – what is it? – your fourth tour to Scotland?'

'Yes, something like that,' she nodded casually.

'Let me introduce the two of you,' he said. 'Maisie, this is Laura, an old friend of mine; Laura Drummond. She used to be our receptionist.'

'Oh, I see...' said Maisie, raising her eyebrows as though this was news to her. The two of them shook hands cordially and said 'How do you do?' 'And are you still a receptionist?' Maisie asked, 'somewhere else perhaps?'

'That's right,' said Laura. 'I'm working up in Inverness now, but I had a fortnight's holiday due, so I decided to come back to Callander for a wee while. And Mr and Mrs Cameron kindly invited me to stay here...' Maisie nodded politely.

'This is my home town, where I was born,' she went on. 'But my parents have just moved to Glasgow. My dad's a bank manager and he's got a promotion, but it's no' a place I would choose to live. I shall go and stay with them, of course, but my roots are here... At the moment I'm looking for a wee place of my own.'

'In Callander...?'

'Aye, or somewhere near...'

'So you don't intend to stay in Inverness?'

'I'll finish the season, and then I'll see,' said Laura, smiling a little mysteriously. 'I don't know how things will work out, but I want a place to call my own, that's for sure.'

Maisie decided she must stop asking questions. It was really none of her business, although she was anxious to know why the young woman was thinking of moving south again. At least she had not exchanged knowing glances with Andy...

She asked Maisie how she was liking Scotland and wanted

to know all about the tour. They had coach parties to stay at the hotel in Inverness, but Galaxy had not yet ventured so far north. Maisie found that she could not help but like her. There was none of the instant animosity that she had felt on first meeting Christine, nor did she sense any possessiveness in Laura's attitude towards Andy. Maybe there had been something between them in the past, but there was no sign of it now. He was behaving towards both of them as though they were good chums, not girlfriends, either past or present.

Maisie sang 'The Bells of Saint Mary's', an old-fashioned song which she enjoyed and the audience enjoyed too; Andy sang a selection of the Hebridean songs; and then, together, they performed 'The Heather on the Hill', which they always included at least once during the three night stay.

'You sing well together,' Laura told them; Maisie noticed that she had applauded enthusiastically at the end of the number.

'Aye, we're no' so bad, are we, Maisie?' Andy winked at her and grinned. 'Now, I must tell you – well, ask you, I mean – about the new duets I have in mind for us…'

The songs that he had chosen – and how could she do anything but fall in with his ideas? – could not have been less romantic. They were both by Irving Berlin; 'A Couple of Swells' from *Easter Parade*, and 'Anything you can do (I can do better)', from *Annie get your Gun*.

'I thought it would make a nice change,' he said. 'A couple of wee comedy numbers. Shall we give them a try?'

'Yes…why not?' she said. 'Judy Garland, eat your heart out. And… Betty Hutton, wasn't she Annie Oakley?'

'To say nothing of Fred Astaire and Howard Keel,' laughed Laura.

She stayed with them later that evening, when nearly all the other guests had retired, whilst they practised their new numbers with Jeanette.

And so it was for the rest of Maisie's stay there. It was as though they were a threesome, during the evenings at any rate. On the second day, of course, she was on her tour of the

Trossachs, but she wondered if, on the final day, Friday, Andy might ask her to go out in the car with him as he had done on the last tour. But he did not do so. Maybe he had gone house hunting with Laura...? But she did not find out.

On the Friday night she could not settle to sleep. She tried to read, but to no avail, and then she tossed and turned for what seemed like hours. And an extra glass of wine, which a man from the tour had insisted on buying her, meant that she needed to pay a visit to the little room along the corridor. She sighed and put on her dressing gown, easing her feet into her slippers, then crept along the passageway. On her way back she caught a glimpse of Laura, also clad in her dressing gown, disappearing down the flight of stairs which led to the first floor. Andy's room was on the first floor...

To her surprise she remained dry-eyed and even managed to sleep. She awoke with a sense of purpose, but not one that cheered her; she was sad at heart and her mind felt numb, but she knew what she had to do. She must forget all about Andy Cameron; she must put him right out of her mind. He was not for her. As it had been with Bruce, it was just an impossible dream.

Laura was with him and his father as they stood by the coach to say farewell to the guests.

'Goodbye; it's been nice meeting you...' Maisie waved to Laura as she stepped on to the coach. She did not give Andy the chance to even kiss her on the cheek. 'Bye, Andy...' she called.

'Yes... Bye, Maisie,' he repeated, rather bemusedly. 'See you in three weeks' time?'

'Yes...see you,' she said. But she was determined not to see him again.

⁓

She was quiet on the return journey, as she usually was. The passengers did not want to hear any more stories or information about the scenery they were passing as they had heard it all on the outward journey. Bob, too, was quiet, concentrating on his driving, and Maisie did not attempt to talk to him until they had their lunch-time stop at a little wayside café near the border.

'Well, Maisie, how's tricks?' he asked her.

'Not too good,' she replied, 'if you are referring to what I think you are.'

'Give the lad a chance,' he remarked. 'From what I could see of yon lass she was hanging on to him like a drowning man to a raft. Talk about a clinging vine...'

'That's what I'm not sure about,' said Maisie. 'I don't know what's going on there... But I've decided to give myself a break. I told you, didn't I, that I made a fool of myself before over a fellow, and I'm not going to do it again.' She paused, then, 'I won't be coming with you on the next tour,' she said.

'Now, Maisie love, you mustn't be hasty. And I don't see why you should run away...'

'I'm not doing, Bob. I'm not saying that I won't go back on the tour sometime...but for the time being I think it's for the best if I give it a miss.'

'Aye...' Bob nodded soberly. 'It might make that young feller-me-lad come to his senses.'

'I doubt it, Bob.' She shook her head. 'I've come to the conclusion that he likes me as a friend, somebody to sing duets with, but as far as anything else is concerned...' She shrugged. 'I can't allow myself to get in any deeper... I told you how I feel about him,' she added quietly.

'I shall miss you, Maisie,' he said. They were both in a pensive mood for the rest of the homeward journey.

＿

She rang Henry Galloway at his home on the Sunday; she was due to set off to Stratford the following day. He listened carefully to her suggestion that Sheila should take over the Scottish tour for a while.

'She could do with the experience, couldn't she?' she asked, 'and I don't want to feel I'm hogging the tour. From what she has said to me, I think Sheila would like the chance to do rather more. And I can perhaps do relief work for a while. You did suggest that at one time...'

If Henry felt there might be another reason for Maisie's request he did not say so. He arranged to meet her in Leeds on the following Saturday, when she returned from her tour in the Midlands.

'I've been thinking about what you said,' he told her, over their lunch table. 'In fact, I have acted upon it already, and Sheila is willing to do the next Scottish tour; I might say she jumped at the chance. The trainee courier, Linda, is experienced enough now to take over Sheila's work, so it should work out very well...

'I don't know if you had any ulterior motive to your request, Maisie, and I am not asking. But it made Trixie and I come to a decision.' He nodded at her in a satisfied way. 'Now, this is what we have decided... You are not going to London on Monday; Sheila is going to do that tour as well. Instead of that you will be on a flight to Paris with Trixie...'

Maisie gasped, both with surprise and delight.

'There are a couple of hotels that we want to "recce" there. And the following week you will be in Amsterdam. We want you to make the most of your time there. As well as assessing the hotels, I want you to get acquainted with the cities and the outlying areas. We will be needing experienced couriers when we start our continental tours next summer...

'Now, have you anything to say, or to ask me about it? I know you may feel you are being thrown in at the deep end, but you did request a change, didn't you?'

'Indeed I did,' she said. 'I'm pleased that you think I'm capable of going abroad. Gosh! How wonderful...' Her personal problems were receding further back in her mind, as she had been trying to make them do for the past week, as she thought about the exciting times that lay ahead. 'Trixie will be with me, though, won't she?'

'She will at first, but not all the time. We both know, Maisie, that you are capable of doing anything that you set your mind to, and we want you to start finding your feet on the continent as well as in our own country. You and Trixie are booked on a flight to Paris with Red Rose Airlines, departing from Leeds airport on Monday morning. So off you go now and start packing...'

—

Henry had insisted she should apply for a passport when she became manageress of the Leeds branch, just in case she might need it. She took it out of the drawer and looked at it wonderingly. Red Rose Airlines was the company that Bruce worked for. She wondered, in passing, if he might be the pilot, and if, on arrival in Paris, the hotel they were to 'recce' might be the one he had mentioned, near to the Tuileries Gardens? But coincidences such as that were unlikely.

She knew it for a fact when she sat in her aeroplane seat with the safety belt fastened and heard the pilot's voice over the intercom.

'Good morning, ladies and gentlemen. This is your captain, John Whitfield speaking...' He promised them a smooth flight with no turbulence ahead.

In a few moments, after the deafening roar of the engines and whizzing of propellers, during which time Maisie kept her eyes tightly closed, they were airborne. From her window seat she watched the houses and factories growing smaller and smaller, and the cars on the roads looking like Dinky models, almost topsy-turvy for a moment as the plane turned. Then they were soaring above the clouds.

She was glad of Trixie's expertise when they arrived, in dealing with the luggage and the taxi to the hotel. Of course it was not anywhere near the Tuileries Gardens, but in a suburb to the east of Paris. Trixie explained that the hotels on the outskirts of the city – in fact, of any city – were far more reasonable in price than those in the centre, an important consideration to the tour managers and to the travellers as well.

They stayed for two nights in two different hotels, and then decided on the first one. It had a more friendly ambience, well cooked food – a simple evening meal as well as the inevitable rolls and butter for breakfast – and a pleasant leafy locality. It was convenient, too, for the excursions that they planned as part of the tour: a visit to Versailles, the palace of the Sun King, Louis the fourteenth; and another to the chateau of Fontainebleau; as well as the city tour of Paris itself.

Maisie, with Trixie as her guide, became familiar with the metro – a quick and easy way of getting around, although the coach passengers would be driven to most of the sights by courtesy of Galaxy – and the familiar landmarks. The Eiffel Tower; the Champs Élysées and Arc de Triomphe; the cathedral of Notre Dame and Sacré Coeur; the river trip along the Seine... So many sights and impressions there were to take in on her first visit. But she would need to know them all thoroughly if she intended to conduct a tour in this glamorous city.

The following week found Maisie and Trixie in the Netherlands, investigating a farmhouse type hotel in the rural Friesian area, to the north of Amsterdam. They agreed that it was perfect. They explored the places they intended to include on the tour; the city of Amsterdam with its tree-lined canals and bridges, cobbled streets and colourful flower markets; the fishing village of Volendam; the picturesque villages of the Iselmeer – once known as the Zuider Zee – Marken, where the elderly people still wore national dress, and Edam, famous for its round red-coated cheese.

This was the week, of course when Maisie would normally have been in Scotland...

Andy Cameron was looking forward to seeing Maisie again. He had known at once, on first meeting her, that he was attracted to her, but as was his wont, he had proceeded with caution. She was a travel courier, here for a few days, and the next week somewhere entirely different. How did he know but that she had male friends – a regular boyfriend, maybe – elsewhere?

The more he saw of her, the more he liked her. He knew it would be easy to fall in love with her; maybe he had done so already? She was friendly – not at all shy – and fun to be with. The coach passengers, each time, obviously took her to their hearts; she was always agreeable and ready to do anything she could to help them. He was even more delighted when he discovered that she could sing, and how harmoniously the two of them sang together… And, apart from all that, she was a stunning looking girl…

Maisie had given him no inkling, however, that she regarded him as anything other than a friend. Occasionally he thought he might have seen a specially tender look in her lovely brown eyes; but then it had changed to one of amusement as the two of them had laughed together at something or other. She was full of fun, and Andy, more accustomed to the dour Scottish outlook of some of his friends and family, found her happy personality was a refreshing change.

It was a pity that Laura had appeared when she did… He had made up his mind that he would say something to Maisie that week. He would find out, first of all, whether there was anyone else in the picture, and then he would know just where he stood. And if there wasn't, then he would invite her out again, hoping that this might lead to more outings together, and then…who could tell? But then Laura had come to stay…

He and Laura had been friends – in fact, more than just friends – for a while, although they had never become engaged. They had known one another since they were at Infant school; they had attended the same church, the same Youth Club, and then, on leaving the sixth form at the age of eighteen, she had come to work as their receptionist. They had come to a mutual decision, though, in the end, that they knew one another too well, if that were possible. They had begun to take one another for granted; there was no excitement, no mystery any more, and so they had brought their relationship to an end. Laura had sought a post elsewhere, ending up, finally, in Inverness. They had agreed, however, that they would remain friends. There was too much shared history and background between them for it to be otherwise.

She had suffered an unhappy love affair a few months ago, and although her damaged heart, so she said, had more or less healed, she had still had a yearning to return to the Lowlands and the scenes of her childhood.

It was a great pity that her visit had coincided with Maisie's tour. The following week Laura had gone to Glasgow to stay with her parents. Whilst she was there, with their help and persuasion, she had decided to settle in Largs, a resort on the Firth of Forth, not too far away from them. She was now in the process of moving into her own flat, and she had already found another post in the town as a hotel receptionist. And Andy had felt obliged to wait until the next tour before speaking to Maisie.

He decided not to go out to the coach to greet the new travellers. That had always been his father's prerogative, but he waited anxiously for the familiar figure to come through the door. But the girl in the red blazer who eventually appeared was as fair as Maisie was dark, shorter too and slightly plumper; a very pleasant girl, seemingly, but she was not Maisie. He knew, however, that he must make her feel welcome. It would be most impolite to say, 'Who are you, and where is Maisie?' which was what he felt like asking.

Bob entered the foyer and he hurried to the girl's side. 'This is Sheila,' he said. 'She is taking over from Maisie for a little while. Sheila, this is Andy, Mr Cameron's son, and our esteemed chef.' They shook hands cordially and Andy did his best to smile warmly at her. Bob edged closer to him.

'I dare say you're wondering where she is,' he said in a low voice, 'our Maisie?' Andy nodded, with one eye on Sheila, who was now chatting amiably to Moira. 'Well, right at this moment she's in Amsterdam...' Bob laughed, seeming to take pleasure in Andy's look of shock and amazement. 'Aye, that took the wind out o' yer sails, didn't it? Listen, Andy...' He put a friendly hand on his arm. 'I think it's time you and me had a bit of a chat; OK?'

'Yes...yes, we must,' replied Andy. 'Shall we meet in the lounge, later this evening?'

'Aye, suits me,' said Bob. 'And don't worry, lad. It'll all turn out all right, believe me.'

———

'You said that Maisie is in Amsterdam?' he asked later. 'What on earth is she doing there? Galaxy don't do tours to Europe, do they?'

'Not at the moment, but they will be doing soon, and Maisie's gone to do a spot of – what's it called? – reconnoitring.'

'But why has she gone? I thought she was here for the rest of the season at least. Was it an order from above?'

'More of a request, I think. She wanted a change; a break, she said, to sort herself out...and I think we can guess why, can't we?' He was looking meaningfully at Andy, who sighed and shook his head.

'I was getting very fond of her. In fact, I was going to tell her so, this week... I couldn't believe it when she wasn't there.'

'Happen you should have told her a bit sooner. She wasn't to know how you felt, was she, if you didn't say 'owt? And then wi' that other lass turning up out o' the blue...'

'Yes, Laura... I know, I know. I was really sorry about that, but there was nothing I could do. And Maisie didn't seem to mind. The two of them got on very well together. Of course, I know that Laura can be rather obtuse at times, and I hadn't told her that Maisie was anything other than a friend. At least, I was hoping she might be more than a friend, very soon... I've made a real mess of things, haven't I?'

'Nothing that can't be put right,' replied Bob. 'By the way, I hope you don't think I'm meddling? Well, I suppose I am really, but I happen to know how that young lass feels about you.'

'You mean...she's actually said so?'

'Aye, she has. In confidence, like, but it's a confidence I don't mind breaking, not if it'll make you come to your senses. She is very fond of you; she told me so herself...and that's all I'm saying.'

Andy smiled. That was wonderful news to hear. 'Will she be coming back, though, on the next tour?' he asked.

'I can't say, Andy, and that's the honest truth. There's talk of Belgium and Brittany and God knows where else... I hear all the gossip from t' other drivers.'

'Do you know her address? She lives in Leeds, doesn't she?'

'I'm not right sure of it, but I can find out for you. It might be better to see her though. As far as I know she's home at the weekends, preparing for her next jaunt.'

Andy knew there was no time to lose. His co-chef, Alistair, was coping very well, and the weekend, after the Galaxy tour departed, would not be too busy. Another coach tour was due in on Monday, from the Newcastle area, but he could be back by then.

'Bob...would you have a spare seat on your coach?' he asked. 'If you do, then I'm coming back with you...'

'Aye, plenty of room for a little 'un,' laughed Bob.

Maisie paid the taxi fare, then let herself into her flat at six o'clock on Saturday evening. Shoes off and slippers on, then fill the kettle and make a cup of tea... Anything else could wait a while. She flopped into an armchair, only rising when she heard the whistle of the kettle. Then she sat down again and sipped at her tea, nibbling at a chocolate biscuit to satisfy her hunger until she felt like making a meal.

What an exciting few days it had been... She opened her travel bag and took out the guide to Belgium and the Netherlands. Next week she would be on her own in

Belgium, without Trixie, looking at two hotels, one in Ostend and the other in the medieval city of Bruges. An hour later she was still sitting there, brought back to the here and now by a ring at the doorbell. She had recently moved to a ground floor flat and she hurried to the door. It might, of course, be someone coming to visit the upstairs tenant.

She gasped when she saw the figure standing on the doorstep. 'Andy! Goodness me, Andy... I don't believe it! What on earth are you doing here?'

'I've come to find you, Maisie,' he said. 'I missed you, and there's such a lot I want to say to you; lots of things I should have said before... Aren't you going to ask me in?'

'Of course,' she laughed. 'Come in, Andy. Oh, it's so lovely to see you...'

He closed the door behind him and put his arms around her. Then he kissed her, their first real kiss, but Maisie knew it would be only the first of many more. And there was all the time in the world for what they needed to say to one another.

# Chapter Twenty-Eight

*'Should auld acquaintance be forgot, an' never
   brought to min'?
Should auld acquaintance be forgot, for the sake of
   Auld Lang Syne?'*

Hogmanay was celebrated each year in the traditional
manner at the Cameron Hotel, and this year Maisie
was there to join in the festivities. Not as a courier, but as a
guest of the family. There were no coach tours from England
that would venture north of the border during the winter
months, when they were liable to be caught in six-foot snow
drifts. But the local folk enjoyed the hospitality and
friendliness of the Cameron family. They came back year
after year, some staying for a night or two, and others from
Callander itself just popping in for the excellent meal and, of
course, the Hogmanay ritual.

Maisie had been enjoying a wonderful, magical time ever
since the moment she had stepped off the train at Callander
station and into Andy's waiting arms. It had been three
weeks since she had seen him. They had each spent
Christmas with their own family and, before that, she had
had her commitments with Galaxy to carry out. Falling in
love could not be allowed to interfere with her work as a
courier.

She had gone back to the Scottish tour, but there had been
only two more tours before they came to an end at the
beginning of October; and since then she had been involved
in her job of appraising the hotels; Reims and Dijon, to
sound out the possibility of a wine tour in France; Rouen and
the chateaux of Normandy; she had even travelled as far as

Remagen on the River Rhine and the Black Forest town of Freiburg.

The war had been over for ages, Henry had assured her, when she had, at first, hesitated at the idea of going to Germany, and we were now all the best of friends. And Maisie had found that it was so. She had been quite proficient at French when she was at school, and that language soon became familiar to her. German, though, was proving much more difficult, and so she had started taking lessons in the subject at night school. The Germans, by and large, spoke English fluently, but she was determined that she would learn to converse with them, and quite soon, too.

But there had been time in between her busy schedule for meeting with Andy. She had taken him to meet her family in Middlebeck; or, to be more accurate, he had taken her, in his car. That was yet another plan she had in mind for the coming year; to learn to drive and to buy her own little car. When she travelled up to Scotland it was by train, and their times together were, alas, soon over and too far apart.

They had both realised, though, that they were very much in love, and that it was a love that would last and last. As she sat with Andy, as part of a carefree laughing crowd, all waiting for the Hogmanay tradition to be acted out, she reflected on the past year, 1950, and the sorrows and heartaches, followed by the joys, that it had brought, especially the happy events of the past few months.

The most memorable of all had been her reunion with Andy at the beginning of September, and the blissful weekend that had followed. They had declared their love for one another...but there were certain things that would have to wait until such time as they could be together for always. Someday, sometime, not too far distant, she hoped...

There had been joyful events in Middlebeck too. Audrey's baby girl had been born on the first day of October. The christening had taken place during the Sunday morning service on Christmas Eve, and the congregation had rejoiced at the welcoming of the newest member into the Christian family. Wendy Patricia, as she was called, was by that time a bonny round-faced child with her mother's fair hair and blue eyes, staring around and smiling at familiar faces. Her godmothers were Maisie and Doris – who was now the mother of two boys, Benjamin and Daniel – and, to the surprise of many, Brian Milner was the godfather.

There had been a few raised eyebrows, and no doubt people were jumping, wrongly, to their own conclusions. But Brian had seemed oblivious to what folk might be thinking. It was clear, though, to anyone who was watching, that his care and attention were focused just as much on Audrey as on her baby daughter.

Patience had held a buffet lunch afterwards at the Rectory, and it was then that two more items of news had been disclosed. Rebecca Tremaine announced that Bruce, that Christmastime, would become engaged to Yvonne, a young lady who worked in a Paris hotel, and whom she and Archie had already met and liked very much.

And Anne – now Ellison – announced, with pink cheeks and loving glances at her husband, that she and Roger were expecting a happy event sometime in June. Her teaching career would come to an end when the school finished for Easter.

'You will miss teaching, won't you?' said Maisie, when she went to visit her at the schoolhouse soon after Christmas. 'At first, I mean, but then I dare say you will be too busy with the baby to even give it a thought.'

'Yes...we couldn't afford to waste any time, Maisie,' she said, a little self-consciously, 'about – you know – about me...conceiving, because I'm already thirty-six; I'll be thirty-seven before the baby arrives, and Roger is turned forty. And we would like to have another one, God willing.'

'You'll be fine, I'm sure,' said Maisie. 'You're fit and healthy, aren't you?'

'Yes; I've never felt better. It will be a wrench at first, not going in to school every day after all these years, but Roger has someone in mind to fill my post. Not as head of Infants

– that will have to be sorted out internally – but as an ordinary teacher. Someone that you know...'

'Do you mean... Audrey?'

'Yes; that is who he had in mind. Not just yet, of course, but...eventually.'

'Mmm... She did very well, didn't she, in her final exams, in spite of circumstances being against her? Two As and a B; a very good result for anyone. But she wouldn't want to leave little Wendy. From what I can see she adores her.'

'No, not yet; but by September Wendy will be nearly a year old... And plans are afoot to have a nursery unit in Miss Thomson's old house. You heard about that, Maisie, didn't you? About Miss Thomson leaving her property to the school?'

'Of course I did. That was a bolt from the blue, all right. Good old Amelia! And she used to be such an old dragon; she didn't seem to like kids at all.'

'Oh, I've seen her standing by the hedge,' said Anne, 'watching them in the playground, even smiling to herself sometimes. There was a softer side to her, and a generous side as well.'

'It's no use to her after she's dead, though...'

Anne smiled. 'No, that's true. She left the house to the school to use in any way they think fit. It's for the Education Committee to decide, of course, but Roger has been consulted. As I said, they are considering a nursery unit, and up-to-date Education offices; they are rather cramped at the moment. It will need a lot of money spending on it, but it is a basically solid house... And you knew about Audrey's legacy too, I suppose?'

'Yes; I was really pleased about that,' said Maisie. 'Miss Thomson became very fond of Audrey. I'm glad Audrey's... er...condition didn't make her change her mind. Yes, it showed that her heart was in the right place after all.' Miss Thomson had left legacies of five hundred pounds to Audrey, and to Daisy, who had been a loyal maid to her for many years, and to Mrs Kitson, Daisy's mother, who had been her daily help ever since Daisy had left the area. The residue of the money she had left to St Bartholomew's church.

'It was sad the way she died,' said Anne. 'Roger and I didn't know until we got back from our honeymoon; it was thoughtful of everyone not to tell us... And we were relieved that Charity was not held responsible.' The result of the inquest had been that it was a tragic accident and that no blame at all was attached to the driver of the car. 'It has made her rather more aware though,' Anne added.

'Is Miss Foster still driving?' asked Maisie.

'Yes, she's started again. She vowed she never would, but she's got guts, has Charity. She's driving with due care and attention now, though, I'm pleased to say.'

'That is something I intend to do next year,' said Maisie. 'I must learn to drive, and buy a little car, of course. It will make it so much easier if I can drive up to Scotland instead of using the train.'

'You are a very busy young woman,' remarked Anne. 'And you are seeing a lot of the world. That is what you had in mind when you were still at school, wasn't it, to widen your horizons? And to think that I have never even been abroad...' she added thoughtfully, 'and I am not likely to do now, not for a good while at any rate.'

'You will one day,' said Maisie with a confident nod. 'It's a changing world, Anne. Henry – that's my boss – says that in ten years' time or so we'll all be nipping on and off aeroplanes as though they were buses.'

Anne laughed. 'That remains to be seen. I'm quite content with Middlebeck at the moment; more than content, in fact...' She smiled serenely. 'And what about you, Maisie? Do you and Andy have any plans? Anything...imminent, I mean?'

Maisie, also, gave a smile of contentment. 'We are just happy to have found one another. At the moment I am enjoying my work; it's exciting; full of surprises, and there's always a new adventure around the next corner; and Andy has always enjoyed what he does... Eventually, yes, we will be together, and when that happens it will be for always, we both know that. But for now we are enjoying the present time. We make the most of every day and hour we spend together, and it's great to know that it's for keeps...'

—

Andy squeezed her hand. 'You were miles away, darling. Where were you?'

'Oh...just thinking,' she replied. 'Thinking how lucky we are. It has been a wonderful evening, Andy. I didn't know much at all about the Scottish New Year until now. You certainly go to town with your celebrations, don't you?'

There had been a magnificent banquet, preceded by Gordon Cameron playing the bagpipes; 'Flowers of the Forest', 'Eriskay Love Lilt', and 'Ye Banks and Braes'. At least, Maisie had thought she recognised those melodies, although she had to admit that they all sounded pretty much the same. He hadn't 'piped in the haggis', Andy explained; that ceremony took place only on Burns' Night on the twenty-fifth of January, but haggis had been included on the menu.

The meal had started with a small portion of that dish; Maisie had found it to be an acquired taste, but she was getting to enjoy it more now. It had been followed by scotch broth; then roast beef for the main course, cooked to perfection in the way she was sure only Andy could do it; and finishing with Queen Mary's tart, a confection of puffed pastry filled with a sweet mixture of eggs, butter, sugar and sultanas, served with an apricot sauce and cream. Truly delicious...

They had danced, she and Andy had sung together, they had watched the local troupe of Scottish dancers who performed there regularly, joining in finally with the familiar reels and jigs; and all the time the whisky and ale had flowed freely.

Now they were awaiting the culmination of the evening's celebrations which would take place when the midnight hour had struck. They listened to Gordon counting down the seconds till twelve o'clock...then there was a deafening cheer and shouts of 'Happy Hogmanay...'

Andy put his arms around Maisie and kissed her, a kiss more of friendship, though, at that moment, than passion. There would be time enough for that later; they were good friends as well as being very much in love.

'Duncan Macleod is doing the honours for us,' Andy told her when they had all settled down again. 'He's an old friend of my father, and he's dark-haired, as he should be, o' course. He's still got his black hair even though he's approaching sixty.'

'So you wouldn't be able to do it, would you?' said Maisie, touching his fair hair. 'It's tradition, is it, that the first person to cross the threshold should be dark? Come to think of it, I've an idea they still do that in some parts of England.'

'Aye, in Northumberland mebbe; they're no so far away. Aye, a dark man, and one who is not a member of the family, so that rules out me and my father as well. Here comes Duncan now...'

There was another cheer as the black-haired man, dressed in the yellow and black tartan of the Macleod clan, entered the room. He carried with him a small loaf of bread, a canister of salt, and a piece of coal, which he placed on a table at the front of the room.

'Happy Hogmanay...' he called, and 'Happy Hogmanay...' they all replied.

'The symbols of life, hospitality and warmth,' said Andy. 'It's a guid auld tradition, and I'm so happy you are here to share it with me. A Happy New Year, darling, and may we have many, many more of them together.'

'A Happy New Year, Andy,' she echoed. Then he kissed her again.

*'For Auld Lang Syne, my dear, for All Lang Syne,*
*We'll tak' a cup of kindness yet, for the sake of*
*Auld Lang Syne.'*